# RESTORATION PROSE FICTION

# Restoration Prose Fiction
# 1666-1700

*An Anthology of Representative Pieces*

*Chosen and Edited by* Charles C. Mish

UNIVERSITY OF NEBRASKA PRESS · LINCOLN

Publishers on the Plains

UNP

PR
1295
M5

Manufactured in the United States of America

# CONTENTS

# INTRODUCTION

Though there has been considerable dispute about the matter, conservative opinion has generally pitched upon Samuel Richardson's *Pamela* (1740) as the first real English novel. As might be expected, however, Richardson's book did not arrive on the scene unheralded; all of its elements can be found in earlier writing, in fiction, in the periodical essay, and even in the drama. The decades preceding 1740 may then be called the seedbed of the modern novel and it was in the late seventeenth century that the seed was first sown that was later to yield such an impressive harvest.

We may date the beginning of the movement leading to Richardson—though not of course consciously—from about 1680. English prose fiction had indeed existed before this date; Caxton published his version of *Reynard the Fox* as far back as 1481, and the great flowering of belles lettres in the Elizabethan age affected prose fiction as well as the other genres of literature. Sidney's *Arcadia* and the tales of Greene and Lodge and Deloney, to name only the most outstanding examples of Elizabethan fiction, offered models that seemed to point the way to a really important achievement in the art of narration. By the year 1600 there seemed every reason to predict that fiction would be one of the most flourishing branches of seventeenth-century imaginative writing. Such a development did not take place, however; whether because the strength of the narrative impulse was drawn off by the drama or whether for some other reason, early seventeenth-century prose fiction did not thrive. It is possible to collect a small group of entertaining stories from the first part of the century, but by and large the work of these years is sterile and static, a mere juggling of techniques and procedures already established, written in a style that is self-consciously precious, stilted and bathetic by turns. What might have been a vital kind of writing sank into a sort of exercise in futility.

Not until halfway through the Restoration period did that new impetus so badly needed come to revive English fiction and to take it out of the doldrums. The new animating spirit when it arrived came from France; under the influence of translations and imitations of French short fiction English fiction found itself transformed. The chief agent in the change was the concept of verisimilitude (called *vraisemblance* in France) which insisted that the elements of a story bear some recognizable resemblance to corresponding elements in contemporary life. The first appearances of this incipient realism are, to be sure, weak and sporadic, but they are there, and with their appearance we are on the way to the full sweep of the English novel as we know it.

The new spirit that remade English fiction was also new and equally powerful in its own homeland, where the previously dominant kind of fiction, the long elaborate heroic romance, came to a fairly abrupt and definite end around 1660. When the heroic romance disappeared in France, its place was taken by various kinds of shorter fiction usually called *nouvelles*, the different subspecies being designated as *nouvelles galantes*, *nouvelles historiques*, and so on. Whatever their designation, however, these *nouvelles* all aimed at some kind of psychological insight and more realistic settings and actions. Plots should seem probable, dialogue should sound like real people talking (seventeenth-century people, of course), characters should behave the way persons in polite society did behave. And of course the states of mind of the characters, especially those of the hero and heroine, should be portrayed as accurately and minutely as possible.

The writers who formed the new French fiction were those who, through translation, also formed the English. Mme de Lafayette, undoubtedly the most important and gifted of these creators of the new French fiction, published her *Princesse de Monpensier* in 1662, thereby laying the foundation for a new sort of love story; it was duly translated in 1666. The *Princesse de Clèves*, usually thought to be her masterpiece and probably the only seventeenth-century story still read in France, appeared in 1678; it was brought into English almost immediately, in 1679. Closely linked with these stories is the sort of work which Marie-Catherine Desjardins, also known as Mme de Villedieu, was producing, much of which also appeared in English. Though Mlle Desjardins was to write nothing as good as *La Princesse de Clèves*, she was by no means without talent and her fairly copious body of work created a new genre, that of the *nouvelle galante*. Her most important contributions to the development of her kind of story were turned (in part at least) into English as *Love's Journal*, 1671; *The Annals of Love*, 1672; and *The Disorders of Love*, 1677.

The classic example in French of the *nouvelle historique* is the *Dom Carlos* (1672) of César Vischard de Saint-Réal, available in English two years later (with a second edition in 1676). Numerous examples of this sort of story based on actual or legendary events in the life of a genuine historical personage appeared in French and were soon transferred to English: *Meroveus, a Prince of the Blood-Royal of France*, 1682; *Don

*Sebastian of Portugal*, 1683; *The Fatal Beauty of Agnes de Castro*, 1688; *The Great Scanderberg*, 1690; *The Life of Count Ulfeld*, 1695. All of these narratives combine fact and fiction to varying degrees, some being almost pure fiction, others almost genuine history. In either case, the genre seemed particularly appealing to readers on the English side of the Channel.

Of considerable influence and interest is the famous *Lettres portugaises*, 1668, an overnight success, around which a whole body of sequels and replies and authorship disputes arose; the letters were turned into English in 1678 as *Five Love-Letters from a Nun to a Cavalier*. These letters, along with the work of Mme de Lafayette, represent the most penetrating depiction to be found in the period of the inner feelings of a woman in love, a fact attested to by their long acceptance as the genuine confessions of their supposed author. Abandoned by her lover, the nun pours out her heart in terms which are the more moving for being somewhat formalized. Mrs. Behn found her a most useful model.

Much more traditional are the oriental tales of the period, for the use of Eastern settings and plot devices had been much used in earlier short fiction: being captured and sold as a slave to a lascivious sultan or being popped into a harem had been a constant danger of any fictional trip by water ever since Heliodorus wrote his *Ethiopian History* in the second or third century of the Christian era. But even here the new interest in psychological analysis makes itself felt. The harem is in some ways the ideal locale for a love story, for the inhabitants of the place have presumably nothing to do day in and day out but to think out and practice love intrigues. Hence minute dwelling on the fluctuations of the emotions of those taking part in the story seems perfectly natural. The author's only problem, then, is to introduce an idealized love affair dealing with "true love" into a milieu which seems much more likely to witness less spiritual feelings. It need hardly be noted that the writers who attempted this genre found a ready acceptance with the reading public; examples of the oriental tale are plentiful. Mme de Lafayette did not disdain using a few oriental motifs in her *Zayde*, 1670, but much more thoroughgoing examples are to be found in such things as Bremond's *Hattige*, 1676 (English version same year), Mlle de La Roche Guilhem's *Almanzaïde*, 1674 (translated into English in 1676 as *Almanzor and Almanzaida*), and the anonymous *Homais, reine de Tunis* [1680?] (translated as *Homais, Queen of Tunis*, 1681). The intensity of the amorous life in these books is quite remarkable.

Finally, among the various kinds of stories founded on a love plot we must reckon the few examples of the novel of manners which made their appearance before 1700. Early French models of this genre are to be found in English translation in *The Husband Forc'd To Be Jealous*, 1668, and *The Gentleman-Apothecary*, 1670. A notable English imitation is *The Fair Extravagant*, 1682, of Alexander Oldys, which reads like a stage comedy in narrative form. If there is not much inward characterization or psychological analysis in Oldys' book, there is a very lively presentation of contemporary settings (coffee-houses, the theater, debtors' prison), and there is above all a great deal of vivacious and lifelike conversation. Verisimilitude, which makes its appearance to a greater or lesser degree in all the stories previously mentioned, here reaches its apogee. It is perhaps a pity that there are so few of these stories depicting manners so directly, but their scarcity will probably occasion little surprise.

Stories like those discussed in the previous paragraphs were also published in collections, the most important of these in the period being without doubt that put together by John Davies of Kidwelly under the title of *Scarron's Novels*, 1665, from the various *nouvelles* of Paul Scarron. In his preface to his *Roman comique*, Scarron himself notes that the Spanish seemed to have the secret of making little stories on the everyday level of humanity and not laden with impossible action or impossible characters. It is hence not surprising that all of Scarron's stories should be based on Spanish originals. The French author re-works his material quite freely, however, adapting rather than translating, and adding one most important ingredient: the voice of the narrator himself, who intervenes often in the course of the story, commenting on the action, attesting to its veracity, adding ironic touches to the whole. The resultant style, more sophisticated than any other of its period, gives an effect of witty urbanity and ironic detachment. It was taken up by a number of imitators in England, particularly by those writing with an anti-romantic intent, such as the anonymous author of *The Art of Cuckoldom*, 1697. It is of some interest that the first periodical fiction, the stories appearing in *The Gentleman's Journal*, 1692–1694, employ this style with notable success. A short "novel," presumably written by Peter Motteux, the editor, appeared in each of the monthly issues. Rather sophisticated and urbane, the stories seem intended, as the title of the periodical indeed indicates, for a masculine rather than a feminine audience, which is to say that they are anti-romantic love stories, ironic rather than passionate. The relations between men and women are looked at in a way that is, if not cynical, at least detached. In a word, these are fabliaux for those with some taste and education, and they necessarily involve some depiction of manners and a realistic viewpoint.

Side by side with the stories so far dealt with, what we may call "polite" fiction, there existed all through the seventeenth century in England another body of fiction, so-called popular fiction, intended for a less educated and cruder group of readers. What stories for this audience lacked in art they often made up in other qualities; the down-to-earth point of view in these unromantic tales, the homeliness of the style, the use of characters and settings drawn from English country life, all gave such fiction a sense of solidity and reality all too often lacking in the stories designed for more cultured classes. In the first half of the century, indeed, these lower-class stories may seem a welcome relief in their forthright gusto when compared with the frequently artificial style and unbelievable events found in their upper-class counterparts. In the latter part of the century, however, this situation alters considerably. Though popular fiction increases in quantity and still continues to offer a rich mine for folklorists and literary sociologists, it no longer has any monopoly on actuality as it once did. Love stories written for the educated now too have a window, if only a small one, on life, and hence the relative literary significance of the popular tale declines somewhat.

The number of new titles in the realm of popular fiction appearing in the years 1660–1700 is remarkable. Most of the horde of little chapbooks, cheap and badly printed, hawked around England by itinerant pedlars during the eighteenth century first saw print in the period of the Restoration. It is of interest that the first prose version of such stories as those of Robin Hood, Guy of Warwick, and Bevis of Hampton first appeared during these years. Stories of other folk heroes, like those of Aurelius, the "valiant London prentice," Dick Whittington, another apprentice, whose cat started him on the road toward becoming Lord Mayor of London, and Sir John Hawkwood, who rose from tailor's boy to the honors of knighthood, all illustrate the careers of men of lowly birth who achieved fame and fortune on a grand scale. Such stories, with their insistent rags-to-riches theme, are very much like the novels with which Horatio Alger regaled readers in America early in our own century. The theme itself, of course, has implications which go far beyond mere entertainment.

Along with new stories, such as that of Aurelius, designed for a popular audience, the Restoration saw the appearance of many abridgements of older long romances, abridgements produced in inexpensive editions for readers of slender means and, it must be added, readers exhibiting a strong cultural lag. Such books as the abridged versions of *Valentine and Orson*, Richard Johnson's *Seven Champions of Christendom*, and Emanuel Forde's *Parismus* can hardly be said to represent a solid if crude grasp on reality; rather they must have been consumed to satisfy the sense of wonder in their readers: this is what life was like in the glorious days when knighthood was in flower, they seem to say.

Akin to such popular material, but probably reaching a wider and more cosmopolitan audience, was a new body of material which began to increase in importance beginning in the 1650's. The criminal biography, that is, the fictionalized life of a highwayman or other law-breaker, a kind of story sitting somewhat uncomfortably in the area between true fiction and true biography, becomes of moment for the first time. There had been, to be sure, lives of rogues and villains appearing as far back as the reign of Queen Elizabeth, but it was the pamphlets connected with the deeds and death of Captain James Hind, a notable highwayman executed September 24, 1652, that mark the beginning of the rise of such material during the latter half of the century.

Earlier historians of the novel were prone to regard the criminal biography as the direct predecessor of the novel. "By grafting character study upon the low-life realism of the original criminal biographies, Defoe produced the first crude specimens of the English novel," says Frank W. Chandler.[1] This would seem to be overstating the case. The novel has many roots rather than a single one, and to look for a direct and simple line of descent will not suffice. Even in the case of Defoe it may be said that military memoirs played as great a part in his creations as the lives of rogues and criminals.

Though several other categories of short fiction, such as moral and religious tales, didactic narratives, political allegories, satire, and so on, are represented in this period by scattered examples, none of them, no matter what their intrinsic interest, can be said to have any real significance in the development of the art of narrative. The writers of travel literature, particularly those who attempted the *voyage imaginaire*, might be expected to pay some attention to methods of gaining the credence of the reader, but since what they relate is usually fantastic rather than realistic, such stories do not seem to do very much in the establishment of realism as a norm. What happens on the outskirts of fiction, so to speak, affects very indirectly the central activity.

[1] *The Literature of Roguery* (Boston and New York: Houghton Mifflin Co., 1907), II, 187.

In summary it may be said that during the Restoration English fiction is dominated by shorter forms, French influence, and a tendency toward realistic presentation of character and setting and action. The heart of the matter is the love story, whose development is central to the development of fiction in general during the period. By 1700 the full-fledged novel is almost in view, needing little more than the addition of the characteristic eighteenth-century ingredients, moralizing and sentimentality, to make its appearance.

The stories included in this collection have been selected with the anthologist's usual three criteria in mind: readability, variety, and representative quality. I am fairly sure that the last two of these criteria have been met, and I fervently hope that readers will agree that the first has been met also. My problem in making a selection was one of exclusion; so many entertaining stories pressed themselves upon me that it was with some difficulty that I finally chose the dozen titles which follow.

## A Note on the Text

The texts contained in this volume have undergone some editorial revision in the direction of modernization. So far as wording and spelling go, they are intended to be faithful reproductions of the original editions. On the few occasions where I felt it necessary to emend a word I have indicated my change by placing the emendation in square brackets; I have done nothing to the spelling. In the matter of punctuation, however, I have ventured on some alterations, since seventeenth-century punctuation is so often misleading or confusing to a twentieth-century reader. I have made such changes only when I thought them particularly necessary, so a good deal of the effect of early punctuation remains. And, finally, I have occasionally re-paragraphed by breaking inordinately long paragraphs in the original into two or even three shorter ones. Here again I have been conservative, and many rather long paragraphs remain. The intention of my changes has been to remove any immediate obstacles to rapid and pleasant reading but to let the original text remain as clear as possible behind the modern reprint.

I am grateful to the several libraries owning the original editions for their gracious permission to reproduce these texts. My thanks go to Harvard College Library for *The Princess of Monpensier, The Maiden-Head*

*Lost by Moon-light*, and *The History of the Golden-Eagle*; to Yale University Library for *The Cimmerian Matron* and *Almanzor and Almanzaida*; to the Folger Shakespeare Library for *Five Love-Letters from a Nun to a Cavalier*, *The Memoires of Monsieur Du Vall*, *London's Glory*, and *Bateman's Tragedy*; to the Henry E. Huntington Library for *The Art of Cuckoldom*; and to the Bodleian Library for *The History of Johnny Armstrong*.

I also wish to express my thanks to the Graduate School of the University of Maryland for a Research Grant which materially aided me in the preparation of this book.

CHARLES C. MISH

*College Park, Maryland*

# SELECTED BIBLIOGRAPHY

ESDAILE, ARUNDELL. *A List of English Tales and Prose Romances Printed Before 1740*. London: The Bibliographical Society, 1912.

MISH, CHARLES C. *English Prose Fiction, 1600–1700: A Chronological Checklist*. Charlottesville, Va.: Bibliographical Society of the University of Virginia, 1967.


DUNLOP, JOHN C. *History of Prose Fiction*. New ed., rev. by Henry Wilson. 2 vols. London, 1888.

MORGAN, CHARLOTTE E. *The Rise of the Novel of Manners: A Study of English Prose Fiction Between 1600 and 1700*. New York: Columbia University Press, 1911.

BAKER, ERNEST A. *The History of the English Novel*. 10 vols. London: H. F. & G. Witherby, Ltd., 1923–1929. (See esp. Vol. III: *The Later Romances and the Establishment of Realism*.)

ERNLE, ROWLAND E., Lord Prothero. *The Light Reading of Our Ancestors*. London: Hutchinson & Co., Ltd., 1927.

MACCARTHY, B. G. *Women Writers: Their Contribution to the English Novel, 1621–1744*. Cork: University Press, 1944.

DAY, ROBERT ADAMS. *Told in Letters: Epistolary Fiction Before Richardson*. Ann Arbor: University of Michigan Press, [1966].

MISH, CHARLES C. "English Short Fiction in the Seventeenth Century," *Studies in Short Fiction*, VI (1969), 233–330.

Mme de Lafayette

# THE PRINCESS OF MONPENSIER

(1666)

THE

# PRINCESS

OF

## Monpenſier.

---

Written Originally in
French, and now newly
rendered into Engliſh.

---

---

London, Printed *Anno Dom.* 1666.

*Mme de Lafayette's* Princess of Monpensier (*French 1662, English trans. 1666*) *is both a little masterpiece in its own right and a landmark in the development of the novel. Both in France and in England it is the first of the new kind of love story which was to make fiction over and lead it in the direction of the modern novel. Simple and unified, using actual historical characters in an invented plot, the book represents a real break with the past in more than in mere length. The story is no longer motivated only by coincidences; the plot no longer moves at the mercy of happenings in the world of external circumstances. Instead it takes its rhythm from the love affair itself, and such events as it contains arise more from the inner lives of the characters than from what they do. The deferment of any attempted consummation of the affair between hero and heroine is not caused by inter-fering parents or intriguing third parties but by the heroine herself because her self-esteem will not permit her to commit adultery. It is perhaps a blemish that the splendid scene at the end where husband, wife, and friend confront each other has been brought about almost solely by accident, but the reactions of the three persons involved and their subsequent behavior are almost wholly dependent upon their characters.*

*The author takes some pains to give the book an air of reality by referring often to the events of contemporary history (the setting is the time of Charles IX of France, 1560–1574, with the events leading up to the St. Bartholomew's Day Massacre of 1572) and to introduce characters who did exist at the French court in the mid-sixteenth century. There is not much explicit analysis of psychological states (and none of the sententious aphorisms which lard other love stories), but there is a convincing display of human emotions to be felt all through the story, an effect largely achieved through the sure-handed presentation of character, the principals being beautifully done with a remarkable economy of touch.*

*It is of course on the heroine that the focus of interest falls. The Princess has too much self-respect to become an adulteress, but she is no longer mistress of her heart nor of her eyes nor of her words, and she realizes that she has ceased to be pure in thought even though she has not given herself to her lover. There is a stain on her honor even though her husband cannot see it or know it. But just as important in giving the book its dominating tone of noble renunciation is the figure of Chabanes; he aids equally in carrying the story line and in emphasizing the theme, and he is in some ways a more striking creation. The sort of love he exhibits—strong, indeed passionate, yet more concerned with its object than with self, a sort of steady adoration intermixed with outbursts of rage and refusal—sets the tone for the whole emotional*

3

*atmosphere of the story and contrasts finely with the completely selfish love of Guise. The love that Chabanes bears for the Princess is the model for what she should have had for her husband, and Chabanes' sufferings both parallel and counterpoint hers.*

*Much of the undoubted power of the story comes from its style, a style which achieves a marvellously quiet, sustained low-keyed intensity, carrying the story on without emotional hyperbole. In its communication of the tension between the calm surface (mirroring the outward behavior of the characters) and the seething emotions underneath it is like the language of Racine or the slow movement of a Mozart concerto. Though the translation is a faithful one, it does not come up to the strength of the French original. It is somewhat better, however, than that made of Mme de Lafayette's great masterpiece,* The Princess of Cleves *(French 1678, English trans. 1679), a book which is so similar in all respects to the present one that it might be called* Monpensier *writ large.*

*The text which follows is based on the copy of the 1666 edition of the book in the possession of Harvard University.*

## The Translator
## to the Reader

Though generally all Translations merit an excuse, and though I am not so much a stranger to my own inabilities, and to the modern Mode of Writing, as to be ignorant, how requisite it is for me to make an Apology for my self, and to beg Pardon for this attempt; yet I shall at present take the liberty upon me, neither to perform the one, nor the other: since, if good, the Translation deserves no excuse; and if bad, it merits no Pardon. I shall only inform the Reader, that this Translation is owing to some vacant hours, and to a Friends request, who having commended the Book to me, & desiring me to translate it, I confess at first (through the small esteem which I have ever had for Romances, since I understood better Books) I made some difficulty to grant his request; But being informed (though the French Stationer, out of his respect to persons descended from those mentioned in this Relation, endeavours to perswade us to the contrary) that this Story was real, and no fiction; I resolved at length to condescend to his desire, and to adventure upon the Translating of a Book, which I heard had received such general commendations; how deservedly (since Mens fancies are so different) I shall not take upon me to determine, but shall leave that, together with the Translation, to be either approved of, or condemned, by the Judicious Reader.

## The French Bookseller
## to the Reader

The respect which we owe to the Illustrious Name which this Book bears for its Title, and the consideration which we ought to have for the Eminent Persons which are descended from them who have born it, obliges me to say (not to fail of respect either towards the one, or the other) that it has not been taken from any Manuscript which is remaining to us of the Time wherein those Persons herein mention'd Liv'd: The Author being willing only for his diversion to write Adventures, invented to please his fancy, has judged it more proper to take names known in our Histories, then to make use of those which are found in Romances; believing that the Reputation of the Princess of *Monpensier* would not be at all blemished by a relation which in effect is fabulous. If this be not his opinion, I have endeavoured to make an amends for it by this Advertisement, which will prove as advantageous to the Author, as it will appear respectfull from me, both towards the Dead, who are interested in it, and towards the Living whom it may concern.

## The Princess of Monpensier

Whil'st the Rage and fury of a Civil War (during the reign of *Charls* the ninth)[1] rent *France* in pieces, Love was not wanting to find room amidst those disorders; and to cause as great in his own Empire, as the Ambition, and self-ends of some Great Ones caused in that Dominion.

The only Daughter of the Marquesse of *Mezieres*, an Heiress very considerable, no less for her great Estate, then for her alliance to the Illustrious House of *Anjou*, from whence she was descended, was promised in marriage to the Duke of *Maine*, a younger Brother to the Duke of *Guise* (since called *Balafre*). The only want of years in this great Heiress seem'd to retard her marriage: during which time the Duke of *Guise*, who saw her often, discovering in her the early appearances of a Beauty (which age in a short time was like to render most accomplish'd), grew exceeding amorous of her, and fortune prov'd so favourable to him that he received a reciprocal return of his affection.

[1] Charles IX ruled from 1560 to 1574.

They long (with care) conceal'd their Love, the Duke of *Guise* (who was not then possest with so much ambition, as since) ardently wished to marry her; but the fear to displease the Cardinal of *Lorrain*, who served him in stead of a Father, hindered him from declaring his intentions.

In this condition were affairs, when as the House of *Bourbon*, who could not but with envy behold the rise of that of *Guise*, perceiving the advantage which they would receive by this marriage, resolved to deprive them of it, and to make it advantageous to themselves, in procuring this Heiress to marry the young Prince of *Monpensier*.

Endeavours were used to execute this design with such success, that the friends of *Madamoiselle de Mezieres*, contrary to the promises which they had made to the Cardinal of *Lorrain*, resolved to bestow her in marriage on that young Prince. The whole house of *Guise* were extreamly surpriz'd at their proceedings, but the Duke, above the rest, seemed to be orewhelm'd with grief; the interest of his Love made him receive this breach of their word as an unsufferable affront; and in spight of all the perswasions and endeavours used to the contrary (by the Cardinal of *Lorrain*, and the Duke of *Aumale*, his Uncles, who would not appear too obstinate in a business which they perceived beyond their power to hinder) his resentment soon appear'd, and with such violence too in the very presence of the Prince of *Monpensier*, that from thence proceeded a hatred between them, which finished not, but with their Lives.

*Madamoiselle de Mezieres*, importun'd by her Relations to marry that Prince, and perceiving otherwise that 'twas impossible for her to marry the Duke of *Guise*, besides her vertue prompting her, that 'twas dangerous to have that Person for a Brother-in-Law, whom she had wished for as a Husband, in the end resolv'd to follow the inclination of her friends, and conjur'd the Duke of *Guise* no longer, by any new obstacle to divert their marriage.

In fine, she married the Prince of *Monpensier*, who shortly after carried her to *Champigni* (the usual seat belonging to the Princes of his family) withdrawing her from *Paris*, where the burthen of the war was like to fall heaviest; that great City being menac'd to sustain a siege from the *Huguenots* Army, of which the Prince of *Conde* was General, who now for the second time had begun to declare War against the King.

The Prince of *Monpensier* even in his childhood had contracted a firm, and particular friendship with the Count of *Chabanes*, who was a man far more advanc'd in years then himself, and a person of extraordinary merit.

This Count had been so sensible of the esteem, and of the confidence which this young Prince reposed in him, that contrary to the engagements which he had made to the Prince of *Conde*, who gave him hopes of considerable imployments in the *Huguenots* party, he declar'd himself for the Catholicks; since he could not resolve to be opposite in any thing to a Person, that was so dear to him. This alteration of Party having no other known foundation, it was doubted whether it were real or no; and the Queen-Mother, *Catherine de Medicis*, had such great suspitions of him, that the War being declar'd by the *Huguenots*, she had a design to arrest him, and to secure his Person, had not the Prince of *Monpensier* endeavour'd to hinder it, and carried *Chabanes* to *Champigni*, in company with his Wife.

The Count being of a very pleasant, and very agreeable humour, he soon gain'd the esteem of the Princess of *Monpensier*, and in a short time she repos'd no less confidence in him, and had no less amity for him, then had the Prince her Husband. *Chabanes* on his side beheld with admiration so much Beauty, Wit, and Vertue; which appear'd in this young Princess, and making use of the friendship which she shewed him to inspire her with the principles of an extraordinary Vertue, and worthy of the greatness of her birth, he in a small time render'd her one of the most accomplish'd Persons in the world.

The Prince being return'd to Court, (call'd thither by the continuation of the War) the Count remain'd alone with the Princess, and began to have a respect, and an amity for her, proportionable both to her quality, and merits. The confidence which they repos'd in each other, augmented on both sides, but grew so great on the Princess of *Monpensiers* part, that she acquainted him with the inclination and affection which she had had for the Duke of *Guise:* but she inform'd him also at the same instant, that her Love was now almost extinct, and that there remain'd no more at present, then what was requisite to defend her heart, from any such other inclination; and that her Vertue, joyning it self to the remainder of this impression, she was not capable to have any thing but disdain and aversion for all those who should dare to have any Love for her.

The Count, who knew the sincerity of this fair Princess, and who perceiv'd in her, dispositions so contrary to be ensnar'd with the inticing baits of gallantry, and courtship, doubted not at all of the verity of her words; Yet notwithstanding his Reason prov'd too weak a defence to protect him from the assaulting charms of a Beauty, in whose company, 'twas his fortune to be every day, so that at length he became passionately enamour'd of this Princess, and whatsoever shame at first posses'd him to be thus vanquish'd, yet in the end he was forc'd to submit, and to affect her with the most sincere, and violent passion, which perhaps ever was; And though he was not Master of his heart, yet he prov'd so of his actions. The alteration of his mind chang'd not at all his humour, so that none suspected him to be in Love.

He took great care, during the space of a whole year, to hide it from the Princess, and he believ'd that he should alwayes have had the same desire to have conceal'd it from her. But Love produc'd the same effects in him which it generally does in all Lovers, causing in him a desire to reveal his affection, and after all those difficulties which are wont to perplex Lovers on the like occasions, he at last took on him the boldness to acquaint her with his affection, being before well prepar'd to endure the violence of that storm, wherewith the haughty humour of this Princess seem'd to menace him. But he found in her a tranquillity, and a coldness worse a thousand times then all the rigour, and ill usage, which he had expected.

She took not so much pains, to put her self in a Passion for what he had say'd; she only in few words represented to him the difference between their Qualities, and Age, the particular knowledge which he had of her vertue, and of the inclination which she had had for the Duke of *Guise*, but, above the rest, what he ow'd to the friendship of the Prince her Husband, and to the confidence which he repos'd in him. The Count (at these words) thought he should have dyed at her feet, through shame and grief; but she indeavour'd to comfort him in assuring him, that she would never remember what he had told her, and that she would never be perswaded to believe a thing which was so disadvantageous to him, and that she would ever still regard him, as her best friend.

These assurances (as may be imagin'd) were some consolation to the Count; but yet he made a sensible discovery of the disdain, and aversion, which the Princess had for him through her words; and the next day, though he beheld her with a countenance as unconcern'd as formerly, yet his grief and affliction much increas'd. The Princess on her part lessen'd not at all the esteem which she before had for him, she us'd him with the same affability as she was accustom'd to do: and often (when occasion serv'd) took an opportunity to discourse of the inclination which she formerly had for the Duke of *Guise:* and Fame beginning then to publish to the world those great and excellent qualities which appear'd in that Prince, she confess'd to him that she was extream glad to hear it, and that she much rejoyc'd to find that he merited the affection which she had had for him.

These signs of confidence, which had been formerly so dear to the Count, became now insupportable to him; yet he durst not shew his displeasure to the Princess, though sometimes he presum'd to put her in mind of that which he had had the boldness to declare to her.

After two years of absence (Peace being made) the Prince of *Monpensier* return'd home to visit the Princess his Wife, cover'd o're with the Lawrels, and honour which he had gain'd at the siege of *Paris*, and at the Battel of St. *Dennis*. He was surpriz'd to find the Beauty of this Princess arriv'd to so great a perfection, and through an inclination of Jealousie (which was natural to him) he seem'd to be troubl'd at it; foreseeing well, that he should not be the only Person, to whom she would appear fair. He much rejoyc'd to see the Count of *Chabanes*, for whom his kindness was not at all diminish'd: he demanded earnestly of him a character of the humour, and conditions of his Wife, who appear'd almost a stranger to him through the small space of time which he had liv'd with her.

The Count with a sincereness as exact, as if he had not been at all in Love, declar'd to the Prince all what he knew of this Princess capable to make him Love her; and he also advertiz'd the Princess of *Monpensier* of all things which she ought to perform fully to gain the heart and estimation of her Husband.

In fine, the Counts Passion so naturally inclin'd him to think of nothing else, but what might augment the prosperity, and happiness of this Princess, that he easily forgot how much it concerns Lovers to hinder Persons they are in Love withall, from keeping a perfect correspondence with their Husbands.

Scarce was the Peace concluded, but the War began to be renew'd again, occasion'd by the design which the King had to arrest at *Noiers* the Prince of *Conde*, and the Admiral of *Chastillon;* and this design having been discover'd, they began on both sides to make new preparations for War, which constrain'd the Prince of *Monpensier* to leave his Wife, and to make his appearance there, where both his honour, and his duty call'd him. *Chabanes* follow'd him to Court, having fully justified himself in the Queens opinion. It was not without extream grief that he departed from the Princess, who on her side remain'd much perplext with the thoughts of those dangers which her Husband was going to expose himself to, in the War.

The Chiefs of the *Huguenots* party retiring themselves to *Rochel, Poictu*, and *Xaintonge* being on their side, the War grew hot, and the King assembl'd together all his forces to suppress their Rebellion. The Duke of *Anjou* his Brother (who was since stil'd *Henry* the Third) acquir'd much honour by several gallant actions which he perform'd, and amongst the rest at the Battel of *Jarnac*, where the Prince of *Conde* was kil'd. In this War, it was that the Duke of *Guise* began first to have considerable imployments, and to make it appear that he surpass'd by much the great hopes which had been conceiv'd of him.

The Prince of *Monpensier*, who hated him, both as his particular enemy, and as that of his Family, beheld with Jealous eyes the Glory of the Duke, as well as the kindness which the Duke of *Anjou* shew'd him.

After that both Armies had tir'd themselves by several small encounters, by a common consent of both Parties, the Troops were licenc'd for some time, to retire to their several Garrisons. The Duke of *Anjou* remain'd at *Loches* to distribute orders to all those places which in probability were like to be attacq'd by the Enemy; the Duke of *Guise* tarried with him, and the Prince of *Monpensier* accompanied with the Count of *Chabanes* return'd to *Champigni*, which was not far distant from thence.

The Duke of *Anjou* went often to visit the Places which he was about to fortifie, and one day as he return'd to *Loches* by a by-way unknown to those of his retinue, the Duke of *Guise*, who bragg'd that he knew it, plac'd himself at the head of the Troop to serve them instead of a Guide; but after that he had rid some time, he lost himself, and found that he was upon the bank of a small River, which was unknown to him. The Duke of *Anjou* rallied with him, and jear'd him for his ill conduct, and making a stop there (being dispos'd to mirth, as usually young Princes are) they perceiv'd a small Boat which stood still in the midst of the River, which not being very broad, they could easily distinguish objects, and perceive in the Boat three or four Women, and amongst the rest, one who appear'd to them very fair, who was in rich apparel, and who attentively regarded two men, who were in the same Boat with her, and were a fishing. This adventure caus'd a new joy both to these young Princes, and to those of their Train. It appear'd to them as a Romance-like accident, some telling the Duke of *Guise* that he had purposely lost them only to make them have a view of this fair Person, others saying that (after what Fortune had done for him) he must of necessity grow amorous of her; and the Duke of *Anjou* maintain'd, that he was oblig'd to become her Lover.

In fine, being resolv'd to see the conclusion of this adventure, they caus'd some of their followers to ride into the River, as far as possible, and to call to that Lady, and tell her, that the Duke of *Anjou* was there, and that he would willingly cross the Water, and intreated her to come and take him in. This Lady (who was the Princess of *Monpensier*) hearing it say'd that the Duke of *Anjou* was there, and not doubting at all (through the quantity of people which she saw on the Rivers-side) but that it was he, caus'd her Boat to advance towards that side of the River, where he was; His graceful Mine[2] made her soon distinguish him from the rest, but yet she sooner took notice of the Duke of *Guise*, whose sight wrought in her such an alteration that it caus'd her to blush, which rather augmented, then decreas'd her Beauty, and made her appear to the Eyes of these Princes, as a Person supernatural, and wholly divine.

The Duke of *Guise* (in spight of that advantageous Alteration which two or three years, since last he saw her, had made in her) immediately knew her, and inform'd the Duke of *Anjou* who she was, who was at first asham'd of the Liberty which he had taken, but perceiving the Princess of *Monpensier* so fair and this adventure so much pleasing him, he resolv'd to compleat it, and after a thousand excuses, and a thousand complements, he invented a story of some considerable business, which he say'd he had to do on the other side of the River, and accepted of the proffer which she made him to carry him over in her Boat; he enter'd it alone acompanied only with the Duke of *Guise*, giving order to those that follow'd them to go, and cross the River at some other place, and to come and meet him at *Champigni*, which the Princess inform'd them was not above two Leagues distant from thence.

As soon as they were in the Boat, the Duke of *Anjou* inquir'd of her, to what propitious Fate it was they ow'd so fortunate an adventure; and what detain'd her there in the midst of the River. She answer'd him, That she came from *Champigni* in company with the Prince her Husband, with a design to hunt; but finding her self too much tir'd, she came for refreshment to the Rivers side; where the curiosity to see a Salmon taken (which had entangl'd it self in a Net) had caus'd her to enter the Boat. The Duke of *Guise* did not at all interest himself in this discourse, but feeling that Passion began to revive again in his breast, which he had formerly had for that Princess, he suspected that he should find it a difficult task to escape from this adventure, without becoming again her captive.

They soon arriv'd to the other side of the River, where they found the Pages, and Servants of the Princess of *Monpensier*, who there attended

---

[2] i.e., mien.

her. The Dukes of *Anjou* and *Guise* assisted her to get on Horsback, where she comported her self with an admirable grace. During the way, she entertain'd them with most exquisite discourse upon several subjects; so that they were no less surpriz'd and charm'd with her excellent parts,[3] then they had been before with her Beauty, and they could not forbear to acquaint her how extreamly they were amaz'd with those extraordinary perfections which they discover'd in her. She answer'd to those commendations which they gave her with all the modesty imaginable, but a little more coldly to those which came from [the] Duke of *Guise;* being willing to use a reserv'dness towards him, which should hinder him from building any hopes upon the inclination which formerly she had for him.

Arriving at the outward-most Court at *Champigni,* they found the Prince of *Monpensier,* who but then return'd from hunting. His amazement was great to behold two men ride on each side of his Wife, but it augmented extreamly, when (approaching nearer) he perceiv'd that they were the Duke of *Anjou,* and the Duke of *Guise.* The hatred which he had for the last, joyning it self to his natural jealousie made him find something so unpleasant to him to see these Princes in company with his Wife, without knowing what accident had brought them together, nor what they came to do at his house, that he could not conceal the disorder which it caus'd in him, though cunningly he rejected the cause of it upon the apprehension which he had, that he should not be able to receive so great a Prince, both according to his quality and to his own wishes.

The Count of *Chabanes* appear'd yet more perplext to see the Duke of *Guise* with the Princess of *Monpensier* than seem'd the Prince himself. The adventure which Fortune had made use of to bring these two Persons together appear'd to him as an unlucky Omen, from whence he prognosticated that this Romance-likebeginning would be follow'd by other accidents of the like nature.

At night the Princess of *Monpensier* entertain'd these Princes very generously, and with a civility which was natural to her. In fine, she pleas'd her Guests but too well. The Duke of *Anjou,* who was a Prince of a comely personage, and very accomplish'd, could not behold a person so worthy of him, without ardently desiring to enjoy her; soon became infected with the same Disease which possest the Duke of *Guise,* and always feigning extraordinary affairs, he remain'd two dayes at *Champigni,* without being oblig'd to stay by any other motive, then by the

---

[3] talents, endowments.

charms of the Princess of *Monpensier*, the Prince her Husband not using any intreaties to retain him there.

The Duke of *Guise*, before he departed, took an opportunity to acquaint the Princess, that he was still the same, which he had ever been, (and since his Passion had never been reveal'd to any) he often told her in publick (without being over-heard by any, but her self) that there was no change in his affection, but that at present he retain'd as much adoration, and respect for her, as ever.

In fine, the Duke of *Anjou*, and he at length departed from *Champigni* with much regret. They rid a long while without speaking one to the other, and remain'd in a profound silence, till at last the Duke of *Anjou*, imagining that perhaps their silence might proceed from one and the same cause, demanded briskly of the Duke of *Guise*, if he meditated upon the beauty, and perfections of the Princess of *Monpensier*. This brisk demand, joyn'd to what the Duke of *Guise* had already observ'd, concerning the inclinations of the Duke of *Anjou*, made him perceive, that infallibly he would become his Rival, and that it extreamly imported him not to discover his Love to that Prince; but to deprive him of all suspition, he answer'd him smiling, That he appear'd himself so much taken up with the imagination, wherewith he accus'd him, that he had judg'd it uncivill to interrupt him; That the Beauty of the Princess of *Monpensier* was no new thing to him; That he had accustom'd himself to gaze on the Luster of her charms, without being dazel'd with them, ever since she was design'd to have been his Sister-in-Law, but that he perceiv'd very well, that all persons were not so well prepar'd against them as himself. The Duke of *Anjou* ingeniously confest to him, that he had never yet seen any thing, which in his opinion, seem'd comparable to this young Princess; and that he found very well, that her presence might prove dangerous to him, if he should often expose himself in her company: he would fain have made the Duke of *Guise* confess, that he apprehended the same Fate himself too: but the Duke (who began now to make a serious affair of his Love) would confess nothing to him.

These Princes returning to *Loches* entertain'd themselves often with a very pleasing discourse of the adventure which had caus'd them to discover the Princess of *Monpensier*: but it prov'd not a subject of so great a diversion at *Champigni*. The Prince of *Monpensier* was discontented at all which had happen'd, without being able to give a Reason wherefore. His Wifes being in the Boat, appear'd to him as an unlucky accident: It seem'd to him, that she had entertain'd these Princes too kindly; and that which displeas'd him most, was to have observ'd that the Duke of *Guise* had regarded her very attentively.

These thoughts caus'd him from that instant, to conceive a furious jealousie, which made him to remember the passion, and resentment, which that Duke had shewn against his Marriage, and he had some thoughts, that from that very time he had been amorous of her. The ill humour which these suspitions put him into, caus'd sometimes but ill usage to the Princess of *Monpensier*. The Count of *Chabanes* (according to his custome) took care to hinder, that their private discontents broke not out into an open quarrel, endeavouring through that, to perswade the Princess how great, and real the passion was, which he had for her, and how disinteress'd from all self-ends.

Yet he could not refrain from asking her the effect which the sight of the Duke of *Guise* had produc'd in her. She acquainted him, That she had been troubl'd at it, through the shame which she had, to remember the kindness which she had formerly shew'd him: she confest that she had found him far more accomplish't now, then at that time; and that his discourse seem'd to intimate, that he would perswade her to believe, that he still affected her; but she assur'd him, that nothing was able to force her to relinquish the resolution which she had taken never to engage her self in so perilous an Affair.

The Count of *Chabanes* was much rejoyc'd to hear this resolution; but nothing could secure him against the suspition which he had of the Duke of *Guise*. He represented to the Princess, that he extreamly fear'd, that the first impressions of her Love would soon return, and made her apprehend the mortal grief which (for their common intrest) he should have, if one day he should see her change her present resolutions. The Princess of *Monpensier* (alwayes continuing her reserv'dness towards him) scarce answer'd to what he said concerning his passion, and never consider'd him, but in the Quality of her faithful'st friend, without doing him the honour to take notice of him as her Lover.

The Armies having quitted their Garrisons, and being again upon their march, the Princes return'd to their several Commands, and the Prince of *Monpensier* found it convenient, that his Wife should come to *Paris*, to be no more so near those places which were the seat of the War. The *Huguenots* besieg'd the City of *Poictiers*, and the Duke of *Guise* cast himself in the Town to defend it, where he perform'd such actions, during the Siege, which alone were sufficient to render for ever famous any other person, but himself.

Soon after, was fought the Battel of *Moncontour*,[4] and the Duke of *Anjou*, after he had taken St. *John d'Angely*, fell sick, and immediately quitted the Army, either through the violence of his distemper, or through the desire which he had to return and take his ease, and to participate of the pleasures and recreations enjoy'd at *Paris*, where the presence of the Princess of *Monpensier* was not the least attracting object that drew him thither.

The Army continued under the command of the Prince of *Monpensier*, and soon after, Peace being concluded, the Court return'd to *Paris*, where the Beauty of the Princess eclips'd, the Luster of all those, who till then had been admir'd; and the charming perfections both of her Wit and Person soon attracted the eyes of all the Court upon her, who consider'd her as a person that surpass'd humanity. The Duke of *Anjou* chang'd not at all, at *Paris*, the inclinations which he had conceiv'd for her at *Champigni;* and he took an extream care to acquaint her with as much through all his actions, taking notwithstanding great heed not to render her too apparent testimonies of his affection, through fear to give jealousie to the Prince her Husband.

The Duke of *Guise* was now become passionately inamour'd of this Princess, and being willing (for several reasons) to conceal his passion, he resolv'd with the first opportunity to declare it privately to her, thereby to avoy'd all those various reports, which generally springs from publick Courtship. Being one day at the Queens appartment at a time when there was small company there (the Queen being retir'd to discourse about business with the Cardinal of *Lorrain*) the Princess of *Monpensier* coming in, he resolv'd to make use of that opportunity which Fortune presented him with, to speak to her; and approaching to her, I go about to surprise you Madam, (said he) and to displease you, in acquainting you, that I have ever preserv'd and cherish'd that passion which formerly was not unknown to you, but which since (through again seeing of you) is so much augmented, that neither the severity nor hatred of the Prince your Husband, nor the Pretensions, and Rivalship of the first Prince of the Realm, are able to reprieve me one moment from its violence. It would indeed have shew'd more respectful from me, to have reveal'd it to you by my actions; but Madam, my actions had discover'd it to others, as well as to your self; and I only desire, that you alone should know, that I am so presumptious to adore you.

The Princess was at first so surpriz'd with this discourse, that she had

4 The Battle of Moncontour took place in 1569.

no power to interrupt him; but recollecting her self, and going about to answer him, the Prince of *Monpensier* enter'd the Room, whose presence, with what the Duke of *Guise* had said to her, so disorder'd and perplext the Princess, that it posses'd him with greater suspitions, then if he had over-heard the Duke of *Guise*'s discourse. The Queen came out of her Closet, and the Duke retir'd himself, to cure the Prince of jealousie.

The Princess of *Monpensier* at night found her Husband possest with the greatest melancholly imaginable, and he behav'd himself so passionately towards her, that he forbid her evermore to speak to the Duke of *Guise*, which caus'd her to retire to her appartment, much possest with sadness, for the adventures which had happen'd to her that day.

The next following, she saw the Duke of *Guise* at the Queens Lodgings; but he kept at a distance, and came not near her, but contented himself to go out of the Room presently after her, to make it appear to her, that he had no business there, when she was absent.

Scarce a day past in which she did not receive a thousand conceal'd assurances of this Dukes passion, without that he ever so much as attempted to mention it to her, but at such a time when none could take notice of it, and as she was well assur'd of the reallity of this passion, she began (notwithstanding all the resolutions which she had made at *Champigni* to the contrary) to feel something of that passion return in her heart, which had formerly possest it.

The Duke of *Anjou* on his part forgot nothing which might declare his Love to her in all places where 'twas his fortune to see her, and made it his business continually to follow her, when she rendred visits to the Queen his Mother.

About this time, it was taken notice of, that the Princess *Margaret* his Sister (who much affected him, and who was since Queen of *Navarr*) had some kindness for the Duke of *Guise*, and that which discover'd it more, was the reservedness which the Duke of *Anjou* shew'd to the Duke of *Guise*. The Princess of *Monpensier* soon learn't this news, which seem'd not indifferent to her, and which made her more sensible of the concern which she had for the Duke of *Guise*, then she thought she had been. *Monsieur de Monpensier* (her Father-in-Law) then marrying *Madamoiselle de Guise* (Sister to that Duke) she was constrain'd to see him often in those places, where the presence of both Parties was requisite to celebrate the Nuptial Ceremonies.

The Princess of *Monpensier* no longer able to endure a man for her Servant, whom all *France* believ'd in Love with the Princess *Margaret*, resolv'd to take on her the boldness to acquaint him, how much she thought her self injur'd. And being offended, and griev'd that she had deceiv'd her self, One day, as the Duke of *Guise* met her at his Sisters, being separated from other company, and being about to speak to her concerning his passion, she briskly interrupted him, with a tone that signified her displeasure and replyed, I cannot comprehend why you should build such hopes upon the weak foundation of a folly, which I was guilty of at thirteen years old, as that you should have the boldness at present to make Love to such a person as my self, but above all, at such a time, when in the view of the whole Court, you appear engag'd to an other.

The Duke of *Guise*, that had a great deal of Wit, and was much in Love, had need to consult with no Oracle to understand the meaning of the Princesses words, answer'd her with much respect; *I confess* Madam, *that I have been too blame, not to despise the honour of being Brother-in-law to my King, rather then to let you suspect one moment, that I could desire to possess any other heart, then yours; but if you will do me the favour as to hear me, I am confident I shall justifie my self in your opinion.*

The Princess of *Monpensier* reply'd nothing, but she remain'd still, and went not away from him, and the Duke perceiving that she granted him the audience, which he had demanded, and wish'd for, acquainted her, That, without any endeavours of his own us'd to gain it, the Princess *Margaret* had honour'd him with her affection; but that having no Love for her, "He had but very ill recompenc'd the favour which she did him, untill such time that she had giv'n him some hopes to marry her; that in truth, the grandure to which this match might raise him, had oblig'd him to render her more observance and respect, then usuall, which it seem'd had giv'n cause of suspition both to the King, and to the Duke of *Anjou*; That the opposition both of the one and the other disswaded him not from his design; but if that design displeas'd her, he would from that very instant abandon it, and never think on it more, during his Life."

This oblation which the Duke of *Guise* made of his own intr'est to please the Princess, soon made her forget all the rigour, and displeasure wherewith she had entertain'd him, when he first began to speak to her. She soon chang'd her discourse, and began to entertain him with the weakness which possest the Princess *Margaret* to Love him first, and of the considerable advantage which he would recieve in marrying her. In conclusion, without saying any thing obliging to the Duke of *Guise*, she discovered to him a thousand charming perfections, which he had formerly ador'd in *Madamoiselle de Meziers*: and though they had not long discours'd together, yet they found themselves so accustom'd to one anothers humours, that Love which was no stranger to their breasts, soon found out a way to return again into its ancient Channel.

They thus finish'd this agreeable conversation, which left a very sensible impression of Joy upon the Duke of *Guise;* nor did the Princess participate a less share than he, to learn that he yet really affected her. But when she was retir'd to her Closet, what reflections did she not make upon the shame which she had, in suffering her self to be so soon or'ecome by the Duke of *Guise*'s excuses; upon that Labyrinth of trouble, which she was agoing about to involve her self into, by engaging her self in a business, which she had regarded with so much horrour, and detestation, and upon the dismal misfortunes, wherewith the jealous humour of her Husband seem'd to threaten her, but these unpleasant thoughts were the next day soon discipated by the Duke of *Guise*'s presence.

He fail'd not to render her an exact account of that which past between the Princess *Margaret* and himself, the new alliance of their Houses often presented him with opportunities to speak to her; but he had no small trouble to cure her of the jealousie which the Beauty of the Princess *Margaret* gave her, against which all his Vows were to weak to secure her from suspition. This jealousie serv'd the Princess of *Monpensier* to defend the remainder of her heart, against the endeavours us'd to gain it by the Duke of *Guise*, who already possest its greatest part.

The Kings marriage with the Princess *Isabella* (Daughter to the Emperour *Maximilian*) fil'd the whole Court with feasts and rejoycings. The King gave a Ball, where the Princess *Margaret*, and the rest of the Princesses danc't, the Princess of *Monpensier* appearing the only person that could dispute the prize of Beauty with her. The Duke of *Anjou*, with the Duke of *Guise*, and four others, which were of their company danc'd an Antick-dance in the shape of *Moors*, their Habits were all alike, and such as are generally us'd on the like occasion.

The first time that the Ball was danc'd, the Duke of *Guise* before he danc'd (not having put on his vizard)[5] say'd something in passing by to the Princess of *Monpensier*, she soon perceiv'd that the Prince her Husband had taken notice of it, which much disturb'd her. Soon after seeing the Duke of *Anjou*, with his Vizard on, and drest like a *Moor*, coming to speak to her, perplex'd through her disorder, she believ'd that it was still

5 mask.

the Duke of *Guise*, and approaching to him, Have no respect too night (said she) but for the Princess *Margaret*. I shall not be jealous, 'tis my command, I am observ'd, approach me no more. As soon as she had finish'd these words, she retir'd, and the Duke of *Anjou* remain'd as surpriz'd, as if he had been Thunder-struck; he perceiv'd at that instant that he had not only a Rival, but a Rival too belov'd; he soon apprehended by the name of the Princess *Margaret*, that that Rival was the Duke of *Guise*, and he made no question, but that the Princess his Sister was the oblation which had render'd the Princess of *Monpensier* favourable to the vows of his Rival.

Jealousie, Despight and Rage joyning themselves to the hatred, which he had already for him, caus'd him to be possest with whatsoever may be imagin'd of a most violent, and impetuous passion, and which had immediately produc'd some bloody Effect of his displeasure, had not that dissimulation which was so natural to him (and which at present was so requisite) soon rescu'd his Reason from those violent motions of his passion, and oblig'd him, for several prevalent reasons, (as affairs then stood) not to attempt any thing against the Duke of *Guise*. Yet nevertheless he could not deprive himself of the satisfaction which he took to tell him, that he knew the secret of his Love; and accosting him in going out of the Room where they had danc'd, 'Tis too much (said he) to dare at once to raise your ambitious thoughts, to pretend to my Sister, and to deprive me of my Mistris. The respect which I bear the King hinders me at present from declaring my resentment; But remember that perhaps the loss of your life shall be the smallest punishment wherewith, some time or other, I shall chastize your temerity. The Duke of *Guise*, though unaccustom'd to such menaces, yet he had no opportunity left him for an answer, because the King who went out at that instant, call'd them both, to speak to them, but they imprinted in his heart a desire of revenge, which he endeavour'd all his life time to satisfie.

From that very Night the Duke of *Anjou* began to render him all sort of ill turns (that lay in his pow'r) with the King: he perswaded him that the Princess his Sister would never consent to marry the King of *Navarre* (with whom it was then propounded to marry her) so long as the Duke of *Guise* was suffer'd to come near her, and that it was a shame to suffer that one of his subjects (to satisfie his own Ambition) should bring any obstacle to a business, which (in probability) might give peace to *France*. The King bore already ill will enough against the Duke of *Guise*, and this discourse so augmented it, that seeing him next day, as he was about to enter the Room, design'd for the Ball, at the Queens Lodgings (adorn'd with an infinite number of Jewels, but yet more adorn'd by this graceful mine) he plac'd himself before the entrance of the door, and tartly demanded of him, where he went. The Duke without being daunted, answer'd, That he came to wait on him (and as it was his duty,) to render him his most humble service; to which the King reply'd, that he had no need of it, and so turn'd from him, without taking any further notice of him.

The Duke of *Guise*, though for all this, did not forbear to enter the room, enrag'd in his heart both against the King and the Duke of *Anjou*, but his grief serv'd but to augment his natural fierceness, and through spight he oftner approach'd the Princess *Margaret*, then he had been accustom'd to do, since what the Duke of *Anjou* had said to him concerning the Princess of *Monpensier* hinder'd him from regarding her.

The Duke of *Anjou* carefully observ'd both one and the other: the countenance of that Princess (though she endeavour'd all she could to conceal it) discover'd the displeasure which she conceiv'd, when the Duke of *Guise* spoke to the Princess *Margaret*. The Duke of *Anjou*, who through what she had said to him, when she mistook him for the Duke of *Guise*, had perceiv'd that she was jealous, hop'd to cause a misunderstanding between them, and setting himself down by her; 'Tis for your intrest, Madam, more then for my own (said he) that I go about to acquaint you, that the Duke of *Guise* merits not that you should make choice of him to my prejudice; let me intreat you not to interrupt me to tell me the contrary of a truth, which I but too well know. He deceives you Madam, he sacrifices you to my Sister, as he has made an oblation of her, to you. 'Tis a man that is only capable of Ambition, but since he has had the good fortune to please you, 'tis enough. I will not hinder him to enjoy a happiness, which without doubt I merited better then he: I should render my self unworthy of it, if I should strive longer to obtain the conquest of a heart, which another possesses, 'tis enough that I have not hitherto, but incurr'd your dislike, and I would not willingly cause hatred to succeed, by any longer importuning you with the most ardent, and faithful passion that ever was.

The Duke of *Anjou*, who was very sensibly wounded both with Love and grief, had scarce power to finish these words, and though he had begun his discourse through a militious intent, and through a desire of vengeance; yet he grew so mollified in considering the Princesses Beauty, and the loss which he receiv'd in loosing the hopes of ever being belov'd, that without attending her answer, he went out from the Ball, feigning that he found himself indispos'd, and went home to his own appartment to muze seriously upon his misfortune.

The Princess of *Monpensier* remain'd afflicted and perplext, as may be easily imagin'd, to see her reputation, and her most important secret, remaining in the hands of a Prince, whom she had treated ill, and to learn from him (what she could now no longer doubt of) that she had been deceiv'd by her Lover. Which added together, prov'd things that did not leave her so much Mistris of her passions, as was requisite she should be, in a place destin'd only to mirth and jollity. Yet she was forc'd to remain there, and afterwards to go and sup at the Dutchess of *Monpensier*'s (her Mother-in-laws) who took her along with her.

The Duke of *Guise* who languish'd with impatience to relate to her what the Duke of *Anjou* had said to him the day before, follow'd her to his Sisters, but how great was his amazement, when going about to entertain this fair Princess with discourse, he found that she reply'd not to what he said, but only made him most fearful reproaches; and her passion caus'd her to make those reproaches so confus'dly, that he could comprehend nothing from them, but only that she accus'd him of infidelity and Treason.

Orewhelm'd with despair to find cause for so great an augmentation of grief, where he had hop'd to find consolation for all his discontents, and affecting the Princess with a passion so violent, which left him not that liberty to remain dubious, whether he were again belov'd, or no; he resolv'd to hazard all at once and to give her an infallible proof of his affection. You shall be satisfied Madam (said he) I will do that for you, which all the Royal-Authority should not have obtain'd from me, nor have forc'd me to perform. It will cost me my Fortune, but that is a thing too inconsiderable to be vallu'd, to satisfie you.

Without remaining any longer at the Dutchess his Sisters, he went immediately to find out the Cardinals his Unkles, and under pretext of the ill treatment which he had receiv'd from the King, he represented to them so great a necessity, to secure his fortune, for him to make it appear, that he had no thoughts to marry the Princess *Margaret*, that he engag'd them to conclude his marriage with the Princess of *Portia*, who had already been propounded to him.

The news of this marriage was soon known throughout all *Paris*, every body seem'd amaz'd at it, and the Princess of *Monpensier* was posses'd at the hearing of it, both with joy, & grief; she was much pleas'd to see the power which she had over the Duke of *Guise;* but at the same instant, she was as much displeas'd to have caus'd him to relinquish a design so advantageous to him, as was his marriage with the Princess *Margaret.*

The Duke of *Guise* who had a mind that Love should recompence him for what he lost by Fortune, prest the Princess to grant him a private audience, to clear himself of the unjust reproaches which she had made him, and he obtain'd from her a promise that she would be at the Dutchess of *Monpensiers* (his Sisters) at such a time when that Dutchess should be absent, and when he might entertain her in private.

The Duke of *Guise* soon receiv'd the effect of this promise, and had the happiness to prostrate himself at her feet, and the freedome to declare to her his passion, and to inform her how much he suffer'd through her suspitions. The Princess, who could not forget what the Duke of *Anjou* had told her, (though the Duke of *Guises* proceedings ought sufficiently to have secur'd her from jealousie) acquainted him with the just cause which she had to believe that he had betray'd her, since the Duke of *Anjou* knew that, which it was impossible for him to have learnt from any other, but himself. The Duke of *Guise* knew not what defence to make for himself, and appear'd as much perplext as the Princess of *Monpensier,* to divine who (in probability) had discover'd their intelligence. In fine, in the remainder of her discourse, as she represented to him that he had been to blame to precipitate his marriage with the Princess of *Portia,* and to abandon that of the Princess *Margaret,* which would have prov'd so advantageous to him, she told him that he might well judge that she was not at all jealouse of it, since that at the Ball she her self had conjur'd him to have no respect for any there, but for that Princess.

The Duke of *Guise* reply'd, that 'twas possible that she might have had an intention to impose that command upon him, but assuredly that she had not done it. The Princess maintain'd the contrary; and in conclusion, at length with disputing, and examining one an others arguments, they found that of necessity, she must have deceiv'd her self, through the resemblance of their habits, and that she her self had reveal'd that to the Duke of *Anjou,* which she accus'd the Duke of *Guise* to have acquainted him with.

The Duke of *Guise,* who was almost justified in her opinion, through his marriage, became entirely so, through this conversation. This fair Princess thought she could not with justice refuse her heart to a man who had formerly possest it, and who but lately had abandon'd all his ambitious pretensions for her sake, she soon consented to accept his services, and permitted him to believe, that she was not insensible of his passion. The arrival of the Dutchess of *Monpensier* (her Mother-in-law) put a conclusion to this discourse, and hinder'd the Duke [of] *Guise* from declaring to her the transports of his joy.

Shortly after the Court removing to *Bloys*, the Princess of *Monpensier* follow'd it thither, where the marriage of the Princess *Margaret*, with the King of *Navarre* was concluded. The Duke of *Guise* knowing nothing more of grandure, and good fortune, then to be belov'd by the Princess of *Monpensier*, beheld, at present, with joy the conclusion of that marriage, which perhaps at another time had o'rewhelm'd him with despair: but yet he could not so well conceal his Love, but that the Prince of *Monpensier* discover'd something of it, who being no longer Master of his jealousie, commanded the Princess his Wife to depart for *Champigni*. This command seem'd very harsh to her, but yet she was forc'd to obey it. She found means to take her leave in private of the Duke of *Guise*, but she was much perplex't to find out a sure way for him to convey Letters to her; in fine, after she had ruminated on several, she at last fixt her thoughts upon the Count of *Chabanes*, who she always accounted for her friend, without considering that he was her Lover.

The Duke of *Guise*, who knew to what degree the Count was a friend to the Prince of *Monpensier*, was amaz'd that she chose him for her confident: but she assured him so much of his fidelity, that she secur'd him from suspition. This discourse ended, he parted from her possest with all the grief which absence and separation (from the belov'd Person) can cause in the breast of an afflicted Lover.

The Count of *Chabanes*, who, during the time of the Princess of *Monpensier* being at *Blois*, had been sick at *Paris*, hearing that she went to *Champigni*, met her upon the way, to wait on her thither: She now began to shew him several tokens of kindness and good will, and testified to him an extraordinary impatiency to discourse with him particularly in private. But what was his surprizal and his grief when he found, that this impatiency only signified to relate to him that she was passionately belov'd by the Duke of *Guise*, and that she had a reciprocal kindness for him: his grief and his astonishment was so great, that it permitted him not to return a reply to what the Princess had said, who was so taken up with her passion, and who found her mind so much eas'd to discourse to him of it, that she took no notice of his silence, but went on with her discourse, and related to him what had happen'd to her, with such exactness, that she forgot not the least circumstance material to her story. She aquainted him how the Duke of *Guise* and her self were agreed to receive through his means the Letters which they had engag'd to write to each other.

These words prov'd like mortal wounds to the Count of *Chabanes*, to see that his Mistris would have him serve his Rival, and that she her self propounded this to him as a thing which would be very pleasing to her. Yet he was so absolutely Master of himself, that he conceal'd from her his resentment, and only acquainted her how much he was surpriz'd to perceive in her so great a change. He hop'd at first that this alteration of her humour, which depriv'd him of all his hopes, would deprive him of his passion too: but he found this Princess so charming, her natural Beauty being lately much augmented by a certain gracefull air and carriage which she had learnt at Court, that he was very sensible that he lov'd her more then ever. The great confidence she reposed in him, in acquainting him with her secret kindness and tenderness she had of Duke of *Guise*'s respect made him discover of what an inestimable value the affection of this Princess was, and caus'd in him an ardent desire to possess it. And as his passion was extraordinary, so it produc'd in him the most extra-ordinary effect imaginable, for it made him undertake to deliver to his Mistris the Letters of his Rival.

The Duke of *Guise*'s absence caus'd the Princess of *Monpensier* to become exceeding pensive, and not hoping to receive any comfort, but from his Letters, she incessantly importun'd the Count of *Chabanes* to know if he receiv'd none, and grew almost passionate with him, that he had not yet deliver'd her any. At last he receiv'd one, brought him by a Gentleman belonging to the Duke of *Guise*, which he immediately carried to the Princess, not to retard her Joy one moment, which was excessive at the receiving of it, and she took no care to conceal it from him, but inviting him to participate of that which was as pleasant as poison to him, she favour'd him with the reading of the Letter to him, and the affectionate and witty Reply which she made to it; this answer he carried to the Gentleman that brought the other, with the same fidelity with which he had render'd to the Princess the Letter which he had receiv'd, but with far more grief. Yet he comforted himself a little with thoughts that this Princess would make some reflection upon what he did for her, and hop'd that she would prove so gratefull to acknowledge it, but finding her aversion to increase more and more every day against him, through the ill humour which she was in for the Duke of *Guise's* absence, he took the liberty upon him to intreat her to be mindful a Little of what he suffer'd for her. The Princess whose inclinations were soly fixt upon the Duke of *Guise*, and who found none (in her opinion) but him alone worthy to adore her, resented so ill that any other should dare to pretend Love to her, that she treated the Count of *Chabanes* worser on this occasion, then she had done at first, when he mention'd Love to her. And though his passion, as well as his patience, was extream, and had appear'd to be so upon all occasions, yet he departed from the Princess, and went to a friends house (not far distant from *Champigni*) from whence he writ to her with all the passion, which so strange a procedure could inspire him with, but yet too with all the respect that was due both to her Quality and Person, and by his Letter took an Eternal farewell of her.

The Princess began to repent her self to have disoblig'd a man, over whom she had such pow'r; and being unwilling to loose him, not only through the amity which she had for him, but also through the int'rest of her Love, (to serve her in which his friendship was extreamly requisite) she sent him word that she desir'd yet once more to speak with him, and that afterwards she left him the liberty to dispose of himself as he pleas'd.

Lovers are generally very weak, and are soon o'recome by any thing that bears but the least shape of incouragement when once in Love. The Count obey'd her message, and return'd, and in less then in the space of one hour the Beauty of the Princess of *Monpensier*, her Wit, and some obliging words, render'd him more submissive, and more her slave then ever. Nay he gave her too immediately the Letters, which he had but then newly receiv'd from the Duke of *Guise*.

About this time, the desire which they had at Court to cause the chief of the *Huguenot*-Party to come thither, to effect that execrable design, which was executed on St. *Bartholomewes* day, made the King (the better to delude them) to send away from about him all the Princes of the house of *Bourbon*, and of the house of *Guise*. The Prince of *Monpensier* return'd to *Champigni*, where his presence serv'd but to o'rewhelm the Princess his Wife with grief.

The Duke of *Guise* retir'd himself in the Countrey to the Cardinal of *Lorrain's* his Unkles, where Love, and want of imployment, caus'd so violent a desire in him to see the Princess of *Monpensier*, that without considering what he did hazard both for her and himself, he feign'd a journey, and leaving all his train at a small village on the way, he took only with him that Gentleman, who already had made several journeys to *Champigni*, and took Post thither: and as he had no other Person to make his address to, but to the Count of *Chabanes*, he caus'd his Gentle-man to write him a Note, by which the Gentleman intreated him to come and meet him at a place which he appointed him.

The Count of *Chabanes*, believing that it was only to receive Letters from the Duke of *Guise*, went and met him, but he was extreamly surpriz'd, and no less afflicted, when he saw the Duke of *Guise*, his affliction equalling his amazement. The Duke, prepossest with his design, took no more notice of the Counts perplexity, then the Princess of *Monpensier* had done of his silence, when she related her Love to him. He began to exagerate his passion to him, and to make him believe that he should infallibly die, if he did not obtain for him from the Princess, the permission to see her. The Count of *Chabanes* answer'd him coldly, That he would acquaint the Princess with all that he desir'd, and that he would come and return him an answer.

Their discourse ended, he return'd to *Champigni* assaulted by such various passions, that sometimes their violence depriv'd him of his Reason, and he often took a resolution to return to the Duke of *Guise* without acquainting the Princess of *Monpensier* with his being there; but the exact fidelity which he had promis'd her soon chang'd that resolution.

He arriv'd at *Champigni*, without knowing what he had best to do, but being inform'd that the Prince of *Monpensier* was gone out a hunting, he went directly to the appartment of the Princess, who seeing him troubled, caus'd her women immediately to retire, to know the subject of that disorder: he told her (moderating his grief as much as possible) that the Duke of *Guise* was within a league of *Champigni*, and that he passionately desir'd to see her.

The Princess at the relation of this unexpected newes gave a great cry, and her disorder seem'd to be a little less then that of the Count. Her love at first represented to her the joy, which she should have to see a man whom she so tenderly affected; but when she consider'd how contrary this action was to those strict rules of vertue which she alwayes practiz'd, and that she could not see her Lover, but by suffering him at midnight to enter her appartment, she found her self perplext extreamly.

The Count of *Chabanes* (who attended her answer as an Oracle to pronounce to him either Life, or Death) judging of the incertainty of the Princesses resolution by her silence, ventur'd to speak to her, to represent to her all those dangers which she would through this interview expose her self to, and being willing that she should perceive that he made her not this discourse upon the account of his own int'rest he told her, If Madam, after all which I have represented to you, your passion is yet more prevalent with you then my Arguments, and that you desire to see the Duke of *Guise*, let not my consideration (if that of your own int'rest does not do it) hinder you from obtaining your wishes. I will not deprive a

Person I adore of so great a satisfaction, nor cause her to search for persons less faithful then my self to procure it for her. Yes Madam if you consent, I will go this very Night, and find the Duke (since 'tis too hazardous to leave him longer where he is) and bring him here to your appartment. But by what way, and how, said the Princess, interrupting him. Ah Madam (cry'd the Count) 'tis done already, since you only deliberate upon the means, that fortunate Lover shall come Madam: I will bring him through the Park, give order only to one of your Women (in whom you most confide) that she should let down precisely at midnight, the little draw-bridge which reaches from your Anti-chamber to the Garden, and do not disquiet your self about the rest. Finishing these words, he rose up from his seat, and without attending any further consent from the Princess of *Monpensier*, he went out and took horse, and went to find out the Duke of *Guise*, who with an extream impatiency expected him.

The Princess of *Monpensier* remain'd so troubl'd at what had happen'd that it was some time before she came to her self again; but as soon as she had recover'd the use of her reason, her first intention was to have had the Count of *Chabanes* call'd back, and to forbid him to bring the Duke of *Guise* thither, but it lay not in her power to put this thought in execution. She imagin'd that without calling of him back again, it was only requisite not to let down the Draw-Bridge to spoil their design, and she believ'd that she should have continued in that resolution, but when the hour of appointment was come, she could no longer resist against the Desire which she had to see a Lover whom she judg'd so worthy to adore her; and she instructed one of her women with all, that was requisite to introduce the Duke of *Guise* into her appartment.

In the interim that Duke & the Count of *Chabanes* approach'd near to *Champigni*, but in a very different condition; the Duke abandon'd his mind only to Joy, and to whatsoever hope and good success, inspires of most agreeable, and pleasing into a Lover: but the Count, on the contrary, abandon'd himself over to dispair and rage, which mov'd him a thousand times (had not his honour, and the Baseness of the action prevented him) to have thrust his Sword through the body of his Rival. At last they arriv'd at *Champigni*, where they left their horses with the Duke of *Guise*'s Page, and passing through the breaches, which were in the wall, they ent'red in the Garden.

The Count of *Chabanes*, amidst his despair, always retain'd some hopes that the Princess of *Monpensiers* reason would at length return, and aid her against her passion, and that in the end she would take a resolution not to see the Duke of *Guise:* but when he saw the Draw-Bridge let down, he could then no longer doubt the contrary, and at that instant his passion grew so violent, and so unruly that he was ready to have executed the last effects of his despair; but recollecting himself, and thinking that if he made a noise, he should apparently be heard by the Prince of *Monpensier* (whose appartment look'd out upon the same Garden) and that all that confusion would in the end light upon the persons whom he most affected, his rage (no longer agitated by the violence of his passion) immediately grew calm, and suffer'd him to accomplish his design, and to conduct the Duke of *Guise* to the feet of his Princess: where not being able to be a witness of their discourse (though the Princess testified to him, that she desir'd it, and though he wish'd it himself) he retir'd into a small passage (which was contingent to the Prince of *Monpensiers* Lodgings) being perplext with the most sad and dismall thoughts, that did ever possess the mind of a disconsolate Lover.

In the mean while, though in their passage over the Draw-bridge they had been careful to make but small noise: yet the Prince of *Monpensier*, (who through misfortune) awak't at that instant, heard them, and caus'd one of his Gentlemen, belonging to his chamber, to rise to see what it was. The Gentleman put his head out of the window, and though the night was dark, yet through its obscurity, he could discover light enough to perceive that the Bridge was let down: he advertiz'd his Master of it, who presently commanded him to go into the Park, and see what was the matter. Immediately after he rose up himself, being disquieted with thinking that he heard some body walk about, and came directly to the appartment of the Princess his Wife, which was opposite against the Bridge.

At the very instant when he approach'd that small passage, where the Count of *Chabanes* was, it chanc'd that the Princess of *Monpensier* who was asham'd to find her self alone with the Duke of *Guise*, intreated the Count several times to enter in her chamber, but he alwayes excus'd himself, and as she continued still pressing him, (possest with grief and passion) he answer'd her so loud, that he was heard by the Prince of *Monpensier*, but so confus'dly, that the Prince only hear'd the voice of a man, without distinguishing that of the Count.

An adventure of the like nature had given cause of suspition to a mind possest with more tranquility, and less jealousie then this Prince: so that it soon produc'd in him an effect both of rage and fury, which made him knock with impetuosity at the Princesses chamber door, and calling aloud to cause it to be open'd, he gave the greatest surprize imaginable to the Princess, the Duke of *Guise*, and to the Count of *Chabanes*, and this last hearing the Princes voice, soon apprehended that it was impossible to hinder him from being perswaded, but that there was some body in the Princess his Wives Chamber, and the greatness of his passion representing to him, that if he found the Duke of *Guise* there, the Princess of *Monpensier* would have the affliction to see him murder'd before her Eyes, and that the very life it self of this Princess would not be secur'd from danger (these thoughts inspiring him with a resolution worthy of himself) he resolv'd by an unparallel'd Generosity, to expose himself to the Princes fury, to save from ruine an ungratefull Mistress and a Beloved Rivall; and whil'st the Prince gave a thousand knocks at the Door, he went to the Duke of *Guise*, who knew not what Resolution to take, and committed to the care of the Princess of *Monpensiers* Woman, who had assisted them to enter by the Draw-bridge, to conduct him out by the same way, whil'st that he oppos'd himself to sustain the Princes fury.

Scarce was the Duke got out of the Anti-chamber, but the Prince, having forc'd the passage door, enter'd in the Chamber as a man possest with rage and fury, and who sought an object against whom he might vent his displeasure. But when he saw no body but the Count of *Chabanes*, and that he saw him remain unmovable, leaning upon the Table, with a countenance in which sadness was represented in its lively colours, he remain'd unmovable as the other, and his surprize was so excessive to find alone, and at mid-night in his Wives Chamber, the only man for whom he had the greatest kindness in the world, that it so disorder'd him, that it left him not the power to speak. The Princess was laid down upon some Cushions, in a condition ready to faint away, and perhaps Fortune never represented three Persons in a state more worthy of Commiseration.

In Fine, the Prince of *Monpensier* who could scarce believe his Eyes, and give credit to what he saw, but imagin'd it to be some fallacy, or some illusion, and who had an intent to disengage himself from that Chaos of confusion in which this adventure had invellopp'd him, and addressing his speech to the Count in a tone which shew'd that he yet retain'd a kindness for him; What is't I see (said he), is't reall, or is't some illusion? Is't possible, that a man whom I have lov'd so dearly, should choose my Wife above all others to seduce her? And you Madam (said he) turning to the Princess, was it not sufficient to deprive me of your heart, and of my honour, without depriving me of the only man capable to comfort me in these misfortunes. Answer me either the one, or the other (continued he) and clear me from the suspitions that I have conceiv'd of an accident, which I cannot believe to be such as it appears.

The Princess remain'd unable to answer, and the Count of *Chabanes* open'd several times his lips, without being able to bring forth a word, but at last, I am criminall (said he) as to what concerns you, and unworthy of the friendship which you have shown me, but 'tis not after the nature which perhaps you may imagine. I am my self more misfortunate, and in a more desperate condition then you. My death shall revenge you, of what I have been culpable of towards you, and if you will deprive me of Life presently, 'tis the only favour which you can bestow upon me that will be acceptable, and welcome to me.

These words (utter'd with a mortall grief, and an air which sufficiently declar'd his innocency) in stead of clearing the Prince of *Monpensier* from his suspitions, perswaded him more and more to believe that there was some hidden mysterie conceal'd in this adventure, which surpast his imagination to divine, and his despair augmenting through this incertainty: Either deprive me of life your self (said he) or give me some explanation of your words. I comprehend nothing, you owe this satisfaction to my moderation, since any other, but my self, before this, would have imprinted characters of vengeance upon your heart for so sensible an affront, and have sacrifiz'd your life, to expiate your crime. The evidences are very false (answer'd the Count in interrupting him,) Ah they are too visible and too apparent (reply'd the Prince), I must revenge my self first, and then search out the mysterie of this adventure at leisure.

In saying these words he drew near to the Count of *Chabanes* with the action of a man possest with rage and fury. The Princess fearing some mischief would follow (which though could not well happen, since her Husband had no Sword about him), rose to cast her self between them, but her faintness was so great, that it forc'd her to sink under this endeavour, for as she approach'd the Prince her Husband, she fell down in a swound at his feet.

The Prince was yet more concern'd at his Wives fainting, then he had been at the tranquility which he found possest the Count when he approach'd him, and not being able longer to endure the sight of two persons who gave him such cause for grief and discontent, he turn'd his head on the other side, and threw himself upon his Wives bed, orewhelm'd with an unimaginable grief.

The Count of *Chabanes* penetrated with repentance, to have abus'd a friend from whom he receiv'd so many tokens of kindness, and finding that he could never make amends for what he had committed, departed hastily out of the Chamber, and passing through the Princes appartment, of which he found the doors open, he descended into the Court, took horse, and guided only by his despair, he wander'd up and down the Countrey till at length he arriv'd at *Paris*.

In the interim, the Prince of *Monpensier*, who saw that the Princess return'd not from her swound, left her to the care of her Women, and retir'd into his Chamber, possest with a mortal grief.

The Duke of *Guise*, who was got safe out of the Park, without almost knowing what he did (so much he was troubl'd at what had happen'd), departed some few Leagues from *Champigni*, but he could go no further, without hearing some news of the Princess; which caus'd him to stay in a Forrest, and to send his Page to enquire of the Count of *Chabanes*, what had succeeded that misfortunate adventure.

The Page could not find the Count of *Chabanes*, but he learnt from others, that the Princess of *Monpensier* was extraordinary ill. The Duke of *Guises* disquiet was much augmented by what his Page related to him, but without being able to hinder it, or to receive any comfort, he was constrain'd to return to his Unkles, least he should give them cause of suspition through his longer absence.

The Duke of *Guises* Page had indeed related to him the truth, in telling that the Princess of *Monpensier* was extream ill, for the truth was, that as soon as her Women had got her to bed, she was seiz'd with so violent a Feaver, and withall began to grow so light-headed, that from the very second day of her sickness, her Life was in extream danger, and her recovery was much fear'd.

The Prince feign'd to be sick too, to the end that none should be amaz'd why he enter'd not into his Wives Chamber, but the order which he receiv'd to return to Court, whither all the Catholick Princes were summon'd to exterminate the *Huguenots*, [helped]⁶ him out of the perplexity into which this adventure had plung'd him, and he return'd to *Paris* not knowing what he ought either to hope, or fear concerning the Princess his Wives distemper. He was but scarce arriv'd there, when they begun to attacque the *Huguenots* in the person of one of the Cheifs of their Party, the Admiral of *Chastillon*, and two dayes after was perform'd that horrible Massacre,⁷ for its execrableness, so famous throughout all *Europe*.

⁶ Original reads "hope," probably a misprint for "holp" (archaic form of helped).
⁷ The St. Bartholomew Massacre took place on August 24, 1572.

The poor Count of *Chabanes*, who came with an intent to conceal himself in one of the remotest parts of the Suburbs of *Paris*, there to abandon himself over entirely to his grief, was invellop'd in the *Huguenots* ruine. The Persons where he lodg'd having known him, and remembring that he had been suspected to be of that Party, murder'd him that very night which prov'd so fatal to several persons. In the morning the Prince of *Monpensier* going out of Town to distribute some orders to keep all in peace and quietness, past through the Street where the murder'd body of *Chabanes* lay. At first he was seiz'd with astonishment at the sight of this deplorable spectacle, but afterwards his friendship reviving, it caused in him some grief, but the remembrance of the affront which he believ'd he had receiv'd from the Count at length gave him joy, and he seem'd contented (without any endeavours of his own) to see himself reveng'd by Fortune.

The Duke of *Guise's* thoughts being taken up with a desire to revenge his Fathers death (and soon after being overjoy'd to have accomplish'd it) his affection by degrees began to diminish, and to grow less and less for the Princess of *Monpensier*, and he began to be less concern'd to hear from her then formerly, and finding that the Marchioness of *Noirmoustier*, a Person possest with a great deal of Wit and Beauty, gave him more encouragement and hopes then that Princess, he engag'd himself entirely to her, and lov'd her with an unexpressable passion, which endur'd till death (which at last frees us from all our passions) put an end to their affection.

In the mean while, after that the Princess of *Monpensiers* disease was arriv'd to the height, it began to decrease, she recover'd again the use of her reason, and finding her self somewhat comforted through the absence of the Prince her Husband, she gave some assurance, and hopes of her recovery, her health notwithstanding return'd not to her but with great trouble, through the ill disposition of her mind, which was again of anew perplext, when she bethought her self, that she had hear'd no news at all of the Duke of *Guise*, during the whole time of her sickness. She enquir'd of her Women, if they had seen no body that came from him, and if they had receiv'd no Letters, and finding nothing which answer'd her expectations, and which she had wish'd for, she imagin'd her self to be the most unhappy Person in the world to have hazzarded all, for a man who in the end forsook her, and it yet prov'd a new addition to her misfortunes, to learn the death of the Count of *Chabanes*, which she soon heard of (through the care which the Prince her Husband took to have her acquainted with it) and the Duke of *Guises* ingratitude made her more sensible of the loss of a man whose fidelity was so well known to her.

Such heavy discontents soon forc'd her to sink under their weight, and reduced her into a condition far more dangerous then that from which she was but lately escap'd, and as the Marchioness of *Noirmoustier* was a Person who took as great care to have the addresses which were made to her taken notice of, as others did to conceal them: those of the Duke of *Guise* soon became so publick, that at as great a distance, and as sick as the Princess of *Monpensier* was, she heard them confirm'd from so many hands, that she could no longer doubt of her misfortune.

This news prov'd fatall to her life, and now her courage grew too weak longer to sustain the weight of her misfortunes, she could no longer resist against the grief which she had to have lost the estimation of her Husband, the heart of her Lover, and the most faithful'st friend that ever was. She dyed in few dayes after in the prime of her age, one of the most Beautiful'st Princesses of the world, and who without doubt had been the most happiest, if Vertue and Prudence had but had the conduct of her actions.

FINIS

# FIVE LOVE-LETTERS
# FROM A NUN TO A CAVALIER

(1678)

# FIVE

# LOVE-LETTERS

## FROM A

# NUN

## TO A

# CAVALIER.

Done out of *French* into *English*,
BY
Sir *ROGER L'ESTRANGE*

*LONDON,*
Printed for *R. Bentley,* at the
*Post-House* in *Russel-street* in
*Covent-Garden.* 1693.

Five Love-Letters from a Nun to a Cavalier (*1678*) *is a translation of the famous* Lettres portugaises *of 1669, a series of five letters purporting to be written by a Portuguese nun to a French army officer who had won her love and then abandoned her. An overnight success in France, the* Letters *were also much read in England, where a number of editions of the translation appeared, not to mention sequels and imitations. No piece of fiction had wider circulation in the late seventeenth century and hence the influence of these letters as a model for the presentation from within of an intensely realized love-story was great.*

*The thoroughgoing use of the epistolary form did two things for the book : it made the love-story, already passionate, much more immediate, and it permitted an intimacy and confessional-like quality which seemed both natural and piquant. Moreover, all but a few readers believed that the unhappy love affair was a true one, that the letters were actually written by a nun in the agony of her broken heart. It was presently "discovered" that the cavalier was one Noel Bouton de Chamilly, Count de St. Leger (1636–1715). The nun's name was a secret until 1810 when she was identified as one Mariana Alcoforado, who had been in the convent at Beja in Portugal. Though these names were accepted as fact until recently, it seems much more likely today that the letters were a literary fabrication, that they constitute a work of fiction, not a true-life confession. Certain expressions, certain parallels to earlier stories, a certain theatrical quality in the exploitation of the situation, all lead to this conclusion. In fact, Rousseau's hunch that they were written by a man seems justified by the evidence, and the author is thought to be that Gabriel-Joseph Lavergne de Guilleragues whose name appeared in a 1669 edition as that of the translator.*

*But the letters themselves are the important thing. They are a remarkable tour de force, apparently giving the reader a direct view into a passionate and suffering heart. There is almost no story ; the important action has already taken place, and though the course of the letters moves the nun from active heartbreak to an even sadder resignation when she realizes finally that she has been abandoned in very truth, little or nothing occurs in the way of action. The nun spreads out her suffering bit by bit, goes over every possible aspect of it minutely, shifts from emotion to emotion, the language everywhere being of the most intense and pathetic kind, a steady anguished outcry.*

*The English translation is fairly free though it regularly manages to render the sense of the original if not the exact wording. The translator, Sir Roger L'Estrange, a journalist with an enormous published output to his credit, seems to have had a strong sense of the difficulty of turning the book into another language. "It is, in* French," *he says in his brief preface,* "*one of the most Artificial* [i.e., *artistic*] *Pieces perhaps of the Kind, that is any where Extant . . .* [and] *cannot be adopted into any other Tongue, without Extream Force, and Affectation."* L'Estrange *was, happily, quite successful in his efforts; the book as he translated it is as pathetic and as apparently unstudied as it is in French.*

*The text which follows is based on the 1693 edition of the* Letters *in the Folger Shakespeare Library. This edition represents a revision of* L'Estrange's *first translation of 1678, and since it presents his second thoughts, as it were, after seeing his earlier work in print, it may be taken as superseding his previous English version.*

## To the Reader

You are to take this Translation very Kindly, for the Author of it has ventur'd his Reputation to Oblige you: Ventur'd it (I say) even in the very Attempt of Copying so Nice an Original. It is, in *French*, one of the most Artificial Pieces perhaps of the Kind, that is any where Extant: Beside the Peculiar Graces, and Felicities of that Language, in the Matter of an *Amour*, which cannot be adopted into any other Tongue, without Extream Force, and Affectation. There was (it seems) an *Intrigue* of Love carry'd on betwixt a *French Officer*, and a *Nun* in *Portugal*. The Cavalier forsakes his Mistress, and Returns for *France*. The Lady expostulates the Business in five Letters of Complaint, which She sends after him; and those five Letters are here at your service. You will find in them the Lively Image of an Extravagant, and an Unfortunate Passion; and that *a Woman may be Flesh and Blood, in a Cloyster, as well as in a Palace.*

## Five Portugaise Letters
## Turn'd into English

### *The first Letter*

Oh my Inconsiderate, Improvident, and most unfortunate Love; and those Treacherous Hopes that have betray'd both Thee, and Me! The Passion that I design'd for the Blessing of my Life, is become the Torment of it: A Torment answerable to the prodigious Cruelty of his Absence that causes it. Bless me! But must this Absence last for ever? An Absence so Hellish, that Sorrow it self wants words to express it? Am I then never to see those Eyes again? Those Eyes, that have so often exchang'd Love with Mine, to the Charming of my very soul with Extacy, and Delight? Those Eyes that were ten thousand worlds to me, and all that I desir'd; the only comfortable Light of Mine, which, since I understood the Resolution of your Insupportable Departure, have Serv'd me only to weep withal, and to lament the sad Approach of my Inevitable fate. And yet in this Extremity I cannot, me-thinks, but have some Tenderness, even for the misfortunes that are of your Creating. My Life was vow'd to you the first time I saw you: and since you would not accept of it as a Present, I am Content to make it a Sacrifice. A Thousand times a day I send my Sighs to hunt you out: And what Return for all my Passionate Disquiets, but the good Counsel of my Cross fortune? that whispers me at every turn; Ah wretched *Mariane!* why do'st thou flatter, and Consume thy self in the vain pursuit of a Creature never to be Recover'd? Hee's gone, hee's gone; Irrevocably gone; h'as past the Seas to fly thee. Hee's now in *France* dissolv'd in pleasures; and does no more think of thee, or of what thou suffer'st for his false sake, then if he had never known any such woman. But hold: Y'ave more of Honour in you then to do so ill a thing; and so have I, then to believe it, especially of a Person that I'm so much concern'd to justify. *Forget me?* 'Tis Impossible. My Case is bad enough at best, without the Aggravation of vain suppositions. No, no: The Care and Pains you took to make me think you lov'd me, and then the Joyes that That Care gave me, must never be forgotten: And should I love you less this Moment, then when I lov'd you most, (in Confidence that you lov'd me so too) I were Ungrateful. 'Tis an Unnatural, and a strange thing, me-thinks, that the Remembrance of those blessed hours should be now so terrible to me; and that those delights that were so ravishing in the Enjoyment, should become so bitter in the Reflection. Your last Letter gave me such a Passion of the heart, as if it would have forc'd its way thorough my Breast, and follow'd you. It laid me three hours senseless: I wish it had been *dead*; for I had Then dy'd of Love. But I reviv'd: and to what End? only to die again, and lose that Life for you, which you your self did not think worth the saving. Beside that there's no Rest for me, while you're Away, any where but in the grave. This fit was follow'd with other Ill Accidents which I shall never be without till I see you: In the mean while, I bear them; and without repining too, because they came from you. But with your Leave: Is this the Recompense that you intend me? Is this your way of treating those that love you? Tho' 'tis no Matter; for (do what you will) I am resolv'd to be firm to you to my last gasp; and never to see the Eyes of any other Mortal. Nay I dare assure you that it will not be the worse for you neither, if you never set your heart upon any other woman: for certainly a Passion under the degree of mine, will never content you. You may find more Beauty perhaps else-where: (tho' the time was when you found no fault with mine) but you shall never meet with so true a heart; and all the rest is nothing.

Let me entreat you not to stuff your Letters with things Unprofitable, and Impertinent to our Affair: and you may save your self the trouble too of desiring me to THINK of you. Why 'tis Impossible for me to forget you: and I must not forget the hope you gave me neither of your Return, and of spending some part of your time here with us in *Portugal.* Alas! and why not your whole Life rather? If I could but find any way to deliver my self from this unlucky Cloyster, I should hardly stand gaping here for the performance of your Promise: but in defiance of all opposition, put my self upon the March, Search you out, follow you, and love you throughout the whole world. It is not that I please my self with this Project as a thing feasible; or that I would so much as entertain any hope of Comfort; (tho' in the very delusion I might find pleasure) but as it is my Lot to be miserable, I will be only sensible of that which is my Doom. And yet after all this, I cannot deny, but upon this Opportunity of writing to you which my Brother has given me, I was surpriz'd with some faint Glimmerings of Delight, that yielded me a temporary Respite to the horrour of my despair. Tell me I conjure you; what was it that made you so solicitous to entangle me, when you knew you were to leave me? And why so bloodily bent to make me Unhappy? why could you not let me alone at quiet in my Cloyster as you found me? Did I ever do you any Injury?

But I must ask your Pardon; for I lay nothing to your Charge. I am not in condition to meditate a Revenge: and I can only complain of the Rigour of my Perverse Fortune. When she has parted our Bodies, she has done her worst, and left us nothing more to fear: Our hearts are inseparable; for those whom Love has United are never to be divided. As you tender my soul let me hear often from you. I have a Right me-thinks to the Knowledg, both of your Heart, and of your Fortune; and to your Care to inform me of it too. But *what-ever you do, be sure to come; and above all things in the world, to let me see you. Adieu.* And yet I cannot quitt this Paper yet. Oh that I could but convey my self in the place on't! Mad fool that I am, to talk at this rate of a thing that I my self know to be Impossible! *Adieu.* For I can go no farther. *Adieu.* Do but love me for ever, and I care not what I endure.

## *The second Letter*

There is so great a difference betwixt the Love I write, and That which I feel, that if you measure the One by the Other, I have undone my self. Oh how happy were I if you could but judge of my Passion by the violence of your own! But That I perceive is not to be the Rule betwixt you, and me. Give me leave however to tell you with an honest freedom, that tho' you cannot love me, you do very ill yet to treat me at this Barbarous Rate: It puts me out of my Wits to see my self forgotten; and it is as little for your Credit perhaps, as it is for my Quiet. Or if I may not say that you are Unjust, it is yet the most Reasonable thing in the World to let me tell you that I am miserable. I foresaw what it would come to, upon the very Instant of your Resolution to leave me. Weak Woman that I was! to expect, (after this) that you should have more Honour, and Integrity then other Men, because I had unquestionably deserv'd it from you, by a transcendent degree of Affection above the Love of other Women. No, no; Your Levity, and Aversion have over-rul'd your Gratitude, and Justice; you are my Enemy by Inclination: whereas only the Kindness of your Disposition can Oblige me. Nay your Love it self, if it were barely grounded upon my Loving of you, could never make me happy. But so far am I even from that Pretence, that in six Months I have not receiv'd one sillable from you; Which I must impute to the blind fondness of my own Passion, for I should otherwise have foreseen that my Comforts were to be but Temporary, and my Love Everlasting. For why should I think that you would ever content your self to spend your whole Life in *Portugal;* and relinquish your Country, and your Fortune, only to think of me? Alas! my sorrows are Inconsolable, and the very Remembrance of my past Enjoyments makes up a great part of my present pain. But must all my hopes be blasted then, and fruitless? Why may not I yet live to see you again within these Walls, and with all those Transports of Extacy, and Satisfaction, as heretofore? But how I fool my self! for I find now that the Passion which on my side, took up all the faculties of my Soul, and Body, was only excited on your part by some loose Pleasures, and that they were to live and die together. It should have been my Business even in the Nick of those Critical, and Blessed Minutes, to have Reason'd my self into the Moderation of so Charming, and deadly an Excess, and to have told my self before-hand, the fate which I now suffer. But my Thoughts were too much taken up with You to consider my self; So that I was not in Condition to attend the Care of my Repose, or to bethink my self of what might poison it, and disappoint me in the full Emprovement of the most Ardent Instances of your Affection. I was too much pleas'd with you, to think of parting with you, and yet you may remember that I have told you now and then by fits, that you would be the Ruin of me. But those Phancies were soon dispers'd; and I was glad to yield them up too; and to give up my self to the Enchantments of your false Oaths and Protestations. I see very well the Remedy of all my Misfortunes, and that I should quickly be at Ease if I could leave Loving you. But Alas! That were a Remedy worse then the disease. No, no: I'le rather endure any thing then forget you. Nor could I if I would. 'Tis a thing that did never so much as enter into my Thought. But is not your Condition now the worse of the two? Is it not better to endure what I now suffer, then to enjoy Your faint satisfactions among your French Mistresses? I am so far from Envying your Indifference, that I Pity it. I defie you to forget me absolutely: and I am deceiv'd if I have not taken such a Course with you, that you shall never be perfectly happy without me. Nay perhaps I am at this Instant the less miserable of the two; in regard that I am the more employ'd. They have lately made me doorkeeper here in this Convent. All the People that talk to me think me mad; for I answer them I know not what; And certainly the rest of the Convent must be as mad as I, they would never else have thought me Capable of any Trust. How do I envy the good Fortune of poor *Emanuel*, and *Francisco!* Why cannot I be with you perpetually as they are? tho' in your Liberty too? I should follow you as Close without dispute, and serve you at least as faithfully; for there is nothing in this World that I so much desire as to see you; But however, let me entreat you to think of me; and I shall Content my self with a bare place in your Memory. And yet I cannot tell neither, whether I should or no? for I know very well that when I saw you every day I should hardly have satisfy'd my self within these Bounds. But you have taught me since, that whatsoever you will have me do, I must do. In the *Interim*, I do not at all repent of my Passion for you; Nay, I am well enough satisfi'd that you have seduc'd me; and your Absence it self tho' never so rigorous, and perhaps Eternal, does not at all lessen the vigour of my Love: which I will avow to the Whole World, for I make no secret on't. I have done many things irregularly 'tis true; and against the Common Rules of good Manners: and not without taking some Glory in them neither, because they were done for your sake. My Honour, and Religion are brought only to serve the Turn of my Love, and to carry me on to my lives end, in the Passionate Continuance of the Affection I have begun. I do not write this, to draw a Letter from you; wherefore never force your self for the Matter: for I will receive nothing at your hands; no, not so much as any Mark of your Affection, unless it comes of its own accord, and in a Manner, whether you will or No. If it may give you any satisfaction, to save your self the trouble of Writing, it shall give me some likewise, to excuse the Unkindness of it; for I am wonderfully enclin'd to pass over all your faults. A *French* Officer, that had the Charity this morning to hold me at least three hours in a discourse of you, tells me that *France* has made a Peace. If it be so; Why cannot you bestow a visit upon me, and take me away with you? But 'tis more then I deserve, and it must be as you please; for my Love does not at all depend upon your Manner of treating me. Since you went away I have not had one Minutes Health, nor any sort of Pleasure, but in the Accents of your Name, which I call upon a Thousand times a day. Some of my Companions that understand the deplorable Ruin you have brought upon me, are so good as to entertain me many times concerning you. I keep as Close to my Chamber as is possible, which is the dearer to me even for the many Visits you have made me there. Your Picture I have perpetually before me, and I Love it more then my Hearts Blood. The very Counterfeit gives me some Comfort: But oh the Horrours too! When I consider that the Original, for ought I know, is lost for ever. But why should it be possible, even to be possible, that I may never see you more? Have you forsaken me then for ever? It turns my Brain to think on't. Poor *Mariane!* But my Spirits fail me, and I shall scarce out-live this Letter. — Mercy — Farewel, Farewel.

### The third Letter

What shall become of me? Or what will you advise me to do? How strangely am I disappointed in all my Expectations! Where are the Letters from you? the Long and Kind Letters that I look'd for by every Post? To keep me alive in the hopes of Seeing you again; and in the Confidence of your Faith, and Justice; to settle me in some tolerable state of Repose, without being abandon'd to any insupportable Extream? I had once cast my Thoughts upon some Idle Projects of endeavouring my own Cure, in case I could but once assure my self that I was totally forgotten. The distance you were at; Certain Impulses of Devotion; the fear of utterly destroying the Remainder of my Imperfect health, by so many restless Nights, and Cares; the Improbability of your Return; The Coldness of your Passion, and the Formality of your last *Adieu's;* Your Weak, and

frivolous pretences for your departure: These, with a thousand other
Considerations, (of more weight, then profit) did all concur to encourage
me in my design, if I should find it necessary; In fine; having only my
single self to encounter I could not doubt of the success, nor could it
enter into my Apprehension what I feel at this day. Alas! how wretched
is my Condition, that am not allow'd so much as to divide the sorrows
with you, of which you your self are the Cause? You are the Offender,
and I am to bear the Punishment of your Crime. It strikes me to the very
heart, for fear you, that are now so Insensible of my Torments, were
never much affected with our mutual delights. Yes, yes; 'Tis now a Clear
Case, that your whole Address to me was onely an Artificial disguise. You
betray'd me as often as you told me, how over-joy'd you were that you
had got me alone: and your Passions, and Transports were only the Effects
of my own Importunities: Yours was a deliberate design to fool me; your
business was to make a Conquest, not a friend; and to triumph over my
Heart, without ever engaging or hazzarding your own. Are not you very
unhappy now, and (at least) Ill-natur'd, if not ill-bred, only to make this
wretched use of so Superlative a friendship? Who would have thought it
possible that such a Love as mine, should not have made you happy?
'Tis for your sake alone if I am troubl'd for the Infinite delights that you
have lost, and might as easily have enjoy'd, had you but thought them
worth the while. Ah! if you did but understand them aright, you would
find a great difference betwixt the Pleasure of Obliging me, and that of
Abusing me; and betwixt the Charming Felicities of Loving violently, and
of being so belov'd. I do not know either what I am, or what I do, or
what I would be at. I am torn to pieces by a Thousand contrary Motions,
and in a Condition deplorable beyond Imagination. I love you to death
and so tenderly too, that I dare hardly wish your heart in the same condition with mine. I should destroy my self, or die with Grief, could I
believe your nights and Thoughts, as restless as I find Mine; your Life
as Anxious and disturb'd; your Eyes still flowing, and all things and
people Odious to you. Alas! I am hardly able to bear up under my own
Misfortunes; how should I then Support the Weight of yours; which
would be a Thousand times more grievous to me? And yet all this While
I cannot bring my self to advise you, not to Think of me. And to deal
freely with you, there is not any thing in *France* that you take pleasure in,
or that comes near your heart, but I'm most furiously jealous of it. I do
not know what 'tis I write for. Perhaps you'l pity me; but what good will
that pity do me? I'le none on't. Oh how I hate my self when I consider

what I have forfeited to oblige you! I have blasted my Reputation; I have
lost my Parents; I have expos'd my self to the Laws of my Country against
Persons of my Profession; and finally, to your Ingratitude, the worst of
my Misfortunes. But why do I pretend to a Remorse, when at this
Instant, I should be glad with all my Soul, if I had run ten thousand
greater hazzards for your dear Sake? and for the danger of my Life and
Honour; the very thought on't is a kind of doleful Pleasure to me, and
all's no more then the delivery of what's your own, and what I hold most
Pretious, into your Disposition; And I do not know how all these risques
could have been better Imploy'd. Upon the whole matter, every thing
displeases me, my Love, my Misfortune; and alas! I cannot perswade
my self that I am well us'd even by You. And yet I Live, (false as I am)
and take as much pains to preserve my Life, as to lose it. Why do I not
die of shame then, and shew you the despair of my Heart, as well as of
my Letters? If I had lov'd you so much as I have told you a thousand
times I did, I had been in my Grave long e're this. But I have deluded
you, and the Cause of Complaint is now on your side. Alas! why did you
not tell me of it? Did I not see you go away? Am I not out of all hopes of
ever seeing you again? And am I yet alive? I have betray'd you, and I beg
your pardon. But do not grant it though; Treat me as severely as you will:
Tell me that my Passion is Weak, and Irresolute. Make your self yet
harder to be pleas'd. Write me word that you would have me die for you.
Do it, I conjure you: and assist me in the Work of surmounting the
Infirmity of my sex; and that I may put an end to all my fruitless delibera-
tions, by an effectual despair. A Tragical Conclusion would undoubtedly
bring me often into your thoughts, and make my Memory dear to you.
And who knows how you might be Affected, with the Bravery of so
Glorious a death? A death Incomparably to be preferr'd before the Life
that you have left me. Farewel then: and *I wish I had never seen the Eyes
of you*. But my heart Contradicts my Pen; for I feel, in the very moment
that I write it, that I would rather choose to Love you in any state of
Misery, then agree to the bare Supposition that I had never Seen you.
Wherefore since you do not think fit, to mend my fortune, I shall chear-
fully submit to the worst on't. *Adieu*; but first promise me, that if I die
of grief, you will have some Tenderness for my Ashes: Or at least that the
Generosity of my Passion shall put you out of Love with all other things.
This Consolation shall satisfie me, that if you must never be mine, I
may be secur'd that you shall never be Anothers. You cannot be so inhumane sure, as to make a mean use of my most Affectionate despairs,

and to recommend your self to any other Woman, by shewing the Power you have had upon me. Once more, *Adieu*. My Letters are long, and I fear troublesome; but I hope you'l forgive them, and dispense with the fooleries of a Sot of your own making. *Adieu*. Me-thinks I run over and over too often with the story of my most deplorable Condition: Give me leave now to thank you from the Bottom of my heart for the Miseries you have brought upon me, and to detest the Tranquility I liv'd in before I knew you. My Passion is greater every Moment than other. *Adieu*. Oh what a World of things have I to tell you!

### The fourth Letter

Your Lieutenant tells me that you were forc'd by foul Weather to put in upon the Coast of *Algarve*. I am afraid the Sea does not agree with you; and my Fears for your Misfortunes make me almost to forget my own. Can you imagine your Lieutenant to be more concern'd in what befals you, than I am? If not, How comes he to be so well inform'd, and not one sillable to me? If you could never find the means of writing to me since you went, I am very Unhappy; but I am more so, if you could have written, and would not. But what should a body expect from so much Ingratitude, and Injustice? And yet it would break my heart, if heaven should punish you upon any account of mine. For I had much rather gratifie my Kindness, than my Revenge. There can be nothing clearer, than that you neither Love me, nor Care what becomes of me; and yet am I so foolish, as to follow the Dictate of a blind, and besotted Passion, in opposition to the Counsels of a demonstrative Reason. This Coldness of yours, when you and I were first acquainted, would have sav'd me many a sorrowful Thought. But where's the Woman, that in my Place, would have done otherwise than I did? Who would ever have question'd the Truth of so pressing and Artificial an Importunity? We cannot easily bring our selves to suspect the Faith of those we Love. I know very well, that a slender Excuse will serve your Turn; and I'le be so kind as to save you even the Labour of that too, by telling you, that I can never consent to conclude you guilty, but in order to the infinite Pleasure I shall take to acquit you, in perswading my self that you are Innocent. It was the Assiduity of your Conversation that refin'd me; your Passion that inflam'd me; Your good humour that Charm'd me; your Oaths, and Vows that confirm'd me; but 'twas my own precipitate Inclination that seduc'd me; and what's the Issue of these fair, and promising beginnings, but Sighs, Tears, Disquiets, nay, and the worst of Deaths too, without either Hope, or Remedy. The Delights of my Love, I must confess, have been strangely surprizing; but follow'd with Miseries not to be express'd: (as whatever comes from you works upon me in Extreams.) If I had either obstinately oppos'd your Address; or done any thing to put you out of humour, or make you jealous, with a design to draw you on: If I had gon any crafty, artificial ways to work with you; or but so much as check'd my early, and my growing inclinations to comply with you, (tho' it would have been to no purpose at all) you might have had some Colour then to make use of your Power, and deal with me accordingly. But so far was I from opposing your Passion, that I prevented[1] it; for I had a kindness for your Person, before you ever told me any thing of your Love; and you had no sooner declar'd it, but with all the joy imaginable I receiv'd it, and gave my self up wholly to that Inclination. You had at that time your Eyes in your Head, tho' I was Blind. Why would you let me go on then to make my self the Miserable Creature which now I am? Why would you train me on to all those Extravagances which to a person of your Indifference must needs have been very Importune? You knew well enough that you were not to be always in *Portugal;* Why must I then be singl'd out from all the rest, to be made thus Unfortunate? In this Country without dispute you might have found out handsomer Women than my self, that would have serv'd your turn every jot as well, (to your course purpose) and that would have been true to you as far as they could have seen you, without breaking their hearts for you, when you were gon; and such as you might have forsaken at last, without either Falseness, or Cruelty: Do you call this the Tenderness of a Lover, or the Persecution of a Tyrant? And 'tis but destroying of your own neither. You are just as easie, I find, to believe ill of me, as I have always been to think better of you then you have deserv'd. Had you but lov'd me half so well as I do you, you would never have parted with me upon so easie Terms. I should have master'd greater Difficulties, and never have upbraided you with the Obligation neither. Your Reasons, 'tis true, were very feeble, but if they had been the strongest imaginable, it had been all one to me: for nothing but Death it self could ever have torn me from you. Your Return into *France* was nothing in the World but a Pretext of your own contriving. *There was a Vessel* (you said) *that was thither bound.* And why could not you let that Vessel take her Course? *Your Relations sent for you away.* You are no stranger sure to the Persecution, that for your sake, I have suffer'd from mine. *Your Honour* (forsooth) *engag'd you to forsake me.* Why did you not think of that scruple,

[1] anticipated.

when you deluded me to the loss of mine? *Well! but you must go back to serve your Prince.* His Majesty, I presume, would have excus'd you in that point? for I cannot learn that he has any need of your Service. But, Alas! I should have been too happy, if you and I might have liv'd, and died together. This only Comfort I have in the bitterness of our deadly separation, that I was never false to you; and that for the whole World I would not have my Conscience tainted with so black a Crime. But can you then, that know the Integrity of my Soul, and the Tenderness that I have for you; can you (I say) find in your heart to abandon me for ever, and expose me to the Terrours that attend my wretched Condition? Never so much as to think of me again, but only when you are to sacrifice me to a new Passion. My Love, you see, has distracted me; and yet I make no complaint at all of the violence of it: for I am so wonted to Persecutions, that I have discover'd a kind of pleasure in them, which I would not live without, and which I enjoy, while I love you, in the middle of a thousand afflictions.

The most grievous part of my Calamity, is the hatred, and disgust that you have given me for all other things: My Friends, my Kindred, the Convent it self is grown intollerable to me; and whatsoever I am oblig'd either to see, or to do, is become odious. I am grown so jealous of my Passion, that methinks all my Actions, and all my Duties ought to have some regard to you. Nay, every moment that is not employ'd upon your service, my Conscience checks me for it, either as misbestow'd, or cast away. My Heart is full of Love, and Hatred; and, Alas! what should I do without it? should I survive this restlessness of thought, to lead a Life of more tranquillity, and ease, such an Emptiness, and such an Insensibility could never consist.[2] Every Creature takes notice how strangely I am chang'd in my Humour, my Manners, and in my Person. My Mother takes me to task about it: One while she speaks me fair, and then she chides me, and asks me what I ail. I do not well know what answers I have made her; but I Phancy that I have told her all. The most severe, even of the Religious themselves, take pity of me, and bear with my Condition. The whole World is touch'd with my Misfortunes; your single self excepted, as wholly unconcern'd: Either you are not pleas'd to write at all; or else your Letters are so cold; so stuff'd with Repetitions; the Paper not half full, and your Constraint so grossly disguis'd, that one may see with half an Eye the pain you are in till they are over. *Dona Brites* would not let me be quiet the other day, till she had got me out of my Chamber, on to the

[2] co-exist.

Balcon that looks (you know) toward *Mertola*: she did it to oblige me, and I follow'd her: But the very sight of the Place struck me with so terrible an Impression, that it set me a Crying the whole day after. Upon this, she took me back again, and I threw my self upon my Bed, where I pass'd a thousand Reflections upon the despairs of my Recovery. I am the worse I find for that which people do to relieve me; and the Remedies they offer me, do but serve to aggravate my Miseries. Many a time have I seen you pass by from this Balcon; (and the sight pleas'd me but too well) and there was I that fatal day, when I first found my self strook with this unhappy Passion. Methought you look'd as if you had a mind to oblige me, even before you knew me; and your Eye was more upon me than the rest of the Company. And when you made a stop, I fool'd my self to think that it was meant to me too, that I might take a fuller view of you, and see how every thing became you. Upon giving your Horse the spur (I remember) my heart was at my mouth for fear of an untoward leap you put him upon. In fine; I could not but secretly concern my self in all your Actions; and as you were no longer indifferent to me, so I took several things to my self also from you; and as done in my favour. I need not tell you the sequel of Matters (not that I care who knows it) nor would I willingly write the whole Story, lest I should make you thought more culpable (if possible) than in Effect (perhaps) you are. Beside that it might furnish your Vanity with subject of reproach, by shewing that all my Labours, and Endeavours to make sure of you, could not yet keep you from forsaking me.

But what a Fool am I, in thinking to work more upon your Ingratitude, with Letters, and Invectives, than ever I could with my Infinite Love, and the Liberty that attended it! No, no: I am too sure of my ill Fortune, and you are too unjust to make me doubt of it; and since I find my self deserted, what mischief is there in Nature which I am not to fear? But are your Charms only to work upon me? Why may not other Women look upon you with my Eyes? I should be well enough content perhaps to find more of my Sex (in some degree) of my Opinion; and that all the Ladyes of *France* had an esteem for you, provided that none of them either doted upon you, or pleas'd you: This is a most ridiculous, and an impossible Proposition. But there's no danger (I may speak it upon sad Experience) of your troubling your head long with any one thing; and you will forget me easily enough, without the help of being forc'd to't by a new Passion. So infinitely do I love you, that (since I am to lose you) I could e'en wish that you had had some fairer colour for't. It is true, that it would have made me more miserable; but you should have had less to answer for then. You'l stay in *France*, I perceive, in perfect Freedom, and perhaps not much to your Satisfaction; The Incommodities of a long Voyage; some Punctilioes of good Manners; and the fear of not returning Love for Love, may perchance keep you there. Oh, you may safely trust me in this Case: Let me but only see you now and then, and know that we are both of us in the same Country, it shall content me. But why do I flatter my self? Who knows but that the Rigour and Severity of some other Woman may come to prevail upon you more than all my favours? Tho' I cannot believe you yet to be a Person that will be wrought upon by ill usage.

Before you come to engage in any powerful Passion, let me entreat you to bethink your self of the Excess of my Sorrows; the Uncertainty of my Purposes; the Distraction of my Thoughts; the Extravagance of my Letters; The Trusts I have repos'd in you; my Despairs, my Wishes, and my Jealousies. Alas! I am affraid that you are about to make your self unfortunate. Take warning, I beg of you, by my Example, and make some Use to your self of the Miseries that I endure for you. I remember you told me in Confidence, (and in great Earnest too) some five or six Months ago, that you had once a Passion for a *French* Lady. If she be any Obstacle to your Return, deal frankly with me, and put me out of my Pain. It will be a kind of Mercy to me, if the faint hope which yet supports me, must never take effect, even to lose my Life, and that together. Pray'e send me her picture, and Some of her Letters, and write me all she says. I shall find Something there undoubtedly that will make me either better, or worse. In the Condition that I am, I cannot long continue; and any Change whatsoever must be to my Advantage. I should take it kindly if you would send me your Brothers and your Sisters pictures too. Whatsoever is dear to you must be so to me; and I am a very faithful Servant to any thing that is related to you: and it cannot be otherwise: for you have left me no power at all to dispose of my self. Sometimes me-thinks I could submit even to attend upon the Woman that you Love. So Low am I brought by your Scorns, and ill Usage, that I dare not so much as say to my self, *Methinks I might be allow'd to be jealous, without displeasing you.* Nay, I chide my self as the most mistaken Creature in the World to blame you: and I am many times convinc'd that I ought not to importune you as I do, with those passages, and thoughts which you are pleas'd to disown.

The Officer that waits for this Letter grows a little impatient: I had once resolved to keep it clear from any possibility of giving you Offence.

But it is broken out into Extravagances, and 'tis time to put an end to't. But Alas! I have not the heart to give it over; when I write to you, methinks I speak to you: and our Letters bring us nearer together. The first shall be neither So long nor So troublesome. But you may venture to open it, and read it, upon the assurance that I now give you. I am not to entertain you, I know, with a Passion that displeases you, and you shall hear no more on't. It is now a year within a few days, that I have delivered my self wholly up to you, without any Reserve. Your Love I took to be both Warm, and Sincere: And I could never have thought you would have been so weary of my favours, as to take a voyage of five hundred leagues; and run the Hazzards of Rocks, and Pirates, only to avoid them. This is a Treatment that certainly I never deserv'd at any mans hands. You can call to mind my Shame, my Confusion, and my Disorders. But you have forgotten the Obligations you had to Love me even in despight of your Aversion. The Officer calls upon me now the fourth time for my Letter. He will go away without it, he Says; and presses me, as if he were running away from another Mistress. Farewell. You had not half the difficulty to leave me (tho' perhaps for ever) which I have, only to part with this Letter. But, *Adieu*. There are a thousand tender names that I could call you now. But I dare not deliver my self up to the freedom of Writing my thoughts. You are a thousand times dearer to me than my Life, and a thousand times more than I imagine too. Never was any thing So barbarous, and so much belov'd. I must needs tell you once again, that *you do not write to me*. But I am now going to begin afresh, and *the Officer will be gone*. Well, and what matters it? Let him go. 'Tis not so much for your sake that I write, as my own; for my Business is only to divert, and entertain my self: Beside that the very Length of this Letter will make you afraid on't: And you'l never read it thorough neither. What Have I done to draw all these Miseries upon me? And why should you of all others be the poisoner of my peace, and blast the Comfort of my Life? Why was I not born in some other Country? forgive me, and farwell. See but to what a Miserable point I am reduc'd, when I dare not so much as intreat you to Love me. *Adieu*.

### The fifth Letter

You will find, I hope, by the different Ayre and stile of this Letter, from all my former, that I have chang'd my Thoughts too; and you are to take this for an Eternal farewell; for I am now at length perfectly con-vinc'd, that since I have irrecoverably lost your Love, I can no longer justify my own. Whatsoever I had of Yours shall be sent you by the first Opportunity: There shall be no more writing in the Case; No, not so much as your Name upon the Pacquett. *Dona Brites* is a Person whom I can trust as my own soul, and whom I have entrusted (as you know very well) Unfortunate Wretch that I am! in Confidences of another Quality betwixt you and me. I have left it to her Care to see your Picture and your Bracelets dispatch'd away to you (those once beloved Pledges of your Kindness) and only in due time to assure me that you have receiv'd them. Would you believe me now, if I should swear to you, that within these five days, I have been at least fifty times upon the very point of Burning the One, and of Tearing the other into a Million of Pieces? But, You have found me too easy a fool, to think me Capable of so Generous an Indignation. If I could but vex you a little in the story of my Misfortunes; it would be some sort of Abatement me-thinks to the Cruelty of them. Those Bawbles (I must confess, both to Your shame, and Mine) went nearer my heart than I am willing to tell you, and when it came to the Pinch of parting with them, I found it the hardest thing in the world to go thorough with it: So Mortal a Tenderness had I for any thing of Yours, even at that Instant when you your self seem'd to be the most Indifferent thing in Nature: But there's no resisting the force of Necessity and Reason. This Resolution has cost me Many, and Many a Tear; A thousand, and a thousand Agonies, and Distractions, more than you can imagine; and more, Undoubtedly, than you shall ever hear of from me. *Dona Brites* (I say) has them in Charge; upon Condition, never to name them to Me again. No, not so much as to give me a sight of them, though I should beg for't upon my Knees; but, in fine, to hasten them away, without one Syllable to Me of their going.

If it had not been for this Trial to get the Mastery of my Passion, I should never have understood the force of it; and if I could have foreseen the pains and the hazzards of the Encounter, I am afraid that I should never have ventur'd upon the Attempt: for I am verily perswaded that I could much better have Supported your Ingratitude it self, though never so foul, and Odious, than the Deadly, Deadly Thought of this Irrevocable Separation. And it is not your Person neither that is so dear to me, but the Dignity of My unalterable Affection. My soul is strangely divided; Your falseness makes me abhor you, and yet at the same time my Love, my Obstinate, and Invincible Love, will not consent to part with you.

What a blessing were it to me now, if I were but endu'd with the Common Quality of other Women, and only Proud enough to despise you? Alas! Your Contempt I have born already: Nay, had it been your Hatred, or the most Raging Jealousie; All this, compar'd with your Indifference, had been a Mercy to me. By the Impertinent Professions, and the most Ridiculous Civilities of your Last Letter, I find that all mine are come to your hand; and that you have read them over too: but as unconcern'd as if you forsooth had no Interest at all in the Matter. Sot that I am, to lie thus at the Mercy of an Insensible, and Ungrateful Creature; and to be as much afflicted now at the Certainty of the Arrival of those Papers, as I was before, for fear of their Miscarriage! What have I to do with your telling me the *TRUTH OF THINGS?* Who desired to know it? Or the *SINCERITY* you talk of; a thing you never practis'd toward me, but to my Mischief. Why could you not let me alone in my Ignorance? Who bad you Write? Miserable Woman that I am! Methinks after so much pains taken already to delude me to my Ruin, you might have streyn'd one point more, in this Extremity, to deceive me to my Advantage, without pretending to excuse your self. 'Tis too late to tell you that I have cast away many a Tender Thought upon the Worst of men, the Most Oblig'd, and the most Unthankful. Let it suffice that I know you now as well as if I were in the heart of you. The only favour that I have now to desire from you, after so many done for you, is This: (and I hope you will not refuse it me) Write no more to me; and remember that I have conjur'd you never to do it. Do all that is Possible for you to do, (if ever you had any Love for me) to make me absolutely forget you. For, Alas! I dare not trust my self in any sort of Correspondence with you. The least hint in the World of any kind Reflection upon the reading of this Letter would perchance expose me to a Relapse; and then the taking of me at my Word, on the other side, would most certainly transport me into an Extravagance of Choler, and Despair. So that in my Opinion it will be your best course not to meddle at all with Me, or my Affairs; for which way so ever you go to work, it must inevitably bring a great disorder upon both. I have no curiosity to know the success of this Letter: Methinks the sorrows you have brought upon me already, might abundantly content you (even if your Design were never so malicious) without disturbing me in my Preparations for my future peace. Do but leave me in my uncertainty, and I will not yet despair, in time, of arriving at some degree of Quiet. This I dare promise you, that I shall never hate you; for I am too great an Enemy to violent Resolutions ever to go about it. Who knows but I may yet live to find a truer friend than I have lost? But, Alas! What signifies any mans Love to me, if I cannot Love him? Why should his passion work more upon my heart, than mine could upon Yours? I have found by sad Experience, that the first Motions of Love which we are more properly said to feel, than to Understand, are never to be forgotten: That our souls are perpetually Intent upon the Idol which we our selves have made: That the first Wounds, and the first Images are never to be cur'd, or defac'd: That all the Passions that pretend to succour us, either by Diversion, or Satisfaction, are but so many vain Promises of bringing us to our Wits again, which, if once lost, are never to be recover'd: And that all the Pleasures that we pursue, (many times without any desire of finding them) amount to no more, than to convince us, that nothing is so dear to us as the Remembrance of our Sorrows. Why must you pitch upon Mee, for the subject of an Imperfect, and Tormenting Inclination; which I can neither Relinquish with Temper, nor Preserve with Honour? The dismal Consequences of an Impetuous Love, which is not Mutual? and why is it that by a Conspiracy of Blind Affection, and Inexorable fate, we are still condemn'd to Love where we are Despis'd, and to Hate where we are Belov'd?

But what if I could flatter my self with the Hope of diverting my Miseries by any other Engagement? I am so sensible of my own Condition, that I should make a very great scruple of Using any other Mortal as you have treated me: and though I am not Conscious of any Obligation to spare you, yet if it were in my Power to take my revenge upon you, by changing you for any other, (a thing very Unlikely) I could never agree to the gratifying of my Passion that way.

I am now telling my self in your behalf, that it is not reasonable to expect, that the simplicity of a Religious should confine the Inclinations of a Cavalier. And yet methinks, if a body might be allow'd to reason upon the Actions of Love, a man should rather fix upon a Mistress in a Convent than any where else. For they have nothing there to hinder them from being perpetually Intent upon their passion: Whereas in the World, there are a thousand fooleries, and Amusements, that either take up their Thoughts intirely, or at least divert them. And what Pleasure is it (or rather how great a Torment, if a body be not Stupid) for a man to see the woman that he loves, in a Continual Hurry of Delights; taken up with Ceremony, and Visits; no discourses but of Balls, Dresses, Walks, &c. Which must needs expose him every hour to fresh jealousies? Who can secure himself that Women are not better Satisfied with these Entertainments than they ought to be? even to the Disgusting of their own Husbands? How can any man pretend to Love, who without examining Particulars, contentedly believes what's told him, and looks upon his

Mistress under all these Circumstances with Confidence, and Quiet? It is not that I am now Arguing my self into a Title to your Kindness, for this is not a way to do my business: especially after the Tryal of a much more probable Method, and to as little purpose. No, no: I know my Destiny, too Well, and there's no strugling with it. My Whole Life is to be miserable. It was so, when I saw you every day; When we were together, for fear of your Infidelity; and at a distance, because I could not endure you out of my sight: My heart ak'd every time you came into the Convent; and my very life was at stake when you were in the Army: It put me out of all Patience to consider that neither my Person, nor Condition were Worthy of you: I was afraid that your pretensions to me might turn to your Damage: I could not love you enough me-thought: I liv'd in dayly Apprehension of some Mischief or other from my Parents: so that upon the Whole Matter, my Case was not much better at that time than it is at present. Nay had you but given me the least Proof of your Affection since you left *Portugal*, I should most certainly have made my Escape, and follow'd you in a disguise. And what would have become of me then, after the loss of my honour, and my friends, to see my self abandon'd in *France* ? What a Confusion should I have been in ? What a plunge should I have been at ? What an Infamy should I have brought upon my family, which I do assure you, since I left loving of you, is very dear to me. Take Notice I Pray'e, that in Cold thoughts I am very Sensible that I might have been much more Miserable than I am; and that once in my Life I have talk'd Reason to you; but whether my Moderation pleases you, or not; and what Opinion soever you entertain of me, I beseech you keep it to your self. I have desired you already, and I do now re-conjure you, never to Write to me again.

Methinks you should sometimes reflect upon the Injuries you have done me; and upon your Ingratitude to the most Generous Obligations in Nature. I have lov'd you to the degree of Madness; and to the Contempt of all other things, and Mortals. You have not dealt with me like a man of honour. Nothing but a Natural Aversion could have kept you even from adoring me. Never was any Woman bewitch'd upon So easy terms. What did you ever do that might entitle you to my favour? What did you ever Lose, or but so much as hazzard for my Sake? Have you not entertain'd your self with a thousand other delights? No, not so much as a Sett at Tennis, or a Hunting-Match, that you would ever forbear upon any Accompt[3] of Mine. Were you not still the first that went to the Army, and the last that came back again? Were you ever the more Careful of your

[3] account.

Person there, because I begg'd it of you, as the greatest Blessing of my Soul? Did you ever so much as offer at the Establishment⁴ of your fortune in *Portugal*? A place where you were so much esteem'd. But one single Letter of your Brothers hurry'd you away, without so much as a moments time to consider of it: and I am certainly inform'd too, that you were never in better humour in your Whole Life, than upon that Voyage. You your self cannot deny, but that I have reason to hate you above all men Living; and yet, in effect, I may thank my Self; for I have drawn all these Calamaties upon my own head. I dealt too openly, and plainly with you at first: I gave you my heart too soon. It is not Love alone that begets Love; there must be Skill, and Address; for it is Artifice, and not Passion, that creates Affection. Your first design was to make me Love you, and there was not any thing in the World which you would not then have done, to compass that End: Nay rather than fail, I am perswaded you would have lov'd Me too, if you had judg'd it necessary. But you found out easier ways to do your Business, and so thought it better to let the Love alone. Perfidious Man! Can you ever think to carry off this affront, without being call'd to an Accompt for't? If ever you set foot in *Portugal* again, I do declare it to you, that I'le deliver you up to the Revenge of my Parents. It is a long time that I have now liv'd in a kind of Licentious Idolatry, And the Concience of it strikes me with horrour, and an Insupportable Remorse; I am Confounded with the Shame of What I have done for your Sake; and I have no longer (alas!) the Passion that kept the foulness of it from my Sight. Shall this tormented heart of Mine never find ease? Ah barbarous Man! When shall I see the End of this Oppression? And yet after all this I cannot find in my heart to wish you any Sort of harm; Nay in my Conscience I could be yet well enough content to see you happy: which as the Case stands, is utterly impossible.

Within a While, you may yet perhaps receive another Letter from me, to shew you that I have outliv'd all your Outrages, and Philosophiz'd my self into a state of Repose. Oh what a Pleasure will it be to me, when I shall be able to tell you of your Ingratitude, and Treacheries, without being any longer concern'd at them my Self! When I shall be able to discourse of you with Scorn; When I shall have forgotten all my Griefs, and pleasures, and not so much as think of your self, but when I have a mind to't.

That you have had the better of me, 'tis true; for I have lov'd you to the very Loss of my Reason: But it is no less true that you have not much

⁴ make an attempt to establish.

cause to be proud on't. Alas I was young, and Credulous: Cloyster'd up
from a Child; and only Wonted to a rude, and disagreeable sort of People.
I never knew what belong'd to fine Words, and Flatteries, till (most
unfortunately) I came acquainted with you: And all the Charms, and
Beauties you so often told me of, I only look'd upon as the Obliging
Mistakes of your Civility, and Bounty. You had a good Character in the
World; I heard every body Speak well of you: and to all this, you made it
your Business to engage me; but you have now (I thank you for't) brought
me to my self again, and not without great need of your Assistance. Your
two last Letters I am resolv'd to keep and to read them over oftner than
ever I did any of the former, for fear of a Relapse. You may well afford
them, I am sure, at the Price that they have cost me. Oh how happy might
I have been, if you would but have given me Leave to Love you for ever:
I know very well that betwixt my Indignation, and your Infidelity, my
present thoughts are in great Disorder. But remember what I tell you: I
am not yet out of hope of a more peaceable Condition, which I will either
Compass, or take some other Course with my self; which I presume, you
will be well enough content to hear of. But I will never have any thing
more to do with you. I am a fool for saying the Same things over, and over
again so often. I must leave you, and not so much as think of you. Now
do I begin to Phansie that I shall not write to you again for all This; for
what Necessity is there that I must be telling of you at every turn how my
Pulse beats?

THE END

Mlle de La Roche Guilhem

# ALMANZOR AND ALMANZAIDA

(1678)

# ALMANZOR,

AND

# ALMANZAIDA.

A

# NOVEL.

---

Written by

Sir *PHILIP SIDNEY*,

And found since his Death amongst his
PAPERS.

---

---

*LONDON,*

Printed for *J. Magnes* and *R. Bentley*,
in *Russel-street*, near the *Piazza*, in
*Covent-garden.* 1678.

A 3

Almanzor and Almanzaida, *translated by an unknown hand from the French original (1674) of Mlle de La Roche Guilhem, is a fine example of the oriental tale.*[1] *In spite of the seraglio setting, the author avoids the overluxurious* dolce far niente *of some similar tales, and produces a plot with sudden reversals and bold strokes of danger—an inheritance, no doubt, from the earlier heroic romances which seem to have been her models. A plot with such possibilities of destruction for the principal characters must depend upon the presence of a determined villain of some sort; in this story the villain is Roxana, the most powerful wife of Abdala, the King of Morocco, who will go to any length to preserve her supremacy. The hero and heroine are both slaves when the story begins, handsome to a fault and much in love with one another. The plot concerns the development of this love: how it is first mutually confessed, then endangered by a rival, then thwarted by the discovery that the two lovers are brother and sister, and finally made possible by the further discovery that they are* not *brother and sister after all. The unrolling of the changing hopes and fears of the lovers, along with the near death of the hero, is managed with considerable economy by the author, and, given the traditions of the genre within which she works, with a certain amount of plausibility.*

*The style in which the story is presented is moderately well polished and very gallant. There is much good exploitation of scenes highly charged with emotional voltage, and a surprising amount of real dialogue, much of it natural sounding. Mlle de La Roche Guilhem is clearly interested in the analysis of emotions and, if her plot and setting do remove the story from the familiar world in which genuine* vraisemblance *is possible, her work is not untouched by the new spirit in fiction which called for probability as a standard. If her characters are not presented from within as much as one might wish, it must be admitted that the sort of story she is writing does not yield very easily to such aims.*

*The text which follows is based on a copy of the 1678 edition in the Yale University Library.*

The Book-Seller
to the Courteous Reader and
Buyer of this Book

It may seem strange how this Book should lie dormant all this time that is elapsed since Sir *Philip Sidney*'s Death; therefore I thought it necessary to acquaint you by what means it came to my Hands.

[1] The false attribution of the story to Sir Philip Sidney in the Bookseller's Introduction may be dismissed summarily as a publisher's trick.

A Gentleman who came in the Train of the Prince of *Orange* when he was last in *England*, brought this *Novel* in an old Manuscript, and presented it to a Lady as a great Rarity of that excellent Authors Sir *Philip Sidney*, and supposed he wrote it when he was Governor of *Flushing;* for soon after his Death it was found amongst his Papers, and hath been several times transcribed for the *English* Gentry there: But this that I print it by, is the Original Copy.

I cannot suppose but I shall do many Persons a kindness in publishing this *Novel*, by reason that they may now buy that for a Shilling, which so many Persons have given Twenty for, and have thought it a Favour to have it at that rate, esteeming any thing of that excellent Authors at what Price soever it should be valued at.

That this Book shall have a good acceptance in the World, I make no doubt of; but if it should be otherwise, I shall not be much concerned, because I have in this considered your Advantage more than my own Profit.

Now let me beg your pardon for detaining you thus long from what is much better, I mean the Book it self; which if you receive with a favourable aspect, I will assure you, you shall get this advantage by it, (which is no very inconsiderable one) That for the future you shall be eased of Prefacing from

*The Humblest of Your Servants,*

R. BENTLEY

## Almanzor and Almanzaida

### A Novel

The Kingdom of *Moroco* had for many years suffered under Tyrannical Powers, when at last it began to breathe, and receive new life, under the just and peaceable Reign of the Great *Abdala*, the most accomplished of all Princes; who having employed his younger years in Arms, had thereby acquired great fame, and assured a peaceful and quiet Seat unto himself, in the most renowned City of *Africa*.

It was there that in a Palace whose Magnificence did surpass even Imagination, the greatest Beauties of the World spent their days under some severity of restraint, being deprived from the sight of all Objects but their own enterview, the presence of a Prince past the flower of his age, and some few young Slaves that were but just stepp'd out of Childhood.

Of all *Abdala*'s Women, there was but one absolute, the birth of a Son had render'd her happy; *Roxana* had the most absolute Authority: yet *Cleonisa* did still preserve such a deserved Power over the Kings heart, as she esteemed infinitely beyond that publick Grandeur, which was the Right of *Roxana*.

Amongst those Slaves appertaining to the King & Princesses, that had the liberty of the Womens Apartments, one onely had attained to his twentieth year: He had been presented to *Abdala* in his Infancy, and some years having given him the opportunity to discover most exquisite Parts of Mind and Body, *Abdala* was taken with them so, that they oblig'd him to bestow his Love and Favours upon the Possessor of them, and distinguished him from the rest, by his tender Affections towards him; and proceeded so far, as to honour him with the Magnificent Name of *Almanzor*, so much in esteem with the Princes of *Moroco*, as having been that of many of their most ancient Kings. The onely Mark that remained with him of his Bondage, was a Chain of Diamonds: and if his Apparel had any thing of *Abdala*'s Liveries yet remaining upon them, they were so obscured under a vast quantity of Jewels, as not to be discernable.

In short, no Captive in the World had a happier Fate; as many as saw him, became his Admirers; none amongst the most considerable, but thought themselves highly favoured with his Friendship; and to wish, was with him the same thing as to enjoy.

Yet notwithstanding all this Happiness, he fell into such a profound melancholy, as became obvious to all Persons; but in a more particular manner, it was observed by the chief and most ancient of *Abdala*'s Eunuchs, unto whose particular care had been committed the Education of his Childhood, of which he had received divers great Advantages, such as were sutable to *Almanzor*'s brave Soul. The extreme affection that this Eunuch had for him, made him with the more extactness observe his Distemper; and not being able to see him in any discontent, it made him enter one evening into *Almanzor*'s Lodgings, where having found him, he spoke to him in this manner: 'I have deserved otherwise from you, than that you should hide your sorrows from me: I cannot see that Person overwhelmed with sorrow, unto whose Childhood I have given all my Cares, and to whose Merits I have sacrificed all my Affections, and be ignorant of the cause of his change. Must I have the trouble to see you hide your Sighs from me? Sir, your Interests are too dear unto me, not to reproch you this reservedness. *Almanzor*, I am not unworthy of your con- fidence; and you ought to believe, that I loving you with that tenderness as I do, I should not desire with so much earnestness the knowledge of what so much disturbs your quiet, but to endeavour the re-establishment of it, even with the hazard of my Life: Therefore I conjure you to speak.'

At this onset, *Almanzor* stood for a while in suspense; after which, casting an obliging look upon the Eunuch, '*Aristan*, (said he) I should become unworthy of your kindness, if I was so ungrateful as to conceal from your knowledge any thing that concerns my Fortune. I do not mistrust a Vertue so well known, and so useful to me as yours has always been: And if I have hid from your knowledge a trouble wholly contained within the narrow limits of my Heart, it was that I might not involve the quiet of a Person to whom I owe a thousand times more than my Life, in such secret Misfortunes as must be suffered by me alone.' 'Do you believe (interrupted *Aristan*) that I can quietly see you suffer, hear your Sighs, and have your troubled Eyes for continual objects, and not be moved? Speak your mind, *Almanzor*, with this assurance, that of whatsoever you can inform me, you will less afflict me in the declaration of it, than you do with your obstinate silence; since there are no such evils, though never so great, but may find remedies: And if there be a necessity of courting you to it, let me conjure you by all that love I have for you.'

'Well (replied the Slave, sighing) you must be satisfied; *Aristan*, I love; it is love that causes all my grief: the onely secret that I would have kept from your knowledge, because of its cruel circumstances.' 'Your informing of me that you love, is defective (replied the Eunuch), except you acquaint me with the Object also.' 'Dear *Aristan* (replied the amorous Captive), if ever you have observed me when near the amiable *Almanzaida*, you could not but perceive it.' '*Almanzaida*, (replied *Aristan*, with an extraordinary emotion) *Roxana*'s Slave!' 'Yes (pursu'd *Almanzor*) it is she that a thousand Charms makes me adore.' 'Remember (replied the Eunuch) that she is destinated to an eternal Servitude; and, if it be possible, fix your heart on some other Object.' 'Dear *Aristan*, (replied *Almanzor*) can *Almanzaida*'s ill Fate make you forget mine of the same nature? Does the glittering of my Apparel so dazel your eyes, as that you cannot see the Badge of my Slavery on me? And does this Chain, because of Jewels, alter my Condition? It is, peradventure, that equality of Fortune, that unites our Souls. Know, *Aristan*, that my Griefs are not the effects of *Almanzaida*'s Rigours; for we having been both together bred in this Palace, with the liberty of seeing and conversing with one another, have kindled such Flames as have grown more furious by the difficulties they have encountered, and which will prove eternal, though of a Slave I should become Master of the whole World: For do not imagine, that none but my single Heart does justice unto *Almanzaida*'s Beauty; the Prince *Abdemar*, Son to the King, and to proud *Roxana*, is her Captive also: That Rival's he which makes me unfortunate; 'tis he, who envious of those Advantages which Love gives me over *Almanzaida*'s Heart, does by a cruel Jealousie disturb the quiet of two Persons whom the Heavens have produced designedly to love one another. The change which I see in your face, *Aristan* (continued he, after a little pause) speaks that particular interest which you take in my misfortunes; therefore to give you still more occasion of exercising your compassion of my miseries, hearken attentively unto the Story of my Love.' The Eunuch did but cast his eyes towards Heaven, and *Almanzor* thus continued.

## *The History of* Almanzor, *and* Almanzaida

I need not give you the Pourtraicture of *Almanzaida*; she is too well known to you, to be ignorant of it; and your eyes have too just a discernment, not to inform you, that she is more beautiful than any thing else they ever yet saw: But, *Aristan*, though I am not ignorant of whatsoever her Person has of amiable, you are not throughly informed of the excellency of her Soul: In the whole World there is not a Vertue more solid than that she is Mistriss of; she has a Generosity beyond all example, such noble Thoughts, such an exact Knowledge, and a quaintness of Wit so little common, that it may boldly be asserted, that her greatest Perfections are wholly unknown to those that have not such familiar Conversations with her, as I have had the happiness to enjoy; in which all is spoken with absolute Liberty.

I was yet so young, and she so innocent, when she was placed with *Roxana*, that all our Pleasures were limited within the bounds of Childrens Sports; yet then was I infinitely pleased with them, when permitted me; and Love was then interwoven with them, in a manner proportionable to our age. It was still my endeavour to insinuate my self in all places that were bless'd with *Almanzaida*'s presence; and the addition of some few years, to those I had pass'd already in that agreeable Commerce, did give [me] to understand, that an innocent complaisancy, and some childish endearments, had been the beginners of a most violent Passion. After that, I had no other thoughts, but such as did absolutely confirm me of the certainty thereof, and would languish in all places that her presence did not grace: I would be out of patience, when *Abdala* would defer some moments in his custom of sending me with an *How do you* to *Roxana*; and I confess, that I would grumble within my self also, when you detained me upon some Lesson longer than my Affections thought reasonable, of which I could reap no benefit at all, but what did happen by meer chance, seeing that I could have no other thoughts but of her: all my Study was bent in endeavouring to please her, and that took up my whole thoughts: she could no sooner desire any thing, but I would with all the earnestness imaginable effect it: And when at last she had learn'd from her own Heart, and from my Eyes, rather than from my Mouth, part of my Intentions, she would frequently blush at the receit of any Services from my hands.

The Prince *Abdemar* went but too frequently unto *Roxana*'s Apartment, not to see her, which he could not do without Love; and I had but too much Interest in that Love, not to take notice of it: and the Princes high Birth, and other Advantages, representing daily a thousand Evils in that Concurrency, I suffered infinitely by it. He was not so reserv'd as I; he would speak of his Love to *Almanzaida* in a most tender manner, even in' my presence, without the least scruple, or any thought that his Fathers Slave durst raise his Pretensions to the same object to which he address'd his. The young Bond-maid would always answer his Sute with such reservedness as would charm me, and conjuring the Prince to spare her, gave him to understand, that if she had heard him make his Addresses to her, he was obliged for it to nothing but his Rank, and *Almanzaida*'s evil Fortune.

Some moments after, he went out, and I remained singly with her, with an impatient desire to learn the cause of a profound reasoning within her self, in which she had fallen immediately upon *Abdemars* departure. Her Complexion was altered, her Eyes were troubled, and her Respiration being more violent than usual, gave me to understand, that her Heart had a great share in this disorder. Good Gods, how heavy did my doubts and my restlessness lie upon me! I look'd upon her for some time with silence; but at last, taking the resolution to inform my self of the very center of this business, which till then I durst not attempt, 'You are surprized, *Almanzaida*, (said I) and what is most sensible to me, is, that I perceive with sorrow it immediately follows the Discourses with which *Abdemar* has entertained you.' '*Abdemars* Discourses (replied she) have nothing in them but what is a trouble to me; and whether what he has said to me be true or feign'd, I think my self very unfortunate in being obliged to hear him.' '*Abdemar* is so great a Prince (I replied) that he thinks he may say any thing without caution; but if he could be what *Almanzor* is, then acting like a Slave, he might, 'tis like, less displease the fair *Almanzaida* in his Addresses.' '*Abdemar* (replied she) cannot become a Slave without a wonder; but though he is the Son of a great Monarch, his Love is no more pleasing to me, than if he were in Chains, or of a mean Rank: For my part (added she) with the unhappiness of an unknown Birth, I have that also of being a Captive; but, *Almanzor*, I know and feel my Heart, and all that it doth inspire me is so great, that not withstanding my low condition, I feel within me a certain natural adversness, which makes me look upon all things that carry any thing of mean and low in them, with horror; which flatters me in an opinion, that I am not inferiour to *Roxana*.' 'I am not happy enough (said I) to have any Intelligence with a Heart whose Motions are so generous: yet, fair *Almanzaida*, though I can judge of it but by the outward appearances, it is long since I am perswaded of the Truth you speak, which makes me look upon you with that respect as is due to a Person whose bare Vertue would prefer her to all the Queens of the World. In a word, *Almanzaida*, you are worthy to Reign in all places, and therefore it is that *Abdemar* does you that justice.' '*Almanzor* (she replied, with some discomposure, that seemed to me as disadvantageous to *Abdemar*) give me leisure to forget his Discourses to me, I conjure you to it; for I declare, I hate that Love which he hath entertained me with; and no doubt but I should hate his Person likewise, should he pursue it.' 'Thus (replied I, in an accent that exprest some disturbance) thus it is, that those that love you must merit your hate; and the Son of *Abdala* is—' 'Are you his Advocate? (interrupted *Almanzaida*, looking fixtly on me) and is it in his behalf that you design to employ that privilege that your Bondage gives you?' 'Ah, *Almanzaida*, (I replied, with such an agitation of mind as she could not but discern) if my better fortune should procure me any with you, it should not be in his, or any others behalf, but my own, that I should employ it. I am not his Agent, Fair one, but his Rival; and give me leave to say, a more bold and more passionate Lover than he, who desires all, but dare not hope any thing.' 'I did not think (replied *Almanzaida*, with much coldness) that *Abdemar* and *Almanzor* should at the same time make their amorous Addresses to me; and I was in hopes that you would have assisted me, in diverting the thoughts of his Courtship, and not thus add to my troubles: And yet I am not angry with you, though I should resent it; that esteem which I have for you, will not permit me; which I promise to continue, notwithstanding what you have declared, provided you repeat it not, and that you confirm me by your future silence of your repentance.'

Divers Persons which were seeking for *Roxana* did interrupt us; I was obliged to withdraw, where making some Reflexions upon *Almanzaida*'s reception of my Declaration of Love, I fancied to find in it more of discomposure than of anger. *Hopes, though small, do pleasingly flatter.* I took enough to perswade me, that I was more happy than *Abdemar*, and that she had impos'd me silence for no other reason, than because she found in her self more disposition to hear and favourably answer me, than she had a mind to discover. I pass'd that night passably well, and the next day having waited on *Abdala* unto *Roxana*'s Apartment, I had the happiness to see *Almanzaida:* She appear'd neither cold nor disagreeing, but as if her Eyes, which I observed to be more languishing than fierce, did take care to shun mine; which I concluded to proceed from a modest bashfulness, that cannot be avoided, when one would hide the motions of the Heart, not being absolutely Master of those of the Eyes.

*Cleonisa* being some few days after at *Roxana*'s Apartment, did tell her so many fine things in the praise of the Weather, that she set her in a humour of going into the Garden: *Almanzaida* took up her Train, and *Cleonisa*, who ever had an obliging goodness for me, seeing me in *Roxana*'s Chamber, and having observed by my assiduous waiting on *Almanzaida*, that her presence was most dear unto me, made me take an *Umbrella*, to give me the happy opportunity of making one in the Walk. It served onely to cross a Plat of Ground that led to the covered Walks, where being got, *Roxana* having made sign to *Almanzaida* to let go her Train, we followed at some distance, under pretence of respect, and so I had the means of entertaining her with liberty.

'*Almanzaida* (said I) those that interrupted us at *Roxana*'s the other day, prevented my answering you, on that severe silence that you would have imposed upon me, and of letting you know, that it is impossible to be silent, and love so passionately as I do.' 'You would not have me have an esteem for you then, (replied she) the Reward of your silence? since you so wilfully relapse into a fault that I was willing to forget?' I was going to reply, but *Almanzaida* continued, saying, 'You abuse my Indulgence, *Almanzor*; I was too little mov'd: but if you knew how dangerous an Enemy I can be, you would doubtless fear me more than you do.' 'There is no resisting of that Power which makes me speak, (I replied) and I am confident that you would pardon me, if you were sensible of it: But am I so criminal onely for loving you? and if it be an offence, are not you more guilty of it than my self? Could my Eyes be pardonable, should they see you without admiration? and would that admiration be as perfect as you deserve it, if it were not followed with all that Passion which I have for you? No, fair *Almanzaida*, none can behold you with quiet thoughts; and I confess, that I shall ever remain a Criminal towards you, if I cannot become innocent without ceasing to love you.' 'I should be very sorry (replied she) that you should cease being my Friend; and to shew you, that it is nor Hatred, nor so little as Indifferency that I require of you, I do protest to you, *Almanzor*, that I wish you were my Brother.' 'This is a modest way of wishing me dead (I replied); for if the amorous *Almanzor* were Brother to the beauteous *Almanzaida*, he would not long out-live that fatal advantage. Judge by these tender resentments, whether it were easie, or rather possible for me to keep silence—' 'Well, (interrupted *Almanzaida*) since you cannot resolve your self to it, see me no more; shun the occasions of being in those places where I shall be, and I shall take care to forbear those of meeting you.' 'Cruel one (said I) were you so unjust as to execute what you mention, you would have much to do to perform it; and in vain would you endeavour to hide your self from such Eyes as seek after no other Object but you.' 'How obstinate you are, (replied *Almanzaida*) and what pains must I take to convince you?' 'Never hope it (said I) since 'tis easier for me to die than not to love you, and let you know it.' 'I must hear you then, it seems, (replied *Almanzaida*, blushing in such a manner as added luster to her Charms) since that I esteem your Life more than what I required from you.' There needed no more to make me apprehend my Happiness: *Almanzaida* being vanquish'd, did from that time no more oppose with fierceness what I would say to her; and I was made sensible of all the Joys that the assurance of being beloved could inspire.

Some short space of time did so confirm me in it, that there was no cause left me to doubt. I am certain, that my Resentments[2] did answer all *Almanzaida*'s Bounties, and I neglected no means to make her sensible of it. *Abdemar* had too much Love not to take notice of mine, and of *Almanzaida*'s tenderness also: He did openly reproch her of it, and came to such threatning terms with me about it, as made her to tremble, and to advise me to constrain my self for my Lifes security.

From that very time forward the Prince did treat me with so much contempt, that no consideration could have made me bear, had not *Almanzaida* forced me to it, by such Orders as I shall ever submit unto:

[2] feelings.

He never more employ'd me on his Messages to *Roxana*; and when I was
sent by the King into her Apartment in his presence, he would take that
Office upon himself: by which, depriving me of my Happiness, he would
bring me almost to despair. Yet I still found some favourable means to
see and entertain *Almanzaida*, whose Bounties were onely capable of
making me happy.

I was one day alone with her, charm'd with the assurance which she
had given me, against some fears that troubled me; too much joy was to
be perceiv'd in my Eyes, when *Abdemar* came in: He perceiv'd it; and
that Pleasure which I could not dissemble, raising a most violent Passion
in him, he forgot the Respect which is due to *Almanzaida*'s Sex, from
which no Rule nor Greatness can ever dispense a gallant Man. I was
concern'd at it, in such a manner, as would have made me run into some
extreme, if *Almanzaida*'s looks had not restrain'd me. 'Retire (said he to
me, in a disdainful manner), shun with diligence not onely the speaking
to this Slave, but the sight of her also; think on those Consequences that
may follow your disobedience, and believe, that it is not in consideration
of your self, that I have spared you till this time.' Ending this word, he
went into his Mothers Closet.[3] *Almanzaida* commanded me to obey, but
not without so much concern for my safety, as forc'd me to sacrifice all
my resentments to her pleasure. My grief did irritate her more against
*Abdemar*, than all that he had said to her; and I was but just gone out,
when he return'd. 'I see (said he) that your heart cannot harbour any
other thoughts than such as are proportionable to its condition; and while
you disdain a Prince, you give a favourable attention to a Slave, by reason
of the proportion which he bears with your condition.' 'I am not to give
you an account of the secrets of my heart, (replied *Almanzaida*, angrily)
and it would please me very much to remain ignorant of yours: Do not
expose your self to the shame of loving a Slave, who has not a Soul large
enough to contain such an esteem as it should have of such a Conquest
as you would be: Leave me and my unworthiness, with the liberty of not
hearing of you; and raise to some higher place those tenders of Services
which I do not, nor never shall deserve.'

*Roxana*'s presence prevented her proceeding; and *Abdemar* retired, so
netled, that his last looks did set *Almanzaida* into a trembling, with the
fears of the result of his Passion: But he never did break out, and the
Prince, as jealous as he is, being vertuous withal, has never attempted
any thing against my Life or Fortune. But, *Aristan*, what has he not done
against my Love? How oft has he most cruelly torn me away from

[3] small private room.

*Almanzaida*'s presence, to possess my room? What Stratagems have I not invented to gain the sight of her, mauger⁴ all those Cautions which his Jealousie did suggest to him? In a word, he has so ordered things, that though I am fully assured of *Almanzaida*'s Heart, the vexations of seeing her but by stealth, and *Abdemar*'s strict observing of my Actions, have reduc'd me unto that restless melancholy which you have taken notice of.

Here did *Almanzor* end his Recital; and perceiving that *Aristan* remained silent, 'Will you not say something to me (said he); is it thus that you have promised to comfort me, and to allay my griefs?' 'Ah, *Almanzor*, (replied the Eunuch) you know them not all yet; and the greatest Fortitude you can be Master of, cannot secure you from trembling, when you learn those that I am oblig'd to inform you of. Oh, what a Love is this that the Fates have inspired you with! and from amongst so many others, what a Person have they chosen to give you a Passion for, such a Passion as cannot be continued but with horror!' 'How, (replied *Almanzor*, strangely moved) what horror, and what repentance ought to follow that Passion which I have for the most amiable Person in the World?' 'I know (replied the Eunuch) that her Beauty, her Merit, her Mind, and her Vertue, render you pardonable for that Error you have been in to this present: but, *Almanzor*, learn, since it must be told you, that she is your Sister, and that one and the same Blood does animate you both.' 'My Sister? (said he, in a great passion) do not deceive me thus, it would be my death, *Aristan*.' 'You must not die, though nothing is more true, (continued the Eunuch) *Abdemar* shall not be happier than you, since that he shares in the same misfortune, and is *Almanzaida*'s Brother, as well as yours. In a word, *Almanzor*, you are *Abdala*'s Child, as he is; and both *Almanzaida* and your self were born of that Prince, and of the generous *Cleonisa*. The King knows it not, *Cleonisa* is also ignorant of it, and I am the onely Depositary of that important Secret. It is that Blood which is ever acting, though by secret motions, which renders you so dear unto *Abdala*. It is the same that affection which *Cleonisa* has for you: and doubtless it is that also which restrains *Abdemar* from acting against you with more vigour than he hath shewn.' *Almanzor* was exceedingly astonish'd at what he heard; never was sorrow comparable to his; he curs'd his Stars, and remain'd in a most deplorable condition, while *Aristan* inform'd him in this manner of the whole Mystery of his Birth.

⁴ in spite of.

*The History of the Births of* Almanzor *and* Almanzaida

There were but two years past, since that the Birth of *Abdemar* had fill'd all the Inhabitants of *Moroco* with joy, and had fortified the imperious *Roxana*'s Credit; when *Haly*, who commanded the Naval Armies of this Kingdom, a Person considerable both to the King and his People, through the important Services which he had rendred, did unfortunately perish by the strength of an infinite number of Pyrates who had combined his destruction, seeing him the Terror of all the Eastern Seas. He was of an Illustrious Birth, and descended from the first Princes that had reign'd over *Moroco*. His unfortunate Death having ruin'd his Fortunes, which had not always been one of the happiest, he left behind him his Family, composed of two Daughters and one Son, without Means or assistance. His Widow felt most sensibly his loss, and finding her self incapable of giving her Son such an Education as would suit with his Birth, she came into this Palace, followed by her three Children, to bring them and her Sorrows at the Feet of *Abdala*, and humbly to implore his Protection and Assistance for the Reliques of a Person who had been so faithful in his Service. Those Objects which accompanied *Haly*'s sad Widow, were too moving not to prevail. The Son was but twelve years of age, the Daughter that preceded him, thirteen, and *Cleonisa*, who was the eldest, was going into her sixteenth. It is easie for you to imagine, that nothing was so beautiful as she: the blackness of her Habit added more Charms unto her Face, and the King found so much in her Eyes, though drowned in Tears, that granting both Means and Dignities unto the young Prince *Haly*, he made a Gift far greater and more precious than all this unto *Cleonisa*, since it was of that Heart over which *Roxana* had till then had an absolute Empire. He had too much Love, to caution himself; and mauger *Roxana*'s Rage and Jealousie, some few days after he espoused *Cleonisa*. Thus *Roxana* had the grief to see her self have a Rival, even an adored one. As she is ingenious, but very dissembling withal, she took upon her the Art of feigning; she conceal'd her Resentments with policy, & frequently visited *Cleonisa* (who presently after grew with Child) and became almost inseparable from her; thus obscuring under a formal and affected Complaisancy, a form'd design of ruining her, she deceived the King and *Cleonisa* also. I was the only Person that distrusted her real intentions, and that feared the evil consequences of this disguised Friendship: *Roxana*'s Endearments were always suspected to me, because I knew her Inclinations: yet all my circumspection could not prevent an accident which had like to have been of a most dreadful consequence. The King did love *Cleonisa* most passionately; but he feared *Roxana*'s evil spirit, and durst not be wanting in his complaisancy: therefore he was highly pleased to see them in a strict union, which to promote the more, he sought all the means imaginable, daily procuring them a thousand various delights.

*Cleonisa*'s great Belly taking away her appetite towards Flesh-meat, she was complaining one day of it to *Roxana*, who caused some Baskets of choice Fruits to be presented unto her, of which she did eat with great delight and satisfaction; but she was scarce retired to her Apartment, when she fell into a Distemper, the violence of which did make us despair of her Life. I found her in the arms of her Slaves, without colour, and almost without motion. The King, almost desperate, came in running. *Roxana* was one of the first, and of the most busied in her assistance; but in her Actions I could observe a malicious Joy mix: and examining more nearly all Circumstances, I concluded that she had been poysoned. I have some skill in the choice of Plants, such as I have found divers times by experience to be great enemies to Poysons; and after I had administred a Remedy to *Cleonisa*, I was confirmed in the suspicion which I had had, of the cause of her Distemper. The Heavens blessed the means, and the young Princess seconded their strength; who after she had vomited the Fruit and Poyson, remained without danger of her Life, but much fatigated with the Pains she had endured.

So soon as she could go forth, she returned to *Roxana*'s Lodgings, with the same assiduity as she did before, without the least distrust: but apprehending the future by the late experience, I resolved to make her Partaker of my jealousies and fears. My Fidelity was well known unto her, and she had reason to confide in it; so that she fell into such an astonishment at my Discourse, as would be difficult for me to express. 'I confess (said she) that not mistrusting in the least *Roxana*'s dissimulation, I should have at some time or other blindly precipitated my self in those ambushes that she laid for me, had I not had this timely advertisement.'[5] 'Madam, you must feign, as she doth (I replied); but let it be so, that she may not have the least distrust of it: Caress the King, who loves you, and to whom I have lately given to understand the same as I have now declared unto you: Secure your own life, and that you go with: for I must tell you, Madam, that *Roxana* is not onely jealous, but highly ambitious also: She hates you mortally, because she sees that you triumph over her in the Kings Heart; and fearing lest you should one day produce a Rival

[5] warning.

for the Throne unto *Abdemar*, as there are no Crimes black enough to strike horror in her, neither will she spare any means to prevent it.'

*Cleonisa* did rellish my Reasons: The King came unto us, and we took our measures accordingly. That which we thought the surest way, was to conceal the time of *Cleonisa*'s delivery, that your death might be feigned. This took happily; you came into the World, I delivered you out of the Palace, into the hands of such Persons which I knew to be very faithful, and which I had managed beforehand to that purpose. *Cleonisa* shed such tears at your absence, as confirmed *Roxana* in the belief of your death, which for the present setled her cruel mind: but within the term of a year, we were again in the same trouble, and *Cleonisa*'s second great Belly did set us in a greater confusion than was the first: In fine, we overcame it. *Cleonisa* is tall, her shape easie; and cruel *Roxana* was not the onely Person that was ignorant of her big Belly; but every body else of the Palace, except the King, two Slaves, and my self. *Almanzaida* came into the World with the same cautions as we had had for you: I took her from hence also, though but a Daughter, that I might hazard nothing. I trusted her unto a Man of my own Country, whose Wife had been delivered about the same time as *Cleonisa*. Mean time, my Lord, the tender *Cleonisa* was not long without entreating me to have you brought secretly into the Palace. I thought my self too weak not to be overcome at some time or other; therefore I rather chose to cause some sorrow to *Cleonisa* for some time, than to hazard your Life, and *Almanzaida*'s also, by telling her that you were dead, and that the young Princess had not outlived you above two Months. She grieved for you both a long time. I told the same story to the King, for fear that through his tenderness to *Cleonisa* he might have undeceived her.

Six years were expired, before I durst introduce you into the Palace. A supposed Merchant presented you to *Abdala* for a Slave: you from that very moment did please him; and that high Recompence which he gave to him that had presented you, was a sufficient testimony of it. He commanded me to take the care upon me of your Education; and you may easily imagine what joy I received with that order. In fine, two years after, by other means, I got the young Princess also into this Place, to whom had been given the name of *Almanzaida* (you bearing that of *Almanzor*) who was presented unto *Roxana*, to endeavour by that means the engagement of her Affections towards her, through a familiar frequentation. She took great care of her; and *Almanzaida* has rendered her self so worthy the affections of all the World, that she could not refuse her

hers. My dear Prince, this is that important Secret, of which your particular Interest made me the particular Depositary: You perceive the
Reasons which made me conceal it, though I fear too long; but I could not
foresee that fatal Engagement, the cause of your afflictions.

'Ah, cruel *Aristan* (cried out *Almanzor*, seeing him silent) why did you
not abandon me to *Roxana*'s fury? You see that the Heavens disapprove
of your pity, since I am fallen into that sad disaster of loving my own
Sister with a more than Brotherly love.—My Sister! (added he, a moment
after) Good Gods! How can I pronounce that word, and live? Oh, thou
too charitable Friend, why did you rescue a Victim from *Roxana*'s fury,
and did not let it fall unto *Roxana*'s satisfaction, for the security of
*Abdemar*'s future Reign? How many evils had you spared me, and sorrows
to your self? What a Life shall I lead for the future? What quiet can I
ever hope for, being thus linked to a Passion, which I find that the name
of Brother will never extinguish in me?' Whatever *Aristan* could oppose
to his Passions, or that he could alledge to moderate the Princes grief,
was all in vain; he could find nothing in him but a rebellious and disturbed
Reason, which would not permit him to hearken to any advice. He
conjur'd *Almanzor* to continue the Secret, and took upon him to inform
*Almanzaida* of all things.

It is easie to imagine what a restless night this miserable Prince had.
The next morning he feign'd himself indisposed, that he might not be
disturbed; and *Aristan* having found out some opportunity of entertaining *Almanzaida*, related unto her the same things which he had done to
*Almanzor* the day before. Though she was less passionate than the Prince
her Brother, yet she was not less sensible;[6] and if she fell into no passion
before *Aristan*, as he had, she, it is very probable, did it in private, and
with as much sorrow. *Aristan* exhorted her to silence, till he had disposed
the minds of the most concerned for the reception of such surprizing
News; and so he left her, as much oppressed with grief, as was *Almanzor*.
He kept his Chamber three days, and *Almanzaida* her Bed during the
same time, the better to conceal a trouble which she could not overcome:
She feared to see a Brother whom she loved with too much passion; and
this unfortunate Prince, still fearing to confound his Sister with his
Mistriss, had not the power to go towards *Roxana*'s Apartment, though
carried on by such powerful Motives.

At last he resolved it. Three days of violent sorrow had made such an

[6] capable of emotion.

impression on *Almanzor*, as was sufficient to perswade any one that he had been sick; and *Almanzaida*'s tears had rendered her eyes so languid, as if she had thus punished them for having carried her Charms into her Brothers very Heart. The disconsolate *Almanzor* found her alone, in *Roxana*'s Chamber; and never two Persons that feared, and yet passionately longed to see one another, did feel more equal Passions at their approch. The Princess did cast down her looks; and *Almanzor*, who under the name of a Lover, as well as of a Brother, did still take the same delight in beholding her, fixed his upon her Face; and after some moments of silence, which were employed in sighing, 'Madam, (said he) have you forgot me? have you not one word for me? will you not speak to me at this time specially that I have so much need of your Vertue, to consolate a Soul so overcome with sorrow, and grown even desperate by that very advantage which will prove fatal to me, though in the same moment infinitely glorious.' 'If I had that pitch of Vertue which you speak of (replied the Princess) it would be very useful to my self at present; and you may well imagine, that being no less surprized, nor less overcome with Sorrow than you are, Consolation would be as necessary for me, as for you: But, dear Brother, we must seek for comfort in constancy; and if I cannot be an example of Fortitude, at the receit of so unfortunate a knowledge as we have lately come to by *Aristan*, but too long concealed from us, I will at least serve you, in helping you to forget that criminal tenderness which ought not to consist between such Persons as are animated with one and the same Blood.' 'Oh, cruel one, (replied the Prince, looking languishingly upon her) I find that it will be easie for you to effect what you say, since that you can pronounce with so little concern that Name which shall never be expressed by me. What (added he), shall a few moments be capable to extinguish those Fires, that I have had so much pains in a long assiduity to kindle? And I foresee that you will easily be brought to look with some indifferency upon that Person, who, though a Slave, you have preferred to a Prince. I see, *Almanzaida*, that you onely thought you loved me, but never did it really. I shall profit but little of the advice you would give me; and though the merciless Fates have determined, that I must never be more than a Brother to you, yet they shall never force my passionate affections from you, but that I shall ever love you, as I have always done: For it is but just, that since you have changed onely in Name, but have preserved all your Beauties, I shou'd likewise preserve my Love, after the loss of all my Hopes.'

'The Heavens (replied *Almanzaida*, sighing) would punish you, shou'd you do what you say; and being what we are, such a Love can remain no longer innocent.' 'Alas! what more cruel Griefs than those I suffer at present, can happen to me? (repli'd the Prince). It is not death that I wish for, though it would be far more welcom to me than life, as I look upon it at present. Know, Madam, that the more I reflect upon what has past, the more horror I have for the future. You know, that through your bounty, forgetting the obscurity of my Birth, and all that could afflict a Man whose Soul was sufficiently raised above the Vulgar, I was become sensible to my Passion onely. You are not ignorant also, Madam, that proud of that preferency which you had given me above *Abdemar*, I esteemed my self incomparably more happy than him with all his Dignities. And can you think, that this so passionate and constant Heart, submitting it self unto a timid Vertue, would sacrifice unto it such a Passion as is to out-last all Sorrows, and even Time it self? In such a case, the Resignation would be a Crime; and doubtless that Love must be but very superficial, that can so soon be laid aside. But you, *Almanzaida*, you that have honoured me with your Love, or that at least would have made me believe such a thing in you, is it possible that you should so soon be at an agreement with that thing called Decency, so that a meer scruple can so suddenly triumph over your Heart? and that in the midst of all my sorrows, I have not so much left me, as the bare comfort to think, that this surprising change has been unwelcom to you?' 'Good my Lord, (replied the Princess) do not thus pierce into a weakness which is so difficult for me to conceal. I seek how to cure, and not how to afflict you. But you, my Lord, do not do me that Justice. I hid my Tears from you; yet you are so cruel as to lay all your Sorrows open to me, and add to them such Reproches as I do not deserve. Can you imagine, that she that preferred you before the Prince *Abdemar*, at that very time also when your Chains were your greatest Ornament, did but indifferently love you? Can you believe, that that Preferency was the effect of a wavering Heart, not firm in its Resolutions? No, Sir, you know not *Almanzaida*: I share your Sorrows, am no less sensible of them than your self; but they are past remedie, and I can see nothing but Time and Reason that can overcome them: Let us wait the one, and endeavour to make use of the other; and in the mean time, my Lord, in pity of me, moderate a Passion that over-comes me, and be assured, that I am not of sufficient strength to bear, without dying, both your Sorrows, and my own.'

*Almanzaida* was going on, when the Prince *Abdemar* came in: He presently cast such Looks on *Almanzor* as were full of indignation; but straight smoothing them up again at the sight of the Princess, whom he had not seen of three days before, he took notice of a change in her Face; and then perceiving *Almanzor*'s trouble, he knew not what to attribute it unto: and being but too well persuaded of their reciprocal Love, he imagined that their sadness proceeded from the despair of ever being happy in the enjoyment of each other: And it is probable, that in this imagination he might have flown into some Passion against *Almanzor*, had not *Roxana* come in.

*Almanzor* withdrew himself, and passing through a Gallery that led into *Cleonisa*'s Apartments, he met her as she was coming out of them. Though she was absolutely ignorant of his Condition, she had a most tender affection for him, and making him sign to draw near, 'As I have always been concerned in your Interest, *Almanzor*, (said she) I must now give you a most important advice, while I have the opportunity of speaking to you in private. You love *Almanzaida; Abdemar* is your Rival, who intends (in order to your eternal separation from her) to get the King to enfranchize you, so to turn you out of the Palace, and out of *Moroco* also. This I learned from his own mouth some days since, I being hid in a place where I overheard him, while he was discoursing of it with *Zais*, who doubtless is of his Secrets. What Charms soever Liberty can put on, I am of opinion that you would find but little content in them, whilst separated from *Almanzaida*. I was glad of the opportunity of giving you this Advertisement, that you may take your measures against *Abdemar* and *Roxana*'s Designs, who will not fail inconsiderately to execute whatever her Son shall require.'

During *Cleonisa*'s Discourse, the Prince found himself agitated in divers manners, and was often upon the point of discovering all *Aristan*'s Secrets unto her; but remembring that he had promised the contrary, he kept them still within himself. 'I am infinitely obliged to your Bounties, Madam, (said he) and I know nothing in the World that I would not do, to render me worthy of it. It is certain, that I love *Almanzaida*; and it is no less true, that *Abdemar* is my Rival in it; But, Madam, neither he nor I can have any further hopes: some day you may learn the surprising cause of it: Mean time, Madam, continue to protect a miserable Person, who is threatned with so many misfortunes; watch also for *Almanzaida*.' *Cleonisa* could return no answer, because some body came by; so that *Almanzor* was forced to retire himself; and she went into *Roxana*'s Apartment, amazed at his Discourse, where she found *Almanzaida* all in tears. *Abdemar*, transported with jealousie, was resolved to break off all

Converse between *Almanzor* and *Almanzaida;* and having found *Roxana* in a fit humour to open his Designs to her, he told her, That they had a confirmed private Intrigue between them, which for some discontents against *Almanzor*, he intreated her to break off, and to forbid him her Apartment. *Roxana* was a declared Enemy to all the Worlds quiet, and glad of the opportunity of troubling two Persons that loved one another, she assured her Son, that she would not onely forbid *Almanzor* her Apartment, but that she would also turn him out of the Palace, for having secret Amours there, and even out of *Moroco* also, if occasion required it.

*Abdemar* went forth well satisfied with this assurance; and *Roxana* having caused *Almanzaida* to be called, 'I should never have believed (said she to her) that forgetting that Vertue in which you have been educated, you would have lent an ear after amorous Propositions, and bound your self in an Intrigue of Love with one of the Kings Slaves: yet it is but too true, that it is so; and the audacious *Almanzor*, abusing of those Privileges which my Bounty and *Abdala*'s Favours had procured him above many others, has been so bold as to seduce your Heart in this very place. I am convinced of this by unquestionable assurances, and it is with trouble that I speak it. I had conceived a sincere affection for you from your very Infancy; and looking upon you with the Eyes of a Mother, rather than of a Mistris, I had designed something more than a Slave for you: But since your Heart has made an unworthy choice, and would not stay for mine, all that you must hope from it, is, that *Almanzor* shall turn out of this Palace, never to enter into it again; and moreover, I shall not onely deprive you of those advantages which I intended you, but of my Esteem and Friendship also.'

*Almanzaida*'s Heart was but too sensible, to endure with patience *Roxana*'s Taunts; she was conscious of her own innocence, and had always lived with *Almanzor* in such a manner, as deserved Praises, rather than Reproches. Therefore looking on *Roxana* as on a Person that would have sacrificed to her own Fury both *Cleonisa* and *Almanzor*, with a boldness that had some mixture of scorn in it; 'Madam, (said she) I neither deserve your Reproches, nor your Menaces; and my Inclinations have ever been so much to Vertue, that peradventure I have even outgone those Lessons which were given me therein. I have no commerce that can make me blush; and I dare tell you, Madam, (what Respects soever I owe you) that you never did perceive in me any thing that could give you any disadvantageous thoughts of *Almanzaida*. I speak with that freedom, Madam, which perhaps is not wholly sutable to my Condition, but which is very conformable to the motions of my Heart, and to those sensible wrongs which I do not deserve, neither know I any Power that can make me to suffer them. I have made no unworthy Choice, Madam; and mauger the obscurity of my Birth, knowing my Soul sufficiently raised above the Vulgar, I leave the success of my Destiny unto the protection of Heaven; I hope the Gods will accept of it, and procure me the means of justifying my self. But, Madam, though you should unhappily deprive me of your Protection, upon such groundless suspicions, I should endeavour to consolate my self of such a disgrace as I had not drawn upon my self, and that I had not deserved.' 'I know not (replied *Roxana*, fretted at *Almanzaida*'s Answer) which of us two is the Queen, and which the Slave: Yet when I consider you, I can see nothing but the effects of my Bounties, and *Almanzor*'s Mistriss.' 'I know what I am, Madam, (replied *Almanzaida*, resolved to justifie her self) I acknowledge my self your Slave: But if my Person is obliged to you, it was for protecting a miserable wretch, destinated to bear your Chains, and to serve you; and I am sensible enough, that this servile condition requires nothing but submission in me: But, Madam, my Heart and my Condition are at odds, and I may say, that the one is the wreck of the other; and if I believe my Heart, which is impatient of suffering wrong, if I am no Queen, at least I am not descended from a place much inferiour to a Throne.' 'A Conquest so Illustrious as that of *Almanzor* (replied *Roxana* scornfully) cannot inspire lower thoughts.' '*Almanzor* (replied the Princess) has a Vertue that would justifie all those that I have for him.' 'I know (interrupted *Roxana*) that Vertue does affect you so, as to make you fancy your self the more considerable for it; but such weak Imaginations move nothing but Commiseration: and for my part, I pitty you, for losing in one day that precious Lovers sight, with all the hopes of ever seeing him again. Go, shut up your shame, and hide it from my sight, and the rest of the Worlds also.'

At these words *Almanzaida* retired, anger drawing a deluge of tears from her fair Eyes, which was the condition that *Cleonisa* had found her in. She endeavoured to comfort her, and to learn the cause of her troubles. *Almanzaida* informed her of it, not mentioning in the least *Aristan*'s Secret, though not without great restraint. *Cleonisa* was moved at it, and embracing the young Princess, 'It is but a moment (said she) since I was advertising *Almanzor* of what you were both to fear: but, my dear *Almanzaida*, what Service can I render you?' 'The most considerable that I can expect from your generosity, Madam, (replied she) is to do me more justice than *Roxana*.' '*Roxana*'s Soul and mine (replied the amiable *Cleonisa*) are too different, to have the same Motives: I have but too much cause to believe her unjust, and though I were not so satisfied as I am of your Vertues, her bare Accusations would be sufficient to confirm your Innocence to me: But once again, what must be done in this juncture?' 'Give notice to *Almanzor* of all that has passed (replied *Almanzaida*); bid him to consult *Aristan*, and that they use all the means they can imagine to deliver me from these aspersions, and from *Roxana*'s and *Abdemar*'s Persecutions. *Almanzor* must no more come into the Palace, Imperious *Roxana* banishes him from thence for ever; and since you have the goodness, Madam, to engage your self in an unfortunate Creatures concerns, be pleased to see *Abdala*'s Slave, tell him my condition: Time presses, and one moment of wrong unto *Almanzaida*'s Vertue is capable of casting her into despair.' *Cleonisa* had no more time, than to assure the Princess, that she would act as she desired; for *Roxana*'s coming in, obliged *Almanzaida* to retire.

*Roxana* said not a word to *Cleonisa* of what had hapned; she designed that the business should break out in publick: her Slaves Answer had so strangely netled her, that she could entertain no other thoughts but of her destruction. *Cleonisa* staid but little with her, being in an impatiency of assisting *Almanzaida*; and because she could not seek out *Almanzor* her self, so soon as she was in her Apartment, she writ him a Note, which she gave to an old Eunuch to deliver unto him, in which were these words.

### *To* Almanzor

*A Most important Business is the cause that I must of necessity see you this day; having such things to impart to you, as are not to be confided to Paper. Meet me within two hours at the Fountain of the Labyrinth: I shall not fail to be there, and to let you know whether your Interests are dear unto me, and what thoughts there are of you in the Bosom of*

Cleonisa

What a World of Troubles did this innocent Letter cause in *Abdala*'s Palace? The Slave *Toxara* did carry it in his Hand so that it might easily be perceived, and was passing into the Kings Apartment to seek out *Almanzor*, when he met *Roxana*, whose suspicious Eyes were immediately cast upon the Note. 'What Message are you going about, *Toxara* (said she to the Slave)? What is that Paper you carry?' He not answering, and seeming perplexed, rendred *Roxana* the more curious, who took the Note

out of his Hand with no further consideration than of her own satisfaction, with which she returned into her Apartment. *Toxara* durst not
inform *Cleonisa* of the truth of the business, but gave her to understand
that he had lost the Note, after he had made a fruitless search for *Almanzor*.

*Roxana*, whose spirit was naturally wicked, presently suspected that
*Cleonisa* had some private concerns with *Almanzor*; and howsoever she
had hitherto concealed her thoughts, it is most certain that she always
hated her, seeing with rage and spite her Merits to reign so powerfully
over *Abdala*'s Heart: being overjoy'd of having this opportunity of ruining
so dreadful an Enemy as she esteemed *Cleonisa*, she put up the Note for
the present, not without a world of revengeful thoughts.

Mean time this accident, and the night coming on, had broke all
*Cleonisa*'s Measures; and what desire soever she had of serving
*Almanzaida*, she was forced to stay till Morning, to advertise *Almanzor*
of her desires to speak with him: While she was musing which way to
compass it, (a Note having already been lost) *Almanzaida* in her solitude
overcome with sorrow, *Almanzor* suffering still at the same rate, un-
capable of comfort, *Roxana* was not idle: *Abdala* coming into her Chamber
that night, according to his custom, she could no longer defer giving the
first onset unto *Cleonisa*'s Happiness: 'My Lord, (said she to *Abdala*,
with an affected sorrow) it is with great reluctancy that I am obliged to
inform you of a Business which will be unpleasing to you; and were not
your Honour interested in it, I would not be thus instrumental in any
trouble to you: But, my Lord, your Glory is concerned in it; and whatsoever be the event, you are not to be long kept from the knowledge that
*Cleonisa* is false to you, and that it is *Almanzor*, whom you love as your
own Child, that insolent Slave, that dishonours you, and entertains a
secret Traffick of Love with her.' 'Ah, Madam, (said the King, struck
with her words as with Thunder) do not distrust *Cleonisa*'s Vertue, and
*Almanzor*'s Fidelity.' 'You know *Cleonisa*'s Character,[7] (replied *Roxana*,
giving him the Note) Read.'

At this sight *Abdala* had much to do to believe his own Eyes: He loved
*Cleonisa* more than ever he had loved *Roxana*, and *Almanzor* had always
been in a manner as dear to him as *Abdemar*; and those kind thoughts he
had for them, making them seem much the more guilty, 'Ah, perfidious,
(cried he) you shall both perish, and your criminal Lives shall revenge me
of so sensible a wrong. Does *Cleonisa* thus betray me? and is it *Almanzor*
that seduces her? This is too much, and I will no longer defer the Decree

7 handwriting.

of their Ruine.' *Roxana*, who politickly weighed all things, did fear that if this Business should break forth more publickly, it might so happen that a Justification would destroy her Designs, retained the King as he was going forth to pronounce their deaths, and craftily gave him to understand, that he was not to publish an Affront which would grow greater by being divulged. This Advice did something allay *Abdala*'s rage, who retired into his Apartment. At the same instant *Abdemar* came in, and *Roxana* renewed her pleasure, in repeating to him what had hapned. He believed nothing of it, and was too well skilled in tender Affections, to believe that those which *Almanzor* had for *Almanzaida* were not real: He therefore would have perswaded his Mother, that *Cleonisa*'s Note was more mysterious than guilty, and that she ought not to expose her to the Fury of the King, without a further search into the Business had first been made: But in stead of receiving this good advice, she accused him of timidity and weakness.

*Abdala* passed that Night without rest; and the great Love he resented[8] for *Cleonisa*, and tenderness for *Almanzor*, made him conclude them the more deserving death, which he was preparing for them. *Aristan* had hitherto been the sole Depositary of all his Secrets; but he would not make him partaker of this last: he was *Almanzors* Adorer, and *Cleonisa*'s faithful Agent, who had too great a liberty with him, not to employ all his Interests in their behalf. Thus did all things concur to both their ruines; who not thinking of what was preparing for them, were entertaining themselves of all that had hapned the day before. *Almanzor* returned a thousand thanks to *Cleonisa*, for what she had done for him; and being sensible of those ill things which *Roxana* was contriving against *Almanzaida*, he took leave of *Cleonisa*, to go seek *Aristan*, to conjure him to declare a Secret that could not have more dangerous Consequences when published, than it had already. The Eunuch, to please the Prince, run immediately to the King, who having resolved not to see him till after he had executed his Designs, feigned to be sick, and pretended to repose; so that the Fates had a full scope to bring this Adventure to the last extremity. *Almanzor* was past all patience at these delays; he durst no longer cast his Eyes towards the place which contained *Almanzaida*: Imperious *Roxana* was insulting over *Cleonisa*; and *Abdemar* durst not complain of not seeing *Almanzaida*, for having drawn this evil upon himself.

Mean time, the incensed King would no longer defer his Revenge; and the evening of that same day the Executioners of such private Deaths had

[8] felt.

Orders given them to deprive *Cleonisa* and *Almanzor* of their Lives. *Roxana* was suddenly informed of the Sentence, and so was feeding her ambitious thoughts with the pleasure of Reigning solely. She would have the satisfaction to acquaint *Almanzaida* first, of that thing which she thought would be the most sensible to her in the World: She sent for her, and not forbearing at *Abdemar*'s arrival, because she no longer feared the revocation of those Orders that had been given, and 'tis probable already executed, she informed the sorrowful *Almanzaida* both of the Deaths and pretended Infidelities of her Lover, and of *Cleonisa*. This unexpected News had like to have cost the Princess her Life; she fell upon a Couch that was near her, without colour or motion. *Abdemar* run to her, and discovered unto his Mother, by that diligence he used, what she had never mistrusted.[9] *Roxana*'s Slaves did second those Cares which he took to succour her; and while some were flinging of Water in her Face, and others tearing off her Clothes, *Abdala*, mortally troubled at what was going to be done, came into *Roxana*'s Chamber, and found *Almanzaida* in that desperate condition: He learned the cause of it, and judged *Almanzor* the more deserving death, in betraying not onely his Bounties, but the beautiful *Almanzaida* also; who at last came out of her swoon, having gathered some strength through an effect of the very same Sorrow that had deprived her of it before: How beautiful did she appear? and how difficult it was to see her in that strange disorder, and not be infinitely moved at it? The discomposing of her Dress, the languidness of her Eyes, her Tears, her sorrowful Complaints, and, in a word, all her Actions, did contribute in exciting both Love and Commiseration at the same time.

The discomposure that she found her self in before the King, did not prevent her from casting her self down at his Feet, 'Ah, Sir, (said she to him) preserve *Cleonisa*, and do not lose *Almanzor*, if you will not expose your self to a remorse more cruel than their deaths.' '*Almanzaida* (replied *Abdala*) I ought to revenge my self of a most ungrateful Woman, and deliver you from a perfidious Man, who is unworthy of your Tears, and that deserves a thousand deaths more cruel than that which is going to punish his Crimes.' 'He is not perfidious, Sir, (cried she); he is your own Blood, your Son, and of unfortunate *Cleonisa*, who by *Roxana*'s treachery, after so many years of distrusts and precautions, falls at last the Victim to her fury. Yes, Sir, *Almanzor* is your Son, and that unfortunate Creature that speaks to you at this present is his Sister, your Daughter, Sir: believe

[9] suspected.

it, Sir, and *Aristan* shall confirm it; it is he who being convinced by experience of what we were to fear from *Roxana*'s rage, deceived you, to preserve us: These are the Criminals that you sacrifice to her satisfaction.'

*Almanzaida*'s Discourse found not any thing in *Abdala*'s Heart that could resist it; and those tender affections which he always had for *Almanzor*, were convincing proofs that he was his Blood: It would be difficult to express his grief; and the first word that he spake, was to bid *Abdemar* hasten to render him a Service more important than his Life, in endeavouring with all diligence to prevent *Cleonisa*'s death, and *Almanzor*'s also, if it were yet time; bidding him remember that he was his Brother, and worthy of that Title by a thousand Vertues. *Abdemar* deferred not a moment to obey; he was generous, and really moved with what he had but just learned, he flew to *Cleonisa*'s Apartment. Mean time *Roxana* seeing *Abdala* busied in giving *Almanzaida* some Testimonies of his Affections, was reflecting with an inward rage on the sudden change that some few words had brought to this business, and was seeking in her Heart and Spirit, ingenious to all evil, some means by which she might invalidate *Aristan*'s Testimony, and render it of no effect, by making it pass for a feigned Story, who in a days space did bring again to life not onely that Child of *Cleonisa*'s which she her self had thought dead coming into the World, but another also, of whose Life she was wholly ignorant.

*Abdemar* came happily to *Cleonisa*'s rescue, who constant in her adversities, was writing her last thoughts unto *Abdala*. He staid with her no longer than to make known that the Orders were reversed, and run immediately to *Almanzor*'s Lodgings; but it was too late, and his Executioners, more diligent than *Cleonisa*'s, having found him upon his Bed, had mercilessly strangled him there.

*Abdemar* moved at so deplorable a fate, could not stay his Eyes on so dreadful a Spectacle; and too certain of a Truth which so afflicted him, he returned to *Roxana*'s Apartment: 'I have staid too long, Sir, (said he to the King) *Cleonisa* lives, but *Almanzor* is breathless.' At these fatal words the King resented[10] his Sorrows to the quick, and repented that he had so lightly given credit to *Roxana*'s perfidiousness: The beauteous *Almanzaida* found her self in the heighth of extremity also. *Abdemar*, whose affections unto her had given way to a real tenderness, did wholly lay upon himself the cause of all these evils, and being moved with a sincere penitency, did reproch unto *Roxana* her barbarousness, unto which the King added his resentments; and certainly nothing in the

[10] felt.

world could be more touching, than to hear all that passed between them. In fine, *Abdala* retired from a place in which *Roxana*'s presence did but augment his sorrow, and went to *Cleonisa*'s Apartment, leading the most afflicted *Almanzaida* along with him; where they found the Princess as composed, as if she had had nothing to fear, but she soon ceased to be so, when she learned at once both the Life and Death of her dear Son: It was her Hand that had sacrificed him, and without that fatal Note *Roxana* could not have destroyed him.

In vain did the King endeavour to recal her Fortitude by his Embraces; *Almanzor* was no more, and though innocent of his death, she looked upon her self as the cause of it. 'Since that your unjust distrusts (said she to the King) have caused me so much sorrow as nothing can ever con-solate me, and that the unfortunate *Almanzor* was not rescued from furious *Roxana*'s rage, but to become a more noble Victim to her cruelty; and that without enjoying the happiness of his Life, I have all the sorrows that such a death could produce, suffer at least that I may give unto his Heart, as cold as it is, such Embraces as I could not give unto him living.' At these words, without staying for *Abdala*'s Answer, she went towards the Slaves Quarters, and had already crossed some Galleries that made the distance between the Kings and the Womens Apartment, when she perceived *Aristan*, with that beloved Son which she was lamenting, and whose supposed loss was going in all probability to cause hers effectually. She was no sooner certain of his Life, but that she gave a full scope to all her Joys, and to the tenderness of her Affections; the King was no less sensible of this Happiness: But *Almanzaida*, not-withstanding her resolutions to the contrary, did resent[11] it in a manner which it is like was yet more eminent than the rest. *Aristan* in few words did clear more amply that Mystery which had preserved two such precious Lives, and did receive such Eulogies from all as his Fidelity did deserve. *Almanzor*, surprised at so many Accidents, could not be taken off from reflecting on the dangers unto which *Cleonisa* had been exposed: As for his part, he found his Soul in such a condition, as made him look upon Death as a refuge, and not as an evil. Embraces and expressions of tenderness were often repeated on all sides; but the Princess *Almanzaida*, who knew by her own experience what Sorrows *Almanzor* did yet feel for her, durst scarcely look upon him.

Mean time it was unhappy *Toxara* who had received that sad fate which was intended for *Almanzor*: He had found the Princes Chamber open,

[11] feel.

and while he was walking with *Aristan* in the Garden, he had thrown himself upon his Bed, where the Executioners had strangled him, taking him for *Almanzor*. *Toxara*'s loss was not significant enough to disturb so much joy. After *Abdala* had left *Cleonisa* in her Apartment, where he also parted with *Almanzaida*, he retired himself unto his also; and *Abdemar*, who had nothing but Brotherly Affection for *Almanzor*, would not part from him; he being not capable of so strong a Passion as his Brother, his Reason overcame his Love: But *Almanzor* was less conformable; he was more in love than ever: and while the rest were at quiet, his share was Tears and Sighs.

The next morning he rendered his Devoirs[12] unto the King, and in the next place to *Cleonisa;* who seeing now her Happiness above her own desires and hopes, did continually ply *Almanzaida* with Caresses. That amiable Princess did answer her Favours with a world of affection, but with as much sadness; so that *Cleonisa* was perswaded, that the knowledge of her Fortune had not restored her Heart to its Liberty, and that *Almanzor* did still hold there a larger place than the name of a Brother would admit of: *Almanzor*'s presence did confirm her in that Opinion; and notwithstanding *Almanzaida*'s reservedness, her Eyes would speak another Language than that of Friendship unto the passionate *Almanzor*. This mutual Affection did not trouble *Cleonisa*, further than as it had relation to their quiet; and being confident in both their Vertues, she knew that she had no cause to fear of that side: therefore she busied her thoughts in healing of such Evils which a long Error had contracted: But he was incapable of it; neither Time, nor *Cleonisa*'s and *Aristan*'s Cares, could obtain any thing upon his strong Impressions; but forgetting every moment that *Almanzaida* was his Sister, he did speak to her of his Love: and the young Princess, being sometimes deluded by a too powerful Charm, did hearken unto him without interruption, and did daily more and more plunge her self into an Abyss, whence it was impossible to retrive her.

Mean time *Roxana* looked upon *Cleonisa*'s Prosperity with rage; and never were so many attempts made for the ruine of her happiness, as then: But all too late; *Abdala* was convinced of the Vertue of the one, and of the others evil Designs: and it is likely that he had resented *Roxana*'s wickedness in an higher measure yet, but that he looked upon her as on *Abdemar*'s Mother.

*Almanzor* of a Slave had taken upon him the Name and Rank of Prince,

[12] duties (paid his respects).

but not the Pride; and as in his mean condition he had the Art of pleasing all the World, it was not difficult for any Person to add to that esteem they had always had for him, those respects due to his Birth. *Aristan* seeing his Designs come so forward, did look upon his good Success with delight; onely *Almanzor*'s obstinate Passion did intermix some discontents with it: He was thinking on the small hopes there was of curing him, when he was advertised, that a Stranger asked to speak with him: He gave order he should be brought in; and no sooner had he cast his Eyes upon him than he knew him to be that Person to whom he had intrusted *Almanzaida*'s first Years. As he had ever found him most faithful to all his Secrets, he did entertain such thoughts of him as were full of Acknowledgments; so that he embraced him, and after the first testimonies of affection, he offered him his Services at *Moroco*, in all that he should desire.

'I am perswaded (replied *Zideus*) that you would generously serve a Person in whom you did once repose the highest confidence: but, as the case stands now, it is on no particular Interest that I come here at present. *Aristan*, I have a business of the highest nature to impart to you, the mystery of which I conjure you to pardon me, since that all my intentions in it have been but to save you from much sorrow. That Child with whom you had intrusted me, was not the same I returned you back, Death bereaved us of it within six months after you had committed it to our care; and I being informed of its Birth, I guess'd at the sorrow that you would have for the loss of it; which to prevent for the present, I supplied the place of the King of *Moroco*'s Daughter, by another young Princess, reduced to seek for succour, and exiled from her very Birth, through extraordinary events, since it had pleased the Heavens to intrust her into our Hands. I did it, *Aristan;* and the Age was so well fitted, that you were not sensible of the change which I had put upon you. But now pray hearken unto the Story of that Person after whom I am now come to inquire.

'You are not ignorant, that *Albenzais* King of *Fez* was driven from his Kingdom some twenty years since, by the ambitious *Morat;* and that he unhappily ended his days, being about to defend the Remains both of his and his Queen *Zaira*'s Liberty. The Queen was then with Child, and near the time of her Delivery, when the deplorable *Albenzais* lost his life; the sorrows of his Queen ended hers also, presently after that she had brought a Daughter into the World. I was born in *Europe*, but had given my self from my youth unto *Albenzais* his Service, and was married unto one of those Persons whom *Zaira* did most consider: We were the onely two that did not abandon them in their Adversities; and it was into our Hands (in the presence of Prince *Ortisis*, Brother unto *Albenzais*, who had never forsaken her) that the dying Queen deposited that innocent Creature which she had newly brought into the World, entreating us to conceal her from *Morat*'s knowledge, and to retire into some unknown place, to wait for a better fortune. *Ortisis* extremely grieved at the Queens death, sent us away without delay, assuring me, that either he would perish in the attempt, or tear *Albenzais* his Scepter from the unjust *Morat*'s Hands, and restore it unto that new-born Babe his Brother's Daughter. Thus we parted from *Ortisis*, who some time after was taken by the Agents of *Morat*, as he was on a Design, and shut up in a close Prison, in which he did languish for a long time.

'In the mean time, that I might not be far from some place where I might hear News from *Fez*, I came to *Moroco*, where I met with you, and where you were pleased to take me into your Friendship: My Wife did appear to you a fit Person to take upon her the care of *Abdala*'s Daughter: but when, after her death, I had given you the Princess of *Fez* in lieu of her, I was well satisfied as to that particular; and finding my self useless at *Moroco*, I took a Voyage, and at my return learned that *Ortisis* had escaped out of Prison. I made some stay at *Fez*, and through my care and diligence did learn the place of his retreat. I came to him, he received me kindly; and I was the more welcome, when I assured him of the Princesses Life. In fine, after divers years of needless Cautions, and of Secret Enterprizes, one has taken effect, in which *Morat* the Usurper has been massacred by the People of *Fez*, tired with the Oppressions of his Tyrannical Government; after whose death, *Ortisis* has no sooner appeared, but the Name of *Albenzais*, and his also, have been repeated a thousand times. He generously refusing the Crown, has assured the Chief amongst them, That there was a Daughter of *Albenzais*'s living, in whom his Memory was to be perpetuated; That for his part, he had taken up the Sword but as its Depositary, till the arrival of the Princess. Thus presenting some Papers to *Aristan;* This is (continued he) the Prince *Ortisis* his Testimony, with a Note of the Queens, which will confirm the truth of my Relation.'

The Eunuch was so amazed at this Discourse, as to remain some time in a profound silence: But after he had read the Letters, being fully perswaded of a thing in which there was so much demonstration of truth, 'Ah, *Almanzor*, (cried he, thinking on the joy this would bring to the Prince)

what happy News are here for you?' And being unwilling to lose a
moments time of publishing them, in few words he informed *Zideus* of
*Almanzaida*'s Condition, and gave him also some light Informations of
what had passed of her Concerns. So conducting him into the Kings
presence, they found *Almanzor* entring the Chamber, with such a consternation of Spirits, as did speak him worse than ever he had been yet.
'Will you thus for ever give your self over to sorrow, Sir, (said *Aristan* to
him)? and will you never endeavour to overcome it?' 'I should attempt
Impossibilities (replied the Prince) should I design it; but as the Cause
has been from my Infancy, and as it were born with me, so neither can it
end but with my Life.' 'Hope better things, my Lord, (replied *Aristan*);
Here is a Man, Sir, that boasts of curing you, if you please; but will not
undertake a Business of such importance, but in the King's presence.'
'Ah, (cried out *Almanzor*) save me at once both the labour and confusion
of informing him of what passes in my Breast.' At these words they entred,
where they found *Abdemar* onely with the King; who presently conceiving,
that this Stranger did not present himself thus without Orders but on
some extraordinary account, expected to learn the occasion, when *Aristan*
informed the King of the business. During the Relation, never was Man
more hearkned unto than he was by *Almanzor*, neither was there ever so
pleasing a surprize as this. *Zideus* his Relation, the Queen of *Fez*'s
Note, and the Letters from *Ortisis*, did joyntly confirm the truth, and
removed all doubts. *Abdala* was the first that congratulated *Almanzor*
with these surprising News, and immediately went with *Aristan* and
*Zideus* unto *Cleonisa*'s Apartment, to inform her and *Almanzaida* of a
thing that would so strangely surprize them.

During their stay in that place, *Almanzor*, in the midst of his Joys,
thinking of *Abdemar*'s concurrency in his Amours, fell into a sudden
melancholy, of which the Prince could not forbear asking him the cause.
*Almanzor* ingenuously confessed, that he feared a return of *Abdemar*'s
amorous Flames, which he might reasonably fear would re-kindle, the
rather because his own had never suffered the least decay. *Abdemar* did
assure him, in so obliging a manner, that he was free, and that he had no
other Affections left for *Almanzaida*, but such as might become a Brother,
that far from opposing in the least his Happiness, he would seek all the
ways imaginable to contribute to it. The King by his return did further
confirm *Almanzor* in his Happiness, in promising him the possession of the
Princess of *Fez;* to that purpose immediately sending back with *Zideus*
some of the most considerable of his Officers, to advertise the Prince

*Ortisis* of the state of things, and to demand of him the Princess of *Fez* for *Almanzor*, he being the onely Person on whom she did depend.

Mean time *Almanzor* run to *Cleonisa*'s Apartment: she took no small part in his contentment, and was somewhat consolated of the loss of her own Daughter, by the consideration that her Son should possess the beautiful *Almanzaida;* to whom he having expressed part of those Joys he felt, he went from her Apartment into that in which was the Princess of *Fez*, whom he found without company: Their contented looks did speak to each other a mutual joy; but being both filled with various thoughts, they kept a profound silence for a considerable time, before they could express themselves; which was first broke by *Almanzor*, in these words: 'Madam, (said he) all my Happiness has its whole dependency on you onely; and the same happy Fate which has brought us out of that confusion in which all my hopes were lost, without the least decay or alteration in my affections, does assist me to bring at your Feet both my Love and my Hopes, here prostrating my self, to demand of the Queen of *Fez* a continuance of those Affections which the beauteous *Almanzaida* did once entertain for the Slave *Almanzor*.' 'My Lord, (replied *Almanzaida*) you should demand with more confidence that which you are sure to obtain: The Slave *Almanzor* was ever dear unto me; *Almanzaida*'s Brother has been the same, peradventure more than he ought to have been; and the Prince of *Moroco* shall ever be more precious than her own Life unto the Daughter of *Albenzais*. I complained against Fortune, when some Circumstances had made me believe that I was *Abdala*'s Daughter, because that Greatness was outragious to the Inclinations of a Heart which could not pardon any thing that did but check its Passions for *Almanzor:* But now I am contented with my change, since that through *Ortisis* his Generosity it gives me a Throne, in which I may have something that may please you. It is you onely, Sir, that I can share it with; and give me leave to tell you, that that which renders it the most considerable to me, is, that I can offer it to you.' 'Generous Princess, (replied the passionate Lover) all that I can boast of, is of a Heart that has been wholly yours since it first knew it self. I have nothing more to repay those precious Favours which you so profusely pour upon me.' 'That Heart you speak of (replied *Almanzaida*) which I esteem above the World, has already acquitted you of all the Favours I could bestow upon you; and no sooner shall *Ortisis* say the word, but—' 'Ah, Madam, (cried out *Almanzor*) can he be the sole Opponent to my Happiness?' 'Hope for better things (replied the Princess); *Zideus* has given us an advantageous account of his Goodness, and his Actions hitherto have been answerable to it: Having so much Vertue, he cannot be ungrateful; and if he is sensible, he will doubtless share in those Obligations which I owe you.' 'It is I that owe you immortal ones (interrupted the Prince) and I should have just cause to fear all things, if I had not more confidence in both your Goodness, than in all my Pretensions.' 'My Lord, (replied the Princess) I hope he will be favourable to you; but should I be deceived in my hopes, that Faith which I at present give you, to be ever yours, shall never be altered.'

These last words elevated *Almanzor* at the heighth of his happiness. *Cleonisa* met him: *Abdemar* came presently after, and did assure them in a handsom manner of the joy he resented at their satisfaction.

In fine, after a tedious expectation for our impatient Lovers (though it was not long) *Abdala*'s Envoys returned with a full consent from *Ortisis*, for *Almanzaida*'s Marriage; which was no longer deferred, than to prepare the Gallantry thereof, which was worthy *Abdala*'s Magnificence, and sutable to those Lovers for whom it was made.

FINIS

Aphra Behn

# THE HISTORY OF THE NUN: OR, THE FAIR VOW-BREAKER

(1689)

# THE
# HISTORY
## OF THE
# NUN:

## OR, *THE*

# Fair Vow-Breaker.

*Written by* Mrs. A. B E H N.

LICENSED,
*Octob.* 22. 1688.      *Ric.* Pocock.

*L O N D O N:*

Printed for *A. Baskervile*, at the *Bible*, the Corner of *Effex-Street*, againft St. *Clement*'s Church , 1689.

*The one big name in Restoration fiction is that of Aphra Behn, whose work, both in quality and in quantity, clearly puts her first among all English writers of the period in the genre. Her production of some dozen varied pieces of short fiction makes her not only the best fiction writer of her time, however, but a nicely representative one. It is almost impossible to single out individual strands of the various influences which she absorbed—though the impress of the novella as written by Paul Scarron and of the drama through her own experience as a playwright seems obvious—but by and large her work stands for the new realism, or the dominance of verisimilitude, whichever we choose to call it, though of course her work is also full of highly romantic material. Her chief contribution to the tendency to realism is the asseveration that she, as narrator, is telling what actually happened in the recent past from first-hand knowledge: either she took part in the events related (or actually witnessed them) or she had the story from the mouth of one of its principals or chief witnesses.*

*In spite of this interest in realism, however, Mrs. Behn's main strength lies elsewhere. The characteristic of her writing that confers excellence upon her beyond mere historical importance is her ability to realize and develop in certain scenes in her stories the emotional potential of the situation. These scenes, in which she has no contemporary rival, are written with depth and real power, and, as might be expected, they are connected with tragic or latently tragic situations. Verisimilitude and an eye for the actual may seem much more adapted to comedy, as manners painting is a device for comic writers, yet it is no paradox to say that tragedy can also benefit from truth to life. Mrs. Behn at times rises nobly, indeed gladly, to the demand her plots put upon her; her characters are on such occasions quite capable of moving the reader to a genuine emotional response.*

The History of the Nun, *a version of the Enoch Arden theme which develops into what one critic has called a "quite remarkable study in the psychology of crime and guilt,"*[1] *is characteristic of Mrs. Behn's best work. There is first of all the insistence on the truth of the story she is about to tell: "it is on the Records of the Town, where it was transacted." Then there is a generalized statement of theme to give the story moral weight and value; the story will be sad but edifying. And then there is the convent setting, a splendid device for keeping lovers separated, perhaps forever, for making them search their hearts with more than ordinary penetration, for forcing them into desperation and rash action, to the deepening of the emotional*

[1] George Woodcock, *The Incomparable Aphra* (London: T. V. Boardman, [1948]), p. 207.

*impact. The first scene between hero and heroine after each knows the other's love is very well done, as is also their next interview, in which Henault, after having expressed a sensible hesitation on economic grounds about running away with Isabella, is quickly brought to share her position that love must leap over all obstacles gladly and blindly to be worthy the name of love. And finally there is the dry, factual close for which Mrs. Behn has been praised—a mere statement of the facts with no final upsurge of that emotion which had carried the story past its various hazards of plot improbability and coincidence.*

*The text which follows is based upon the copy of the 1689 edition in the British Museum.*


### To the Most Illustrious Princess,
### The Dutchess of Mazarine

MADAM,

There are none of an Illustrious Quality, who have not been made, by some Poet or other, the Patronesses of his Distress'd Hero, or Unfortunate Damsel; and such Addresses are Tributes, due only to the most Elevated, where they have always been very well receiv'd, since they are the greatest Testimonies we can give, of our Esteem and Veneration.

Madam, when I survey'd the whole Toor of Ladies at Court, which was adorn'd by you, who appear'd there with a Grace and Majesty, peculiar to Your Great Self only, mix'd with an irresistible Air of Sweetness, Generosity, and Wit, I was impatient for an Opportunity, to tell Your Grace, how infinitely one of Your own Sex ador'd You, and that, among all the numerous Conquests, Your Grace has made over the Hearts of Men, Your Grace has not subdu'd a more entire Slave; I assure you, Madam, there is neither Compliment nor Poetry, in this humble Declaration, but a Truth, which has cost me a great deal of Inquietude, for that Fortune has not set me in such a Station, as might justifie my Pretence to the honour and satisfaction of being ever near Your Grace, to view eternally that lovely Person, and hear that surprizing Wit; what can be more grateful to a Heart, than so great, and so agreeable, an Entertainment? And how few Objects are there, that can render it so entire a Pleasure, as at once to hear you speak, and to look upon your Beauty. A Beauty that is heighten'd, if possible, with an air of Negligence, in Dress, wholly Charming, as if your Beauty disdain'd those little Arts of your Sex, whose Nicety alone is their greatest Charm, while yours,

Madam, even without the Assistance of your exalted Birth, begets an Awe and Reverence in all that do approach you, and every one is proud, and pleas'd, in paying you Homage their several ways, according to their Capacities and Talents; mine, Madam, can only be exprest by my Pen, which would be infinitely honour'd, in being permitted to celebrate your great Name for ever, and perpetually to serve, where it has so great an inclination.

In the mean time, Madam, I presume to lay this little Trifle at your Feet; the Story is true, as it is on the Records of the Town, where it was transacted; and if my fair unfortunate *Vow-Breaker* do not deserve the honour of your Graces Protection, at least, she will be found worthy of your Pity; which will be a sufficient Glory, both for her, and,

Madam,
Your Graces most humble,
and most obedient Servant,
A. BEHN

### The History of the Nun:
### or, The Fair Vow-Breaker

Of all the Sins, incident to Human Nature, there is none, of which Heaven has took so particular, visible, and frequent Notice, and Revenge, as on that of *Violated Vows*, which never go unpunished; and the *Cupids* may boast what they will, for the encouragement of their Trade of Love, that Heaven never takes cognisance of Lovers broken Vows and Oaths, and that 'tis the only Perjury that escapes the Anger of the *Gods:* But I verily believe, if it were search'd into, we should find these frequent Perjuries, that pass in the World for so many Gallantries only, to be the occasion of so many unhappy Marriages, and the cause of all those Misfortunes, which are so frequent to the Nuptiall'd Pair. For not one of a Thousand, but, either on his side, or on hers, has been perjur'd, and broke Vows made to some fond believing Wretch, whom they have abandon'd and undone. What Man that does not boast of the Numbers he has thus ruin'd, and who does not glory in the shameful Triumph? Nay, what Woman, almost, has not a pleasure in Deceiving, taught, perhaps, at first, by some dear false one, who had fatally instructed her Youth in an Art she ever after practis'd, in Revenge on all those she could be too hard for, and conquer at their own Weapons? For, without all dispute, Women are by Nature more Constant and Just, than Men, and did not their first

Lovers teach them the trick of Change, they would be *Doves*, that would never quit their Mate, and, like *Indian* Wives, would leap alive into the Graves of their deceased Lovers, and be buried quick with 'em. But Customs of Countries change even Nature her self, and long Habit takes her place: The Women are taught, by the Lives of the Men, to live up to all their Vices, and are become almost as inconstant; and 'tis but Modesty that makes the difference, and, hardly inclination; so deprav'd the nicest Appetites grow in time, by bad Examples.

But, as there are degrees of Vows, so there are degrees of Punishments for Vows, there are solemn Matrimonial Vows, such as contract and are the most effectual Marriage, and have the most reason to be so; there are a thousand Vows and Friendships, that pass between Man and Man, on a thousand Occasions; but there is another Vow, call'd a *Sacred Vow*, made to God only; and, by which, we oblige our selves eternally to serve him with all Chastity and Devotion: This Vow is only taken, and made, by those that enter into Holy Orders, and, of all broken Vows, these are those, that receive the most severe and notorious Revenges of God; and I am almost certain, there is not one Example to be produc'd in the World, where Perjuries of this nature have past unpunish'd, nay, that have not been persu'd with the greatest and most rigorous of Punishments. I could my self, of my own knowledge, give an hundred Examples of the fatal Consequences of the Violation of Sacred Vows; and who ever make it their business, and are curious in the search of such Misfortunes, shall find, as I say, that they never go unregarded.

The young Beauty therefore, who dedicates her self to Heaven, and weds her self for ever to the service of God, ought, first, very well to consider the Self-denial she is going to put upon her Youth, her fickle faithless deceiving Youth, of one Opinion to day, and of another to morrow; like Flowers, which never remain in one state or fashion, but bud to day, and blow[2] by insensible degrees, and decay as imperceptibly. The Resolution, we promise, and believe we shall maintain, is not in our power, and nothing is so deceitful as human Hearts.

I once was design'd an humble Votary in the House of Devotion, but fancying my self not endu'd with an obstinacy of Mind, great enough to secure me from the Efforts and Vanities of the World, I rather chose to deny my self that Content I could not certainly promise my self, than to languish (as I have seen some do) in a certain Affliction; tho' possibly, since, I have sufficiently bewailed that mistaken and inconsiderate

[2] bloom.

Approbation and Preference of the false ungrateful World, (full of nothing but Nonsense, Noise, false Notions, and Contradiction) before the Innocence and Quiet of a Cloyster; nevertheless, I could wish, for the prevention of abundance of Mischiefs and Miseries, that Nunneries and Marriages were not to be enter'd into, 'till the Maid, so destin'd, were of a mature Age to make her own Choice; and that Parents would not make use of their justly assum'd Authority to compel their Children, neither to the one or the other; but since I cannot alter Custom, nor shall ever be allow'd to make new Laws, or rectify the old ones, I must leave the Young Nuns inclos'd to their best Endeavours, of making a Virtue of Necessity; and the young Wives, to make the best of a bad Market.

In *Iper*, a Town, not long since, in the Dominions of the King of *Spain*, and now in possession of the King of *France*, there liv'd a Man of Quality, of a considerable Fortune, call'd Count *Henrick de Vallary*, who had a very beautiful Lady, by whom he had one Daughter, call'd *Isabella*, whose Mother dying when she was about two years old, to the unspeakable Grief of the Count, her Husband, he resolv'd never to partake of any Pleasure more, that this transitory World could court him with, but determin'd, with himself, to dedicate his Youth, and future Days, to Heaven, and to take upon him Holy Orders; and, without considering, that, possibly, the young *Isabella*, when she grew to Woman, might have Sentiments contrary to those that now possest him, he design'd she should also become a Nun: However, he was not so positive in that Resolution, as to put the matter wholly out of her Choice, but divided his Estate; one half he carried with him to the Monastery of *Jesuits*, of which number, he became one; and the other half, he gave with *Isabella*, to the Monastery, of which his only Sister was Lady *Abbess*, of the Order of St. *Augustine;* but so he ordered the matter, that if, at the Age of Thirteen, *Isabella* had not a mind to take Orders, or that the Lady *Abbess* found her Inclination averse to a Monastick Life, she should have such a proportion of the Revenue, as should be fit to marry her to a Noble Man, and left it to the discretion of the Lady *Abbess*, who was a Lady of known Piety, and admirable strictness of Life, and so nearly related to Isabella, that there was no doubt made of her Integrity and Justice.

The little *Isabella* was carried immediately (in her Mourning for her dead Mother) into the Nunnery, and was receiv'd as a very diverting Companion by all the young Ladies, and, above all, by her Reverend Aunt, for she was come just to the Age of delighting her Parents; she was the prettiest forward Pratler in the World, and had a thousand little

Charms to please, besides the young Beauties that were just budding in her little Angel Face: So that she soon became the dear lov'd Favourite of the whole House; and as she was an Entertainment to them all, so they made it their study to find all the Diversions they could for the pretty *Isabella;* and as she grew in Wit and Beauty every day, so they fail'd not to cultivate her Mind, and delicate Apprehension, in all that was advantageous in her Sex, and whatever Excellency any one abounded in, she was sure to communicate it to the young *Isabella;* if one could Dance, another Sing, another play on this Instrument, another on that; if this spoke one Language, and that another; if she had Wit, and she Discretion, and a third the finest Fashion and Manners; all joyn'd to compleat the Mind and Body of this beautiful young Girl; Who, being undiverted with the less noble, and less solid, Vanities of the World, took to these Virtues, and excell'd in all; and her Youth and Wit being apt for all Impressions, she soon became a greater Mistress of their Arts, than those who taught her; so that at the Age of eight or nine Years, she was thought fit to receive and entertain all the great Men and Ladies, and the Strangers of any Nation, at the *Grate;*[3] and that with so admirable a Grace, so quick and piercing a Wit, and so delightful and sweet a Conversation, that she became the whole Discourse of the Town, and Strangers spread her Fame, as prodigious, throughout the Christian World; for Strangers came daily to hear her talk, and sing, and play, and to admire her Beauty; and Ladies brought their Children, to shame 'em into good Fashion and Manners, with looking on the lovely young *Isabella.*

The Lady *Abbess,* her Aunt, you may believe, was not a little proud of the Excellencies and Virtues of her fair *Niece,* and omitted nothing that might adorn her Mind; because, not only of the vastness of her Parts and Fame, and the Credit she would do her House, by residing there for ever; but also, being very loth to part with her considerable Fortune, which she must resign, if she returned into the World, she us'd all her Arts and Stratagems to make her become a *Nun,* to which all the fair Sisterhood contributed their Cunning, but it was altogether needless; her Inclination, the strictness of her Devotion, her early Prayers, and those continual, and innate Stedfastness, and Calm, she was Mistress of, her Ignorance of the World's Vanities, and those that uninclos'd young Ladies count Pleasures and Diversions being all unknown to her, she thought there was no Joy out of a *Nunnery,* and no Satisfactions on the other side of a *Grate.*

The Lady *Abbess,* seeing that of her self she yielded faster than she

[3] the grating separating the nuns' side of the visiting room from that of the public.

could expect, to discharge her Conscience to her Brother, who came frequently to visit his Darling *Isabella*, would very often discourse to her of the Pleasures of the World, telling her how much happier she would think her self, to be the Wife of some gallant young Cavalier, and to have Coaches and Equipages; to see the World, to behold a thousand Rarities she had never seen, to live in Splendor, to eat high, and wear magnificent Clothes, to be bow'd to as she pass'd, and have a thousand Adorers, to see in time a pretty Offspring, the products of Love, that should talk, and look, and delight, as she did, the Heart of their Parents; but to all, her Father and the Lady *Abbess* could say of the World, and its Pleasures, *Isabella* brought a thousand Reasons and Arguments, so Pious, so Devout, that the *Abbess* was very well pleased, to find her (purposely weak) Propositions so well overthrown; and gives an account of her daily Discourses to her Brother, which were no less pleasing to him; and tho' *Isabella* went already dress'd as richly as her Quality deserv'd, yet her Father, to try the utmost that the World's Vanity could do upon her young Heart, orders the most Glorious Clothes should be bought her, and that the Lady *Abbess* should suffer her to go abroad with those Ladies of Quality, that were her Relations, and her Mother's Acquaintance; that she should visit and go on the Toore, (that is, the Hide Park there) that she should see all that was diverting, to try, whether it were not for want of Temptation to Vanity, that made her leave the World, and love an inclos'd Life.

As the Count had commanded, all things were performed; and *Isabella* arriving at her Thirteenth Year of Age, and being pretty tall of Stature, with the finest Shape that Fancy can create, with all the Adornment of a perfect brown-hair'd Beauty, Eyes black and lovely, Complexion fair; to a Miracle, all her Features of the rarest proportion, the Mouth red, the Teeth white, and a thousand Graces in her Meen and Air; she came no sooner abroad, but she had a thousand Persons fighting for love of her; the Reputation her Wit had acquir'd, got her Adorers without seeing her; but when they saw her, they found themselves conquer'd and undone; all were glad she was come into the World, of whom they had heard so much, and all the Youth of the Town dress'd only for *Isabella de Valerie*, she rose like a new Star that Eclips'd all the rest, and which set the World a gazing. Some hop'd and some despair'd, but all lov'd, while *Isabella* regarded not their Eyes, their distant darling Looks of Love, and their signs of Adoration; she was civil and affable to all, but so reserv'd, that none durst tell her his Passion, or name that strange and abhorr'd thing,

*Love,* to her; the Relations, with whom she went abroad every day, were fein to force her out, and when she went, 'twas the motive of Civility, and not Satisfaction, that made her go; whatever she saw, she beheld with no admiration, and nothing created wonder in her, tho' never so strange and Novel. She survey'd all things with an indifference, that tho' it was not sullen, was far from Transport, so that her evenness of Mind was infinitely admir'd and prais'd. And now it was, that, young as she was, her Conduct and Discretion appear'd equal to her Wit and Beauty, and she encreas'd daily in Reputation, insomuch that the Parents of abundance of young Noble Men made it their business to endeavour to marry their Sons to so admirable and noble a Maid, and one whose Virtues were the Discourse of all the World; the *Father,* the Lady *Abbess,* and those who had her abroad, were solicited to make an Alliance; for the *Father,* he would give no answer, but left it to the discretion of *Isabella,* who could not be persuaded to hear any thing of that nature; so that for a long time she refus'd her company to all those, who propos'd any thing of Marriage to her; she said, she had seen nothing in the World that was worth her Care, or the venturing the losing of Heaven for, and therefore was resolv'd to dedicate her self to that; that the more she saw of the World, the worse she lik'd it, and pity'd the Wretches that were condemn'd to it; that she had consider'd it, and found no one Inclination that forbad her immediate Entrance into a Religious Life; to which her Father, after using all the Arguments he could, to make her take good heed of what she went about, to consider it well; and had urg'd all the Inconveniences of Severe Life, Watchings, Midnight Risings in all Weathers and Seasons to Prayers, hard Lodging, course[4] Diet, and homely Habit, with a thousand other things of Labour and Work us'd among the *Nuns;* and finding her still resolv'd and inflexible to all contrary persuasions, he consented, kiss'd her, and told her, She had argu'd according to the wish of his Soul, and that he never believ'd himself truly happy, till this moment that he was assur'd, she would become a Religious.

This News, to the Heart-breaking of a thousand Lovers, was spread all over the Town, and there was nothing but Songs of Complaint, and of her retiring, after she had shewn her self to the World, and vanquish'd so many Hearts; all Wits were at work on this Cruel Subject, and one begat another, as is usual in such Affairs. Amongst the number of these Lovers, there was a young Gentleman, Nobly born, his name was *Villenoys,* who was admirably made, and very handsom, had travell'd and accomplish'd

4 coarse

himself, as much as possible for one so young to do; he was about Eighteen, and was going to the Siege of *Candia*, in a very good Equipage, but, overtaken by his Fate, surpriz'd in his way to Glory, he stopt at *Ipers*, so fell most passionately in love with this Maid of Immortal Fame; but being defeated in his hopes by this News, was the Man that made the softest Complaints to this fair Beauty, and whose violence of Passion oppress'd him to that degree, that he was the only Lover, who durst himself tell her, he was in love with her; he writ Billets[5] so soft and tender, that she had, of all her Lovers, most compassion for *Villenoys*, and dain'd several times, in pity of him, to send him answers to his Letters, but they were such, as absolutely forbad him to love her; such as incited him to follow Glory, the Mistress that could noblest reward him; and that, for her part, her Prayers should always be, that he might be victorious, and the Darling of that Fortune he was going to court; and that she, for her part, had fix'd her Mind on Heaven, and no Earthly Thought should bring it down; but she should ever retain for him all Sisterly Respect, and begg'd, in her Solitudes, to hear, whether her Prayers had prov'd effectual or not, and if Fortune were so kind to him, as she should perpetually wish.

When *Villenoys* found she was resolv'd, he design'd to persue his Journy, but could not leave the Town, till he had seen the fatal Ceremony of *Isabella*'s being made a *Nun*, which was every day expected; and while he stay'd, he could not forbear writing daily to her, but receiv'd no more Answers from her, she already accusing her self of having done too much, for a Maid in her Circumstances; but she confess'd, of all she had seen, she lik'd *Villenoys* the best; and if she ever could have lov'd, she believ'd it would have been *Villenoys*, for he had all the good Qualities, and grace, that could render him agreeable to the Fair; besides that he was only Son to a very rich and noble Parent, and one that might very well presume to lay claim to a Maid of *Isabella*'s Beauty and Fortune.

As the time approach'd, when he must eternally lose all hope, by *Isabella*'s taking *Orders*, he found himself less able to bear the Efforts of that Despair it possess'd him with; he languish'd with the thought, so that it was visible to all his Friends, the decays it wrought on his Beauty and Gaity: So that he fell at last into a Feaver; and 'twas the whole Discourse of the Town, That *Villenoys* was dying for the Fair *Isabella;* his Relations, being all of Quality, were extreamly afflicted at his Misfortune, and joyn'd their Interests yet, to dissuade this fair young Victoress from an act so cruel,

5 love notes.

as to inclose her self in a *Nunnery*, while the finest of all the youths of Quality was dying for her, and ask'd her, If it would not be more accept-able to Heaven to save a Life, and perhaps a Soul, than to go and expose her own to a thousand Tortures? They assur'd her, *Villenoys* was dying, and dying Adoring her; that nothing could save his Life, but her kind Eyes turn'd upon the fainting Lover, a Lover that could breath nothing but her Name in Sighs, and find satisfaction in nothing but weeping and crying out, *I dye for Isabella!* This Discourse fetch'd abundance of Tears from the fair Eyes of this tender Maid; but at the same time she besought them to believe, these Tears ought not to give them hope, she should ever yield to save his Life by quitting her Resolution of becoming a *Nun;* but, on the contrary, they were Tears that only bewail'd her own Misfortune, in having been the occasion of the death of any Man, especially a Man who had so many Excellencies, as might have render'd him entirely Happy and Glorious for a long race of Years, had it not been his ill fortune to have seen her unlucky Face. She believ'd it was for her Sins of Curiosity, and going beyond the Walls of the Monastery, to wander after the Vanities of the foolish World, that had occasion'd this Mis-fortune to the young Count of *Villenoys*, and she would put a severe Penance on her Body, for the Mischiefs her Eyes had done him; she fears she might, by something in her looks, have intic'd his Heart, for she own'd she saw him with wonder at his Beauty, and much more she admir'd him, when she found the Beauties of his Mind; she confess'd, she had given him hope, by answering his Letters; and that when she found her Heart grow a little more than usually tender, when she thought on him, she believ'd it a Crime that ought to be check'd by a Virtue, such as she pretended to profess, and hop'd she should ever carry to her Grave; and she desired his Relations to implore him, in her Name, to rest contented in knowing he was the first, and should be the last, that should ever make an impression on her Heart; that what she had conceiv'd there, for him, should remain with her to her dying day, and that she besought him to live, that she might see he both deserv'd this Esteem she had for him, and to repay it her, otherwise he would dye in her debt, and make her Life ever after reposeless.

This being all they could get from her, they return'd with Looks that told their Message; however, they render'd those soft things *Isabella* had said, in so moving a manner, as fail'd not to please, and while he remain'd in this condition, the Ceremonies were compleated, of making *Isabella* a *Nun;* which was a Secret to none but *Villenoys*, and from him it was carefully conceal'd, so that in a little time he recover'd his lost health, at least so well as to support the fatal News, and upon the first hearing it, he made ready his Equipage, and departed immediately for *Candia*, where he behav'd himself very gallantly under the Command of the Duke De *Beaufort*, and with him return'd to *France*, after the loss of that noble City to the *Turks*.

In all the time of his absence, that he might the sooner establish his Repose, he forbore sending to the fair Cruel *Nun*, and she heard no more of *Villenoys* in above two years; so that giving her self wholly up to Devotion, there was never seen any one, who led so Austere and Pious a Life, as this young *Votress;* she was a Saint in the Chapel, and an Angel at the *Grate:* She there laid by all her severe Looks, and mortify'd Discourse, and being at perfect peace and tranquillity within, she was outwardly all gay, sprightly, and entertaining; being satisfy'd, no Sights, no Freedoms, could give any temptations to worldly desires; she gave a loose to all that was modest, and that Virtue and Honour would permit, and was the most charming Conversation that ever was admir'd; and the whole World that pass'd through *Iper*, of Strangers, came directed and recommended to the lovely *Isabella;* I mean, those of Quality: But however Diverting she was at the *Grate*, she was most exemplary Devout in the Cloister, doing more Penance, and imposing a more rigid Severity and Task on her self, than was requir'd, giving such rare Examples to all the *Nuns* that were less Devout, that her Life was a Proverb, and a President,[6] and when they would express a very Holy Woman indeed, they would say, *She was a very ISABELLA.*

There was in this *Nunnery*, a young *Nun*, call'd Sister *Katteriena*, Daughter to the Grave *Vanhenault*, that is to say, an Earl, who liv'd about six Miles from the Town, in a noble *Villa;* this Sister *Katteriena* was not only a very beautiful Maid, but very witty, and had all the good qualities to make her be belov'd, and had most wonderfully gain'd upon the Heart of the fair *Isabella*. She was her Chamber-Fellow and Companion in all her Devotions and Diversions, so that where one was, there was the other, and they never went but together to the *Grate*, to the Garden, or to any place, whither their *Affairs* call'd either. This young *Katteriena* had a Brother, who lov'd her intirely, and came every day to see her; he was about twenty Years of Age, rather tall than middle Statur'd, his Hair and Eyes brown, but his Face exceeding beautiful, adorn'd with a thousand Graces, and the most nobly and exactly made, that 'twas possible for

[6] precedent.

Nature to form; to the Fineness and Charms of his Person, he had an Air in his Meen and Dressing, so very agreeable, besides rich, that 'twas impossible to look on him, without wishing him happy, because he did so absolutely merit being so. His Wit and his Manner was so perfectly Obliging, a Goodness and Generosity so Sincere and Gallant, that it would even have aton'd for Ugliness. As he was eldest Son to so great a Father, he was kept at home, while the rest of his Brothers were employ'd in Wars abroad; this made him of a melancholy Temper, and fit for soft Impressions; he was very Bookish, and had the best Tutors that could be got, for Learning and Languages, and all that could compleat a Man; but was unus'd to Action, and of a temper Lazy, and given to Repose, so that his Father could hardly ever get him to any Exercise, or so much as ride abroad, which he would call, Losing Time from his Studies: He car'd not for the Conversation of Men, because he lov'd not Debauch, as they usually did; so that for Exercise, more than any Design, he came on Horseback every day to *Iper* to the *Monastery*, and would sit at the *Grate*, entertaining his Sister the most part of the Afternoon, and in the Evening, retire; he had often seen and convers'd with the lovely *Isabella*, and found, from the first sight of her, he had more Esteem for her, than any other of her Sex: But as Love very rarely takes Birth without Hope, so he never believ'd that the Pleasure he took in beholding her, and in discoursing with her, was Love, because he regarded her as a Thing consecrate to Heaven, and never so much as thought to wish she were a Mortal fit for his Addresses; yet he found himself more and more fill'd with Reflections on her which was not usual with him; he found she grew upon his Memory, and oftner came there than he us'd to do, that he lov'd his Studies less, and going to *Iper* more; and, that every time he went, he found a new Joy at his Heart that pleas'd him; he found, he could not get himself from the *Grate*, without Pain, nor part from the sight of that all-charming Object, without Sighs; and if, while he was there, any persons came to visit her, whose Quality she could not refuse the honour of her sight to, he would blush, and pant with uneasiness, especially if they were handsom, and fit to make Impressions: And he would check this Uneasiness in himself, and ask his Heart, what it meant, by rising and beating in those Moments, and strive to assume an Indifferency in vain, and depart dissatisfy'd, and out of humour.

On the other side, *Isabella* was not so Gay as she us'd to be, but, on the sudden, retir'd her self more from the *Grate* than she us'd to do, refus'd to receive Visits every day, and her Complexion grew a little pale and languid; she was observ'd not to sleep, or eat, as she us'd to do, nor exercise in those little Plays they made, and diverted themselves with, now and then; she was heard to sigh often, and it became the Discourse of the whole House, that she was much alter'd: The Lady *Abbess*, who lov'd her with a most tender Passion, was infinitely concern'd at this Change, and endeavour'd to find out the Cause, and 'twas generally believ'd, she was too Devout, for now she redoubled her Austerity; and in cold Winter Nights, of Frost and Snow, would be up at all Hours, and lying upon the cold Stones before the Altar, prostrate at Prayers: So that she receiv'd Orders from the Lady *Abbess*, not to harass her self so very much, but to have a care of her Health, as well as her Soul; but she regarded not these Admonitions, tho' even persuaded daily by her *Katteriena*, whom she lov'd every day more and more.

But, one Night, when they were retir'd to their Chamber, amongst a thousand things that they spoke of, to pass away a tedious Evening, they talk'd of Pictures and Likenesses, and *Katteriena* told *Isabella*, that before she was a *Nun*, in her more happy days, she was so like her Brother *Bernardo Henault*, (who was the same that visited them every day) that she would, in Men's Clothes, undertake, she should not have known one from t'other, and fetching out his *Picture*, she had in a Dressing-Box, she threw it to *Isabella*, who, at the first sight of it, turns as pale as Ashes, and, being ready to swound, she bid her take it away, and could not, for her Soul, hide the sudden surprise the *Picture* brought: *Katteriena* had too much Wit, not to make a just Interpretation of this Change, and (as a Woman) was naturally curious to pry farther, tho' Discretion should have made her been silent, for Talking, in such cases, does but make the Wound rage the more. 'Why, my dear Sister, (said *Katteriena*) is the likeness of my Brother so offensive to you?' *Isabella* found by this, she had dis-cover'd too much, and that Thought put her by all power of excusing it; she was confounded with Shame, and the more she strove to hide it, the more it disorder'd her; so that she (blushing extremely) hung down her Head, sigh'd, and confess'd all by her Looks. At last, after a considering Pause, she cry'd, 'My dearest Sister, I do confess, I was surpriz'd at the sight of Monsieur *Henault*, and much more than ever you have observ'd me to be at the sight of his Person, because there is scarce a day wherein I do not see that, and know beforehand I shall see him; I am prepar'd for the Encounter, and have lessen'd my Concern, or rather Confusion, by that time I come to the *Grate*, so much Mistress I am of my Passions, when they give me warning of their approach, and sure I can withstand the greatest assaults of Fate, if I can but foresee it; but if it surprize me, I find I am as feeble a Woman as the most unresolv'd; you did not tell me you had this Picture, nor say you would shew me such a Picture; but when I least expect to see that Face, you shew it me, even in my Chamber.'

'Ah, my dear Sister! (reply'd *Katteriena*) I believe, that Paleness, and those Blushes, proceed from some other cause, than the Nicety of seeing the Picture of a Man in your Chamber.'

'You have too much Wit, (reply'd *Isabella*) to be impos'd on by such an Excuse, if I were so silly to make it; but oh! my dear Sister! it was in my Thoughts to deceive you; could I have conceal'd my Pain and Sufferings, you should never have known them; but since I find it impossible, and that I am too sincere to make use of Fraud in any thing, 'tis fit I tell you from what cause my change of Colour proceeds, and to own to you, I fear 'tis Love. If ever therefore, oh gentle pitying Maid! thou were a Lover, if ever thy tender Heart were touch'd with that Passion, inform me, oh! inform me, of the nature of that cruel Disease, and how thou found'st a Cure?'

While she was speaking these words, she threw her Arms about the Neck of the fair *Katteriena*, and bath'd her Bosom (where she hid her Face) with a shower of Tears: *Katteriena*, embracing her with all the fondness of a dear Lover, told her, with a Sigh, that she could deny her nothing, and therefore confess'd to her, she had been a Lover, and that was the occasion of her being made a *Nun*, her Father finding out the Intrigue, which fatally happen'd to be with his own Page, a Youth of extraordinary Beauty. 'I was but Young, (said she) about Thirteen, and knew not what to call the new-known Pleasure that I felt; when e're I look'd upon the young *Arnaldo*, my Heart would heave, when e're he came in view, and my disorder'd Breath came doubly from my Bosom; a Shivering seiz'd me, and my Face grew wan; my Thought was at a stand, and Sense it self, for that short moment, lost its Faculties: But when he touch'd me, oh! no hunted Deer, tir'd with his flight, and just secur'd in Shades,[7] pants with a nimbler motion than my Heart; at first, I thought the Youth had had some Magick Art, to make one faint and tremble at his touches; but he himself, when I accus'd his Cruelty, told me, he had no Art, but awful Passion, and vow'd that when I touch'd him, he was so; so trembling, so surpriz'd, so charm'd, so pleas'd. When he was present, nothing could displease me; but when he parted from me, then 'twas rather a soft silent Grief, that eas'd it self by sighing, and

[7] reached the safety of a shady retreat.

by hoping, that some kind moment would restore my Joy. When he was absent, nothing could divert me, howe're I strove, howe're I toyl'd for Mirth; No Smile, no Joy dwelt in my Heart or Eyes; I could not feign, so very well I lov'd; impatient in his absence, I would count the tedious parting Hours, and pass them off like useless Visitants, whom we wish were gon; these are the Hours, where Life no business has, at least a Lover's Life. But, oh! what Minutes seem'd the happy Hours, when on his Eyes I gaz'd, and he on mine, and half our Conversation lost in Sighs, Sighs, the soft moving Language of a Lover!'

'No more, no more, (reply'd *Isabella*, throwing her Arms again about the Neck of the transported *Katteriena*) thou blow'st my Flame by thy soft Words, and mak'st me know my Weakness, and my Shame: I love! I love! and feel those differing Passions!'—Then pausing a moment, she proceeded, — 'Yet so didst thou, but hast surmounted it. Now thou hast found the Nature of my Pain, oh! tell me thy saving Remedy.' 'Alas! (reply'd *Katteriena*) tho' there's but one Disease, there's many Remedies: They say, Possession's one, but that to me seems a Riddle; Absence, they say, another, and that was mine; for *Arnaldo* having by chance lost one of my Billets, discover'd the Amour,[8] and was sent to travel, and my self forc'd into this Monastery, where at last, Time convinc'd me I had lov'd below my Quality, and that sham'd me into Holy Orders.' 'And is it a Disease, (reply'd *Isabella*) that People often recover?' 'Most frequently, (said *Katteriena*) and yet some dye of the Disease, but very rarely.' 'Nay then, (said *Isabella*) I fear, you will find me one of these Martyrs; for I have already oppos'd it with the most severe Devotion in the World: But all my Prayers are vain, your lovely Brother persues me into the greatest Solitude; he meets me at my very Midnight Devotions, and interrupts my Prayers; he gives me a thousand Thoughts, that ought not to enter into a Soul dedicated to Heaven; he ruins all the Glory I have achiev'd, even above my Sex, for Piety of Life, and the Observation of all Virtues. Oh *Katteriena!* he has a Power in his Eyes, that transcends all the World besides: And, to shew the weakness of Human Nature, and how vain all our Boastings are, he has done that in one fatal Hour, that the persuasions of all my Relations and Friends, Glory, Honour, Pleasure, and all that can tempt, could not perform in Years; I resisted all but *Henault*'s Eyes, and they were Ordain'd to make me truly wretched: But yet with thy Assistance, and a Resolution to see him no more, and my perpetual Trust in Heaven, I may, perhaps, overcome

[8] let the love affair become known to others.

this Tyrant of my Soul, who, I thought, had never enter'd into holy Houses, or mix'd his Devotions and Worship with the true Religion; but, oh! no Cells, no Cloysters, no Hermitages, are secur'd from his Efforts.'

This Discourse she ended with abundance of Tears, and it was resolv'd, since she was devoted for ever to a Holy Life, That it was best for her to make it as easy to her as was possible; in order to it, and the banishing this fond and useless Passion from her Heart, it was very necessary, she should see *Henault* no more: At first, *Isabella* was afraid, that in refusing to see him, he might mistrust her Passion; but *Katteriena*, who was both Pious and Discreet, and endeavour'd truly to cure her of so violent a Disease, which must, she knew, either end in her death or destruction, told her, She would take care of that matter, that it should not blemish her Honour; and so leaving her a while, after they had resolv'd on this, she left her in a thousand Confusions. She was now another Woman than what she had hitherto been; she was quite alter'd in every Sentiment, thought and Notion; she now repented, she had promis'd not to see *Henault;* she trembled and even fainted, for fear she should see him no more; she was not able to bear that thought, it made her rage within, like one possest, and all her Virtue could not calm her; yet since her word was past, and, as she was, she could not without great Scandal break it in that point, she resolv'd to dye a thousand Deaths, rather than not perform her Promise made to *Katteriena;* but 'tis not to be express'd what she endur'd; what Fits, Pains, and Convulsions, she sustain'd; and how much ado she had to dissemble to Dame *Katteriena*, who soon return'd to the afflicted Maid. The next day, about the time that *Henault* was to come, as he usually did, about two or three a Clock after Noon, 'tis impossible to express the uneasiness of *Isabella;* she ask'd a thousand times, 'What, is not your Brother come?' When Dame *Katteriena* would reply, 'Why do you ask?' She would say, 'Because I would be sure not to see him.' 'You need not fear, Madam, (reply'd *Katteriena*) for you shall keep your Chamber.' She need not have urg'd that, for *Isabella* was very ill without knowing it, and in a Feaver.

At last, one of the *Nuns* came up, and told Dame *Katteriena*, that her Brother was at the *Grate*, and she desired, he should be bid come about to the Private *Grate* above stairs, which he did, and she went to him, leaving *Isabella* even dead on the Bed, at the very name of *Henault:* But the more she conceal'd her Flame, the more violently it rag'd, which she strove in vain by Prayers, and those Recourses of Solitude to lessen; all this did but augment the Pain, and was Oyl to the Fire, so that she now could hope, that nothing but Death would put an end to her Griefs, and her Infamy. She was eternally thinking on him, how handsome his Face, how delicate every Feature, how charming his Air, how graceful his Meen, how soft and good his Disposition, and how witty and entertaining his Conversation. She now fancy'd, she was at the *Grate*, talking to him as she us'd to be, and blest those happy Hours she past then, and bewail'd her Misfortune, that she is no more destin'd to be so Happy, then gives a loose to Grief; Griefs, at which, no Mortals, but Despairing Lovers, can guess, or how tormenting they are; where the most easie Moments are, those, wherein one resolves to kill ones self, and the happiest Thought is Damnation; but from these Imaginations, she endeavours to fly, all frighted with horror; but, alas! whither would she fly, but to a Life more full of horror? She considers well, she cannot bear Despairing Love, and finds it impossible to cure her Despair; she cannot fly from the Thoughts of the Charming *Henault*, and 'tis impossible to quit 'em; and, at this rate, she found, Life could not long support it self, but would either reduce her to Madness, and so render her an hated Object of Scorn to the Censuring World, or force her Hand to commit a Murder upon her self. This she had found, this she had well consider'd, nor could her fervent and continual Prayers, her nightly Watchings, her Mortifications on the cold Marble in long Winter Season, and all her Acts of Devotion abate one spark of this shameful Feaver of Love, that was destroying her within.

When she had rag'd and struggled with this unruly Passion, 'till she was quite tir'd and breathless, finding all her force in vain, she fill'd her fancy with a thousand charming *Idea's* of the lovely *Henault*, and, in that soft fit, had a mind to satisfy her panting Heart, and give it one Joy more, by beholding the Lord of its Desires, and the Author of its Pains: Pleas'd, yet trembling, at this Resolve, she rose from the Bed where she was laid, and softly advanc'd to the Stair-Case, from whence there open'd that Room where Dame *Katteriena* was, and where there was a private *Grate*, at which, she was entertaining her *Brother;* they were earnest in Discourse, and so loud, that *Isabella* could easily hear all they said, and the first words were from *Katteriena*, who, in a sort of *Anger*, cry'd, 'Urge me no more! My Virtue is too nice, to become an Advocate for a Passion, that can tend to nothing but your Ruin; for, suppose I should tell the fair *Isabella*, you dye for her, what can it avail you? What hope can any Man have, to move the Heart of a Virgin, so averse to Love? A Virgin, whose Modesty and Virtue is so very curious, it would fly the very word, Love, as some monstrous Witchcraft, or the foulest of Sins, who would loath me for bringing so lewd a Message, and banish you her Sight, as the Object of her Hate and Scorn; is it unknown to you, how many of the noblest Youths of *Flanders* have address'd themselves to her in vain, when yet she was in the World? Have you been ignorant, how the young Count *De Villenoys* languish'd, in vain, almost to Death for her? And, that no Persuasions, no Attractions in him, no worldly Advantages, or all his Pleadings, who had a Wit and Spirit capable of prevailing on any Heart, less severe and harsh, than hers? Do you not know, that all was lost on this insensible fair one, even when she was a proper Object for the Adoration of the Young and Amorous? And can you hope, now she has so entirely wedded her future days to Devotion, and given all to Heaven; nay, lives a Life here more like a Saint, than a Woman; rather an Angel, than a mortal Creature? Do you imagin, with any Rhetorick you can deliver, now to turn the Heart, and whole Nature, of this Divine Maid, to consider your Earthly Passion? No, 'tis fondness, and an injury to her Virtue, to harbour such a Thought; quit it, quit it, my dear Brother! before it ruin your Repose.' 'Ah, Sister! (reply'd the dejected *Henault*) your Counsel comes too late, and your Reasons are of too feeble force, to rebate those Arrows, the Charming *Isabella*'s Eyes have fix'd in my Heart and Soul; and I am undone, unless she know my Pain, which I shall dye, before I shall ever dare mention to her; but you, young Maids, have a thousand Familiarities together, can jest, and play, and say a thousand things between Railery and Earnest, that may first hint what you would deliver, and insinuate into each others Hearts a kind of Curiosity to know more; for naturally, (my dear Sister) Maids are curious and vain; and however Divine the Mind of the fair *Isabella* may be, it bears the Tincture still of Mortal Woman.'

'Suppose this true, how could this Mortal part about her Advantage you, (said *Katteriena*) all that you can expect from this Discovery, (if she should be content to hear it, and to return you pity) would be, to make her wretched, like your self. What farther can you hope?' 'Oh! talk not, (reply'd *Henault*) of so much Happiness! I do not expect to be so blest, that she should pity me, or love to a degree of Inquietude; 'tis sufficient, for the ease of my Heart, that she know its Pains, and what it suffers for her; that she would give my Eyes leave to gaze upon her, and my Heart to vent a Sigh now and then; and, when I dare, to give me leave to speak, and tell her of my Passion. This, this, is all, my Sister.' And, at that word, the Tears glided down his Cheeks, and he declin'd his Eyes, and set a Look so charming, and so sad, that *Isabella*, whose Eyes were

fix'd upon him, was a thousand times ready to throw her self into the
Room, and to have made a Confession, how sensible she was of all she
had heard and seen: But, with much ado, she contain'd and satisfy'd her
self, with knowing, that she was ador'd by him whom she ador'd, and,
with a Prudence that is natural to her, she withdrew, and waited with
patience the event of their Discourse. She impatiently long'd to know, how
*Katteriena* would manage this Secret her Brother had given her, and was
pleas'd, that the Friendship and Prudence of that Maid had conceal'd her
Passion from her Brother; and now contented and joyful beyond imagination, to find her self belov'd, she knew she could dissemble her own
Passion and make him the first Aggressor; the first that lov'd, or, at least,
that should seem to do so. This Thought restores her so great a part of
her Peace of Mind, that she resolv'd to see him, and to dissemble with
*Katteriena* so far, as to make her believe, she had subdu'd that Passion,
she was really asham'd to own; she now, with her Woman's Skill, begins
to practise an Art she never before understood, and has recourse to
Cunning, and resolves to seem to reassume her former Repose: But
hearing *Katteriena* approach, she laid her self again on her Bed, where
she had left her, but compos'd her Face to more chearfulness, and put on a
Resolution that indeed deceiv'd the Sister, who was extreamly pleased,
she said, to see her look so well: When *Isabella* reply'd, 'Yes, I am another
Woman now; I hope Heaven has heard, and granted, my long and humble
Supplications, and driven from my Heart this tormenting God, that has so
long disturb'd my purer Thoughts.' 'And are you sure, (said Dame
*Katteriena*) that this wanton Deity is repell'd by the noble force of your
Resolution? Is he never to return?' 'No, (replied *Isabella*) never to my
Heart.' 'Yes, (said *Katteriena*) if you should see the lovely Murderer of
your Repose, your Wound would bleed anew.'

At this, *Isabella* smiling with a little Disdain, reply'd, 'Because you
once [did] love, and *Henault*'s Charms defenceless found me, ah! do you
think I have no Fortitude? But so in Fondness lost, remiss in Virtue, that
when I have resolv'd, (and see it necessary for my after-Quiet) to want the
power of keeping that Resolution? No, scorn me, and despise me then,
as lost to all the Glories of my Sex, and all that Nicety I've hitherto
preserv'd.' There needed no more from a Maid of *Isabella*'s Integrity and
Reputation, to convince any one of the Sincerity of what she said, since,
in the whole course of her Life, she never could be charg'd with an
Untruth, or an Equivocation; and *Katteriena* assur'd her, she believ'd
her, and was infinitely glad she had vanquish'd a Passion, that would have

prov'd destructive to her Repose: *Isabella* reply'd, She had not altogether vanquish'd her Passion, she did not boast of so absolute a power over her soft Nature, but had resolv'd things great, and Time would work the Cure; that she hop'd, *Katteriena* would make such Excuses to her Brother, for her not appearing at the *Grate* so gay and entertaining as she us'd, and, by a little absence, she should retrieve the Liberty she had lost: But she desir'd, such Excuses might be made for her, that young *Henault* might not perceive the Reason. At the naming him, she had much ado not to shew some Concern extraordinary, and *Katteriena* assur'd her, She had now a very good Excuse to keep from the *Grate*, when he was at it; 'For, (said she) now you have resolv'd, I may tell you, he is dying for you, raving in Love, and has this day made me promise to him, to give you some account of his Passion, and to make you sensible of his Languishment: I had not told you this, (reply'd [*sic*] *Katteriena*) but that I believe you fortify'd with brave Resolution and Virtue, and that this knowledge will rather put you more upon your Guard, than you were before.'

While she spoke, she fix'd her Eyes on *Isabella*, to see what alteration it would make in her Heart and Looks; but the Master-piece of this young Maid's Art was shewn in this minute, for she commanded her self so well, that her very Looks dissembled, and shew'd no concern at a Relation, that made her Soul dance with Joy; but it was, what she was prepar'd for, or else I question her Fortitude. But, with a Calmness, which absolutely subdu'd *Katteriena*, she reply'd, 'I am almost glad he has confess'd a Passion for me, and you shall confess to him, you told me of it, and that I absent my self from the *Grate*, on purpose to avoid the sight of a Man, who durst love me, and confess it; and I assure you, my dear Sister! (continu'd she, dissembling) You could not have advanc'd my Cure by a more effectual way, than telling me of his Presumption.' At that word, *Katteriena* joyfully related to her all that had pass'd between young *Henault* and her self, and how he implor'd her Aid in this Amour; at the end of which Relation, *Isabella* smil'd, and carelessly reply'd, 'I pity him': And so going to their Devotion, they had no more Discourse of the Lover.

In the mean time, young *Henault* was a little satisfy'd, to know, his Sister would discover his Passion to the lovely *Isabella;* and though he dreaded the return, he was pleas'd that she should know, she had a Lover that ador'd her, though even without hope; for though the thought of possessing *Isabella*, was the most ravishing that could be; yet he had a dread upon him, when he thought of it, for he could not hope to accomplish that, without Sacrilege; and he was a young Man very Devout, and even bigotted in Religion; and would often question and debate within himself, that, if it were possible, he should come to be belov'd by this Fair Creature, and that it were possible for her to grant all that Youth in Love could require, whether he should receive the Blessing offer'd? And though he ador'd the Maid, whether he should not abhor the *Nun* in his Embraces? 'Twas an undetermin'd Thought, that chill'd his Fire as often as it approach'd; but he had too many that rekindled it again with the greater Flame and Ardor.

His impatience to know, what Success *Katteriena* had, with the Relation she was to make to *Isabella* in his behalf, brought him early to *Iper* the next day. He came again to the private *Grate*, where his Sister receiving him, and finding him, with a sad and dejected Look, expect what she had to say; she told him, That Look well became the News she had for him, it being such, as ought to make him both Griev'd, and Penitent; for, to obey him, she had so absolutely displeas'd *Isabella*, that she was resolv'd never to believe her her Friend more, 'Or to see you, (said she) therefore, as you have made me commit a Crime against my Conscience, against my Order, against my Friendship, and against my Honour, you ought to do some brave thing; take some noble Resolution, worthy of your Courage, to redeem all; for your Repose, I promis'd, I would let *Isabella* know you lov'd, and, for the mitigation of my Crime, you ought to let me tell her, you have surmounted your Passion, as the last Remedy of Life and Fame.'

At these her last words, the Tears gush'd from his Eyes, and he was able only, a good while, to sigh; at last, cry'd, 'What! see her no more! see the Charming *Isabella* no more!' And then vented the Grief of his Soul in so passionate a manner, as his Sister had all the Compassion imaginable for him, but thought it great Sin and Indiscretion to cherish his Flame: So that, after a while, having her Counsel, he reply'd, 'And is this all, my Sister, you will do to save a Brother?' 'All!' (reply'd she) I would not be the occasion of making a *NUN* violate her Vow, to save a Brother's Life, no, nor my own; assure your self of this, and take it as my last Resolution: Therefore, if you will be content with the Friendship of this young Lady, and so behave your self, that we may find no longer the Lover in the Friend, we shall reassume our former Conversation, and live with you, as we ought; otherwise, your Presence will continually banish her from the *Grate*, and, in time, make both her you love, and your self, a Town Discourse.

Much more to this purpose she said, to dissuade him, and bid him

retire, and keep himself from thence, till he could resolve to visit them
without a Crime; and she protested, if he did not do this, and master his
foolish Passion, she would let her Father understand his Conduct, who
was a Man of temper so very precise, that should he believe, his Son
should have a thought of Love to a Virgin vow'd to Heaven, he would
abandon him to Shame, and eternal Poverty, by disinheriting him of all
he could: Therefore, she said, he ought to lay all this to his Heart, and
weigh it with his unheedy Passion. While the Sister talk'd thus wisely,
*Henault* was not without his Thoughts, but consider'd as she spoke, but
did not consider in the right place; he was not considering, how to please
a Father, and save an Estate, but how to manage the matter so, to establish
himself, as he was before with *Isabella;* for he imagin'd, since already she
knew his Passion, and that if after that she would be prevail'd with to
see him, he might, some lucky Minute or other, have the pleasure of
speaking for himself, at least, he should again see and talk to her, which
was a joyful Thought in the midst of so many dreadful ones: And, as if
he had known what pass'd in *Isabella*'s Heart, he, by a strange sympathy,
took the measures to deceive *Katteriena*, a well-meaning young Lady, and
easily impos'd on from her own Innocence, he resolv'd to dissemble
Patience, since he must have that Virtue, and own'd, his Sister's Reasons
were just, and ought to be persu'd; that she had argu'd him into half his
Peace, and that he would endeavour to recover the rest; that Youth ought
to be pardon'd a thousand Failings, and Years would reduce him to a
condition of laughing at his Follies of Youth, but that grave Direction was
not yet arriv'd: And so desiring, she would pray for his Conversion, and
that she would recommend him to the Devotions of the Fair *Isabella*, he
took his leave, and came no more to the *Nunnery* in ten Days; in all which
time, none but Impatient Lovers can guess, what Pain and Languishments
*Isabella* suffer'd, not knowing the Cause of his Absence, nor daring to
enquire; but she bore it out so admirably, that Dame *Katteriena* never
so much as suspected she had any Thoughts of that nature that perplex'd
her; and now believ'd indeed she had conquer'd all her Uneasiness: And
one day, when *Isabella* and she were alone together, she ask'd that fair
Dissembler, if she did not admire at the Conduct and Resolution of her
Brother? 'Why!' (reply'd *Isabella* unconcernedly, while her Heart was
fainting within, for fear of ill News:) With that, *Katteriena* told her the
last Discourse she had with her Brother, and how at last she had persuaded
him (for her sake) to quit his Passion; and that he had promis'd, he would
endeavour to surmount it; and that, that was the reason he was absent

now, and they were to see him no more, till he had made a Conquest over himself. You may assure your self, this News was not so welcom to *Isabella*, as *Katteriena* imagin'd; yet still she dissembled, with a force, beyond what the most cunning Practitioner could have shewn, and carry'd her self before People, as if no Pressures had lain upon her Heart; but when alone retir'd, in order to her Devotion, she would vent her Griefs in the most deplorable manner, that a distress'd distracted Maid could do, and which, in spite of all her severe Penances, she found no abatement of.

At last *Henault* came again to the *Monastery*, and, with a Look as gay as he could possibly assume, he saw his Sister, and told her, He had gain'd an absolute Victory over his Heart; and desir'd, he might see *Isabella*, only to convince, both her, and *Katteriena*, that he was no longer a Lover of that fair Creature, that had so lately charm'd him; that he had set Five thousand Pounds a Year, against a fruitless Passion, and found the solid Gold much the heavier in the Scale: And he smil'd, and talk'd the whole Day of indifferent things, with his Sister, and ask'd no more for *Isabella;* nor did *Isabella* look, or ask, after him, but in her Heart. Two Months pass'd in this Indifference, till it was taken notice of, that Sister *Isabella* came not to the *Grate*, when *Henault* was there, as she us'd to do; this being spoken to Dame *Katteriena*, she told it to *Isabella*, and said, 'The *NUNS* would believe, there was some Cause for her Absence, if she did not appear again': That if she could trust her Heart, she was sure she could trust her Brother, for he thought no more of her, she was confident; this, in lieu of pleasing, was a Dagger to the Heart of *Isabella*, who thought it time to retrieve the flying Lover, and therefore told *Katteriena*, She would the next Day entertain at the Low *Grate*, as she was wont to do, and accordingly, as soon as any People of Quality came, she appear'd there, where she had not been two Minutes, but she saw the lovely *Henault*, and it was well for both, that People were in the Room, they had else both sufficiently discover'd their Inclinations, or rather their not to be conceal'd Passions; after the General Conversation was over, by the going away of the Gentlemen that were at the *Grate*, *Katteriena* being employ'd elsewhere, *Isabella* was at last left alone with *Henault;* but who can guess the Confusion of these two Lovers, who wish'd, yet fear'd, to know each others Thoughts? She trembling with a dismal Apprehension, that he lov'd no more; and he almost dying with fear, she should Reproach or Upbraid him with his Presumption; so that both being possess'd with equal Sentiments of Love, Fear, and Shame, they both stood fix'd with dejected Looks and Hearts, that heav'd with stifled Sighs. At last, *Isabella*, the softer and tender-hearted of the two, tho' not the most a Lover perhaps, not being able to contain her Love any longer within the bounds of Dissimulation or Discretion, being by Nature innocent, burst out into Tears, and all fainting with pressing Thoughts within, she fell languishly into a Chair that stood there, while the distracted *Henault*, who could not come to her Assistance, and finding Marks of Love, rather than Anger or Disdain, in that Confusion of *Isabella*'s, throwing himself on his Knees at the *Grate*, implor'd her to behold him, to hear him, and to pardon him, who dy'd every moment for her, and who ador'd her with a violent Ardor; but yet, with such an one, as should (tho' he perish'd with it) be conformable to her Commands; and as he spoke, the Tears stream'd down his dying Eyes, that beheld her with all the tender Regard that ever Lover was capable of; she recover'd a little, and turn'd her too beautiful Face to him, and pierc'd him with a Look that darted a thousand Joys and Flames into his Heart, with Eyes, that told him her Heart was burning and dying for him; for which Assurances he made Ten thousand Asseverations of his never-dying Passion, and expressing as many Raptures and Excesses of Joy, to find her Eyes and Looks confess, he was not odious to her, and that the knowledge he was her Lover, did not make her hate him: In fine, he spoke so many things all soft and moving, and so well convinc'd her of his Passion, that she at last was compell'd by a mighty force, absolutely irresistible, to speak.

'Sir, (said she) perhaps you will wonder, where I, a Maid brought up in the simplicity of Virtue, should learn the Confidence, not only to hear of Love from you, but to confess I am sensible of the most violent of its Pain my self; and I wonder, and am amazed at my own Daring, that I should have the Courage, rather to speak than dye, and bury it in silence; but such is my Fate. Hurried by an unknown Force, which I have endeavoured always, in vain, to resist, I am compell'd to tell you, I love you, and have done so from the first moment I saw you; and you are the only Man born to give me Life or Death, to make me Happy or Blest; perhaps, had I not been confin'd, and, as it were, utterly forbid by my Vow, as well as my Modesty, to tell you this, I should not have been so miserable to have fallen thus low, as to have confess'd my Shame; but our Opportunities of Speaking are so few, and Letters so impossible to be sent without discovery, that perhaps this is the only time I shall ever have to speak with you alone.' And, at that word, the Tears flow'd abundantly from her Eyes, and gave *Henault* leave to speak. 'Ah Madam! (said he) do not, as soon as you have rais'd me to the greatest Happiness in the World, throw me with one word beneath your Scorn, much easier 'tis to dye, and know I am lov'd, than never, never, hope to hear that blessed sound again from that beautiful Mouth: Ah, Madam! rather let me make use of this one opportunity our happy Luck has given us, and contrive how we may for ever see, and speak, to each other; let us assure one another, there are a thousand ways to escape a place so rigid, as denies us that Happiness; and denies the fairest Maid in the World, the privilege of her Creation, and the end to which she was form'd so Angelical.' And seeing *Isabella* was going to speak, lest she should say something that might dissuade from an Attempt so dangerous and wicked, he persu'd to tell her, it might be indeed the last moment Heaven would give 'em, and besought her to answer him what he implor'd, whether she would fly with him from the *Monastery?* At this Word, she grew pale, and started, as at some dreadful Sound, and cry'd, 'Hah! what is't you say? Is it possible, you should propose a thing so wicked? And can it enter into your Imagination, because I have so far forgot my Virtue, and my Vow, to become a Lover, I should therefore fall to so wretched a degree of Infamy and Reprobation? No, name it to me no more, if you would see me; and if it be as you say, a Pleasure to be belov'd by me; for I will sooner dye, than yield to what . . . Alas! I but too well approve!' These last words she spoke with a fainting Tone, and the Tears fell anew from her fair soft Eyes. 'If it be so,' said he, (with a Voice so languishing, it could scarce be heard) 'If it be so, and that you are resolv'd to try, if my Love be eternal without Hope, without expectation of any other Joy, than seeing and adoring you through the *Grate*; I am, and must, and will be contented, and you shall see, I can prefer the Sighing to these cold Irons, that separate us, before all the Possessions of the rest of the World; that I chuse rather to lead my Life here, at this cruel Distance from you, for ever, than before the Embrace of all the Fair; and you shall see, how pleas'd I will be, to languish here; but as you see me decay, (for surely so I shall) do not triumph o're my languid Looks, and laugh at my Pale and meager Face; but, Pitying, say, How easily I might have preserv'd that Face, those Eyes, and all that Youth and Vigour, now no more, from this total Ruine I now behold it in, and love your Slave that dyes, and will be daily and visibly dying, as long as my Eyes can gaze on that fair Object, and my Soul be fed and kept alive with her Charming Wit and Conversation; if Love can live on such Airy Food, (tho' rich in it self, yet unfit, alone, to sustain Life) it shall be for ever dedicated to the lovely *ISABELLA:* But, oh! that time cannot be

long! Fate will not lend her Slave many days, who loves too violently, to
be satisfy'd to enjoy the fair Object of his Desires, no otherwise than at a
*Grate.*'

He ceas'd speaking, for Sighs and Tears stopt his Voice, and he begg'd
the liberty to sit down; and his Looks being quite alter'd, *Isabella* found
her self touch'd to the very Soul, with a concern the most tender, that
ever yielding Maid was oppressed with: She had no power to suffer him
to Languish, while she by one soft word could restore him, and being
about to say a thousand things that would have been agreeable to him,
she saw her self approach'd by some of the *Nuns*, and only had time to
say, 'If you love me, live and hope.' The rest of the *Nuns* began to ask
*Henault* of News, for he always brought them all that was Novel in the
Town, and they were glad still of his Visits, above all other, for they
heard, how all Amours and Intrigues pass'd in the World, by this young
Cavalier. These last words of *Isabella*'s were a Cordial to his Soul, and he,
from that, and to conceal the present Affair, endeavour'd to assume all the
Gaity he could; and told 'em all he could either remember, or invent, to
please 'em, tho' he wish'd them a great way off at that time.

Thus they pass'd the day, till it was a decent hour for him to quit the
*Grate*, and for them to draw the Curtain; all that Night did *Isabella*
dedicate to Love, she went to Bed, with a Resolution, to think over all
she had to do, and to consider, how she should manage this great Affair
of her Life: I have already said, she had try'd all that was possible in
Human Strength to perform, in the design of quitting a Passion so
injurious to her Honour and Virtue, and found no means possible to
accomplish it: She had try'd Fasting long, Praying fervently, rigid
Penances and Pains, severe Disciplines, all the Mortifications, almost to
the destruction of Life it self, to conquer the unruly Flame; but still it
burnt and rag'd but the more; so, at last, she was forc'd to permit that to
conquer her, she could not conquer, and submitted to her Fate, as a thing
destin'd her by Heaven it self; and after all this opposition, she fancy'd
it was resisting even Divine Providence, to struggle any longer with her
Heart; and this being her real Belief, she the more patiently gave way to
all the Thoughts that pleas'd her.

As soon as she was laid, without discoursing (as she us'd to do) to
*Katteriena*, after they were in Bed, she pretended to be sleepy, and
turning from her, setled her self to profound Thinking, and was resolv'd
to conclude the Matter, between her Heart, and her Vow of Devotion,
that Night, and she, having no more to determine, might end the Affair

accordingly, the first opportunity she should have to speak to *Henault*, which was, to fly, and marry him; or, to remain for ever fix'd to her Vow of Chastity. This was the Debate; she brings Reason on both sides: Against the first, she sets the Shame of a Violated Vow, and considers, where she shall shew her Face after such an Action; to the Vow, she argues, that she was born in Sin, and could not live without it; that she was Human, and no Angel, and that, possibly, that Sin might be as soon forgiven, as another; that since all her devout Endeavours could not defend her from the Cause, Heaven ought to execute the Effect; that as to shewing her Face, so she saw that of *Henault* always turned (Charming as it was) towards her with love; what had she to do with the World, or car'd to behold any other?

Some times, she thought, it would be more Brave and Pious to dye, than to break her Vow; but she soon answer'd that, as false Arguing, for Self-Murder was the worst of Sins, and in the Deadly Number. She could, after such an Action, live to repent, and, of two Evils, she ought to chuse the least; she dreads to think, since she had so great a Reputation for Virtue and Piety, both in the *Monastery*, and in the World, what they both would say, when she should commit an Action so contrary to both these, she posest; but, after a whole Night's Debate, Love was strongest, and gain'd the Victory. She never went about to think, how she should escape, because she knew it would be easy, the keeping of the Key of the *Monastery*, [was] often intrusted in her keeping, and was, by turns, in the hands of many more, whose Virtue and Discretion was Infallible, and out of Doubt; besides, her Aunt being the Lady *Abbess*, she had greater privilege than the rest; so that she had no more to do, she thought, than to acquaint *Henault* with her Design, as soon as she should get an opportunity. Which was not quickly; but, in the mean time, *Isabella*'s Father dy'd, which put some little stop to our Lover's Happiness, and gave her a short time of Grief; but Love, who, while he is new and young, can do us Miracles, soon wip'd her Eyes, and chas'd away all Sorrows from her Heart, and grew every day more and more impatient, to put her new Design in Execution, being every day more resolv'd. Her Father's Death had remov'd one Obstacle, and secur'd her from his Reproaches; and now she only wants Opportunity, first, to acquaint *Henault*, and then to fly.

She waited not long, all things concurring to her desire; for *Katteriena* falling sick, she had the good luck, as she call'd it then, to entertain *Henault* at the *Grate* oftentimes alone; the first moment she did so, she entertain'd him with the good News, and told him, She had at last vanquish'd her Heart in favour of him, and loving him above all things, Honour, her Vow or Reputation, had resolv'd to abandon her self wholly to him, to give her self up to love and serve him, and that she had no other Consideration in the World; but *Henault*, instead of returning her an Answer, all Joy and Satisfaction, held down his Eyes, and Sighing, with a dejected Look, he cry'd, 'Ah, Madam! Pity a Man so wretched and undone, as not to be sensible of this Blessing as I ought.' She grew pale at this Reply, and trembling, expected he would proceed: ' 'Tis not (continued he) that I want[9] Love, tenderest Passion, and all the desire Youth and Love can inspire; But, Oh, Madam! when I consider, (for raving mad in Love as I am for your sake, I do consider) that if I should take you from this Repose, Nobly Born and Educated, as you are; and, for that Act, should find a rigid Father deprive me of all that ought to support you, and afford your Birth, Beauty, and Merits, their due, what would you say? How would you Reproach me?' He sighing, expected her Answer, when Blushes overspreading her Face, she reply'd, in a Tone all haughty and angry, 'Ah, *Henault!* Am I then refus'd, after having abandon'd all things for you? Is it thus, you reward my Sacrific'd Honour, Vows, and Virtue? Cannot you hazard the loss of Fortune to possess *Isabella*, who loses all for you!' Then bursting into Tears, at her misfortune of Loving, she suffer'd him to say, 'Oh, Charming fair one! how industrious is your Cruelty, to find out new Torments for an Heart, already press'd down with the Severities of Love? Is it possible, you can make so unhappy a Construction of the tenderest part of my Passion? And can you imagin it want of Love in me, to consider how I shall preserve and merit the vast Blessing Heaven has given me? Is my Care a Crime? And would not the most deserving Beauty of the World hate me, if I should, to preserve my Life, and satisfy the Passion of my fond Heart, reduce her to the Extremities of Want and Misery? And is there any thing, in what I have said, but what you ought to take for the greatest Respect and tenderness!'

'Alas! (reply'd *Isabella* sighing) young as I am, all unskilful in Love, I find but what I feel, that Discretion is no part of it; and Consideration inconsistent with the Nobler Passion, who will subsist of its own Nature, and Love unmixed with any other Sentiment. And 'tis not pure, if it be otherwise: I know, had I mix'd Discretion with mine, my Love must have been less, I never thought of living, but my Love; and, if I consider'd at

[9] lack.

all, it was, that Grandure and Magnificence were useless Trifles to Lovers, wholly needless and troublesom. I thought of living in some loanly Cottage, far from the noise of crowded busie Cities, to walk with thee in Groves, and silent Shades, where I might hear no Voice but thine; and when we had been tir'd, to sit us down by some cool murmuring Rivulet, and be to each a World, my Monarch thou, and I thy Sovereign Queen, while Wreaths of Flowers shall crown our happy Heads, some fragrant Bank our Throne, and Heaven our Canopy: Thus we might laugh at Fortune, and the Proud, despise the duller World, who place their Joys in mighty Show and Equipage. Alas! my Nature would not bear it, I am unus'd to Worldly Vanities, and would boast of nothing but my *Henault;* no Riches, but his Love; no Grandure, but his Presence.' She ended speaking, with Tears, and he reply'd, 'Now, now, I find my *Isabella* loves indeed, when she's content to abandon the World for my sake; Oh! thou hast named the only happy Life that suits my quiet Nature, to be retir'd, has always been my Joy! But to be so with thee! Oh! thou hast charm'd me with a Thought so dear, as has for ever banish'd all my Care, but how to receive thy Goodness! Please think no more what my angry Parent may do, when he shall hear how I have dispos'd of my self against his Will and Pleasure, but trust to Love and Providence; no more! be gone all Thoughts, but those of *Isabella!*'

As soon as he had made an end of expressing his Joy, he fell to consulting how, and when, she should escape; and since it was uncertain, when she should be offer'd the Key, for she would not ask for it, she resolv'd to give him notice, either by word of Mouth, or a bit of Paper she would write in, and give him through the *Grate* the first opportunity; and, parting for that time, they both resolv'd to get up what was possible for their Support, till Time should reconcile Affairs and Friends, and to wait the happy hour.

*Isabella*'s dead Mother had left Jewels, of the value of 2000£ to her Daughter, at her Decease, which Jewels were in the possession now of the Lady *Abbess*, and were upon Sale, to be added to the Revenue of the *Monastery;* and as *Isabella* was the most Prudent of her Sex, at least, had hitherto been so esteem'd, she was intrusted with all that was in possession of the Lady *Abbess*, and 'twas not difficult to make her self Mistress of all her own Jewels; as also, some 3 or 400£ in Gold, that was hoarded up in her Ladyship's Cabinet, against any Accidents that might arrive to the *Monastery;* these *Isabella* also made her own, and put up with the Jewels; and having acquainted *Henault* with the Day and Hour of her Escape, he got together what he could, and waiting for her, with his Coach, one Night, when no body was awake but her self, when rising softly, as she us'd to do in the Night to her Devotion, she stole so dexterously out of the *Monastery*, as no body knew any thing of it; she carry'd away the Keys with her, after having lock'd all the Doors, for she was intrusted often with all. She found *Henault* waiting in his Coach, and trusted none but an honest Coachman that lov'd him; he receiv'd her with all the Transports of a truly ravish'd Lover, and she was infinitely charm'd with the new Pleasure of his Embraces and Kisses.

They drove out of Town immediately, and because she durst not be seen in that Habit, (for it had been immediate Death for both) they drove into a Thicket some three Miles from the Town, where *Henault* having brought her some of his younger Sister's Clothes, he made her put off her Habit, and put on those; and, rending the other, they hid them in a Sand-pit, covered over with Broom, and went that Night forty Miles from *Iper*, to a little Town upon the River *Rhine*, where, changing their Names, they were forthwith married, and took a House in a Country Village, a Farm, where they resolv'd to live retir'd, by the name of *Beroone*, and drove a Farming Trade; however, not forgetting to set Friends and Engines at work, to get their Pardon, as Criminals, first, that had transgress'd the Law; and, next, as disobedient Persons, who had done contrary to the Will and Desire of their Parents: *Isabella* writ to her Aunt the most moving Letters in the World, so did *Henault* to his Father; but she was a long time, before she could gain so much as an answer from her Aunt, and *Henault* was so unhappy, as never to gain one from his Father; who no sooner heard the News that was spread over all the Town and Country, that young *Henault* was fled with the so fam'd *Isabella*, a *Nun*, and singular for Devotion and Piety of Life, but he immediately setled his Estate on his youngest Son, cutting *Henault* off with all his Birthright, which was 5000£. a Year. This News, you may believe, was not very pleasing to the young Man, who tho' in possession of the loveliest Virgin, and now Wife, that ever Man was bless'd with; yet when he reflected, he should have children by her, and these and she should come to want, (he having been magnificently Educated, and impatient of scanty Fortune) he laid it to Heart, and it gave him a thousand Uneasinesses in the midst of unspeakable Joys; and the more he strove to hide his Sentiments from *Isabella*, the more tormenting it was within; he durst not name it to her, so insuperable a Grief it would cause in her, to hear him complain; and tho' she could live hardly, as being bred to a

devout and severe Life, he could not, but must let the Man of Quality
shew it self; even in the disguise of an humbler Farmer: Besides all this,
he found nothing of his Industry thrive, his Cattel still dy'd in the midst
of those that were in full Vigour and Health of other Peoples; his Crops
of Wheat and Barly, and other Grain, tho' manag'd by able and knowing
Husbandmen, were all, either Mildew'd, or Blasted, or some Misfortune
still arriv'd to him; his Coach-Horses would fight and kill one another, his
Barns sometimes be fir'd; so that it became a Proverb all over the Country,
if any ill Luck had arriv'd to any body, they would say, 'They had
Monsieur *BEROONE'S* Luck.' All these Reflections did but add to his
Melancholy, and he grew at last to be in some want, insomuch, that
*Isabella*, who had by her frequent Letters, and submissive Supplications,
to her Aunt, (who lov'd her tenderly) obtain'd her Pardon, and her
Blessing; she now press'd her for some Money, and besought her to
consider, how great a Fortune she had brought to the *Monastery*, and
implor'd, she would allow her some Sallary out of it, for she had been
marry'd two Years, and most of what she had was exhausted. The Aunt,
who found, that what was done, could not be undone, did, from time to
time, supply her so, as one might have liv'd very decently on that very
Revenue; but that would not satisfy the great Heart of *Henault*. He was
now about three and twenty Years old, and *Isabella* about eighteen, too
young, and too lovely a Pair, to begin their Misfortunes so soon; they
were both the most Just and Pious in the World; they were Examples of
Goodness, and Eminent for Holy Living, and for perfect Loving, and yet
nothing thriv'd they undertook; they had no Children, and all their Joy
was in each other; at last, one good Fortune arriv'd to them, by the
Solicitations of the Lady *Abbess*, and the *Bishop*, who was her near
Kinsman, they got a Pardon for *Isabella's* quitting the *Monastery*, and
marrying, so that she might now return to her own Country again.
*Henault* having also his Pardon, they immediately quit the place, where
they had remain'd for two Years, and came again into *Flanders*, hoping,
the change of place might afford 'em better Luck.

*Henault* then began again to solicit his Cruel Father, but nothing
would do, he refus'd to see him, or to receive any Letters from him; but,
at last, he prevail'd so far with him, as that he sent a Kinsman to him,
to assure him, if he would leave his Wife, and go into the *French* Campagn,
he would Equip him as well as his Quality requir'd, and that, according
as he behav'd himself, he should gain his Favour; but if he liv'd Idly at
home, giving up his Youth and Glory to lazy Love, he would have no

more to say to him, but race[10] him out of his Heart, and out of his Memory.

He had setled himself in a very pretty House, furnished with what was fitting for the Reception of any Body of Quality that would live a private Life, and they found all the Respect that their Merits deserv'd from all the World, every body entirely loving and endeavouring to serve them; and *Isabella* so perfectly had the Ascendent over her Aunt's Heart, that she procur'd from her all that she could desire, and much more than she could expect. She was perpetually progging[11] and saving all that she could, to enrich and advance her, and, at last, pardoning and forgiving *Henault*, lov'd him as her own Child; so that all things look'd with a better Face than before, and never was so dear and fond a Couple seen, as *Henault* and *Isabella;* but, at last, she prov'd with Child, and the Aunt, who might reasonably believe, so young a Couple would have a great many Children, and foreseeing there was no Provision likely to be made them, unless he pleas'd his Father, for if the Aunt should chance to dye, all their Hope was gone; she therefore daily solicited him to obey his Father, and go up to the Camp; and that having atchiev'd Fame and Renown, he would return a Favourite to his Father, and Comfort to his Wife: After she had solicited in vain, for he was not able to endure the thought of leaving *Isabella*, melancholy as he was with his ill Fortune; the *Bishop*, kinsman to *Isabella*, took him to task, and urg'd his Youth and Birth, and that he ought not to wast both without Action, when all the World was employ'd; and, that since his Father had so great a desire he should go into a Campagn, either to serve the *Venetian* against the *Turks*, or into the *French* Service, which he lik'd best; he besought him to think of it; and since he had satisfy'd his Love, he should and ought to satisfy his Duty, it being absolutely necessary for the wiping off the Stain of his Sacrilege, and to gain him the favour of Heaven, which, he found, had hitherto been averse to all he had undertaken: In fine, all his Friends, and all who lov'd him, joyn'd in this Design, and all thought it convenient, nor was he insensible of the Advantage it might bring him; but Love, which every day grew fonder and fonder in his Heart, oppos'd all their Reasonings, tho' he saw all the Brave Youth of the Age preparing to go, either to one Army, or the other.

At last, he lets *Isabella* know, what Propositions he had made him, both by his Father, and his Relations; at the very first Motion,[12] she

---

[10] erase.          [11] begging alms.

[12] proposition.

almost fainted in his Arms, while he was speaking, and it possess'd her
with so intire a Grief, that she miscarry'd, to the insupportable Torment
of her tender Husband and Lover, so that, to re-establish her Repose, he
was forc'd to promise not to go; however, she consider'd all their Circumstances, and weigh'd the Advantages that might redound both to his
Honour and Fortune, by it; and, in a matter of a Month's time, with the
Persuasions and Reasons of her Friends, she suffer'd him to resolve upon
going, her self determining to retire to the *Monastery*, till the time of his
Return; but when she nam'd the *Monastery*, he grew pale and disorder'd,
and obliged her to promise him, not to enter into it any more, for fear
they should never suffer her to come forth again; so that he resolv'd not
to depart, till she had made a Vow to him, never to go again within the
Walls of a Religious House, which had already been so fatal to them. She
promis'd, and he believ'd.

*Henault*, at last, overcame his Heart, which pleaded so for his Stay,
and sent his Father word, he was ready to obey him, and to carry the
first Efforts of his Arms against the common Foes of Christendom, the
*Turks;* his Father was very well pleas'd at this, and sent him Two
thousand Crowns, his Horses and Furniture sutable to his Quality, and a
Man to wait on him; so that it was not long e're he got himself in order
to be gone, after a dismal parting.

He made what hast he could to the *French* Army, then under the
Command of the Monsignior, the Duke of *Beaufort*, then at *Candia*, and
put himself a Voluntier under his Conduct; in which Station was
*Villenoys*, who, you have already heard, was so passionate a Lover of
*Isabella*, who no sooner heard of *Henault's* being arriv'd, and that he was
Husband to *Isabella*, but he was impatient to learn, by what strange
Adventure he came to gain her, even from her Vow'd Retreat, when he,
with all his Courtship, could not be so happy, tho' she was then free in
the World, and Unvow'd to Heaven.

As soon as he sent his Name to *Henault*, he was sent for up, for *Henault*
had heard of *Villenoys*, and that he had been a Lover of *Isabella;* they
receiv'd one another with all the endearing Civility imaginable for the
aforesaid Reason, and for that he was his Country-man, tho' unknown to
him, *Villenoys* being gone to the Army, just as *Henault* came from the
*Jesuits* College. A great deal of Endearment pass'd between them, and
they became, from that moment, like two sworn Brothers, and he receiv'd
the whole Relation from *Henault*, of his Amour.

It was not long before the Siege began anew, for he arriv'd at the beginning of the Spring, and, as soon as he came, almost, they fell to Action; and it happen'd upon a day, that a Party of some Four hundred Men resolv'd to sally out upon the Enemy, as, when ever they could, they did; but as it is not my business to relate the History of the War, being wholly unacquainted with the Terms of Battels, I shall only say, That these Men were led by *Villenoys*, and that *Henault* would accompany him in this Sally, and that they acted very Noble, and great Things, worthy of a Memory in the History of that Siege; but this day, particularly, they had an occasion to shew their Valour, which they did very much to their Glory; but, venturing too far, they were ambush'd, in the persuit of the Party of the Enemies, and being surrounded, *Villenoys* had the unhappiness to see his gallant Friend fall, fighting and dealing of Wounds around him, even as he descended to the Earth, for he fell from his Horse at the same moment that he kill'd a *Turk;* and *Villenoys* could neither assist him, nor had he the satisfaction to be able to rescue his dead Body from under the Horses, but, with much ado, escaping with his own Life, got away, in spite of all that follow'd him, and recover'd the Town, before they could overtake him: He passionately bewail'd the Loss of this brave young Man, and offer'd any Recompence to those, that would have ventur'd to have search'd for his dead Body among the Slain; but it was not fit to hazard the Living, for unnecessary Services to the Dead; and tho' he had a great mind to have Interr'd him, he rested content with what he wish'd to pay his Friends Memory, tho' he could not: So that all the Service now he could do him, was, to write to *Isabella*, to whom he had not writ, tho' commanded by her so to do, in three Years before, which was never since she took Orders. He gave her an Account of the Death of her Husband, and how Gloriously he fell fighting for the Holy Cross, and how much Honour he had won, if it had been his Fate to have outliv'd that great, but unfortunate, Day, where, with 400 Men, they had kill'd 1500 of the Enemy. The General *Beaufort* himself had so great a Respect and Esteem for this young Man, and knowing him to be of Quality, that he did him the honour to bemoan him, and to send a Condoling Letter to *Isabella*, how much worth her Esteem he dy'd, and that he had Eterniz'd his Memory with the last Gasp of his Life.

When this News arriv'd, it may be easily imagin'd, what Impressions, or rather Ruins, it made in the Heart of this fair Mourner; the Letters came by his Man, who saw him fall in Battel, and came off with those few that escap'd with *Villenoys;* he brought back what Money he had, a few Jewels, with *Isabella's* Picture that he carry'd with him and had left in his

Chamber in the Fort of *Candia*, for fear of breaking it in Action. And now *Isabella's* Sorrow grew to the Extremity, she thought, she could not suffer more than she did by his Absence, but she now found a Grief more killing; she hung her Chamber with Black, and liv'd without the Light of Day: Only Wax Lights, that let her behold the Picture of this Charming Man, before which she sacrific'd Floods of Tears. He had now been absent about ten Months, and she had learnt just to live without him, but Hope preserv'd her then; but now she had nothing, for which to wish to live. She, for about two Months after the News arriv'd, liv'd without seeing any Creature but a young Maid, that was her Woman; but extream Importunity oblig'd her to give way to the Visits of her Friends, who endeavour'd to restore her Melancholy Soul to its wonted Easiness; for, however it was oppress'd within, by *Henault's* absence, she bore it off with a modest Chearfulness; but now she found, that Fortitude and Virtue fail'd her, when she was assur'd, he was no more: She continu'd thus Mourning, and thus inclos'd, the space of a whole Year, never suffering the Visit of any Man, but of a near Relation; so that she acquir'd a Reputation, such as never any young Beauty had, for she was now but Nineteen, and her Face and Shape more excellent than ever; she daily increas'd in Beauty, which, joyn'd to her Exemplary Piety, Charity, and all other excellent Qualities, gain'd her a wonderous Fame, and begat an Awe and Reverence in all that heard of her, and there was no Man of any Quality, that did not Adore her. After her Year was up, she went to the Churches, but would never be seen any where else abroad, but that was enough to procure her a thousand Lovers; and some, who had the boldness to send her Letters, which, if she receiv'd, she gave no Answer to, and many she sent back unread and unseal'd: So that she would encourage none, tho' their Quality was far beyond what she could hope; but she was resolv'd to marry no more, however her Fortune might require it.

It happen'd, that, about this time, *Candia* being unfortunately taken by the *Turks*, all the brave Men that escap'd the Sword, return'd, among them, *Villenoys*, who no sooner arriv'd, but he sent to let *Isabella* know of it, and to beg the Honour of waiting on her; desirous to learn what Fate befel her dear Lord, she suffer'd him to visit her, where he found her, in her Mourning, a thousand times more Fair, (at least, he fancy'd so) than ever she appear'd to be; so that if he lov'd her before, he now ador'd her; if he burnt then, he rages now; but the awful Sadness, and soft Languishment of her Eyes, hinder'd him from the presumption of speaking of his Passion to her, tho' it would have been no new thing; and his first Visit was spent in the Relation of every Circumstance of *Henault's* Death; and, at his going away, he begg'd leave to visit her sometimes, and she gave him permission: He lost no time, but made use of the Liberty she had given him; and when his Sister, who was a great Companion of *Isabella's*, went to see her, he would still wait on her; so that, either with his own Visits, and those of his Sister's, he saw *Isabella* every day, and had the good luck to see, he diverted her, by giving her Relations of Transactions of the Siege, and the Customs and Manners of the *Turks:* All he said, was with so good a Grace, that he render'd every thing agreeable; he was, besides, very Beautiful, well made, of Quality and Fortune, and fit to inspire Love.

He made his Visits so often, and so long, that, at last, he took the Courage to speak of his Passion, which, at first, *Isabella* would by no means hear of, but, by degrees, she yielded more and more to listen to his tender Discourse; and he liv'd thus with her two Years, before he could gain any more upon her Heart, than to suffer him to speak of Love to her; but that, which subdu'd her quite was, That her Aunt, the Lady *Abbess*, dy'd, and with her, all the Hopes and Fortune of *Isabella*, so that she was left with only a Charming Face and Meen, a Virtue, and a Discretion above her Sex, to make her Fortune within the World; into a Religious House, she was resolv'd not to go, because her Heart deceiv'd her once, and she durst not trust it again, whatever it promis'd.

The death of this Lady made her look more favourably on *Villenoys;* but yet, she was resolv'd to try his Love to the utmost, and keep him off, as long as 'twas possible she could subsist, and 'twas for Interest she married again, tho' she lik'd the Person very well; and since she was forc'd to submit her self to be a second time a Wife, she thought, she could live better with *Villenoys*, than any other, since for him she ever had a great Esteem; and fancy'd the Hand of Heaven had pointed out her Destiny, which she could not avoid, without a Crime.

So that when she was again importun'd by her impatient Lover, she told him, She had made a Vow to remain three Years, at least, before she would marry again, after the Death of the best of Men and Husbands, and him who had the Fruits of her early Heart; and, notwithstanding all the Solicitations of *Villenoys*, she would not consent to marry him, till her Vow of Widowhood was expir'd.

He took her promise, which he urg'd her to give him, and to shew the height of his Passion in his obedience, he condescends to stay her appointed time, tho' he saw her every day, and all his Friends and

Relations made her Visits upon this new account, and there was nothing talk'd on, but this design'd Wedding, which, when the time was expir'd, was perform'd accordingly with great Pomp and Magnificence, for *Villenoys* had no Parents to hinder his Design; or if he had, the Reputation and Virtue of this Lady would have subdu'd them.

The Marriage was celebrated in this House, where she liv'd ever since her Return from *Germany*, from the time she got her Pardon; and when *Villenoys* was preparing all things in a more magnificent Order at his Villa, some ten Miles from the City, she was very melancholy, and would often say, She had been us'd to such profound Retreat, and to live without the fatigue of Noise and Equipage, that, she fear'd, she should never endure that Grandeur, which was proper for his Quality; and tho' the House, in the Country, was the most beautifully Situated in all *Flanders*, she was afraid of a numerous Train, and kept him, for the most part, in this pretty City Mansion, which he Adorn'd and Enlarg'd, as much as she would give him leave; so that there wanted nothing, to make this House fit to receive the People of the greatest Quality, little as it was: But all the Servants and Footmen, all but one *Valet*, and the Maid, were lodg'd abroad, for *Isabella*, not much us'd to the sight of Men about her, suffer'd them as seldom as possible, to come in her Presence, so that she liv'd more like a *Nun* still, than a Lady of the World; and very rarely any Maids came about her, but *Maria*, who had always permission to come, when ever she pleas'd, unless forbidden.

As *Villenoys* had the most tender and violent Passion for his Wife, in the World, he suffer'd her to be pleas'd at any rate, and to live in what Method she best lik'd, and was infinitely satisfy'd with the Austerity and manner of her Conduct, since in his Arms, and alone, with him, she wanted nothing that could Charm; so that she was esteemed the fairest and best of Wives, and he the most happy of all Mankind. When she would go abroad, she had her Coaches Rich and Gay, and her Livery ready to attend her in all the Splendour imaginable; and he was always buying one rich Jewel, or Necklace, or some great Rarity or other, that might please her; so that there was nothing her Soul could desire, which it had not, except the Assurance of Eternal Happiness, which she labour'd incessantly to gain. She had no Discontent, but because she was not bless'd with a Child; but she submits to the pleasure of Heaven, and endeavour'd, by her good Works, and her Charity, to make the Poor her Children, and was ever doing Acts of Virtue, to make the Proverb good, *That more are the Children of the Barren, than the Fruitful Woman.* She liv'd in this

Tranquility, belov'd by all, for the space of five Years, and Time (and perpetual Obligations from *Villenoys*, who was the most indulgent and indearing Man in the World) had almost worn out of her Heart the Thought of *Henault*, or if she remember'd him, it was in her Prayers, or sometimes with a short sigh, and no more, tho' it was a great while, before she could subdue her Heart to that Calmness; but she was prudent, and wisely bent all her Endeavours to please, oblige, and caress, the deserving Living, and to strive all she could, to forget the unhappy Dead, since it could not but redound to the disturbance of her Repose, to think of him; so that she had now transferr'd all that Tenderness she had for him, to *Villenoys*.

*Villenoys*, of all Diversions, lov'd Hunting, and kept, at his Country House, a very famous Pack of Dogs, which he us'd to lend, sometimes, to a young Lord, who was his dear Friend, and his Neighbour in the Country, who would often take them, and be out two or three days together, where he heard of Game, and oftentimes *Villenoys* and he would be a whole Week at a time exercising in this Sport, for there was no Game near at hand. This young Lord had sent him a Letter, to invite him fifteen Miles farther than his own *Villa*, to hunt, and appointed to meet him at his Country House, in order to go in search of this promis'd Game; So that *Villenoys* got about a Week's Provision, of what Necessaries he thought he should want in that time; and taking only his *Valet*, who lov'd the Sport, he left *Isabella* for a Week to her Devotion, and her other innocent Diversions of fine Work, at which she was Excellent, and left the Town to go meet this young Challenger.

When *Villenoys* was at any time out, it was the custom of *Isabella* to retire to her Chamber, and to receive no Visits, not even the Ladies, so absolutely she devoted her self to her Husband: All the first day she pass'd over in this manner, and Evening being come, she order'd her Supper to be brought to her Chamber, and, because it was Washing-day the next day, she order'd all her Maids to go very early to Bed, that they might be up betimes, and to leave only *Maria* to attend her; which was accordingly done. This *Maria* was a young Maid, that was very discreet, and, of all things in the World, lov'd her Lady, whom she had liv'd with, ever since she came from the *Monastery*.

When all were in Bed, and the little light Supper just carry'd up to the Lady, and only, as I said, *Maria* attending, some body knock'd at the Gate, it being about Nine of the Clock at Night; so *Maria* snatching up a Candle, went to the Gate, to see who it might be; when she open'd the

Door, she found a Man in a very odd Habit, and a worse Countenance, and asking, Who he would speak with? He told her, Her Lady: My Lady (reply'd *Maria*) does not use to receive Visits at this hour; Pray, what is your Business? He reply'd, That which I will deliver only to your Lady, and that she may give me Admittance, pray, deliver her this Ring: And pulling off a small Ring, with *Isabella's* Name and Hair in it, he gave it *Maria*, who, shutting the Gate upon him, went in with the Ring; as soon as *Isabella* saw it, she was ready to swound on the Chair where she sate, and cry'd, Where had you this? *Maria* reply'd, An old rusty Fellow at the Gate gave it me, and desired, it might be his Pasport to you; I ask'd his Name, but he said, You knew him not, but he had great News to tell you. *Isabella* reply'd, (almost swounding again) Oh, *Maria!* I am ruin'd. The Maid, all this while, knew not what she meant, nor, that that was a Ring given to *Henault* by her Mistress, but endeavouring to recover her, only ask'd her, What she should say to the old Messenger? *Isabella* bid her bring him up to her, (she had scarce Life to utter these last words) and before she was well recover'd, *Maria* enter'd with the Man; and *Isabella* making a Sign to her, to depart the Room, she was left alone with him.

*Henault* (for it was he) stood trembling and speechless before her, giving her leisure to take a strict Survey of him; at first finding no Feature nor Part of *Henault* about him, her Fears began to lessen, and she hop'd, it was not he, as her first Apprehensions had suggested; when he (with the Tears of Joy standing in his Eyes, and not daring suddenly to approach her, for fear of encreasing that Disorder he saw in her pale Face) began to speak to her, and cry'd, Fair Creature! is there no Remains of your *Henault* left in this Face of mine, all o'regrown with Hair? Nothing in these Eyes, sunk with eight Years Absence from you, and Sorrows? Nothing in this Shape, bow'd with Labour and Griefs, that can inform you? I was once that happy Man you lov'd! At these words, Tears stop'd his Speech, and *Isabella* kept them Company, for yet she wanted Words. Shame and Confusion fill'd her Soul, and she was not able to lift her Eyes up, to consider the Face of him, whose Voice she knew so perfectly well. In one moment, she run over a thousand Thoughts. She finds, by his Return, she is not only expos'd to all the Shame imaginable; to all the Upbraiding, on his part, when he shall know she is marry'd to another; but all the Fury and Rage of *Villenoys*, and the Scorn of the Town, who will look on her as an Adulteress: She sees *Henault* poor, and knew, she must fall from all the Glory and Tranquility she had for five happy Years triumph'd in; in which time, she had known no Sorrow, or Care, tho' she had endur'd a thousand with *Henault*. She dyes, to think, however, that he should know, she had been so lightly in Love with him, to marry again; and she dyes, to think, that *Villenoys* must see her again in the Arms of *Henault;* besides, she could not recal her Love, for Love, like Reputation, once fled, never returns more. 'Tis impossible to love, and cease to love, (and love another) and yet return again to the first Passion, tho' the Person have all the Charms, or a thousand times more than it had, when it first conquer'd. This Mistery in Love, it may be, is not generally known, but nothing is more certain. One may a while suffer the Flame to languish, but there may be a reviving Spark in the Ashes, rak'd up, that may burn anew; but when 'tis quite extinguish'd, it never returns or rekindles.

'Twas so with the Heart of *Isabella;* had she believ'd *Henault* had been living, she had lov'd to the last moment of their Lives; but, alas! the Dead are soon forgotten, and she now lov'd only *Villenoys*.

After they had both thus silently wept, with very different sentiments, she thought 'twas time to speak; and dissembling as well as she could, she caress'd him in her Arms, and told him, She could not express her Surprize and Joy for his Arrival. If she did not Embrace him heartily, or speak so Passionately as she us'd to do, he fancy'd it her Confusion, and his being in a condition not so fit to receive Embraces from her; and evaded them as much as 'twas possible for him to do, in respect to her, till he had dress'd his Face, and put himself in order; but the Supper being just brought up, when he knock'd, she order'd him to sit down and Eat, and he desir'd her not to let *Maria* know who he was, to see how long it would be, before she knew him or would call him to mind. But *Isabella* commanded *Maria*, to make up a Bed in such a Chamber, without disturbing her Fellows, and dismiss'd her from waiting at Table. The Maid admir'd,[13] what strange, good, and joyful News, this Man had brought her Mistress, that he was so Treated, and alone with her, which never any Man had yet been; but she never imagin'd the Truth, and knew her Lady's Prudence too well, to question her Conduct. While they were at Supper, *Isabella* oblig'd him to tell her, How he came to be reported Dead; of which, she receiv'd Letters, both from Monsieur *Villenoys*, and the Duke of *Beaufort*, and by his Man the News, who saw him Dead? He told her, That, after the Fight, of which, first, he gave her an account, he being left among the Dead, when the Enemy came to

[13] wondered about.

Plunder and strip 'em, they found, he had Life in him, and appearing as an Eminent Person, they thought it better Booty to save me, (continu'd he) and get my Ransom, than to strip me, and bury me among the Dead; so they bore me off to a Tent, and recover'd me to Life; and, after that, I was recover'd of my Wounds, and sold, by the Soldier that had taken me, to a Spahee,[14] who kept me a Slave, setting a great Ransom on me, such as I was not able to pay. I writ several times, to give you, and my Father, an account of my Misery, but receiv'd no Answer, and endur'd seven Years of Dreadful Slavery: When I found, at last, an opportunity to make my Escape, and from that time, resolv'd, never to cut the Hair of this Beard, till I should either see my dearest *Isabella* again, or hear some News of her. All that I fear'd, was, That she was Dead; and, at that word, he fetch'd a deep Sigh; and viewing all things so infinitely more Magnificent than he had left 'em, or, believ'd, she could afford; and, that she was far more Beautiful in Person, and Rich in Dress, than when he left her: He had a thousand Torments of Jealousie that seiz'd him, of which, he durst not make any mention, but rather chose to wait a little, and see, whether she had lost her Virtue: He desir'd, he might send for a Barber, to put his Face in some handsomer Order, and more fit for the Happiness 'twas that Night to receive; but she told him, No Dress, no Disguise, could render him more Dear and Acceptable to her, and that to morrow was time enough, and that his Travels had render'd him more fit for Repose, than Dressing.

So that after a little while, they had talk'd over all they had a mind to say, all that was very indearing on his side, and as much Concern as she could force, on hers; she conducted him to his Chamber, which was very rich, and which gave him a very great addition of Jealousie: However, he suffer'd her to help him to Bed, which she seem'd to do, with all the tenderness in the World; and when she had seen him laid, she said, She would go to her Prayers, and come to him as soon as she had done, which being before her usual Custom, it was not a wonder to him she stay'd long, and he, being extreamly tir'd with his Journy, fell asleep. 'Tis true, *Isabella* essay'd to Pray, but alas! it was in vain, she was distracted with a thousand Thoughts what to do, which the more she thought, the more it distracted her; she was a thousand times about to end her Life, and, at one stroke, rid her self of the Infamy, that, she saw, must inevitably fall upon her; but Nature was frail, and the Tempter strong: And after a thousand Convulsions, even worse than Death it self, she resolv'd upon

[14] Spahi, a native African cavalryman.

the Murder of *Henault*, as the only means of removing all Obstacles to her future Happiness; she resolv'd on this, but after she had done so, she was seiz'd with so great Horror, that she imagin'd, if she perform'd it, she should run Mad; and yet, if she did not, she should be also Frantick, with the Shames and Miseries that would befal her; and believing the Murder the least Evil, since she could never live with him, she fix'd her Heart on that; and causing her self to be put immediately to Bed, in her own Bed, she made *Maria* go to hers, and when all was still, she softly rose, and taking a Candle with her, only in her Night-Gown and Slippers, she goes to the Bed of the Unfortunate *Henault*, with a Penknife in her hand; but considering, she knew not how to conceal the Blood, should she cut his Throat, she resolves to Strangle him, or Smother him with a Pillow; that last thought was no sooner borne, but put in Execution; and, as he soundly slept, she smother'd him without any Noise, or so much as his Strugling; But when she had done this dreadful Deed, and saw the dead Corps of her once-lov'd Lord, lye Smiling (as it were) upon her, she fell into a Swound with the Horror of the Deed, and it had been well for her she had there dy'd; but she reviv'd again, and awaken'd to more and new Horrors, she flyes all frighted from the Chamber, and fancies, the Phantom of her dead Lord persues her; she runs from Room to Room, and starts and stares, as if she saw him continually before her. Now all that was ever Soft and Dear to her, with him, comes into her Heart, and, she finds, he conquers anew, being Dead, who could not gain her Pity, while Living.

While she was thus flying from her Guilt, in vain, she hears one knock with Authority at the Door: She is now more affrighted, if possible, and knows not whither to fly for Refuge; she fancies, they are already the Officers of Justice, and that Ten thousand Tortures and Wrecks[15] are fastening on her, to make her confess the horrid Murder; the knocking increases, and so loud, that the Laundry Maids believing it to be the Woman that us'd to call them up, and help them to Wash, rose, and, opening the Door, let in *Villenoys;* who having been at his Country *Villa*, and finding there a Footman, instead of his Friend, who waited to tell him, His Master was fallen sick of the Small Pox, and could not wait on him, he took Horse, and came back to his lovely *Isabella;* but running up, as he us'd to do, to her Chamber, he found her not, and seeing a Light in another Room, he went in, but found *Isabella* flying from him, out at another Door, with all the speed she could, he admires at this

[15] racks.

Action, and the more, because his Maid told him Her Lady had been a Bed
a good while; he grows a little Jealous, and persues her, but still she
flies; at last he caught her in his Arms, where she fell into a swound, but
quickly recovering, he set her down in a Chair, and, kneeling before her,
implor'd to know what she ayl'd, and why she fled from him, who ador'd
her? She only fix'd a ghastly Look upon him, and said, She was not well:
'Oh! (said he) put not me off with such poor Excuses, *Isabella* never fled
from me, when Ill, but came to my Arms, and to my Bosom, to find a
Cure; therefore, tell me, what's the matter?' At that, she fell a weeping
in a most violent manner, and cry'd, She was for ever undone: He, being
mov'd with Love and Compassion, conjur'd her to tell what she ayl'd:
'Ah! (said she) thou and I, and all of us, are undone!' At this, he lost all
Patience, and rav'd, and cry'd, 'Tell me, and tell me immediately, what's
the matter?' When she saw his Face pale, and his Eyes fierce, she fell on
her knees, and cry'd, 'Oh! you can never Pardon me, if I should tell
you, and yet, alas! I am innocent of Ill, by all that's good, I am.' But her
Conscience accusing her at that word, she was silent. 'If thou art
Innocent,' said *Villenoys*, taking her up in his Arms, and kissing her wet
Face, 'By all that's Good, I Pardon thee, what ever thou hast done.'
'Alas! (said she) Oh! but I dare not name it, 'till you swear.' 'By all that's
Sacred, (reply'd he) and by whatever Oath you can oblige me to; by my
inviolable Love to thee, and by thy own dear Self, I swear, whate're it
be, I do forgive thee; I know, thou art too good to commit a Sin I may
not with Honour, pardon.'

With this, and hearten'd by his Caresses, she told him, That *Henault*
was return'd; and repeating to him his Escape, she said, She had put him
to Bed, and when he expected her to come, she fell on her Knees at the
Bed-side, and confess'd, She was married to *Villenoys;* at that word (said
she) he fetch'd a deep Sigh or two, and presently after, with a very little
struggling, dy'd; and, yonder, he lyes still in the Bed. After this, she
wept so abundantly, that all *Villenoys* could do, could hardly calm her
Spirits; but after, consulting what they should do in this Affair, *Villenoys*
ask'd her, Who of the House saw him? She said, Only *Maria*, who knew
not who he was; so that, resolving to save *Isabella's* Honour, which was
the only Misfortune to come, *Villenoys* himself propos'd the carrying him
out to the Bridge, and throwing him into the River, where the Stream
would carry him down to the Sea, and lose him; or, if he were found,
none could know him. So *Villenoys* took a Candle, and went and look'd
on him, and found him altogether chang'd, that no Body would know

who he was; he therefore put on his Clothes, which was not hard for him to do, for he was scarce yet cold, and comforting again *Isabella*, as well as he could, he went himself into the Stable, and fetched a Sack, such as they us'd for Oats, a new Sack, whereon stuck a great Needle, with a Pack-thread in it; this Sack he brings into the House, and shews to *Isabella*, telling her, He would put the Body in there, for the better convenience of carrying it on his Back. *Isabella* all this while said but little, but, fill'd with Thoughts all Black and Hellish, she ponder'd within, while the Fond and Passionate *Villenoys* was endeavouring to hide her Shame, and to make this an absolute Secret: She imagin'd, that could she live after a Deed so black, *Villenoys* would be eternal[ly] reproaching her, if not with his Tongue, at least with his Heart, and embolden'd by one Wickedness, she was the readier for another, and another of such a Nature, as has, in my Opinion, far less Excuse, than the first; but when Fate begins to afflict, she goes through stitch[16] with her Black Work.

When *Villenoys*, who would, for the Safety of *Isabella's* Honour, be the sole Actor in the disposing of this Body; and since he was Young, Vigorous, and Strong, and able to bear it, would trust no one with the Secret, he having put up the Body, and ty'd it fast, set it on a Chair, turning his Back towards it, with the more conveniency to take it upon his Back, bidding *Isabella* give him the two Corners of the Sack in his Hands; telling her, They must do this last office for the Dead, more, in order to the securing their Honour and Tranquility hereafter, than for any other Reason, and bid her be of good Courage, till he came back, for it was not far to the Bridge, and it being the dead of the Night, he should pass well enough. When he had the Sack on his Back, and ready to go with it, she cry'd, Stay, my Dear, some of his Clothes hang out, which I will put in; and, with that, taking the Pack-needle with the Thread, sew'd the Sack, with several strong Stitches, to the Collar of *Villenoy's* Coat, without his perceiving it, and bid him go now; and when you come to the Bridge, (said she) and that you are throwing him over the Rail, (which is not above Breast high) be sure you give him a good swing, least the Sack should hang on any thing at the side of the Bridge, and not fall into the Stream; I'le warrant you, (said *Villenoys*) I know how to secure his falling. And going his way with it, Love lent him Strength, and he soon arriv'd at the Bridge; where, turning his Back to the Rail, and heaving the Body over, he threw himself with all his force backward, the better to swing the Body into the River, whose weight (it being made fast to his

[16] goes right through to the bitter end without stopping.

Collar) pull'd *Villenoys* after it, and both the live and the dead Man falling into the River, which, being rapid at the Bridge, soon drown'd him, especially when so great a weight hung to his Neck; so that he dy'd, without considering what was the occasion of his Fate.

*Isabella* remain'd the most part of the Night sitting in her Chamber, without going to Bed, to see what would become of her Damnable Design; but when it was towards Morning, and she heard no News, she put herself into Bed, but not to find Repose or Rest there, for that she thought impossible, after so great a Barbarity as she had committed; No, (said she) it is but just I should for ever wake, who have, in one fatal Night, destroy'd two such Innocents. Oh! what Fate, what Destiny, is mine? Under what cursed Planet was I born, that Heaven it self could not divert my Ruine? It was not many Hours since I thought my self the most happy and blest of Women, and now am fallen to the Misery of one of the Worst Fiends of Hell.

Such were her Thoughts, and such her Cryes, till the Light brought on new Matter for Grief; for, about Ten of the Clock, News was brought, that Two Men were found dead in the River, and that they were carry'd to the Town-Hall, to lye there, till they were own'd: Within an hour after, News was brought in, that one of these Unhappy Men was *Villenoys;* his *Valet*, who, all this while, imagin'd him in Bed with his Lady, ran to the Hall, to undeceive the People, for he knew, if his Lord were gone out, he should have been call'd to Dress him; but finding it, as 'twas reported, he fell a weeping, and wringing his Hands, in a most miserable manner, he ran home with the News; where, knocking at his Lady's Chamber Door, and finding it fast lock'd, he almost hop'd again, he was deceiv'd; but, *Isabella* rising, and opening the Door, *Maria* first enter'd weeping, with the News, and then brought the *Valet*, to testify the fatal Truth of it. *Isabella*, tho' it were nothing but what she expected to hear, almost swounded in her Chair; nor did she feign it, but felt really all the Pangs of Killing Grief; and was so alter'd with her Night's Watching and Grieving, that this new Sorrow look'd very Natural in her. When she was recover'd, she ask'd a thousand Questions about him, and question'd the Possibility of it; for (said she) he went out this Morning early from me, and had no signs, in his Face, of any Grief, or Discontent. Alas! (said the *Valet*) Madam, he is not his own Murderer, some one has done it in Revenge; and then told her, how he was found fasten'd to a Sack, with a dead strange Man ty'd up within it; and every body concludes, that they were both first murder'd, and then drawn to the River, and thrown both in.

the Relation of this Strange Man, she seem'd more amaz'd than before, At and commanding the *Valet* to go to the Hall, and to take Order about the Coroner's sitting on the Body[17] of *Villenoys*, and then to have it brought home: She called *Maria* to her, and, after bidding her shut the Door, she cry'd, Ah, *Maria!* I will tell thee what my Heart imagins; but first, (said she) run to the Chamber of the Stranger, and see, if he be still in Bed, which I fear he is not; she did so, and brought word, he was gone; then (said she) my Forebodings are true. When I was in Bed last Night, with *Villenoys*, (and at that word, she sigh'd as if her Heart-Strings had broken) I told him, I had lodg'd a Stranger in my House, who was by, when my first Lord and Husband fell in Battel; and that, after the Fight, finding him yet alive, he spoke to him, and gave him that Ring you brought me last Night; and conjur'd him, if ever his Fortune should bring him to *Flanders*, to see me, and give me that Ring, and tell me— (with that, she wept, and could scarce speak) a thousand tender and endearing things, and then dy'd in his Arms. For my dear *Henault's* sake, (said she) I us'd him nobly, and dismiss'd you that Night, because I was asham'd to have any witness of the Griefs I paid his Memory: All this I told to *Villenoys*, whom I found disorder'd; and, after a sleepless Night, I fancy he got up, and took this poor Man, and has occasion'd his Death: At that, she wept anew, and *Maria*, to whom all that her Mistress said was Gospel, verily believ'd it so, without examining Reason; and *Isabella* conjuring her, since none of the House knew of the old Man's being there, (for Old he appear'd to be) that she would let it for ever be a Secret, and to this she bound her by an Oath; so that none knowing *Henault*, altho' his Body was expos'd there for three Days to Publick View: When the Coroner had Set on the Bodies, he found, they had been first Murder'd some way or other, and then afterwards tack'd together, and thrown into the River.

They brought the Body of *Villenoys* home to his House, where, it being laid on a Table, all the House infinitely bewail'd it; and *Isabella* did nothing but swound away, almost as fast as she recover'd Life; however, she would, to compleat her Misery, be led to see this dreadful Victim of her Cruelty, and, coming near the Table, the Body, whose Eyes were before close shut, now open'd themselves wide, and fix'd them on *Isabella*, who, giving a great Schreek, fell down in a swound, and the Eyes clos'd again; they had much ado to bring her to Life, but, at last, they did so, and led her back to her Bed, where she remain'd a good while. Different Opinions and Discourses were made, concerning the opening of the Eyes

[17] A coroner's jury must be called to consider suspicious deaths.

of the Dead Man, and viewing *Isabella*; but she was a Woman of so admirable a Life and Conversation, of so undoubted a Piety and Sanctity of Living, that not the least Conjecture could be made, of her having a hand in it, besides the improbability of it; yet the whole thing was a Mystery, which, they thought, they ought to look into: But a few Days after, the Body of *Villenoys* being interr'd in a most magnificent manner, and, by Will, all he had, was long since setled on *Isabella*, the World, instead of Suspecting her, Ador'd her the more, and every Body of Quality was already hoping to be next, tho' the fair Mourner still kept her Bed, and Languish'd daily.

It happen'd, not long after this, there came to the Town a *French* Gentleman, who was taken at the Siege of *Candia*, and was Fellow-Slave with *Henault*, for seven Years, in *Turky*, and who had escap'd with *Henault*, and came as far as *Liege* with him, where, having some Business and Acquaintance with a Merchant, he stay'd some time; but when he parted with *Henault*, he ask'd him, Where he should find him in *Flanders?* *Henault* gave him a Note, with his Name, and Place of Abode, if his Wife were alive; if not, to enquire at his Sister's, or his Father's. This *French* Man came at last, to the very House of *Isabella*, enquiring for this Man, and receiv'd a strange Answer, and was laugh'd at; He found, that was the House, and that the Lady; and enquiring about the Town, and speaking of *Henault*'s Return, describing the Man, it was quickly discover'd, to be the same that was in the Sack: He had his Friend taken up, (for he was buried) and found him the same, and, causing a *Barber* to Trim him, when his bushy Beard was off, a great many People remember'd him; and the *French* Man affirming, he went to his own Home, all *Isabella*'s Family, and her self, were cited before the Magistrate of Justice, where, as soon as she was accus'd, she confess'd the whole Matter of Fact, and, without any Disorder, deliver'd her self in the Hands of Justice, as the Murderess of two Husbands (both belov'd) in one Night: The whole World stood amaz'd at this, who knew her Life a Holy and Charitable Life, and how dearly and well she had liv'd with her Husbands, and every one bewail'd her Misfortune, and she alone was the only Person, that was not afflicted for her self; she was Try'd, and Condemn'd to lose her Head; which Sentence, she joyfully receiv'd, and said, Heaven, and her Judges, were too Merciful to her, and that her Sins had deserv'd much more.

While she was in Prison, she was always at Prayers, and very Chearful and Easie, distributing all she had amongst, and for the Use of, the Poor of the Town, especially to the Poor Widows; exhorting daily the Young and the Fair, that came perpetually to visit her, never to break a Vow; for that was first the Ruine of her, and she never since prosper'd, do whatever other good Deeds she could. When the Day of Execution came, she appear'd on the Scaffold all in Mourning, but with a Meen so very Majestick, and Charming, and a Face so surprizing Fair, where no Languishment or Fear appear'd, but all Chearful as a Bride, that she set all Hearts a flaming, even in that mortifying Minute of Preparation for Death: She made a Speech of half an Hour long, so Eloquent, so admirable a warning to the *Vow-Breakers*, that it was as amazing to hear her, as it was to behold her.

After she had done with the help of *Maria*, she put off her Mourning Vail, and, without any thing over her Face, she kneel'd down, and the Executioner, at one Blow, sever'd her Beautiful Head from her Delicate Body, being then in her Seven and Twentieth Year. She was generally Lamented, and Honourably Bury'd.

FINIS

Walter Charleton (or P. M.)

# THE CIMMERIAN MATRON

(1668)

# THE
# Cimmerian
# MATRON,
To which is added,
## THE
# MYSTERIES
And
# MIRACLES
OF
# LOVE.

By *P. M.* Gent.

---

*Qui cavet, ne decipiatur ; vix cavet, etiam cum cavet :*
*Etiam cum cavisse ratus eft, is cautor captus eft.*
Plautus.

---

In the *SAVOY* :
Printed for *Henry Herringman* at the Sign of the
*Anchor* in the Lower-walk of the
*New-Exchange.* 1668.

Dr. *Walter Charleton (1619–1707) was a genuine seventeenth-century polymath; a physician, an antiquary, and a Fellow of the Royal Society, he was the author of many books whose variety well indicates the extent of his wide-ranging intellectual interests. Among the list of some twenty-odd works ascribed to him are two excellent short stories, both translated from Latin originals and both dealing with women of a somewhat openly erotic nature (the implication seems to be that they are quite typical of their sex). The story of the Ephesian matron, the earlier of the two to be published, comes from Petronius. An account of the triumph of sexual desire over mourning for a dead husband, the story can be pushed in any one of several directions according to the teller's fancy and can be made to seem cynically misogynistic, frankly realistic, or even sturdily hopeful (life conquers death, as it were). The essence of the plot is fairly simple: a widow, disregarding the entreaties of her friends, determines to stay in the burial vault with the body of her husband, there to perish of grief. But a soldier, charged with guarding the body of a certain malefactor executed nearby, sees the light in the tomb, enters, captures her attention and her emotions almost at once, and makes love to her. The soldier then finds that the body he has been told to watch has been carried off, but the widow, formerly so tender of her late husband's memory, gladly permits her new lover to substitute the body she had been mourning over for the one he had lost.*

*The other story, again exhibiting a woman who has the courage of her amorous convictions, is that of the Cimmerian matron; it has also been attributed to Charleton in the standard bibliographies. The original of this story is an inset tale in the* Comus of Erycius Puteanus *first published in 1608, a Latin satire condemning in Stoic terms excessive sensuality, especially in the matters of eating and drinking.*[1] *The story is, however, much older than the version given in Puteanus; it had appeared in Boccaccio, where it figures as the eighth story of the seventh day, and before that it can be found as far back as the collection of Indian tales called the* Pantchatantra. (*The tale is K1512 in the Stith Thompson* Motif-Index.)[2] *Again a simple incident*

[1] A somewhat abridged English version of the original, the work of one Bryce Blair, appeared in English in 1671 as *The Vision of Theodorus Verax*. Comus contains three inset tales, the first of these that of the Cimmerian matron, the third the *novella* which follows in this anthology. For the relationship between the Latin *Comus* and Milton's masque, see Ralph H. Singleton, "Milton's *Comus* and the *Comus* of Erycius Puteanus," *PMLA*, LVIII (1943), 949–957.

[2] Stith Thompson, *Motif-Index of Folk Literature* (rev. ed.; Bloomington: Indiana University Press, 1957), 6 vols. This reference book classifies and locates the folklore motifs found in narrative prose.

*comprises the whole story: the husband of a certain Cimmerian lady suspects (and rightly) that she is about to have an assignation and ties her to a post in the back of his house to prevent her sneaking off to meet her lover; the lady's go-between is induced to take the lady's place; the husband is then moved during the night to cut off the nose of the go-between on the assumption that he was punishing his wife; when next morning the wife appears whole of face she claims that divine intercession restored her nose and hence has established her innocence of intention; the husband can only accept this explanation of the apparent miracle and apologize for his unjust suspicions.*

*It is however quite possible that Charleton was not the translator of this second tale, in spite of the fact that the two stories were published together in 1668 and in spite of the additional fact that the two tales share much the same style and technique of narration. The* Ephesian Matron *was first published in 1659; the* Cimmerian Matron *joined it as a companion piece in the next edition, that of 1668, being there provided with its own separate title page which quite clearly says it is by "P. M. Gent."[3] This title page is then followed by a dedication inscribed "To the Author of The Ephesian Matron." The evidence of this title page and the dedication seems to indicate that it was some hand other than Charleton's that rendered the second story into English, but the identity of P. M. remains mysterious.[4]*

*In any case the translators (or translator) of both stories treat their originals with care but are also able to introduce a contemporary style into their work, a style which is simultaneously grave, elegant, and somewhat mocking. The writers of both stories pretend to believe that they are telling a true anecdote, comment on the veracity of one or two details (P. M. speaks of a mantle but adds "some will have it to be only a blanket"), offer some sententious morals, and produce some comments of their own from time to time on the action as it unrolls. The style is, indeed, exactly what one would expect from a scholar who mixed with the best wits of Restoration London, as Charleton and presumably P. M. also undoubtedly did.*

*The text which follows is based on the copy of the 1668 edition in Yale University Library; it omits the dedicatory preface mentioned above.*

---

[3] *Gent.* is an abbreviation for "Gentleman."

[4] It has been very tentatively suggested that the initials are those of one Patrick Malan, apparently, like Charleton, a medical man with philosophical tendencies. See Gretl Katchen, "*Comus* Once More," *Milton Newsletter*, II (1968), 46.

## The Cimmerian Matron

On the Confines of *Cimmeria*,[5] there not long since lived a certain Gentlewoman, of shape more exact than a Statue formed by all the rules of *Leon Battista Alberti*; of features and complexion more sweet and delicate then those of *Venus* her self; of reputation as clear and immaculate as *Diana*. Wife she was to one, whom Usury had made Rich, and Riches eminent; with whom she enjoy'd all the pleasures of conjugal Love and Fidelity; not so much as dreaming of any content but in his indulgence and embraces.

But, ah! how mutable are human Affections! how many faults doth time discover, which were before concealed! This Woman had but newly acquired the Fame of a chaste and obsequious Wife, when Lust succeeding into the place of honesty wrought so unhappy a change in her, that now she began to nauseate the wholsome viands of the Marriage bed and long for strange and forbidden delicates, insomuch that her former humor of complacency and fondness by degrees degenerated into a perfect abhorrence of the Person and Company of her most uxorious Husband.

For, having by accident cast her eyes upon a young *Soldier*, naked and bathing himself, Love entred into them together with the image of the tempting object.

> She saw the man, that he was like a Knight,
> And suffisaunt of person and of might,
> And like to been a very Gentilman,
> And well his words he beset can,
> And had a noble visage for the nones,
> And formed well of brawne and of bones;
> And after *Venus* had soche faireness,
> That no man might be halfe so faire I gesse;
> And well a Lord he seemed for to be.
> And for he was a stranger, som what she
> Liked him the bet; as God do bote,
> To some folk often new thing is sote.[6]

[5] a mythical country characterized by darkness.

[6] rather inaccurately quoted from Chaucer's *Legend of Good Women*, ll. 1066–1077. *Beset can* means "arrange, organize"; *for the nones*, "indeed"; *as God do bote*, "as God offers salvation" (a pious tag); *sote*, "sweet."

Yet be not too severe in condemning the passion of a frail Woman, you who know how strong and quick assaults *Cupid* often makes upon Forts so weakly man'd, and with what unresistable Artillery he is provided. Her *Husband* observing a change in her, at first admired what should be the cause of her discontent and coldness toward him, using in the mean time all imaginable caresses and endearments to sweeten her melancholly, and dispel those gloomy clouds that had overcast her joys. After all his Courtship and Arts of Kindness proving unsuccessful, he grew suspicious (what was indeed too true) that she had removed her Affection from him, and fix'd it upon some other person. For, though she carefully conceal'd from him her flame, and often endeavour'd to suppress it, even with showrs of tears, especially when 'twas newly kindled; yet that, like wild-fire, raging the more by opposition, and breaking forth in flashes of discontent, she was not able so to hide it, but that he perceived her heart was scorch'd: Her melancholly had quite altered the graceful and charming Aire of her face, consumed her spirits, destroyed the Roses in her cheeks, bedimm'd the lustre of her sparkling eyes, and reduced her to a dejected and languishing condition. To these symptoms you may add restless nights, broken discourses, love of solitude, suddain startings, unwilling sighs, and all other signs by which a wounded heart is forced to betray it self. No wonder then, if the vigilant *Usurer* soon became confirmed in his jealousie; which yet he used as much cunning to obscure from her, as she had to conceal her passion from him. But Love is no less difficult to be resisted, than to be disguised: and now our impatient *Matron* can no longer live without the help of her Gallant.

Having therefore some knowledge of a certain wise Woman of the same Town, one of the Grand-daughters of *Pandarus*, such as the *French* call *Messageurs d'Amour*, a *Bawd* of Quality, she addresses to her, and without much difficulty engages her to go Ambassadress to the Man of Arms, and negotiate with him about a firm League of Love, and a private interview upon the first fair opportunity. In this Treaty, there needed not much of Rhetorick on the part of this *Oratrix*, the Soldier (who was indeed so handsome and proper a Fellow, that *Diana* her self might without any disparagement to her judgement have preferred him to *Endymion*; and wanted not wit enough to serve himselfe of so advantagious an occasion) accepting and assenting to the conditions proposed with all alacrity and gratitude imaginable. So that now nothing was wanting to the mutual ratification of the amorous Ligue, but an opportunity for the two *Princes* (for such their *hopes* had made them) interchangeably to *sign* and

*Seal*, which the watchfulness of the jealous *Husband* made extreamly difficult: he making it his main business to observe, not only all the motions of her feet, and whither she went at any time, but those also of her eies; so that you would have thought the beatious *Io* once again committed to the custody of *Argus*.

Among a thousand other plots and stratagems his troubled Imagination suggested to him, towards the discovery of what he equally fear'd and desir'd to know, he at last fixes upon this, as most hopeful, to pretend a journey from home, and by an unexpected return to surprize his wife; confident, by this artifice, he should at length arrive at the certain knowledge both of the nature and cause of her disease. According to this politick resolution, he prepares for a long journey, and dissembling a sad valediction to his dear *Fidessa* (who, you may believe, as truly counterfeited sorrow as himselfe, and moistned her parting kisses with artificial tears) sets forth early in the morning, in an hour long wish't for on both sides, nor unlucky to either.

No sooner was the *Husband* gone, than the glad *Wife*, thinking that now the propitious time drew near when her desires should be crown'd with solid pleasures, and her imaginary embraces exchanged for real ones, soon gave Commission to her *Emissary*, who was the very buckle and thong of *Venery*, instantly to advertise[7] her *Paramore*, that the Festival of Love was come, and that the Husbands departure had open'd the door to their meeting with freedom and security. This welcome message was as speedily delivered as received, and an *Assignation* made, that immediately after the wearied Sun had resigned his Empire in the upper Hemisphere to Night, and mortals began to supply his absence with an artificial day of Candle-light, our valiant and well provided Lover should come to the back door of his *Saints* Chappel, by which he should be introduced and conducted into the *Chancel*, and thence to the *Altar*, upon which he was to offer up his Sacrifice and pay his vows; and that done, return to his quarters, without the least suspicion of the Neighbours. In the mean time, lest the Incense he brought with him might not be sufficient to maintain the flame of love the whole night, and his zeal cool through too much fervency at first, the provident *Matron* made ready a *Collation* of generous Wines, Conserves,[8] and other restorative *quelques Choses*,[9] to help carry on the work; and set them in order upon a little Table in her bed-chamber. She contrived also her affair so circumspectly, as to send

[7] let him know.          [8] preserves (made of fruit).
[9] other dainties.

her *Chamber-maid*, who was indeed the Husbands principal spie over her, to the wedding of a Neighbours Daughter, not without reason presuming that the wenches curiosity to pry into the pleasant rites of the Bridal night, and her ambition to be most lucky in the superstitious sport of throwing the Brides stocking, would long enough divert her from her charge at home. And thus far all things went on according to their wishes, nor did any thoughts disquiet the calmer breasts of our pair of Lovers but such as usually arise from vehement *expectation;* the Soldier dreaming of nothing but Victory, Triumph, and Spoils; and the Lady of high content in having her Fort new man'd, and making the Assailant her Captive. But, Oh, the capriciousness of *Fortune!* or rather the vigilance of *Jealousie!*

The appointed hour being at length come, the punctual *Soldier* making haste to enter upon his Duty, to guard the fair *Matron* from Spectres and Goblins, in the absence of her Husband, advanceth to the postern door of her house, as he had been directed, but finding it shut, and hearing no noise within, he made a halt, and very discreetly forbearing to knock, fell to the posture of a diligent *Sentinel,* softly walking to and fro in the narrow Alley that led to the house from the Street, where while he was exercising his patience, it most unluckily hapned that the no less vigilant and impatient *Husband* (who had conceal'd himself at a Friends in the Neighbourhood) returned by the same Alley, and stealing along as softly and warily as a Thief to commit Burglary, takes good notice of the night-walker, whom he immediately concluded within himself to be the *Mars,* on whom his *Venus* was so *furiously* ennamour'd; whereupon, entring his house, and locking the door behind him, with as little noise as a Pick-lock, he finds his wife in a dress of neat and rich night-linnen, like a Bride going to bed, which adding more Fewel to his suspicion, and exasperating the sense of his wrong, he puts on the countenance of rage and terror, with enflamed and threatning eyes staring, as *Caesars* Ghost upon *Brutus,* upon his poor surprised wife, who stood as still, by reason of her astonishment, as if she had been congealed by lightning, or transformed into a Statue. For *shame upon the unexpected frustration of an evil design, doth usually produce confusion.* Her soul, conscious of infidelity hitherto only in imagination and design, began to presage more evils, than it could have deserved, had her design succeeded into Act, the violence of her passion being favourably considered. But, could she so soon have recollected her disordered spirits, and recovered the use of her tongue, her Husband's fury would have restrain'd her, and he yet could only breath revenge, not utter it in words. After a little pause, going into her bed-chamber, he there encounters with fresh causes of suspicion: the dressing-Table by the bed-side richly furnisht with provoking delicates, clean sheets, perfum'd pillows, and above all, his spie, the *Chambermaid*, conjur'd out of the way; confirm'd in his jealousie by these convincing signs, he now meditates upon nothing but Revenge, and how to effect it with the more security and apparence of justice. Resolved, therefore, by cruelty to extort a Confession, and so make her her own accuser, without speaking a word, he strips her to her snow-white skin, and carrying her down into the Porch, there binds her delicate Arms to one of the Pillars: had you been so happy to have beheld her in that deplorable posture, doubtless you would have thought you had seen the beautiful *Andromede* a second time chained naked to a Rock, and one, though perhaps not quite so chaste as she, yet, if Beauty had its due,

> *She could not merit any bonds, beside*
> *Those, with which Lovers mutualy are tyed;*

and well worthy another *Perseus* to deliver, love and enjoy her. The hard-hearted *Usurer*, fancying to himself some satisfaction in this first Act of the Tragedy he intended, retires to his bed (though likely to have but a melancholy night of it without his Consort) hoping by sleep to recompose his troubled mind.

In the mean time, our *Man of War*, who had promised to himselfe the height of all enjoyments, lay (Soldier like) perdue[10] in the open Air; and when he had till almost midnight in vain watched his Mistresses door, which still continued as fast shut, as the Temple of *Janus* in time of peace, he returns back to the house of his *She-Officer* the *Bawd*, whom he found halfe naked, and prepared to keep one of *Venus*'s *Vigils* with a *Client* of hers (for her Clients were often forced to gratifie her, for solliciting their Love-causes, with such Fees), whom at that very hour she expected. Ho, Mother, says he, with what tedious hope do I purchase from the Lady the pleasure promised me? I have already consumed a whole hour (longer indeed than a whole winters night) in fruitless expectation; while she, who sought my Love, and made the Assignation, hath not vouchsafed to open the door. 'Tis very strange, methinks, unless having forgot both her self and her appointment, she hath buried her amour in sleep. Go thy ways, dear Mother, and enquire the cause of my disappointment, and what commands the Lady hath for me; if to readvance, lo, I am ready for the combat; if to retreat, I am as ready to march off with flying Colours, and

---

[10] placed (as a sentinel) in a hazardous position; hidden away.

deferr the encounter till another night. Scarcely were these last words
out of his mouth, when the *Bawd*, incited partly by the sense of her
honour (for those of her Trade must be punctual in their assignations)
and partly by commiseration of his impatience, hastily casting a *Mantle*
(a most useful garment in such cases) over her shoulders, catches the
*Soldier* by the hand, and conducts him back to the door, which she opens
with a Key given her by the *Matron* some while before, for her private
access upon occasion, and entreating him to stand close and silent for a
few minutes without, she passes on through the Wood-yard and a little
Garden, till she arrived at the walk under the Porch, where groping along,
she had almost run her head against the living Statue there bound to a
Pillar; which she no sooner discern'd, but surpriz'd with horror, as at
sight of a Ghost or Apparition, she stood still and gazed with affrighted
eyes. The milky whiteness of the *Matrons* skin to some degree overcame
the darkness of the moonless night, nor would it suffer her to be longer
unperceived; so that the *Bawd* soon recovering her self out of her first
consternation, boldly approaches to the *Lady*, and, omitting to enquire
into the cause of her being in that strange and lamentable condition,
delivers in few words the *Soldiers* message, even at that time not ungrateful
to the receiver; for, the *Lady* finding the chains of Love more intollerable
than those of her barbarous Husband; and endowed with a *Wit* no whit
inferior to her Beauty, soon apprehended that now she had an opportunity
to convert this her misfortune into a benefit, and that she ought not to
despond, nor despair of reaping the delights which the jealousie of her
Husband had hitherto prevented. Thus reanimated with fresh hope, she
begins to wheadle the *Engineer of Lust*, and pouring the oyl of good
language and endearing expressions into her ears, My dearest Mother,
says she, my good Angel, I can bear this my affliction with patience
becoming the undaunted resolution of a Lover; yea more, I can change
it into a complete Felicity, if you will but vouchsafe me your assistance;
I know no way to revenge my Husbands cruelty, but to deserve it by
acting what he so much fears. Help me then to meet and embrace my
Lover, that he who hath so kindly entertain'd my invitation, so justly
observed our appointment, may neither accuse me of breach of faith, nor
want the reward due to his Fidelity. Let your courteous hands untie the
knots that hamper mine, and for a few minutes free me from these bonds,
that I may really deserve them. These charms soon wrought upon the
good nature of the *Bawd*, who was the very *Renet*[11] of Concupiscence; so

[11] i.e., rennet, anything used to curdle milk; the bawd can turn anything to lust.

that she readily disingaged her Daughter from the cold embraces of the Pillar.

Who being thus happily at liberty, assumes more Courage and Wit from her adventure, and falls to perswade her deliverer to suffer her self to be bound with the same Cord, and to supply her room only while she hasted to her *Gallant*, to give him an assurance of her constancy; she told her there could be no hazard in the enterprize, since her Husband was in his bed and fast asleep, and all the world but themselves at quiet, and within two minutes she would return and relieve her: Hereto she added such golden promises, as might have overcome a mind much more obstinate and doubtful than the *Bawds*, who boggled at no danger to oblige a friend; but accordingly shifting her *Mantle* (some will have it to be only a *Blanket*) from her own shoulders to the *Matrons*, readily yielded her self to be bound to the Pillar, in the same manner as she had found her Predecessor. This certainly was a most pleasant Scene, well worthy a Theatre, and might make a good plot for a *Tragicomedy*. The *Matron* leaving her Deputy thus bound and naked, yet without impeachment of her modesty; and mounting on the wings of love, fled in an instant to her *Paramour:* 'Twas a bold and adventurous Act this, for a Woman so lately surprized, so cruelly treated, so miraculously delivered, nay, not yet delivered from danger of greater torments, and perhaps of death, thus to throw her self into the Arms of her Adulterer, to force even destiny it self to give way to the satisfaction of her desires. But *Love inspires Audacity and Contempt of all perils into the Weakest and most timorous hearts.*

Hardly had the greedy *Matron* with silence express'd her joy, and tasted the first dish of Loves Banquet, *Kisses*, a dish that doth at once satisfie and provoke the Appetite, when the *Soldier*, deceived by the *Mantle* she had borrowed, and mistaking her for the true owner thereof, began to put her from him, as scorning to use his Arms against so base and impudent an Enemy; but she soon guessing at the cause of his aversion, by her harmonious voice, which yet she durst not raise above a whisper, convinced him of his error, and restored him to a due assurance that he had the person he look'd for, and no *Changeling:* Whereupon, omitting all further ceremonies, he did his devoir[12] to verifie the good opinion she had at first sight, when he was bathing himself, conceived of his *good parts*; and she, on the other side (if at least there were now any distinction of sides) did hers, to fix him in a confidence that her Love was *true* and unfeigned.

[12] duty.

While these our zealous votaries to the Goddess of Pleasures are at their silent devotions, the silly *Cuckold* (now I think we may call him so), her *Husband*, who is an example of that Sentence in *Seneca*, that *many times by seeking to avoid dangers we run headlong into the midst of them*, was in a slumber wherein his perturbed imagination presented to him dismal and infaust[13] visions: he dreamed that he saw his wife sacrificing her honour, and doing that odious Act that drew an indelible stain and reproach upon him and his whole Family, having broken her bonds asunder and mixing her self with her armed Adulterer in closest embraces; that himself, while he was labouring to revenge the contumelious injury, was transformed into a *Satyr:* The horror of this ominous dream interrupting his slumber, and his Fancy retaining a deep impression of those dire Phantasmes, he begins to believe his transformation to be real, and feels his Nose, if it were not grown crooked like a *Satyr*'s; his Forehead, if it were not armed with Antlers; his Thighs, if they were cloth'd with shaggy hair; his feet, if they were not cloven, and his Toes turned into hoofs; then still credulous of the first part of his vision, he leaps out of his bed, throws open the window, and calls aloud upon his wife, who was now either out of hearing, or not at leasure to give answer to his curses and reproaches. But alas! the Reverend *Bail*,[14] her *Confident*, heard and trembled; she now, though too late, found the error of her kindness, and saw no way to safety but by obstinate silence, which she with more resolution and constancy kept, than one of *Pythagoras* Scholars during his novitiate, in spite of the ingeminated exclamations of the inraged *Malbecco*,[15] who exasperated by that Contempt (for so he understood it) and fancying some Divine suggestions to revenge from the *Genius* of the Marriage-bed, snatches up a Razor that lay in the Window, runs down the Stairs in the dark, and flying most furiously at the very face of his wifes Deputy catches her fast by her Nose, and with one well-guided slash cuts it quite off, then flinging the same in her face, Thou worst of Women, saith he, worthy of a greater brand of infamy, there, take that token of my hate, and send it for a present to thy Adulterer, who perhaps will either grow more enamour'd upon this change of thy forme, this new-modell'd face, or confess thee to have a better Title to his love by the suffrings for his sake. Thus insulting over the miserable wretch, and triumphing in his

[13] unlucky, ill-omened.
[14] pledge left as guarantee of return.
[15] betrayed husband in Spenser's *Faerie Queene* (Book III) who turns into Jealousy itself.

revenge, he returns to his thorny bed, there with sleep to ease his head, now in truth much *heavier* than before: What shall I say of the poor mangled and noseless *Bawd*? only this: that her fear of a worse accident, if she were known to her Tormentor, made her undergoe her pains and loss with more than a *Spartan* patience: Unhappy friendship! sad Exchange! it was her lot to be drencht with the Gall of Love, while the Matron suck'd the Honey of it; her evil destiny to be besmear'd with her own blood, while the more guilty wife was anointed with the Butter of Joy. Thus in *Duels*, we see, often the *seconds* are wounded while the *Principals* remain unhurt.

The Schismatical *Nose* was scarcely grown cold when our *Faustina*,[16] having finished her first trial of skil with her *Gladiator*, and with a thousand parting kisses dismiss'd him to recruit his spirits lost in the conflict, returns with the joys of a double victory to her Post. But how short-lived a thing is sensual delight! how evanid[17] are all our triumphs! when she understood the sufferings of her *Martyr*, the Sun-shine of her content was in a moment darkned with clouds of grief and dreadful apprehensions, and all her exulting smiles exchanged for tears and dejection of Mind. But *Grief and Fear are almost as bad Counsellors as Love*, which our witty *Matron* well understanding, and remembring withal that Nature had furnished her whole Sex with a faculty of quick invention, how to evade approaching danger and to conceal faults, re-assures her self, and sets her brain on work how to palliate this wound, which was past her cure. She hath recourse, therefore, to the Art of Consolation, and endeavours to mitigate the *Bawds* dolours with an *Anodyne* of kind and commiserating language. She bids her not to be cast down with her misfortune, which, carried with bravery and discretion, might turn to her advantage, and prove a noble experiment of her Fidelity among all the *Cimmerians*; that the segment of her Nose would be to *Venus* an offering as grateful and propitiatory as locks of hair to other *Deities;* that if in a Soldier, wounds in the face were honourable witnesses of his courage and bravery, why should not those received in the service of *Venus* be likewise accounted marks of Gallantry and a daring spirit? that though the now mortified *Nose* could not be set on again (for *Tagliacotius*[18] lived a great

[16] wife of the emperor Marcus Aurelius Antoninus (121–180 A.D.), famous for her debaucheries.

[17] evanescent; faint, weak.

[18] Gaspero Tagliacozzi (1546–1599), an Italian surgeon whose skill became legendary.

way off *Cimmeria*) yet the wound would be easily cured; and at worst if she were so foolish to resolve not to live without one (a thing many a person of greater quality had done before her), she would cause a new one to be made for her of much more value, and better mettal than the first. This last promise mollified more than all the consolatory reasons precedent, and the *Bawd* (who had a Soul so abject and Mercenary, that she would for Money have sold her eyes, and ears too into the bargain) becom's pacified and comforted therewith; then being loosed from the Pillar, and binding the *Matron* (who desired it) to the same, she gropes out the piece of her Nose, wraps it up in a corner of her Mantle, and away she trudges in quest of a *Chirurgeon*,[19] locking the back door very carefully after her, and reflecting upon the ill success of her *obligation*.

King *Salomon* reckoning *Conies*[20] among the four sorts of Animals that being little are yet exceeding wise saith of them that *being a generation not strong, they make holes for themselves among the Rocks*. The same may be said of *Women*, who, wanting strength to assert their faults, yet have cunning enough to hide them; they make burrows of excuses and run into them when in danger to be taken: Like Statesmen, who have for their Impress a Glass Bee-hive with this Motto, *Nulli patet opus;*[21] they do their business in the dark, or (as a witty *Italian* expresseth it) *desmienten lo transparente con un vanno de cera,*[22] they smear over their Hives with wax, so that no eye can pry into the secrets of their workings, or be able to trace them in their amorous stealths; if you doubt of this, you shall see it verified in the fourth Act of this our Tragicomedy, which we are now arrived at.

The *Bawd* being handsomly conjur'd away, the coast clear, and all the world at rest, our subtle *Matron*, after a short meditation, hath found out a way, if it succeed, not only to dissemble her joyful Treason, but to appear still innocent and faithful to her *Husband;* yea, yet farther, to invert the guilt upon him, and bring him at last to confess himself to have been in an error. This, you'l say, is somewhat difficult: but, remember she is a *woman* and in *Love*, and then you'l conceive it to be facil. Having formed the design, she delays not to put it in execution: Counterfeiting therefore an appeal to the *Moon* (then newly risen above the verge of the Horizon) with a voice raised by degrees from a low whisper to a pitch

[19] surgeon.
[20] rabbits: a term of endearment for women, somewhat indecent; a dupe or gull.
[21] literally, the work lies open to no one.
[22] they conceal transparent things with a covering of wax.

high enough to reach the poor *Cuckolds* ears, she invocates her help and protection in such verses as these.

Sister of *Jove*, Queen Regent of the night,
From whom the meaner Stars derive their light;
Or wouldst be worship by great *Juno's* name,
*Joves* Wife, or Sister, thou art still the same.
That Sov'raign Dame, who art the Deity
Of wedlock rites and femal Chastity,
Why with auspicious Omens did I pay
My Nuptial vows upon my Marriage day?
If with an unconcern'd and even face
Thou dost behold the Mischiefs of this place.
And you, bright Planets, Heavens unerring eyes,
With which by night he things on earth descries,
You witnesses of my pure innocence
(Who yet, as Judges, my hard fate dispense),
Don't you grow dimm with horror, thus to see
A jealous Husbands causeless cruelty?
See, naked, bound, and mangled here I grone,
And expiate offences not my own.
If then the vertuous you can thus torment,
For these rewards, who would be innocent?
   Methinks I now seem but my own pale Ghost.
Beauty and Fame (a Womans soul) are lost.
Though pure from Thought, or Act, yet wretched I
Must wear a face that gives my heart the lie.
Why live I thus? why does this mangled shape
Confine that soul, which would so fain escape?
To die is better, and one blow to give,
Than rob'd of Honour, nay and Beauty, live.
To die is best indeed; but, oh, the hands
That should performe my freer Wills commands,
Alas, are fetter'd!—.
For death, when courted, from us then to flie,
Forcing to live, 'tis then he makes us die.

   Ah, cruel Man! here thou hast torments found
Beyond these bonds, beyond this horrid wound.

Happy *Lucretia*, since thou could'st attest
Thy innocence, by piercing of thy breast,
Whilst thus expiring in thy Husbands arms,
Ev'n in thy death couldst gain more pow'rful charms.
Thou Chast are call'd, because thou couldst but die,
Whilst death to me doth that relief deny.

Thou Goddess were severe unto thy *Jove*,
And Heav'n couldst purge from his unlawful love:
If to bad Women thou so just art known,
Wilt thou not vindicate one honest one?
Behold with pity, and do not despise
Tears mixt with blood, which flow from mournful eyes.
Punish the jealous Man, and make him feel
The sad effects of his own cruel steel.
Shew him his crime, and what 'tis let him know,
T'offend a Woman, and a Goddess too.
At least be just, and my late form restore
With my lost fame, or let me be no more.

Having breath'd forth this supplication in a languishing tone, and made it seem more pathetical by interposing now and then a profound sigh or two (and indeed of all our Passions none are more easily counterfeited then *Zeal* and *Sorrow*), on a suddain changing the key of her voice into a confused murmur, and then to that of a civil conference, she dissembled a familiar Dialogue with the *Deity*, whose ayd she had newly implored: and in fine, as if her prayer had been heard, and her petition miraculously granted, with an elevated voice she makes an *Apostrophe* to her Husband, exclaiming against his improsperous tyranny in these words.

Ho, thou most barbarous of men, thou Fury in human shape, thy bloody rage against thy chastest wife hath prov'd thy own undoing. The mercy of the Celestial Powers hath overcome thy Cruelty, lest my virtue might suffer by thy undeserved and base suspicions. Now shalt thou be forced to confess what thy impiety made thee doubt of, that I am innocent, and that there is a God who sees and notes our deeds. I am convinced, I am convinced; it is none but *Juno*, *Protectress of conjugal Chastity*, who compassionating my sufferings, hath by Miracle restored that amiable form of mine, which thou, distracted with jealousie, had'st destroy'd. Goe then, desperate Villain, and sheath that bloody knife of thine in thy own inhuman bowels, that so unworthy a wretch may no longer enjoy the happiness of so faithful and spotless a Wife. Having obtained so signal a favour from the immortal Gods, well may I contemn and bid defiance to the anger of a Mortal Man, especially one so wicked, so degraded by his crimes. —O night! more illustrious than the brightest day. O hour! more fortunate than that of my birth. —Now flow on, flow on, officious Tears, but from a different passion. But thou, execrable Hangman, sacrilegious Thief, hasten hither to be convinced of my purity, and thy crime; make hast, I say, that, if it be possible, thou maist make attonement for the innocent blood thou hast spilt, and for the sacrilege thou hast committed, and so in time appease the wrath of an offended Goddess.

This triumphant *Harangue* arriving at the ears of the poor *Cornuto*[23] her *Husband* (whom disquiet of mind kept from sleep), it alarmed all his Faculties and put him into so great a confusion, that giving but little credit to his sense, he lay a good while considering the probability of what he heard. At first he thought it an *Illusion* (since to Nature it is much easier to make a man dream impossibilities, than to effect them) and began therefore to feel if his Eyes were open, that he might thereby be certified whether he were awake or not. Then finding it to be no dream, and hearing his Wife continue her Speech, and denouncing a deluge of dire Judgments against him, his rage and jealousie began at once to give place to as vehement Fear and Remorse. Rising therefore hastily from his bed, and lighting a candle, down he goes, resolved to make his eyes judges of the truth of what he durst not believe upon the single testimony of his ears. Arrived at the fatal Pillar, the scene of such prodigious accidents, and beholding his Wifes face attentively, he found it perfect, and without the least sign of hurt, nay not so much as stain'd with a drop of blood, and her hands still tied as he had at first left them. Whereat astonish't, and persuaded in himself, that so supernatural an event as the restauration of a. Nose cut off, could not come to pass but by power *Divine*, he sunk down into an abhorrence of his wicked fact, and of the no less abominable motive thereof, his jealousie, dreading withall some dire punishment from the just anger of the Gods. Then casting himself upon the pavement, in token of his sorrow and contrition, he washes out the bloody stains thereof with penitential tears. Which done, he kneels in adoration of so manifest a *Miracle*, and in humble but fervent prayers, begs pardon first of Heaven, then of his Wife (too wise to be inexorable) for the horrid effect of his outragious Passion. Which when she, *good Soul*, had graciously promised

[23] wearing the traditional horns of the cuckold.

upon a solemn vow of reformation of Manners on his part, transported with joy, he unties the cord, sets her at liberty, kisses her all over, and leads her to bed, there to seal his reconciliation to her, now a rare Example of unspotted Chastity. Thus, blest be the God of Love! Our witty *Matron* hath at once recovered three most precious things, her *Nose*, her *Honour*, and her Husbands *Love*.

Not long after this happy conclusion or *Catastrophe*, the *Bawd*, well rewarded with a purse of money for her loss and secresy, and hoping to mend her fortunes by removing to a place of better trading, packs up her baggage and marches away to the Court of *Comus*, King of the *Cimmerians*, where she now lives no small Favourite, and exercising her talent every day in laying new designs and managing the close intrigues of Love betwixt Ladies and their Gallants. Wherein long practice hath made her so excellent that if any Woman in that Court, be she Maid, Wife, or Widow, please you, and if you commit the matter to her contrivement and intercession, you need not doubt the success.

As for the *Souldier*, though my *Author* says no more of him but what I have recounted, yet, considering that he was a man of honour, a Son of *Mars*, it is not to be doubted but that he continued secret and faithful to his *Venus*. Nor is it less probable that *She*, a gracious and obliging Mistress, continued to love him better than she did her *Usurer*, notwithstanding her remission of his cruel usage and readmission of him to her grace and favour. Whereupon I cannot at any time reflect, without acknowledging the goodness of *Proserpine* in keeping her promise made to the Lady *May* in *Chaucer*, which was this, in her answer to *Pluto*, who would fain restore to *January*, her Husband, his sight, that he might see his Esquire, *Damian*, making him *Cuckold* in a Pear-tree.[24]

> You shall (quoth *Proserpine*) and well ye so?
> Now by my Mothers Soul, Sir, I swere,
> That I shall yeven her sufficient answere,
> And all women after for her sake;
> That though they ben in any gilte itake,
> With face bolde, they shullen hemselve excuse,
> And bere hem doun, that wold hem accuse.

[24] a reference to Chaucer's *Merchant's Tale;* the following lines are quoted from Chaucer; they are lines 2264–2276 in F. N. Robinson's edition (Boston: Houghton Mifflin Co., 1957). *Yeven* means "give"; *hem*, "them"; *dien*, "die"; *sey*, "saw"; *leude*, "ignorant"; *what recketh me of*, "what do I care about."

For lack of answere, non of hem shull dien,
All had he sey a thing with both his eyen
Yet should we women so visage it hardely,
And wepe, and swere, and chide subtelly,
That men shall ben as leude as Gees.
What recketh me of your auctoritees, &c.

*Explicit Historia*

Joseph Kepple

# THE MAIDEN-HEAD
# LOST BY MOON-LIGHT

(1672)

# THE
# MAIDEN-HEAD
## LOST BY
# Moon-light:
## OR THE
# ADVENTURE
## OF THE
# MEADOW.

*Written by* JOSEPH KEPPLE.

LONDON,
Printed for *Nathaniel Brooke* at the *Angel* in
*Cornhil.* MDCLXXII.

*Joseph Kepple's* The Maiden-Head Lost by Moon-Light *is a successful tour de force. Basically a translation of an inset tale from a Latin satire, the* Comus *of Erycius Puteanus, first published in 1608, Kepple's work keeps nearly all the material of his original yet shifts the emphasis and the tone so as to make the resulting story a genuine piece of Restoration fiction. The change is achieved by giving the story an intrusive narrator who affects to tell his tale from personal knowledge (a considerable piece of irony since the action is said to have taken place in the time of Tiresias) and who reminds us frequently of his presence by interposing his own comments on the action or by explaining how he knew such-and-such a thing to be true. Equally important in effecting the change is the style, which, consistent with the persona of the narrator, is both self-conscious and sophisticated, being full of satirical ironies, deliberately mock hyperboles and comparisons, the overall effect being both chatty and detached: an urbane and worldly man is telling a story to equally urbane and worldly listeners. The style (and general manner of narration) may owe something to Charleton's* Ephesian and Cimmerian Matrons, *to which indeed Kepple makes specific if not explicit reference in his opening pages headed "To the Ladies," but if it does the later writer goes far beyond his model in bright colloquial effect. Kepple has undoubtedly picked up a few tricks from the short stories of Scarron too.*

*The plot, along with the names of the characters, comes straight from Puteanus and bears much resemblance to the sort of novella written by Boccaccio. The action moves rapidly, the basic pattern being the simple but effective one of the cross-loves of two couples. The central episode, as one might expect from the amusingly provocative title, is the one in which the successful rival soft-talks the lady into yielding. At this point the author draws a veil over his lovers and proceeds to offer, instead of an epithalamion, some reasons why sex al fresco is better than "staying the Parson's leisure." The reasons may be mock-serious, but the reader can feel that they are offered at least partially in earnest, since the author has told us in his preface that his story portrays an honester kind of love than the usual venal coquetry so in vogue in the 1670's, which makes love a piece of art rather than a natural occurrence. Indeed, we can if we wish regard the story as an Horatian attack on the times, or at least on one phase of them.*

*The text which follows is based on the copy of the edition of 1672 in the Harvard University Library.*

## To the Ladies

You have in this Romance in *Querpo*[1] (although I believe having read it, you will allow it a better Title, and at least, swear 'tis pity it was not True) the perfect Representation of the state of *Innocence ;* I don't mean the time when our first Parents, for want of Drapers, made use of Leaves, but the Age that not long after follow'd; in which *Love*, which is now made a piece of Art, was Natural; when Mens Affections were not byass'd with the Desire of a great Estate, and without huge heaps of Gold were contented with the innocent lightness of their Mistresses; I mean that Air, Mine[2] and Gayety they esteem'd, and did not as we do, censure their sprightly Gestures, as if Mirth and Honesty were inconsistent. Then how would they have laugh'd to hear of a Lady, that made her Servant follow the Sent two whole Years, when perhaps she is more in love with the Gallant, than he with her, who in his apish Apprentiship (for he must be a Slave to her Will) has spent more Money in the *Mulberry Garden*, and the *Parks*, than would build an *Hospital*; has seen more *Plays* than are good, and been acquainted with all the Coach-men in Town; whose Estate at last being spent, *Victoria, Victoria*, the Day's our own, he at last has vanquish'd his Mistresses Affections, is marry'd, and with her Portion is just flush'd for the visit of another Lady; and then who can blame our *Prophetick Gentlewomen?* They are like to enjoy little Pleasure, after the Man in black has conjur'd them together, except to tell how many *Rhenish-wine* Glasses have been drank in drinking her *Health*, by the Good-man her Husband, who is now perhaps, lest he should forget his Courtship, paying his *Devoirs* to a new Madam.

I know the Ladies having read it (But not for the good of the Book-seller, let us contrive how that may be; why, it is but feeing the Chamber-maid to pretend Ignorance, and get the Foot Boy to buy her the new Book of the Maid that was so Blind as to Lose her self in a *Moon shine Night*, and then convey it to her Lady, who will by the Title, expect it should be horrible Bawdy, when a starch'd Puritan I think would not groan in Spirit to be call'd the Owner of it), I say the Ladies that read it will be cursed angry with me, that *Myrtilla* was so easily gain'd, and that she did not, like our foolish Females, oppose what she most desir'd. For the first I dare oppose her Constancy to any of their Ladyships; and for

---

[1] *in cuerpo:* without the cloak or upper garment, hence in undress; (humorously) naked.
[2] mien.

the other, you shall see I am so much a Gentleman, as to help a young Lady over the Stile. I know her Accusers Argument is, that she ought to have taken some time to try her Servants Affection; but pray direct me to that foolish Fop (and I'le procure him a Mistress of Clouts,[3] for he deserves no better) who when he is wooing, will offer to be deficient in his Duty, that will quarrel at an angry look, and will threaten to bang her[4] if she will not say she loves, which is as ridiculous to think, as that a lame Beggar should Hector out[5] an Alms. For my part, I think our *Myrtilla* is to be commended for her Policy; she does by this oblige her Lover, and he must bely the shape of a man, and be worse than a Devil, that will wrong a Lady that so confidently commits her Honour to his keeping. Well, however the Ladies quarrel at me and *Myrtilla*, *Circe* and I shall be sure to scape with the Chambermaids, their good hearts will only envy a little her fortune, and it may be say their Prayers every Night, and lie cross-legg'd in expectation of the like.

It is now fit to tell you why I undertook this harmless piece of Mirth, which was for this Reason; I saw how well one Story out of the same Authour took, beeing turn'd into *English*, that is out of the incomparable *Erycius Puteanus*,[6] and thinking this no way inferiour to it in it self, having nothing to do, I adventur'd upon the Translation of it. I confess it comes so short of the Pen of that ingenious person that wrote the other, that [I] fear I have done the witty *Italian* an unpardonable Injury in daring to render it so pitifully. But to excuse him of all those faults my Translation may make him seem guilty of, I assure you the Cloaths are my own; If you ask why I made 'em no better, I assure you I could not, 'twas done for the aforesaid Reason to avoid idleness, and then I think I am a little more excusable, than the person that having nothing to do, went and hir'd in the Market a Drudgery at the expence of a great Sum. If I have offended the Ladies, I beg their pardon, and assure them that I am their

Humble Servant,

*J. K.*

---

[3] a mere rag-doll in garb of a woman.
[4] hit her.
[5] to force by threats or insolence.
[6] presumably a reference to Charleton's *Cimmerian Matrons*.

### The Maiden-head
### Lost by Moon-Light
### or, The Adventure of the Meadow

My little Skill in Geography will not let me give you any better Account, then that in part of the Dominions of the great *Comus*,[7] dwelt a young Gentleman, by Name *Cherestratus;* I shall not trouble my self nor you with a tedious Relation of his Ancestors, and how many of them were *Lord Mayors;* but I am something like a Woman, and now I think on't, can't but tell you that one of them was hang'd, which I had not done, but that I thought it would not be any disparagement to him, who was so well accomplish'd, that his first actions had quitted the disgrace had they all suffer'd the like fate; He was not at all behind hand with the Gallants of these times, either for Learning or Valour, besides Singing, and composing of Madrigals, which seemed in those days to have been in great use; for the Ladies being not over coy, were not so great Enemies to the Progress of Musick, as to deny themselves or Servant the pleasure of an early *Serenade*, which the next day was rewarded with some signal favour, except the Lady so courted had been wak'd out of some pleasant Dream, and then too she durst hardly chide, for fear lest being one with the men (who were chiefly concern'd in the Comedy) her Dream should prove but a Dream, and she should never be made happy with the Reality. Besides this, he could Dance incomparably well, by which the Ladies might ghess he had not been under the Surgeon's hands, nor had much skill in *Maiden-heads* (a thing very much to be deplor'd in our days, for our Gallants not finding the first night what they look for (but they are fools that do) seldome continue Loving above the first Month; and seem not so much to be married as to keep a Mistress with a little more Ceremony). I am loath to tell you that with these Perfections he was rich, for I would be unwilling to put in any thing that might make you suspect the truth of this Relation; and I am sure you will never believe, that a person so well accomplish'd, and of a sufficient Estate should find so cruel a Lady, as not to admit of his Addresses. But you must consider the time, which according to the best Chronologers was in *Tiresias*'s days, and the women would not deny his Doctrine, *viz.* That they take as much pleasure or more in doing the Gentleman a good turn, than the person that receiv'd it. This made the Ladies then, contrary to what they are now a days, count it an unpardonable Sin to take a Reward for their mutual pleasures,

---

[7] god of revelry, feasting, and nocturnal entertainments.

and this made *Cherestratus* not prove so successful in his Amours, as he might have done had he liv'd now.

But to come to the Story, it was the unhappiness of this incomparable Gallant, to place his Affection on a Person that disdain'd his frequent Suits, which she did with a kind of Reluctancy, for she her self nor any body else could tell why she would not let him pay his *Devoirs* to her, as well as any other Gallant of the Town, to whom he was no way inferiour. But the mysteries of Love are as blind as himself, whose hidden Causes can never be understood, and I should rather be content to be kept in ignorance, then endeavour of a discovery of *Medea's Video meliora proboque, Deteriora sequor.*[8] However the Lady continued very obstinate, whether because she was prepossess'd with the Love of *Hyleus* (Rival only in Love to our noble *Cherestratus*, for, for other things he could not stand in competition with him) or for some other Reason, I know not. For I do not think that the comparing of a Ladie's Favours to Shadows always holds true, for then *Hyleus* had been as unhappy as our unfortunate Gentleman, who ply'd his Business as hotly as *Cherestratus* could possibly do.

By this time *Cherestratus* was grown a perfect Votary of Love, which made him like the rest of that mad Religion abandon the society of men, and endeavouring as it were to be free from himself, he would often be singing some lamentable Ditty, of which he had store, but above all, this was the chief:

> *Whatever I think or whatever I do,*
> *My* Phillis *is still in my mind :*
> *When in anger I mean not to* Phillis *to go*
> *My feet of themselves the way find,* &c.

Now you'l say this is very like a modern Song of ours, but I assure you what follows, could I but remember it, was not at all like it, and it was only by chance, that he thought of the first Stave, for it is certain there are common notions, which are obvious to all that make upon the same Subject. In hitting on which some have been so happy, that they have wrote whole Poems, and things of greater bulk so like other men, that if compar'd, it was not easily told which was which. But let this pass, sometimes you should have our *Inamorato* under the reverend shade of a well-spread Oak, beseeching it's senseless Divinity to give him leave to inscribe

[8] I see what is right and I approve it, but I do what is wrong.

the Name of his dear *Myrtilla* there (for so was the hard-hearted Lady call'd,) and then taking out a Pen Knife, which had never been put to any servile office, as cutting of Corns, or the like, he ingraves on the bark with florishing Letters, which scarce a Writing Master in those parts could mend, the Name of his Saint. This done, like a meer heathenish Gentleman he falls down, and worships the work of his own hands; then with a tedious Harangue he twits the poor Tree in the teeth of the benefit he had done it, saying that it should be now more famous for bearing the Name of the incomparable *Myrtilla*, then it was for *Jupiter*, and that were not corn yet found out, he might not at all fear a rape of his ripe Acorns, for as soon as people came, and saw those Letters, rapt up in admiration, they would forget to eat, and with fixed eyes gaze till some envious Dryades forc'd 'em from their Devotion. Besides these works of supererogation, our Gallant (which was the only comfort he had) was almost continually walking by the door of the cruel Lady, whom he seem'd to watch or rather guard with as much diligence, as *Argus* did *Io*, or the mortify'd Ghost of some lately departed Usurer his musty baggs, but yet he durst not (as being forbid by his Mistress, and fearing to displease her) hang Garlands at her Posts so artificially woven with Enigmatical Flowers,[9] that she might there read his fervent affection. This and several other Love-tricks that the Youths of those times us'd, to accomplish their wishes, he was forc'd to forbear.

His Friends by this began to have small hopes of his Estate, or Legacies; for his not eating nor drinking any thing, made them suspect he was grown immortal. Amongst the rest of his acquaintance one *Paneutus*, a Yeoman ith' Country some ten miles of the City where our pining Lover now was, hearing of the deplorable condition his Friend lay in, and being himself a boon Companion, did not doubt, but if he could get him into the Countrey, he cou'd make him quit his humour. To effect which he wrote this Letter.

*Paneutus* to his *Cherestratus*

Sir,

Rather then suspect your wisdome, I must needs think, that the Lady which hath brought you into the sad condition I hear you are in, must needs be one of so divine a Beauty, that she would make *Cato*[10] in love with her, and convert the severest Woman-hater. However, I am so far Interess'd in you, as my second self, that knowing a Remedy, I could

---

[9] flowers used symbolically to carry a message.
[10] a strict moralist.

not but prescribe it you, which being follow'd will either make you happy with your Love, or without it. Your City Air will something obstruct the Cure, and hinder your Physick from working. If therefore you will accept of my House, you know you may command

*Paneutus*

This Letter in *Cherestratus's* absence arriv'd at his City House, who was just now gone, as his custome was, to take a view of his Lady's Lodgings, which he did so eagerly, that he had like to have paid for his gaping. For some of the Neighbours observing him how narrowly he ey'd the House, thinking he had some bad design, acquainted the old Gentlewoman, Mother to the young Lady; who could hardly be perswaded from carrying our Gallant before the Justice, to which her Daughter encourag'd her, which went to the very heart of *Cherestratus*, for she knew well enough though she seem'd ignorant of the cause. But the old Lady, having no witness to prove any thing, dismiss'd him, with a severe charge never to trouble her door again. What remains now to the desperate Lover, but to make away with himself, and fall a Sacrifice to her disdain? which certainly he had done, had not his hasty desire to visit *Myrtilla's* House made him forget to put on his Shash[11] that morning. A thousand miserable thoughts offer'd themselves to him in his way home, whither he was no sooner come, but throwing himself upon his Bed, he began to bewail his hard fortune, with tears and sighs. Scarce had he begun his Soliloquy, but his Servant came into the Room, and presented him with the Letter; which having read, and taking a turn or two in the Chamber, the reflecting on his Lady's incivilities made him resolve to accept his Friend's Offer. To which end setling his Houshold Affairs, he commands all things to be made ready for his next days intended Journey, which accordingly he took, wisely choosing rather to ride a mile about, then to come by *Myrtilla's* House, by which he should have passed; being safe come to his journey's end we will leave him with his merry Friend *Paneutus*, who entertain'd him with all the kindness imaginable, always endeavouring his diversion with some pastime, as Hawking, Hunting, and the like, and return to *Myrtilla*, whose Mother, you must know, knowing what care and caution is to be us'd over young Maids, made the Daughter grow weary of her Government, counting it too severe, as depriving her of those Pleasures that young Ladies would willingly accept of. For her Mother keeping a Dairy would often set her to make Butter and Cheese

11 sash.

for fear of the green Sickness,[12] which he knew how to cure as well as any Doctor in *Europe*, had her Mother been as willing as she, whereas she had rather have been reading of some brisk Romance, or Story of the strange Metamorphosis of a Maid into a Woman. Besides, her Mother began now to oppose *Hyleus*'s Visits, the only comfort her Daughter had, for she being a pretty while in her Teens, had the same desire as all her Contemporaries had, to mind nothing but the end for which they were made, which caus'd her, encourag'd by her Mothers rigour, to think on some way to obtain her desires, and free her self from the old Lady's Tyranny, which was very much encreas'd since the death of her Husband, to whose Education he left his Girl *Myrtilla*.

Long you may imagine she had not studied before she found out a Plot (for Women's Wits on such occasions are very quick, and for my part I believe that had not *Jupiter* quickly put in Execution his golden Project, *Danae* for all the Tower would have found the way to his Embraces:) well a Plot is now found, which was this, to venture her Maiden-head into *Hyleus*'s hands, rather then endure the slavery she was in. This she resolv'd to put in practice, and contrary to a Woman, kept constant too. But she saw no way of effecting it without making some body privy to it, and then she thought no one fitter then her maid *Circe*, a loving Girle, and welwisher to Gentlemen, for before she happen'd into her Mistresses Service, she waited on a Lady, and like the rest of that trade, very often chose before[13] her Mistress, otherwise she would not speak a good word for a Gallant. *Myrtilla's* Mother being call'd to a Womans Labour, she thought it a very fit time to communicate her Design to her Maid. Where upon coming down to look for *Circe* she found her in the Garden tumbling on a Camomile bed, lying on her back a Star-gazing, but seeing her young Mistress starting up she quickly quitted that posture, and ask'd her if she had any service to command her. Ah *Circe* (said she sighing) I have, could I but be assur'd of thy Secrecy. Of mine, Madam? (reply'd *Circe*) why, there be a great many Gallants in Town, would be Surety for me if need requir'd. Why, 'tis the only thing I am good for. Why then (said *Myrtilla* sitting down with her Maid) you must needs have observ'd how my Mother pryes into all my Actions, debarring me of all I take delight in. I have now thought how to mend this, would'st thou consent to aid and assist me. *Circe*, who now thought she should get an opportunity to be reveng'd on her old Mistress for making her rise so

[12] anemic disease of pubescent girls.
[13] tested him in bed first.

early, not admitting of her Sweet-hearts company, and hindring her from wearing her best Clothes, and going to Church a Sunday (for let me tell you Preaching is of very old standing) made all Protestations possible to give her Mistress a good opinion of her Secrecy, which *Myrtilla*, being put to a strait, soon believ'd, and ask'd her what she thought of running away with *Hyleus*, without her Mothers consent. To which *Circe* answered, I believe he is an honest Gentleman, and were it to me I should take his word; now all the difficulty will be to make him acquainted with the Design. For that too (crys *Myrtilla*) I've contriv'd, and now my Mother's out of the way thou shalt be the happy Messenger to inform my dear *Hyleus* of mine Intent. I am certain he will gladly embrace the opportunity, which I would never have given him, but that I'm confident his Honour will not let him stain mine. Mad *Circe* would have taken up her Mistress, but the short time she had, fearing her Mother's return, would not let *Myrtilla* admit of her fooling. Take here, said she, this Jewel (in which was neatly wrought in Diamonds) the Story of the Rape[14] of *Proserpine* by *Pluto*, (and you cannot imagine *Hyleus* so much a fool as not at first sight to understand the Hieroglyphick) which I have got wrought on purpose. Deliver it to him as a token of my Affection (dear Creature) and tell him I shall with impatience expect his coming to fetch me away at Night.

*Circe*, who was not a stranger to these Love Embassies, willingly apply'd her self to her Task immediately, took her Pattins[15] and away to *Hyleus*, who was not at home just when she came, but the Servants told her he would be presently. It was the Butlers fortune to see her first, who seeing her young and handsome, could not but offer the Civility of the Cellar. *Circe* was very willing to accept his offer, the weather being hot, and having come a good way, she took off her Liquor, that the Butler began to conceive some hopes from the effect of the Drink. But they were scarce acquainted, when *Hyleus* came in from Fishing, and presently *Circe* deliver'd her message very diligently, and if I am not very much mistaken, 'twas just thus: Sir, my Lady, Madam *Myrtilla*, by me acquaints you she hath hitherto endeavour'd to find out the means of rewarding your Affection and constancy, which you may assure your self had been done before this, but that the old Gentlewoman her Mother hath such an aversion to any thing that she hath an inclination for, and seeing there is no way to quit scores with you but by running away, she doth this night

14 abduction.
15 footgear (maybe overshoes or sandals for protection).

intend to make her self happy with your good company, and for a token of her Love she hath sent you this Jewel, and desires you not to fail waiting for her with a Horse, at her Mother's door, where you may privately carry away your own *Myrtilla*.

This unexpected News was extreamly surprising to *Hyleus*, who before was much fretted with the sport he but just now came from, for his ill success in it. And is it so then, ye kind Deities (cry'd he out) that my *Myrtilla* will thus freely put her self into my hands. I should never deserve any success in my Love, should I neglect this happiness. Nor am I one of those foolish foppish Lovers, who having lay'd siege to a Ladies Affections, then begin to throw off all respect, when she begins to throw off all her cruelty, and when she is coming to answer their expectations. Then turning to *Circe*, Assure the divine *Myrtilla* from me, I will not fail to expect her, and am only sorry that she order'd nothing more difficult, that she might see my Love in daring to compass it; take this (continu'd he giving her a Piece,[16] and then kissing her) and carry this Kiss to thy Mistress, and assure her again I will not fail.

With this Answer departed *Circe*, who was got home before she was aware, who was extreamly taken with *Hyleus*, and thinking on the Token she had for *Myrtilla*, whom she now began to envy, and long as much for the forbidden fruit as her Mistress; coming to *Myrtilla*, she told her the good success of her Message, and how effectually it had wrought upon the Heart of *Hyleus*, who would not fail two hours after Sun-set; this done she enter'd on the not unpleasant Panegyrick of the expected Gentleman. The ill connection[17] of it, as all other Chambermaids discourses, makes me I can't remember it, only this I am sure was in it, that he was a fine proper Man, handsom Leg'd, and she'd warrant as good a Woman's Man as any in the Shire. But the old Lady coming home made her unwillingly break off her Discourse.

*Hyleus* by this time had got all things in readiness for his Love-adventure, and setting out with two Servants he had towards the City, which was about three miles from his House, his great desire of the Prey made him there something of the soonest, which he had not been, but that *Myrtilla* and *Circe* were at difference; for her Mistress could not perswade her to stay behind, if she went, although she urg'd the unlikeliness of their Escape together; however she would not be contented till she had promis'd to send one of *Hyleus*'s Servants for her.

[16] i.e., of money.
[17] incoherence.

Now we are forc'd to a small digression, to make you acquainted that the Countrey and all it's Sports, with all the perswasions of his Friend *Paneutus*, could not make *Cherestratus* leave off thinking on his Mistress, and it so happen'd that his Friend being engag'd in some Business, our melancholy Lover being left to himself, who was now taking a turn in the Garden, began to recollect his former Affection, one while chiding himself for spending so long a time in a vain pursuit; another while angry with himself for leaving off now, when he was so far engag'd, and then a few musty Apothegms got in his Head, *viz.* Maids say No, and take it, *&c.* he resolves to renew the Onset, for which he could not have met with a convenienter time, *Paneutus* being out of the way, for had he been at home, he could not have been brought to have parted with *Cherestratus*, whose company he took very much delight in: This being resolv'd on, he marched to the Stable, and charges the Groom immediately to make ready his Gelding, under pretence of breathing him that Evening, and indeed so he did, for in half an hour and two minutes, he reach'd the door of his dearly belov'd *Myrtilla*.

*Hyleus*, you must know, thinking he had been too soon, had taken a turn down to view the Castle, thinking immediately to come back, and indeed it was not long e're he did, but however this is the critical minute, when out came *Myrtilla* in a riding Dress, making signs of dispatch to *Cherestratus*, who was staring on the Windows as he us'd to do, not dreaming what good luck was approaching him; Make hast, make hast my Dear (cryes the kind Lady) my Mother else will be here immediately. Our Gallant could scarce believe his Eyes or Ears, and thought certainly he was a dreaming, for he could never hope for such a happiness as to have his cruel Lady submit her self to him; but he now began to smell out the Plot, and without more adoe helpt the Lady up, who had not as yet discern'd the mistake. Having got his rich Prize behind him, he thought it not safe to tarry there long, wherefore spurring on his free Beast, away he rides, and met with no obstacle, for the City gates were kept open for *Hyleus*, by the appointment of the Servants, who had brib'd the Watch-men (for you may assure your self in *Comus*'s City, they keep very good Hours, although the Citizens are commonly scandaliz'd for Revelling, or letting their Wives tarry up longer then themselves.)

*Hyleus* was now return'd back to *Myrtilla's* Door, to which he was no sooner come, but he heard all the House in an uproar; for it seems the old Lady had mist her Daughter, and began to ghess at the Business, for which she was schooling *Circe* most bitterly, who being in her riding

Clothes, expecting *Hyleus*'s man, could not possibly frame any thing like an Excuse, at which her Mistress was so enrag'd, she began to seek for something to chastice the poor Maid. *Circe* therefore seeing her scarce avoidable Doom, runs out pulling the door after her, which hinder'd her Executioners pursuit. *Hyleus* who had been all this while in an Agony for his Lady, to think what would become of her, seeing *Circe* escaping out so boldly, and taking her for *Myrtilla*, lights strait off his Horse to help her up, which done, away he rides. He was no sooner got through the City Gate, but his Servants that accompany'd him thither, came out to congratulate his good fortune; he was so overjoy'd with his Booty, he could scarce find time to thank them, making homewards with all the speed imaginable. Whither he was scarce come, when by his order three Maids met them strowing Flowers all the way home, while others there were busied in providing the Cake and Sack-Posset;[18] at the Gate stood a proper Gentleman Usher to take down the Lady, Madam Chamber-maid; that done, off leaps *Hyleus* to salute her, and bid her welcome to her Own.

And now at last it was that the miserable man perceiv'd his Errour, but he was wonderfully surpriz'd to see *Circe*, where he expected *Myrtilla ;* he began now to consider how improbable it was, that she should give her self up to him so easily, and now concludes it was a Plot of *Circe's*, to whom he addresses himself to be clear'd of the doubt. And is it thus, base Slut, thou hast abus'd me, and thy Mistress? was it for your embraces I have taken all this pains and care? were the numerous Pages about Town, that us'd to accompany their Masters to visit my dear *Myrtilla*, grown so scarce, that I must be made a Property? I wonder thy impudence could ever harbour such a thought, so prejudicious to thy Lady, as to think I was reserv'd for thy tooth; how cam'st thou by this Jewel, which I am confident belong'd once to *Myrtilla* ? For none sure would buy thy favour at the vast expence of so rich a Diamond? He would have gone on in his tedious Harangue, but being always kind hearted to Females, he began to consider how unmanly it was to quarrel with a Woman, and for a fault Love had made her commit. However, his passion proceeded so far that he call'd her Whore: Poor *Circe*, who all this while stood shivering for fear (though it seem'd to her a pleasant pain, being in the company of her sweet *Hyleus*) was something mov'd at the last word, which made a deeper impression on her mind, then all had past before (for though I

[18] a stimulating wedding-drink.

will not swear for her, yet I think she was honest)[19] she makes him this Answer. My kindness in helping young Gentlemen in Addresses to my Lady, could never deserve that name. No, no, Sir, you have here no Whore, nor one that had any designs upon you, but what were innocent and devoted to the Service of my young Mistress. I will not indeed so far bely my Conscience, as to deny I lov'd you; but I was so far from promoting my love, that I quite despair'd of it; and therefore resolv'd to be happy in the next degree, namely, in mediating with you for my Mistress. The desire of following her hath thus betray'd me to your censure. And is *Myrtilla* gone before, then? said *Hyleus;* Yes Sir, answered *Circe*, she is, and had not your Passion transported you, you might e're this have been in a Capacity of recovering my Lady, who cannot be gone far.

*Circe's* Answer you'l say was very excusable, and indeed *Hyleus* could not but approve of it, although anger for his ravish'd Mistress would not let him at present acknowledge it. For he immediately commanded his Horses to be brought out of the Stable again; but hold, I think they were not yet put in, and with his other Fellow Travellers like a Knight Errant, resolves to go to rescue the Lady, leaving poor *Circe* again to the mercy of the Butler, who was now resolv'd to try the utmost strength of his strong Beer Philter on the weak Virgin. But she, contrary to his expectation, seem'd more coy, as having more hopes than ever of marrying *Hyleus*, in case her Mistress could not be found out. But we must be found as uncivil as *Hyleus*, and leave her to the Butlers managing, and mad he to his Progress, and return to *Cherestratus:*

Who by this being ten miles out of Town, was impatient to see and salute his sweet Prey, whose Maiden-modesty not suffering her to speak first, very much wonder'd at her silent Lover. They were scarce gone a quarter of a mile further; but the transparent Rays of the bright Queen of Night (a rare expression for Moon shine, this same) made discovery of a delicate pleasant Meadow, which lay just by the Road-side. *Cherestratus* could not for his life pass by this opportunity, he light and gently taking *Myrtilla* off the Horse, began the amorous Prologue with a Kiss. That done, Madam, said he, how happy have you made the late miserable *Cherestratus!* At the name of *Cherestratus*, *Myrtilla* started, and looking upon him seriously, knew him to be the person nam'd. The poor Lady was so extreamly troubled at this unexpected Accident, that she swouned

[19] chaste.

away in *Cherestratus*'s Arms, and truly me thinks it was ominous, for ever since that night the Lady was troubled with Qualms. But I fear I shall be censur'd for playing thus with a Gentlewomans misfortunes; all I have to excuse it is, that knowing the fifth Act of the Play and how they came off, it is pardonable to be merry, and laugh before as she did after sufficiently.

*Cherestratus* you may imagine was in a sweet kind of taking to think that he had lost his Mistress before he had her (which was true enough, if you can make it out); besides a Constable and a grave ignorant Jury came in his head, for some might think he had kill'd her, besides the plaguy fear of being wrote against, like *Philaster*[20] for being the death of his pretty Miss. All this consider'd, the poor man was extreamly put to his shifts, what to do. And though men say our wits are best in cases of necessity, he at present could not think of a better Remedy, then *Hudibras*'s,[21] so that he was forc'd to give her a gentle twinge oth' Nose, for Water in that place there was none, nor any thing else that might conduce to the recovering of a Lady out of that sad condition. *Myrtilla* by this was something come again to her self, and gave *Cherestratus* some small hopes of her, to whom in a lamentable tone she said, By what Magick, Villain, hast thou depriv'd me of the company of my dear *Hyleus*? who were he but present, would teach you better manners, then to lie Evesdropping thus, to betray the secrets of miserable Lovers. But alas, why blame I you? It was my own rashness, for which I am justly punish'd, since I could not distinguish betwixt the Worthy *Hyleus* and the base *Cherestratus*. Our Gallant, that thought himself well enough to pass, as never having a Rupture, or any thing else that might reduce him to the using the Wedding Ring the wrong way, in case Art had conquer'd Nature, could not endure to hear *Myrtilla* preferr *Hyleus* so much before him, and was going to vindicate himself when thus she continued. O my unhappy Fate! have I for this prov'd disobedient, and left my old Mother? to fall into the hands of him I so much hated, who is in pretence only a Lover? if it be not so as I say, prove your Affection, and redeem your fault by killing the miserable *Myrtilla*.

Faintly he thought she spoke, for all the while—stay, I think there was no smile in the case; however *Cherestratus* who came *communi Animantium appetitu*,[22] did not care to satisfie his Lady in that point, and had rather

---

[20] hero of Beaumont and Fletcher's play of the same name.

[21] eponymic hero of Butler's burlesque poem.

[22] with the appetite common to living beings (i.e., sexual desire).

get the King a Souldier, then lose him a Subject, for Ladies do good Service. No, Madam, said he, that were to injure you, and rob my self of the greatest happiness in the world. Your misfortunes are not such as to make you boldly wish for Death, that Bug-Bear to all Ladies. 'Tis time enough for it yet, you have no reason to think on't, being in the hands of a Person, of whose incivility you never yet had any proof. I cannot imagine you are really angry, when if you are pleas'd to remember I took you up in a ready Dress for the March, as if you as well as Heaven were willing to make me happy. For doubtless, Madam, it was not by meer chance I left my Friend in the Countrey at so unseasonable time of Night to come and visit your door, where unlookt for, my good Genious had prepar'd me a sight of my divine *Myrtilla*. No, no, the Powers above, whose will we ought not to resist, ordain'd this, to see how happy they could make a mortal Man by the presence of a person so nigh their Divinities as your incomparable self. This done, he put his Handkerchief to his Eyes, and us'd such comforting expressions to the Lady, that they dissipated her clouds of Sorrows. Her Eyes shot such lustre, that the Moon with all the noise of Brass Pots and Kettles that could be rung out fear'd an Eclipse. To be short, she seem'd so well satisfy'd, that *Cherestratus* tying his Horse to a Tree, did not much offend her, in desiring her to repose her self on a neighbouring Bank. They were no sooner sat down, but our Gallant began before his Mistress to admire the works of Nature in that pleasant place, in whose commendations he insisted so far, that soon after he forc'd her to yield to some Arguments he brought. He show'd her all the pretty Sceletons, the fair Flowers I mean, that once were Bodies of young Men and Ladies, and turn'd into that fading condition for denying their Admirers some small Curtesie or other. He might have gone on longer, for seriously the place was so pleasant that it is impossible to imagine any thing beyond it in natural Bravery. *Adonis*'s Garden,[23] and whatever Antiquity hath made famous for Pleasures, could not reach it. I would have strove for a little Poetry, but that at present I am not in the Humour, but if I make a modern Poet of ours describe it better than perhaps I should have done, I suppose 'tis all one.

> *Nature is wanton here, and the high way*
> *Seem'd to be private, though it open lay,*
> *As if some swelling Lawyer for his health,*

[23] perhaps a reference to the Garden of Adonis in Spenser's *Fairie Queene* (Book III, canto vi).

*Or frantick Usurer to tame his wealth,*
*Had chosen out ten miles — — to try*
*Two great effects of Art and Industry.*

*The ground they trod, was Meadow fertile land,*
*New trim'd and levell'd by the Mowers hand,*
*Above it grew a Rock, rude, steep and high,*
*Which claims a kind of Reverence from the Eye,*
*Betwixt 'em both there glides a lovely stream*
*Not loud but swift. Meander was a Theam*
*Crooked and rough, but had the Poets seen*
*Strait and even (for I have forgot the name) it had immortal been.*
*This side the open Plain admits the Sun,*
*To half the River then did Silver run:*
*The other half ran clouds, where the curl'd Wood*
*With his exalted head threatned the flood,* &c.

They had not been in this delightful Scene long, but *Cherestratus* found his Lady's mind to sympathize with the pleasantness of the place, which so reviv'd on a sudden her drooping Spirits, that she seem'd so brisk, airy and gay, as gave our Gallant good hopes that the thoughts of *Hyleus* were remov'd, and that she had no small Affection for him, who was now musing how to compass the great design, for the obtaining which he thought nothing more efficacious, then the disparagement of *Hyleus*, his Rival. Madam, cries he, you cannot now but be satisfied how noble all my actions have been to you, far beyond *Hyleus*'s, by whose unpardonable neglect I have now the happiness of seeing my dear *Myrtilla*. Lovers, Lady, are seldome slow when invited by their Mistresses, which makes me confident *Hyleus* had only an intent to abuse and disgrace you, who had not the hours above sent me to that happy Station, your door, had been expos'd to the censure of the Neighbours, besides the Anger you might have incurr'd from the old Gentlewoman your Mother. Ungrateful man, that could disesteem so great an obligation!

These words so wrought upon her, that she became more obliging than before, so that she very complaisantly render'd thanks to her Lover for his true Affection, and vow'd she would never have an esteem for his Rival, which was all the recompense she could make him. No, Madam, (reply'd *Cherestratus*) if I have deserv'd any thing of you, you may soon think of a better way of rewarding your Lover; who for all those favours he saw you daily heap on the unworthy *Hyleus*, could not diminish his Affections to you, which must now be rewarded, or he will sacrifice his miserable life before you. Then taking out a true *Bilbo* blade,[24] that had never kill'd a man yet, and therefore wanted seasoning, he set it to his Breast, and desir'd his Sentence. The tender-hearted Lady that but just now desir'd to die her self could not endure to see her Lover fall a Victim at her feet, and resolv'd to withstand manslaughter, said, Hold, Sir, your case is not so desperate, nor I hope your love for me so little, as to kill him I esteem, thy self I mean, my dear *Cherestratus*. And assure your self, that you or no man, shall be the Person that shall make me happy. Our young Gentleman could not have desir'd a more satisfactory Answer from his Lady, to whom (putting up his naked tool) he reply'd, Then, Madam, assure your self, you have bestow'd your favours on one that will study to deserve them, while the careless *Hyleus* shall die with envy at my good fortune: After the Peace thus concluded between both parties, there pass'd many amorous Dialogues, all which were begun and ended with a sweet Kiss.

*Myrtilla*, you must understand, whether entic'd by his pretty discourse, or mov'd with an equal desire, seem'd extraordinary loving, so that *Cherestratus* could not but put forward, had he been less modest then he was. At my first view I was extreamly amaz'd, for, but that I had seen the Moon with all her twinkling Attendance, I should have sworn I saw the Lady *Aurora* in one of her richest Vermilion Sutes. For it seems something that *Cherestratus* had said in her Ear, had dy'd her Cheeks with a Rosie blush. I expected now she should have rattled[25] him soundly, but it seems she was not so angry as I took her for: They continued their Discourse for some time, which though I could not hear, I soon perceiv'd it was no Treason they spoke; for soon after I saw *Myrtilla* with small reluctancy receive a Green Gown[26] from her lusty Lover, who was now preparing to make his Lady amends to the utmost of his power for her former Favours. We will leave 'em in mutual Embraces, and instead of an *Epithalamium* (for I am loth to be idle) make an Apology for their not staying the Parson's leisure. To which these grave Reasons induce them.

First, Here the Bride-groom is sure next morning to have all his Ribbons upon his Breeches.

[24] originally a fine sword noted for its excellent temper, but since come to mean a bully or swashbuckler.
[25] scolded at, railed at.
[26] symbol of loss of virginity.

Secondly, The Bride, or the Woman lay with, will not be at a loss to find her Stockings, which at Ceremonious Weddings are thrown over her Head, nor will her Pins be lost to dress her with.

Thirdly, While they lie on the Grass, they need not fear cutting the Bed-cords,[27] or sowing the Sheets together.

Fourthly, There can be no Bell under their Bed, unless a natural Blew-bell.

Fifthly, The Lady need not be put to the blush the next morning by a company of her Chronies with asking her how she does, and how she likes it.

Sixthly and lastly, No troublesome crowd of Fidlers betimes in the morning, to spoil better sport with their miserable scraping. For these and some other Reasons, our Lovers may deserve your pardon, which I question not but you will give them without petitioning for.

*Cherestratus* now began to fail in his vigour, and was sounding a Reatreat in a whole Volly of Kisses, which she return'd very willingly, as being now conscious of the Obligation she had to him. And then they setled themselves for a gentle Repose, which they did in so sweet a posture, she infolding his Neck in her delicate Arms, that they seem'd like *Cynthia* and her belov'd *Endymion*, whose soft Embraces she so oft courted. They had not lain long thus, but a sweet Sleep seiz'd them both, in which they dream'd over again what they had just now been the real partakers of. Where we will leave them to their natural Rest, and return to *Hyleus* and his three Companions, who just now unfortunately arriv'd at this Scene of Love, whither they were no sooner arriv'd, but *Hyleus* spy'd out the Pair of Lovers in that loving Condition, that I describ'd them in.

*Hyleus* was enrag'd to see his *Myrtilla* as it were with her own Consent given up to another. He immediately draws his Rapier, and swears most damnably that he will be the death of *Cherestratus*, as in effect he had, but that those who accompany'd him, having a kindness for his happy Rival, perswaded him to desist from his purpose, at least they told him he ought to stay till he wak'd, for then he might force him nobly either to resign up his Life, or his Mistress, supposing he had forc'd her against her Will (as the loving posture they were in, was proof enough to the contrary); for otherwise, it was not worth the while. Well, with much adoe, *Hyleus* was at last perswaded to stay till he wak'd, but then he swore to be reveng'd on him.

---

[27] The bed cords supported the mattress; to cut them almost through was a prank played on newlyweds.

Hereupon for this purpose lighting off their Horses, they all sat down by our sleeping Lovers. It had been you'l say, a great temptation to his fellow Travellers to lie by so handsome a Lady, but being weary with accompanying their Master in his wilde pursuit, they thus seem'd with him rather to have a desire to sleep, than any thing else; they strove indeed a great while against the drowsie Distemper, but *Morpheus*[28] at last arrested them, in the King's name, and charg'd them to keep the Peace, which they had broken with their loud Jangling.

They had not been long under the Leaden Scepter'd Gentleman's hands, but the two Lovers awak'd very much troubled to see any Company there, but much more when they knew them to be *Hyleus* and his men. *Cherestratus* bid his *Myrtilla* not be affraid, but prepare for her Journey, by which he doubted not, but they should escape the Enemy, which *Myrtilla* as much now endeavour'd to avoid, as not long before she coveted the Sight of *Hyleus*. *Cherestratus* that had before learn'd of *Myrtilla*, that *Hyleus* had receiv'd a rich Diamond of her, which was to be worn in his Hat, was unwilling to leave that Token of his Ladies former Affection behind him, wherefore he advanc'd towards *Hyleus*, and did without any difficulty find out the Jewel by the extream lustre of it. Having got this, he and *Myrtilla* march with full speed together towards his Friend's House, with whom he had lodg'd being invited, the honest trusty Soul *Paneutus*.

They had not been long gone, but *Hyleus* and his men awake, and find the Pair of Lovers gone, to the satisfaction of all but *Hyleus*, who was so much troubled at their escape, that they had much adoe to keep him from laying violent hands on himself, but his rage was very much encreas'd when he saw the Jewel was gone too, and now he resolves to pursue *Cherestratus*, not as a Rival only, but as a profest Enemy. The Servants did all they could to pacifie their furious Master, telling him he ought not to be so incens'd against *Cherestratus*, since he had done nothing but what a Lover in the like case would have done, and that doubtless it was not his fault, but *Myrtilla* either by her free consent, or the treachery of *Circe*, that lov'd him her self, had deliver'd her up to him. And that since 'twas so, he ought not to despise the innocent flames of pretty *Circe*, who excepting her Birth, seem'd altogether as worthy his Bed, as the scornful, faithless *Myrtilla*. What though she sent that Diamond, yet *Circe* brought it, by whom he might reckon it given too, seeing there was no Remedy left, and there appear'd not the least hopes of overtaking the happy couple.

[28] the god of sleep.

*Hyleus*'s passion was now pretty well over, when he took Horse for Home, intending to follow his Servants Counsel, and make poor *Circe* happy, who all this while was crying, and deploring her condition. As soon as he came in, he call'd for her, and with a Kiss told her, his Intention was to marry her that Night, telling her the mad Adventures of his rash Journey. *Circe* you may easily imagine, was very well pleas'd to hear her Mistress had sped so well, and that she was now to enjoy her belov'd *Hyleus. Hyleus* immediately sent for the man in Black,[29] and gave order for making ready that very Night for the Wedding, which was done with all speed, and they two huddled to Bed together, for better for worse, where I suppose they had as much satisfaction of one another, as *Cherestratus* and *Myrtilla* did before, besides the advantage they had of a softer Bed.

The next day early, *Hyleus* sent to bespeak the Wedding Dinner five miles off, where also *Cherestratus* with his Lady were that day to be merry together; and as good luck would have it, they were in the next Room to one another, though neither Company knew of it, till about Dinner time. *Myrtilla* hearing *Hyleus*'s Voice in the next Room, swouned, *Cherestratus* and all his Company wonder'd at the suddeness of her sickness, and suspected there was something in it more then ordinary; and as soon as she came to her self again, she told them the Reason, *viz.* That she heard *Hyleus*, and fear'd lest he should know of *Cherestratus*, and there might some mischief be done. They cheer'd her up, and told her there was no fear of any such thing, especially in that place. While they were comforting *Myrtilla*, a Gentleman that was equally a Friend to both of them, ran to tell *Hyleus*, having first engag'd him to be civil, since things could not be alter'd. *Hyleus* was at first surprized, but then one glance of *Circe's* dispell'd his anger, and he was resolv'd to joyn Companies, which he presently did, to the satisfaction of both Parties. Where I'le leave them drinking their Ladies Healths, besides some odd Brushers[30] to the little Country Gentleman, or *Myrtilla's Hans en Kelder.*[31]

FINIS

[29] parson.
[30] exceedingly full glasses of wine.
[31] the baby she was already carrying.

# THE ART OF CUCKOLDOM

## (1697)

# THE
# Art of Cuckoldom:
## OR, THE
# INTRIGUES
## OF THE
# City-Wives.

❀❀❀❀
❀❀❀❀

*LONDON:*
**Printed in the Year, 1697.**

The Art of Cuckoldom, or, The Intrigues of the City-Wives, *is an anonymous collection of four short stories that are, as the subtitle suggests, strongly middle-class in outlook, which is to say that they are anything but romantic in their treatment of the relationship between men and women. The focus is not on the delicious passages of love leading up to marriage but on the rather frank acceptance of the necessary economic basis of marriage and the resultant consequences, infidelity being presented as the absolute necessity for making a marriage between a young wife and an old husband (a situation presumably of frequent occurrence in a class without inherited wealth) a going concern. Adultery then becomes, ironically enough, the refuge of true love.*

*In three of the four stories in the book the young wife–old husband marriage is the groundwork of the story (older men have money and a girl is a fool to marry for love and starve). The fourth story has a stupid husband and a wife who prizes wit in a man above all things. Infidelity is the theme in all four and only one of them (the third) has anything like what might be called an acceptable moral, and even there it sounds more like lip-service than a genuine desire to edify. In all four stories the plot is organized in the same general way : the unsatisfied wife seeks extra-marital solace and finds it. The complications arise in getting the lover admitted to the house and to her bed, and in preventing discovery when the husband returns unexpectedly or becomes too suspicious or when some unforeseen contretemps takes place. A certain degree of ingenuity is displayed in contriving excuses and in hiding lovers, a characteristic indeed of the whole genre of the fabliau no matter when composed or by whom. And the usual fabliau point is made here too : nothing can prevent a determined wife from outwitting her spouse when she really sets her mind to it.*

*The story which follows is the first of the collection ; it has no name, being called simply "Intriegue I." The second and fourth stories are much like this one in length and in plan ; in the second, for instance, the lover is hidden in a grandfather clock, but his being in it unfortunately stops the mechanism and when the old husband attempts to wind it discovery is prevented only by the lover's knocking the clock over on the old man and escaping during the ensuing confusion. The third story, over twice as long as any of the others, has a much more complicated plot involving two pairs of lovers and a longer duration of time. Nevertheless, the basic situation during most of the tale revolves around the deception of an old husband by his young wife and her lover, the situation being moralized to the extent of containing the comment that only those who love innocently can hope for blessings on their love.*

*The text which follows is based on the copy of the book in the Henry E. Huntington Library.*

## The Art of Cuckoldom

### Intriegue I

There was a very pretty young Virgin Gentlewoman, whose whole Patrimony was her Face, together with a very handsome competency of Wit, the bounty of Nature on one part, and a genteel Education bestow'd her by her Friends on the other. For to tell Truth, Providence had not been over generous in any other worldly Capacity: Not but that so much Beauty deserved a fair and ample Fortune, suitable to her other Accomplishments, and indeed she was Born to such a one, had not the over profuseness of a prodigal Parent (her Fathers sower Grapes) imbitter'd her unlucky Circumstances, and thereby intail'd some Frowns in the World upon her, her forementioned Education being indeed the whole Portion she had left her.

This young Lady a little turn'd of Sixteen, (an Age that generally furnishes the fair Sex with some little speculative Knowledge into the great Work of their Creation, the End they were Born for,) felt an extraordinary Passion for a young Gentleman on this side Twenty, a very zealous Adorer of hers; and one that (not to render the conquer'd Virgin a Prize too easie) had fairly Sieged her Heart, and had as nobly won it.

But for another Persecution of Fortune, this Gentleman a younger, or rather youngest Brother, of not an over-Rich, though otherwise Honourable Family, had as little to trust to, or expect from the unkind World as his Mistress. For as she had only her Eyes and Charms to raise her Fortunes in it, so he had little else but his Sword to raise his; a Commission abroad, or perhaps some Court-favour at home, being indeed the whole Foundation of his Hopes.

These unhappy Obstacles to their Felicity being duly considered, especially on the Ladies side, (not but she lov'd him to a hight, even to run all Hazards for his sake;) she durst not, or rather would not Marry him, out of a principle of pure Affection; as well remembring an old Proverb, That *when Poverty comes in at the Door, Love creeps out at the Window;* insomuch that, that only Check, *viz.* Her loving him too well to run the risque of loving him less, restrain'd her Inclinations from so dangerous a push as Matrimony.

All Things being thus duly weigh'd, she took an occasion one day with her kind Arms round his Neck, and a dropping Pearl in her Eye, to burst out into an extravagant Complaint against the cruelty of their Stars, that such true Love as theirs should be excluded from the Bed of Honour,

*Marriage:* That she was intirely his own, her Love, her Life, and what not. However, she cou'd no ways consent to a long miserable Life, (for that wou'd be their Nuptial Portion) only for a few short liv'd Bridal Joys—with infinite more tender Expressions upon this Melancholy Subject.

The young Lover who in all his Passion for so darling a Mistress, was still Master of some Reason also, cou'd not but acquiesce in the Justice of her Complaints and the mutual Resentments of both their Misfortunes, under this cruel Bar to their Felicities.

Some little Time after it happen'd that a very eminent Merchant in *Lime-street*, of the reverend Age of Fifty Eight, was Captivated with this young Fair One; a Man of a true City Complexion, Naturally very Jealous, and as Naturally Covetous, being a Person of a very low Extract, though otherwise blest with the extraordinary Smiles of the World, having heaped together more than double an Aldermans Estate.

This superannuated *Inamorato*, being now entred into the Rivals List to our young Gallant, makes his bold and open Addresses to the fair *Phillis* (let that pass for her Name) For though the disparity of their Age might have rendred him a more modest Intruder, Nevertheless, as Wealth never wants Front, the consideration of that single Advantage so amply atoned for all other Imperfections, that well knowing his Endowments that way, he accosted her with all the Courage of an Heroick Lover.

This new Victory was no sooner obtain'd, but her first *Io pean*[1] was sounded in her young Gallants Ears: She immediately run to her dear *Strephon* (for so we'll call him) big with the Triumph of so doughty a Conquest as her new *Lime-street* Captive. As formidable a Rival as his City Figure might make him, nevertheless, so antiquated a Pretender to so young a Bed-fellow, created no great Jealousies on the young *Strephon*'s Side. But to shorten this heaviest part of our History, the young Lovers in an Amorous Consult between 'em, come to this Resolve, *viz.* That the Man of Gold shall carry the Dame: She shall Marry our grave Citizen, and her contented *Strephon* wear the Willow. However, not to make a too mortifying Divorce between the young Lovers, 'tis agreed, that the Virgin Prize, *viz.* The First-Fruits of Love shall be *Strephon*'s, and the old Gentleman shall only be admitted Tenant to her Reversion. In short, she'll condescend to make a City Husband of one, and a Court Friend of the other; the good old Gentleman, the titular Lord of the Soyl, like old

[1] O Apollo! (a cry of triumph).

*Jupiter*, shall shower *Gold* into her *Danae*'s Lap, and *Strephon* shower *Love*.

Accordingly all reasonable Advances are made on her side, to her Small-Ware Merchant, her *Lime-street* humble Servant. His Addresses are favourably heard, his Suit received, and the Preliminaries soon settled for the great, and now easy, Work of Consummation; easy indeed, for the happy *Strephon* has opened the Blooming-Rose, done his aged Rival that Favour, that the Bridal Night Drudgery is not like to be too hard a tug for his Fifty eight. Thus whilst all three Parties are rapt up in equal Felicities, the young Wantons in their substantial Joys, and the old Fondling in his imaginary *Paradice*, the nuptial Day and the bridal Robes are all fixt and prepared: Our *Strephon* and *Phillis* having first Sworn an inviolable Correspondence, the Golden *Fleece* to be at his faithful Service, as often as 'tis possible to lull the watchful *Dragon* to give 'em the Opportunity.

To pass over the matrimonial Ceremony; for indeed 'tis little else but Ceremony; at least on the feminine side: After she has received all the congratulary Compliments from the most eminent City Matrons, and took her Seat of Honour amongst them, suitable to the Dignity of the fair Partner of Magistracy, the Bride of such an Honourable Metropolitan Member; After her first due provision of all Perquisites of State, Equipage, and Grandeur, equal to her Character; The next and indeed most important Study, is the performance of Covenants with her dear *Strephon*, for as to her Vows at Home, she left them at the Altar. Love is resolved to make strong Work here, whatever Cobweb Lawn[2] it makes there.

But now under her nuptial Yoke she sees a great part of her Hopes defeated; 'tis almost impossible for her to find that happy Minute of meeting her *Strephon*: For her doating City Sir Politick is so fond, or at least so cautious of such young Flesh, that he is never out of her Sight. 'Tis true, she keeps a Coach, but she can never go abroad in it, without his Luggage to load it: If she pretends to go to Church, he is in earnest with her there; and whatever Powers she prays to, he resolves she shall never be upon her Knees without him. If she pretends a Visit to any Relation of what Degree of Sex soever, 'tis a downright Affront to his Years and Person to be left behind her; so that she must either carry him along with her, wherever she goes; Or, plainly tell him, she is either ashamed of him, or has Designs upon him, which is neither consistent

[2] a very delicate kind of fabric.

with her Honour, nor the great Game she has to Play; for the Hope of a Rich Widowhood will not permit her to put any Slights upon him, lest it might endanger his Death-Bed good Graces, and a kind last Will and Testament. In fine, it was a full Month (which Lovers call an Age) before she could have one half Hour with her dear *Strephon*, and that very difficultly obtained.

What use was made of the short Minutes, the Reader may guess. But more particularly they laid this Plot together, that her Spark, being of a perfect Beau shape, fair Complexion'd, and as yet wholly Beardless, he should Dress himself in Womens Apparel, and by passing for a dear Country she-Cozen of hers (to whose admission it should be her Business to pave his way) he should be received into her House; and by Living under her Roof, have all the private Hours of stoln Delight, that their own Hearts could Wish. This Design so well laid was decreed for speedy Execution, the Lady equipping him with a fair Yellow-lined Purse (a small Token of her brighter Golden Favours in store) to furnish him with all the Feminine Accoutrements requisite, &c.

Accordingly, about Six Days after, by which time the young Spark had not only rig'd himself *Capapee*[3] for a *Virago*,[4] but also practised some necessary Graces in his Looking glass, more cleverly to carry on the Masque; and likewise his kind *Phillis* had rapt up her believing Spouse into wonderful expectations of a visiting Cozen of hers shortly look'd for in Town: With this preparation the bonny Lass makes her Entry into our Alderman's Roof, with all the welcome Reception imaginable. Her Lodging Apartment is immediately very Respectfully, and no less Prudently provided, being a large Room on the same Floor, only a Stair head between that and her new City Cozen's the Alderman's Bed-chamber. By this Domestick freedom how many riotous Joys were tasted, though no set Feasts of Love, but only so many running Banquets (a snap and away) may easily be imagined. However, as our *Phillis*'s whole Extasies were all bounded in her *Strephons* Embraces, it was a little shackle upon her Delights, to think that she could no ways furnish out more plentiful Revels, *viz.* A whole Nights Regale in those darling Arms. However, the two Lovers contriv'd a very pretty Stratagem to gain that Enjoyment. For which purpose one Evening by a small slight of Hand she conveyed a small quantity of Jallop[5] into the Alderman's Supper-broth, which Operating as soon as ever he came to Bed, the poor Man was forced

[3] from head to foot.     [4] a man-like maiden.
[5] a purgative (today spelled jalap).

to rise several Times in the Night, which unseemly mischance made him so ashamed, as well as surprized at the suddenness of the Indisposition, that with a kind of a Blush, to have so tender and Nice a Stomach as his young Brides offended by so unsavoury a Society, as his at present is; he desired her to make bold with her Cozens Bed for that Night, whilst his Servants sat up with him, and some learned Assistance was called from abroad to take care of him.

The poor young Lady with a great deal of Tenderness for him, and passionate concern at this sudden Irruption, was very hardly prest to desert him in this Condition, till his absolute Commands compelled her to withdraw; and accordingly, she trips over to her expecting *Strephon*, where we'll leave her to as little Sleep as her sick Man she left behind her, the operations of warm Love on this side affording as little time for Rest here, as the Jallop does there. 'Tis true she has the Misfortune now and then to hear some unmusical Gruntings and Grumblings, from the tother side of the Stairhead, a very melancholy Discord to her tender Ears, had not some sweeter Harmony in her *Strephons* Embraces a little softened those ungrateful sounds, together with the private Titillation of so successful an Intrigue.

All Matters thus go on rarely: This ravishing Night on the young Lovers side has eased a great many hideous Sighs and Longings, now all amply satisfied by this favourable occasion. In short, not a shadow of Suspicion disturbs their mutual Joys. Nay, not only the old Gentleman's, but likewise another younger and more penetrating Rival's Eyes are deluded by this Female Masque of the happy *Strephon*. For I had forgot to tell my Reader, that our *Phillis*'s Charms had captivated our Merchant's elder Prentice, a young Spark within Three Months out of his Time, and by Birth a Gentleman, a very accomplisht Youth; who to tell the Truth, from the first Day of his Masters Marriage, had not only entertained an extraordinary Veneration for his fair young Mistress, but likewise naturally imagining that such dry Bones as her old Husband, could not be over-extraordinary satisfactory to such young Veins, had one Day assumed the confidence to Breathe a few passionate Sighs to her, and to throw himself a perfect Adorer at her Feet. 'Tis true the Fair Offended gave him but a cold Answer, and perhaps repremanded him very severely for so bold an Attempt, against so much Virtue and Honour, as could not but be highly profaned by such insolent Language. However, this Repulse had not wholly dasht him but that he both continued his Devoirs, and perhaps not wholly despaired of a more smiling Beam, that might one Day shine a little warmer upon him; not at all doubting, but as louring[6] an Ascendent as her rigid Virtue yet held, that still she was Flesh and Blood, and that the present fond Hony-moon of her cold Fifty Eight, would not last always.

As prying a Hawks Eye as this more dangerous Critick might have upon her, yet still, as I said before, neither our young *Strephon*'s Behaviour or Deportment had any thing that in the least look'd like Masculine, so very artfully was the fair Imposture carried on.

One Afternoon a little time after, it fell out, that the young Lady was called to a City Matrons, an eminent Neighbours Labour. And as this particular occasion gave her the freedom of going abroad, unhaunted by her troublesome Persecutor, she whispered her dear *Strephon* in the Ear, that as in all likelyhood she should return pretty late in the Night, when the good Man would be asleep, so in Compliment to him, she was resolved at her return to slip to Bed to her dear Cozen, upon pretence that at so unseasonable an Hour, she was afraid she might hazard the Waking him, and so breaking his Rest.

The fair Cozen to make all due preparation for so dear a Bed-fellow took the occasion that Evening to pretend some small indisposition, and so went to Bed a little sooner than ordinary, with a design to have taken a short Sleep before hand, to be the better Fortified for those sprightlier waking Hours she should have occasion to melt in Raptures afterwards.

The young *Strephon* having thus bid good Night, it fell out that a young Girl a Neice of the old Gentleman's, that lived somewhere towards *Westminster*, a very honest poor Creature, whose whole Fortunes depended upon her rich Uncles gracious Favour, came to pay her Duty to her honourable Uncle and Aunt, the Aunt being at that time abroad, and consequently that part of her duteous Devoirs yet unpaid, the old Gentleman resolves she should stay all night, as being uncertain of her Aunts return. And not to make any Ceremony with making another Bed for her, by way of good Husbandry and saving that trouble, he resolved to make bold with his Wives Cozen's, who was just gone to Bed before, being withall charged that she should disturb the young Ladies Rest as little as possibly she could, because she was gone a little Indisposed to Bed.

The poor Innocent Girl, without any more Attendance than a Candle in her own Hand to light her up, accordingly prepares for Bed, where entring very softly, she finds the young Lady faln fast asleep, and therefore in Obedience to her Commission, the Bed being large, and the young Lady

6 frowning, forbidding (today spelled lowering).

lodged on the further side, she pulls off her Cloaths and puts out her Light, and creeps very silently into Bed, as cautious of Waking the sleeping Lady.

By this time the whole Family were all gone to Bed, excepting a small Domestick that waited below for the return of the Mistress from her Christian Visit abroad. The young *Westminster* Lass was no sooner in Bed, but, what by Virtue of a good Supper of somewhat better Fare than her own Commons at home, together with the Fatigue of a long Foot-walk from *Charing-cross* to *Lime-street*, was faln into a very sound Sleep. At this time the young *Strephon* waking, and his roving Arms being the first Member that moved, he felt a soft Bedfellow lodged by him; hereupon being not only Transported to find his dear *Phillis* so near him, not Dreaming a Mistake, but likewise hearing by her Breath, that she was faln asleep, notwithstanding his impatience for the unutterable Joys, however he was resolved he would not Wake her too rudely; and therefore first gently stealing his warm Hand into her Bosom, the soft Temptation soon grew so powerful, that he could not forbear rambling it a little farther still, to which her sound Sleep gave him all the free Accesses his most libertine Fancy could reach. These preliminary Blisses having now intirely fired him all over for more substantial Extasies, he could not forbear clasping her round in his Arms, when with those burning Kisses sealed to her Lips, and Embracing her so close, her Face happening to lye towards him, and not so much as the least Bar between the nearest touch of all her softest Charms; (for his own roving Hand before had removed and unveil'd all interposing Skreens) these too ardent Arms about her, and some other yet more surprizing pressure so very near her tenderest Virgin Treasury, the poor Girl was immediately startled out of her sleep, into that hideous Terror, that she presently shriek'd out, crying, *Help, Murder, Help. I am Betray'd, I am Ruin'd;* and so leap'd from him out of the Bed, the poor *Strephon*'s Amazement no ways hindering her flight (for the change of the Voice soon distinguish'd his fatal mistake, and put him into no small Disorder and Astonishment.) This uproar of the poor frighted Maiden alarm'd the whole House, insomuch that not only the Husband from his Bed, but likewise several of the Servants from theirs (particularly the Elder Prentice we spoke of, who run down from his Chamber above in his night Gown,) all bolted into the Room where the poor Girl, under little less Apprehension than downright Ravishment still continued her Outcry; when her Uncle asking her what was the Reason of all this noise, *Oh Sir*, says she, *you have put me to Bed to a Man, a filthy, lewd, wicked, lascivious, wild Man. Lord have Mercy upon us,* reply'd the old Gravity, *a Man! Yes Sir,* cryes the young thing, *this impudent pretended Neece of yours, is a* He *Devil in Petticoats, a meer* Tarquin,[7] *a downright Rampant Limb of* Lucifer.

Just in the height of all this dismal Outcry (the poor *Strephon* being little less than Thunderstruck, and having only time to leap out of the Bed, and skreen himself in a large Night Gown that lay upon the Table,) it happend that the gossiping Lady was just returned home too, and entred in the nick, full in the middle of the whole hideous Impeachment against her poor discover'd Sham-Neece, to her no little Mortification and Confusion. However with a little more Presence of Mind, and somewhat a larger Talent of Assurance than the poor mute *Strephon,* she fell very Magisterially upon this clamorous young Roarer, and askt her with what Impudence she durst talk at this wild rate, or what Bedlam Frenzy had possest her, to run on with all this Noise and Nonsense? *Nay Madam,* answered the Girl, *dont think to fright me out of my Reason; what I say is Truth: I say again, and again, 'tis a Man; and though I thank my Stars, I am a pure spotless Virgin; yet I am not so Ignorant at these years, but I have my feeling about me, and know what's what, Madam. And if I had not had Grace enough to cry out as I did, but been as willing as he, I might have been Ravish'd before this time. In short, if I understand a Spindle from a Wheel, or a Pestle from a Mortar, or any thing in this World; nay, if there be a Cock Sparrow in all the Hedges between High-Gate and Hamstead, or a Whoremaster between Aldgate and Westminster, I tell you once more, this impudent She Cozen of yours, is a downright He Rogue, Madam.*

Before the Lady cou'd make answer to this crying Charge against her dear *Strephon,* the old Gentleman took up the Alarm; *She Cozen! with a Pox,* cries he, *Ay, I am He-cozen'd and She-cozen'd too in the Devils Name; betwixt your Ladyship, and your Ladyship's Neece, I am sweetly brought to Bed, I thank you; I have nurst a Snake with a Sting in his Tail indeed. Yes, you Jezebel, with your Mr.* Horner[8] *in Petticoats, I have been finely Cornuted.*

Before the poor Lady cou'd speak in her Justification (as indeed it was but a very barren Subject) the poor Elder Prentice, who by this time had fully smelt the whole Intrigue, and saw his dear Mistress in this inextricable Plunge and Labyrinth, very generously fell down upon his

---

[7] the ravisher of Lucretia (called Lucrece a little later).

[8] the protagonist of Wycherley's *Country Wife* (1674) who pretends to be impotent to deceive husbands into trusting him with their wives.

Knees, beseeching Pardon both from Heaven and his Master, when his own Guilt and Confusion must unravel this whole Mystery of Iniquity, and unfold the whole Riddle that had occasion'd all this Alarm and Distraction: And hereupon with a great deal of Penitence and Shame, he very formally told them, That he himself was the true and only *Tarquin*, the intended Ravisher, that the young Woman had accused, and who had made all this wicked Assault upon her Virgin Innocence, and that by an unhappy, tho' no less guilty Mistake; for what through the Instigation of the Devil, and his own Brutal Lust, he had a long time conceived a Design upon the Chastity of his Mistress's fair and vertuous Cozen, and this Night intending to put his wicked Purposes in Execution, he had stolen down from his own Bed to surprize her in her sleep, and not knowing of this Stranger's being Lodged with her, through the darkness of the Night he had mistaken his Prey, and only through his Bestial violence, had been the whole and sole Author of all this Disturbance. And though at the young Gentlewoman's first Out-cry he had leap'd out of the Bed again, and stole back into his own Chamber; yet his own, now too accusing Conscience had made him return to confess his intended Villany, and implore all their Forgiveness. The old Man who had scarce Patience to hear out the Story, notwithstanding the satisfaction it gave him in clearing his dear Spouse's and Cozen's Innocence, nevertheless cou'd not forbear a great deal of very violent and opprobrious Language against his wicked Servant for this outragious Fault. But his good Lady, who by a private wink to her kind Deliverer, had partly acknowledged his witty and [generous]⁹ Ingenuity in this defence of her endanger'd Honour, very modestly reprimanded her Husband's too vehement Indignation. She told him, That truly she had as much, or more Reason to be angry than he, for her Virtue and Reputation lay at stake; not but her Cozen, if occasion had been, should have strain'd a Point of Virgin Modesty, even to a more ample Demonstration of her true Sex. But as Heaven had been pleased to clear the Innocent without any such unseemly proofs, and the Criminals true Penitence had made some part of an Expiation for his Fault, it was their Christian Duty to endeavour both to forget and forgive.

All Parties being thus fully convinced, and all Clouds intirely dissipated, the fair She-cozen was likewise graciously pleased to grant her Pardon to the penitent Offender, (for now we may restore her her feminine Epithite) declaring, That she was heartily sorry, that she should carry any of those fatal Charms in her Eyes, as could have power to provoke

⁹ original text reads "geneous."

any such lewd Attempts against her Virtue; not but had the young, too Violent, Gentleman addrest himself to her by any Modest and Honourable Tenders of Passion towards her, perhaps upon fair and virtuous Terms, she might not have been wholly insensible nor invincible.

All Things thus hush'd, the good old Man took his harmless and spotless Lady to his Embraces, and his *Westminster* Neece lay down again by her late Ravishers side, who took care to play the *Lucrece* not the *Tarquin*, the remainder of the Night.

The next Day our fair Guest, took an occasion to take her leave of the Family, in order to her pretended return into the Country, out of a Point of Virgin Honour, as not seemly for her to remain any longer under that Roof, and so near that Person by whom such Violence had been only offer'd to her.

Though her *Strephon*'s absence was highly regretted by his dear *Phillis*, yet she was forced to consent to it, as not willing to have so dangerous a Spy upon her Actions, as the Rival Prentice, who she was now satisfied was no longer a stranger to her whole Masquerade. However she comforted her self, that this dangerous Rival had not above two Months to serve, and then she might have fairer Liberty for her disguis'd *Strephon*'s safe return again to her Embraces.

No sooner was the false Cozen and true *Strephon* departed, but the poor blushing *Phillis*, out of a principle of Gratitude, took an opportunity to make some farther acknowledgments to the kind Prentice for her protected Honour in that unlucky Exigence. To which he reply'd, That truly as he had had the Fortune to relieve a Distressed Lady, he hoped her Goodness and Smiles (for he was so far mercenary) would be pleased to reward his Service: And now if he was so impudent a Beggar, as to ask a return of Love from her, however the boldness of such a Petitioner was so far excusable, that the niceties of Virtue cou'd be no Bar to his Ambition, and nothing but her Aversion, cou'd deny him that Bliss. To conclude, he prest the Subject so home, that notwithstanding her vow'd Fidelity to her dear *Strephon*, she cou'd not tell how to refuse him: She was Conscious to her self, that her Frailty was discovered, and (if for no other Reason) she ought to consult the preservation of her Honour, by hushing the Silence of the Discoverer, though at no less price than her last Favours; besides the Merit of the Service he did her, in sheilding both her self from inevitable Ruin, and her dear *Strephon* from eternal Exposure and Shame, demanded her kindest Retaliation; and therefore the Invasion of her *Strephon*'s Right was, at least in this Case, a venial Trespass.

Walter Pope

# THE MEMOIRES OF
# MONSIEUR DU VALL

(1670)

# THE
# MEMOIRES
OF
# Monſieur Du Vall:
CONTAINING THE
# HISTORY
OF HIS
# LIFE and DEATH.
Whereunto are Annexed

## His laſt Speech and Epitaph.

————————————————————*Si quis*
*Opprobriis dignos latraverit, integer ipſe,*
*Solventur riſu tabulæ.*————————
Horat.

*LONDON*,
Printed for *Henry Brome*, at the Gun near the
*Weſt-End* of St. *Pauls*, 1670.

*In the 1650's a hitherto minor sort of semi-fictional story became increas-*
*ingly important. The criminal biography, a genre sitting rather uncomfortably*
*in the area between true fiction and true biography, became of moment for*
*the first time. Though examples of this kind of narrative can be easily traced*
*back into the sixteenth century, the pamphlets connected with the deeds and*
*death of Captain James Hind, executed as a highwayman on September 24,*
*1652, mark the rise of the genre in the latter half of the century. The popularity*
*of such lives continued unabated into the eighteenth century, as witness the*
*great success of Gay's* Beggar's Opera *(1728) and the classic compilations of*
*Alexander Smith,* History of the Lives of the Most Noted Highwaymen
*(1714, reprinted 1926), Theophilus Lucas,* Memoires of the Lives . . . of
the Most Famous Gamesters and Celebrated Sharpers *(1714), and* The
Tyburn Chronicle *(1768).*

The Memoires of Monsieur Du Vall, *however, is a criminal biography*
*with a difference. The author, Dr. Walter Pope, a doctor of medicine and a*
*Fellow of the Royal Society who died in 1714, made use of the genre in a novel*
*and probably unique way—he turned his book into a satire in which he*
*inveighed against the fashionable over-valuation of all things French, and*
*particularly the hysterical worship of French men on the part of English*
*ladies. Perhaps too he was alarmed at the idolizing of highwaymen as*
*heroes, just as later writers felt alarm at what they thought was the dubious*
*morality of Gay's ballad opera. (The eighteenth-century reaction is nicely*
*exhibited in a short tale entitled* Thievery A-la-mode: or the Fatal
Encouragement, *1728, in which the author professes himself shocked that the*
*town prefers the "cant of Newgate" to the great examples drawn from heroes*
*of antiquity, such as Henry V and the Black Prince.) Though a modern*
*reader quickly discovers that the book was written tongue-in-cheek, Pope's*
*narrative was for a long while accepted as literal truth, and was the founda-*
*tion on which subsequent discussions of Du Vall, like that in the* Dictionary
of National Biography, *were based.*

*Whether the very few anecdotes that Pope gives about the career of his*
*subject really took place is impossible to say, but over and over he gives*
*warning that his book is not exactly what it seems to be. It is, indeed, a*
*parody of the genre it represents, and it tells us less about Du Vall than about*
*its author's own opinions. That Pope does not idolize Du Vall is clear right*
*along, but his real attitude is especially amusingly shown in his comment*
*about the gentlemanly qualities his protagonist displayed in the course of the*
*robbery on the heath during which he danced with the lady. Pope's own*
*feelings of outrage come out clearly in his description of the obsequies of his*

*highwayman, at the Tangier Tavern and later. Perhaps Pope's satirical bent is best displayed in the book's appendix, where he explains how his whole life has been blighted because in his younger years he had once dared to suggest in female society the proposition that an English gentleman is superior to a French lackey.*

*The text which follows is based on the copy of the 1670 edition in the Folger Shakespeare Library. An amusing and highly readable account of Du Vall and other highwaymen is to be found in Patrick Pringle,* Stand and Deliver: The Story of the Highwaymen (*London: Museum Press, 1951*).

## The Life and Death
## of Claude Du Vall

*Claude Du Vall* was born *Anno* 1643 at *Domfront* in *Normandy*, a place very Famous for the Excellency and Healthfulness of the Air, and for the production of *Mercurial wits:* at the time of his Birth (as we have since found by Rectification of his Nativity by Accidents) there was a Conjunction of *Venus* and *Mercury*, certain Presages of very good Fortune, but of a short Continuance. His Father was *Pierre du Vall*, a Miller, his Mother *Marguerite de la Roche*, a Taylors Daughter. I hear no hurt of his Parents, they lived in as much Reputation and Honesty, as their Conditions and Occupations would permit.

There are some that confidently averr he was born in *Smock-Ally* without *Bishopsgate;* that his Father was a Cook, and sold boyled Beef and Pottage: But this report is as false, as it is defamatory and malicious; and 'tis easie to disprove it several ways: I will only urge one Demonstrative Argument against it. If he had been born there he had been no *Frenchman*, but if he had not been a *Frenchman*, 'tis absolutely impossible he should have been so much beloved in his life, and lamented at his Death by the English Ladies.

His Father and Mother had not been long Married when *Marguerite* long'd for Pudding and mince-Pye, which the good man was fain to beg for her at an English Merchants in *Rouen:* which was a certain sign of his inclination to *England*. They were very merry at his Christning, and his Father without any grumbling paid also then the Fees for his Burial, which is an extraordinary custom at *Domfront*, not exercis'd anywhere else in all *France*, and of which I count my self obliged to give the Reader a particular account.

In the days of *Charles* the ninth of that name, the Curate of *Domfront* (for so the *French* name him whom we call Parson and Vicar) out of his own head began a strange innovation and oppression in that Parish; that is, he absolutely denyed to baptize any of their Children, if they would not at the same time pay him also the Funeral Fees; and, what was worse, he would give them no reason for this alteration, but only promised to enter Bond for himself and his successors, that hereafter all persons paying so at their Christning, should be buried *gratis:* What think ye the poor people did in this case? they did not pull his *Surplice* over his *ears*, nor *tear* his *Mass-Book*, nor throw *Crickets* at his *head;* no, they humbly desired him to alter his resolution, and amicably reason'd it with him; but he being a capricious fellow, gave them no other answer, but, What I have done, I have done: take your remedy where you can find it, 'tis not for men of my *Coat*, to give an account of my Actions to the *Laity*. Which was a surly and quarrelsome answer, and unbefitting a Priest. Yet this did not provoke his Parishioners to speak one ill word against his person or function, or to do any illegal Act. They only took the Regular way of complaining of him to his Ordinary, the Archbishop of *Rouen*. Upon summons he appears, the Archbishop takes him up roundly, tells him he deserves deprivation, if that can be proved which is objected against him, and askes him, What he has to say for himself? After his due reverence, he answers, that he acknowledges the fact, to save the time of examining witnesses, but desires his Grace to hear his reasons, and then do unto him as he shall see cause. I have been, saies he, Curate of this Parish these seven years; in that time I have one year with another baptized a hundred children, and buried not one. At first I rejoyced at my good fortune to be placed in so good an air: But looking into the Register Book I found for a hundred years back near the same number yearly baptiz'd, and not one above five year old buried. And, which did more amaze me, I find the number of the Communicants to be no greater now than they were then: this seem'd to me a great mystery, but upon further inquiry I found out the true cause of it, for all that are born at *Domfront* were hanged at *Rouen*. I did this to keep my Parishioners from hanging, incouraging them to die at home, the burial duties being already paid.

The Archbishop demanded of the Parishioners, Whether this was true or not? they answered, That too many of them came to that unlucky end at *Rouen*. Well then, said he, I approve of what the Curate has done, and will cause my Secretary in *Perpetuam rei memoriam* to make an Act of it; which Act the Curate carried home with him, and the Parish cheerfully submitted to it, and have found much good by it; for within less than twenty years there died fifteen of natural Deaths, and now there die three or four yearly.

But to return to *Du Vall*, 'twill not, I hope, be expected that I should in a true History, play the Romancer, and describe all his Actions from his Cradle to his Saddle, telling what childish Sports he was best at, and who were his play-fellows; that were enough to make the Truth of the whole Narration suspected, only one important Accident I ought not to omit.

An old Frier, counted very expert in Physiognomy and Judicial Astrology, came on a time to see *Pierre Du Vall* and his Wife, who had then by extraordinary good Fortune some *Norman* Wine, that is, Cider in their house, of which they were very liberal to this old Frier, whom they made heartily welcome, thinking nothing too good for him.

For those silly people, who know no better, count it a great honour and favour, when any religious person, as Priest or Frier, are pleas'd to give them a visit, and to eat and drink with them. As these three were sitting by the fire, and chirping over their Cups, in comes *Claude*, and broke the Friers Draught, who fix'd his eyes attentively upon him, without speaking one word for the space of half an hour, to the amazement of *Claude*'s Parents, who seeing the Frier neither speak nor drink, imagined he was sick, and courteously askt him, Brother, what ails you? are you not well? why do you so look upon our Son? The Frier having rous'd himself out of his Ecstasie, Is that Stripling, saies he, your Son? to which after they had replied, Yes; Come hither Boy, quoth he, and looking upon his head, he perceived he had two Crowns, a certain sign that he should be a Traveller: This Child, saies he, will be a Traveller, and he shall never, during his life, be long without money; and wherever he goes, he will be in extraordinary favour with Women of the highest Condition. Now from this Story, the certainty of Physiognomy and Judicial Astrology is evidently proved; so that from henceforward, who ever shall presume to deny it, ought not to be esteemed a person in his right Wits.

*Pierre* and *Marguerite* look'd upon the Frier as an Oracle, and mightily rejoyced at their Sons fortune; but it could not enter into their imagination, how this should come to pass, having nothing to leave him as a Foundation to build so great a Structure upon.

The Boy grew up, and spoke the Language of the Country fluently, which is, *Lawyers French;* and which (if I should not offend the Ladies in comparing our Language with theirs) is as much inferiour to that at *Paris*, as *Devonshire* or *Somersetshire* English to that spoken at *White-hall*.[1]

[1] i.e., at court.

I speak not this to disgrace him, for could he have spoke never so good *French*, it is not in such high esteem there as it is here; and it very rarely happens that, upon that account alone, any great mans Daughter runs away with a Lacquey.

When he was about thirteen or fourteen years old, his Friends muster'd their Forces together to set him up in the World; they bought him shoos and stockins, for (according to the laudable Custom of that Country of inuring their youth to hardship) till then he had never worn any; they also bought him a Suit of the Brokers, gave him their Blessing, and twenty *Sous* in his Pocket, and threw an old shoo after him, and bid him go seek his fortune: This throwing of an old shoo after him was looked upon as a great piece of *Prodigality* in *Normandy*, where they are so considerable a *Merchandize;* the Citizens Wives of the best quality, wearing old shoos chalked; whence, I suppose, our custom of wearing white shoos derives its original.

His Friends advised him to go to *Paris*, assuring him he would not fail of a Condition there, if any could be had in the *World;* for so the French call *Paris*. He goes to *Rouen*, and fortunately meets with Post-horses which were to be returned, one of which he was profer'd to ride *gratis*, only upon promise to help to dress them at night: And, which was yet more fortunate, he meets several young English Gentlemen with their Governours going to *Paris*, to learn their Exercises to fit them to go a-woing at their return home, who were infinitely ambitious of his Company, not doubting but in those two daies travels, they should *pump* many *considerable things* out of him, both as to the *Language* and *Customs* of *France;* and upon that account they did very willingly defray his Charges.

They arrive at *Paris*, and light in the *Fauxbourg* St. *Germain*, the quarter wherein generally the English lodge, near whom also our *Du Vall* did earnestly desire to plant himself. Not long after by the intercession of some of the English Gentlemen (for in this time he had indear'd himself to them) he was admitted to run on errants, and do the meanest Offices at the St. *Esprit* in the *Rue de Boucherie:* A house in those daies betwixt a Tavern, and an Ale-house, a Cooks-shop and a Bawdy-house; and, upon some of those accounts, much frequented by the English his Patrons. In this condition he lived unblamably during some time, unless you esteem it a fault to be *scabby*, and a little given to *filching*, qualities very frequent in persons of his Nation and condition.

The Restauration of his Majesty, which was in 1660, brought multitudes of all Nations into *England*, to be spectators of our *Jubilee;* but more

particularly it drein'd *Paris* of all the English there, as being most concern'd in so great a happiness: One of them, a person of Quality, entertained *Du Vall* as his Servant, and brought him over with him.

What fortunes he ran through afterwards, is known to every one, and
how good a proficient he was in the laudable qualities of *Gaming* and
*making Love*. But one Vice he had which I cannot pardon him, because
'tis not of the *French* growth, but *Northern* and ungenteele, I mean, that
of drinking; for that very night he was *surpriz'd*, he was *overtaken*.[2]

By these Courses (for I dare not call them Vices) he soon fell into
want of Money to maintain his Port; That, and his Stars, but chiefly his
Valour, inclined him to take the Generous way of *Padding;*[3] in which he
quickly became so famous, that in a Proclamation, for the taking several
notorious Highway-men, he had the *honour* to be named first.

This is the place where I should set down several of his Exploits, but
I omit them, both as being well known, and because I cannot find in
them more ingenuity than was practiz'd before by *Hind* and *Hannum*,
and several other *meer English* Thieves.

Yet, to do him right, one Story there is that savours of Gallantry, and
I should not be an honest Historian if I should conceal it.

He, with his Squadron, overtakes a Coach which they had set over
night,[4] having intelligence of a booty of Four Hundred Pounds in it:
In the Coach was a *Knight*, his *Lady*, and only *one serving Maid*, who
perceiving five Horsemen making up to them, presently imagin'd they
were beset, and they were confirmed in this apprehension, by seeing them
whisper to one another, and ride backwards and forwards: The Lady, to
shew she was not affraid, takes a Flageolet[5] out of her pocket and plays.
*Du Vall* takes the hint, plays also, and excellently well, upon a Flageolet
of his own, and in this posture he rides up to the Coach side. Sir, sayes
he, to the person in the Coach, your Lady playes excellently, and I doubt
not but that she Dances as well; will you please to walk out of the Coach,
and let me have the honour to Dance one Corant with her upon the
Heath? Sir, said the person in the Coach, I dare not deny any thing to
one of your Quality and good *Mine;*[6] you seem a Gentleman, and your
request is very reasonable: Which said, the Lacquey opens the Boot,[7] out
comes the Knight, *Du Vall* leaps lightly off his Horse, and hands the

---

[2] i.e., he was drunk the night he was caught.
[3] being a highwayman, a footpad.
[4] planned the night before to rob.                    [5] a little flute.
[6] mien, appearance.                    [7] part of a coach.

Lady out of the Coach. They Danc'd and here it was that *Du Vall* performed marvels; the best Master in *London*, except those that are *French*, not being able to shew such *footing* as he did in his great riding *French* Boots. The Dancing being over, he waits on the Lady to her Coach; as the Knight was going in, sayes *Du Vall* to him, Sir, You have forgot to pay the Musick: No, I have not, replies the Knight, and putting his hand under the Seat of the Coach, puls out a Hundred pounds in a bag, and delivers it to him: Which *Du Vall* took with a very good grace, and courteously answered, Sir, You are liberal, and shall have no cause to repent your being so; this liberality of yours shall excuse you the other Three Hundred Pounds; and giving him the Word that, if he met with any more of the Crew, he might pass undisturb'd, he civily takes his leave of him.

This story, I confess, justifies the great kindness the Ladies had for *Du Vall;* for in this, as in an Epitome, are contain'd all things that set off a man advantageously, and make him appear, as the phrase is, *much a Gentleman.* First, here was *Valour*, that he and but four more durst assault a *Knight*, a *Lady*, a *Waiting Gentlewoman*, a *Lacquey*, a *Groom* that rid by to open the Gates, and the *Coach-man*, they being *Six* to *Five*, *odds* at *Foot-ball;* and besides *Du Vall* had much the worst cause, and reason to believe, that whoever should arrive, would range their selves on the Enemies party. Then he shewed his *Invention* and *Sagacity* that he could *sur le Champ*,[8] and without studying, make that advantage of the Ladies playing on the Flageolet. He evidenced his *Skill in Instrumental Musick*, by playing on his Flageolet; in *Vocal* by his Singing; for, (as I should have told you before,) there being no Violins, *Du Vall* sung the Corant[9] himself. He manifested his *Agility of Body*, by lightly dismounting off his Horse, and with ease and freedome getting up again, when he took his leave; his *excellent Deportment*, by his incomparable Dancing, and his graceful manner of taking the Hundred Pound; his *Generosity* in taking no more, his *Wit* and *Eloquence*, and *readiness at Reparties*, in the whole discourse with the Knight and Lady, the greatest part of which I have been forced to omit.

And here (could I dispense with truth and impartiality, necessary ingredients of a good History) I could come off with flying colours, leave *Du Vall* in the Ladies *Bosomes*, and not put my self out of a possibility of ever being in favour with any of them.

[8] on the spot.
[9] a dance tune.

But I must tell the story of the *Sucking-Bottle;* which, if it seem to his disadvantage, set that other against it which I come from relating. The adventure of the *Sucking-Bottle* was as follows.

It happened another time, as *Du Vall* was upon his *Vocation* of Robbing, on *Black-Heath*, he meets with a Coach richly fraught with Ladies of Quality, and with one Child who had a Silver *Sucking-Bottle;* He robs them rudely, takes away their Money, Watches, Rings, and even the little Childs *Sucking-Bottle:* Nor would, upon the Childs tears, nor the Ladies earnest intercession, be wrought upon to restore it; till at last one of his Companions (whose Name I wish I could put down here, that he may find friends when he shall stand in need of them) a good natured person (for the *French* are strangers both to the name and thing) forced him to deliver it. I shall make no reflexions upon this story, both because I do not design to render him odious, or make this Pamphlet more prolix.

The noise of the Proclamation, and the Rewards promised to those who should take any therein named, made *Du Vall* retire to *France*. At *Paris* he lives highly, makes great boastings of the success of his Armes and Amours in *England*, proudly bragging, He could never incounter with any of either Sex that could resist him. He had not been long in *France*, but he had a fit of his old disease, Want of Money, which he found to be much augmented by the thin air of *France;* and therefore by the advice of his Physicians, lest the disease should *seise upon his Vitals*, and make him *lie by it*, he resolves to transport himself into *England;* which accordingly he did: For, in truth, the air of *France* is not good for persons of his constitution, it being the custom there to Travel in great Companies well Armed, and with little Money; the danger of being resisted, and the danger of being Taken is much greater there; and the *Quarry* much lesser than in *England;* For if by chance a Dapper Fellow with fine *black Eyes*, and a *white Peruke*, be taken there, and found guilty of Robbing, all the Women in the Town don't presently take the Alarm, and run to the King to beg his life.

To *England* he comes, but alas! his Reign proves but short; for, within few months after his return, before he had done any thing of great glory, or advantage to himself, he fell into the Hands of Justice, being taken Drunk at the Hole in the Wall[10] in *Chandois-street:* And well it was for the Baily,[11] and his men, that he was Drunk, otherwise they had tasted of his prowess; for he had in his pocket three Pistols, one whereof would

[10] a cheap tavern.
[11] bailiff.

shoot twice, and by his side an excellent Sword, which managed by such a hand and heart, must without doubt have done wonders. Nay, I have heard it attested by those that knew how good a Marks-man he was, and his excellent way of Fencing, that had he been Sober 'twas impossible he could have kill'd less than ten. They farther add, upon their own knowledge, he would have been cut as small as herbs for the Pot, before he would have yielded to the Bayly of *Westminster;* that is to say, he would have died in the place, had not some *Great person* been sent to him to whom he might with *Honour* have delivered his *Sword* and *himself.* But taken he was, and that too *a bon Marche,*[12] without the expense of blood or Treasure, committed to *Newgate,* Arraigned, Convicted, Condemned, and on Friday *Jan.* 21.[13] Executed at *Tiburn* in the 27th. year of his Age, (which number is made up of three times nine) and left behind him a sad instance of the irresistible influence of the Stars, and the fatality of Climacterical years.

There were a great Company of Ladies, and those not of the meanest Degree, that visited him in Prison, interceded for his Pardon, and accompanied him to the Gallows; a Catalogue of whose Names I have by me, nay, even of those who when they visited him, durst not pull off their Vizards for fear of shewing their *Eyes swoln,* and their *Cheeks blubbered* with *tears.*

When I first put Pen to Paper, I was in great indignation, and fully resolved, nay, and I think I swore, that I would Print this Muster-role. But upon second thoughts, and calmer considerations, I have alter'd my fierce resolution, partly because I would not do my Nation so great a disgrace, and especially that part of it to whom I am so intirely devoted. But principally because I hoped milder Physick might cure them of this *French Disease,* of this inordinate *Appetite* to *Mushromes,*[14] of this Degenerous *doating* upon *Strangers.*

After he had hang'd a convenient time, he was cut down, and by persons well dress'd, carried into a Mourning Coach, and so conveyed to the *Tangier Tavern* in St.*Gile*'s, where he lay in State all that night, the Room hung with black cloath, the Hearse cover'd with Scutcheons, eight wax Tapers burning, as many tall Gentlemen with long black Cloaks attending; *Mum* was the word, great silence expected from all that visited, for fear of disturbing this sleeping Lion: And this Ceremony had

[12] cheaply.
[13] 1660.
[14] upstarts.

lasted much longer, had not one of the Judges (whose name I must not mention here lest he should incur the displeasure of the Ladies) sent to disturb this *Pageantry*. But I dare set down a mark, whereby you ʀay guess at him; 'Tis one betwixt whom and the Highway-men there's little love lost, one who thought the *Filou*[15] lay in *State* enough in not being *buried* under the *Gallows*.

This story of lying in State seem'd to me so improbable, and such an audacious *mocquerie* of the Laws, that, till I had it *again* and *again* from several Gentlemen who had the curiosity to see him, I durst not put it down here for fear of being accounted a *notorious Lyer*.

The night was stormy and rainy, as if the Heavens had sympathiz'd with the Ladies, and *ecchoed* again their *Sighs*, and *wept* over again their *Tears*.

As they were undressing him, in order to his lying in State, one of his Friends put his hands in his pocket, and found therein the Speech which he intended to have made, written with a very fair hand; a Copy whereof (though I have with much cost and industry procured) I do freely make it publick, because I would not have any thing wanting in this Narration.

## *Du Vall*'s Speech

I should be very ungrateful (which, amongst persons of Honour, is a greater Crime than that for which I die) should I not acknowledge my Obligation to you fair *English* Ladies. I could not have hoped that a person of my *Nation, Birth, Education*, and *Condition*, could have had so many and powerful *Charms*, to *captivate* you all, and to tie you so firmly to my interest; that you have not abandon'd me in *distress* or in *prison*, that you have accompanied me to this place of *Death*, of *Ignominious Death*.

From the experience of your true *Loves* I speak it; nay, I know I speak *your hearts*, you could be content to die with *me now*, and even *here*, could you be assured of enjoying your beloved *Du Vall* in the other world.

How *mightily* and how *generously* have you rewarded my *little* Services? Shall I ever forget that *universal Consternation* amongst you when I was taken, your *frequent*, your *chargeable Visits* to me at *Newgate*, your *Shreeks*, your *Swoonings* when I was *Condemned*, your *Zealous Intercession* and *Importunity* for my *Pardon*?

[15] thief.

You could not have erected fairer pillars of Honour and respect to me, had I been a *Hercules*, and could have got *fifty Sons* in a night.

It has been the Misfortune of several *English* Gentlemen, in the times of the late Usurpation, to die at this place upon the *Honourablest Occasion* that ever *presented* itself, the indeavouring to restore their *Exil'd Sovereign:* Gentlemen indeed, who had ventured their *Lives*, and lost their *Estates* in the Service of their Prince; but they all died *unlamented* and *un-interceded* for, because they were *English*. How much greater therefore is my Obligation, whom you love better than your own *Country-men*, better than your own *dear Husbands?* Nevertheless, Ladies, it does not grieve me, that your Intercession for my life prov'd ineffectual; For now I shall die with *little pain*, a *healthful body*, and I hope a *prepared mind.* For my Confessor has shewed me the Evil of my way, and wrought in me a true Repentance; witness these *tears*, these *unfeigned tears.* Had you prevail'd for my life, I must in gratitude had devoted it wholly to you, which yet would have been but short; for, had you been sound, I should have soon died of a *Consumption;* if otherwise, of the POX.[16]

He was buried with many *Flambeaux*, and a numerous train of Mourners, most whereof were of the Beautiful Sex: He lies in the middle Ile in *Covent-Garden* Church under a plain white marble stone, whereon are curiously ingrav'd the *Du Valls* Arms, and under them written in black this Epitaph.

### *Du Vall*'s Epitaph

*Here lies* Du Vall: *Reader, if* Male *thou art,*
*Look to thy* purse; *if* Female, *to thy* heart.
*Much havock has he made of both : For all*
Men *he made* stand,[17] *and* Women *he made* fall.
*The Second Conquerour of the* Norman *Race,*
Knights *to his* Arms *did yield, and* Ladies *to his* Face:
*Old* Tiburns *Glory,* Englands *Illustrious Thief,*
Du Vall *the Ladies Joy,* Du Vall *the Ladies Grief.*

### The Author's Apology
### why he Conceals his Name

Some there are without doubt, that will look upon this harmless Pamphlet as a Libell, and invective Satyre; because the Author has not

[16] syphilis, of course, not the small pox.
[17] from the robber's cry: "Stand and deliver!"

put his Name to it. But the Book-sellers Printing his true name,[18] and place of abode, wipes off that objection.

But, if any person be yet so curious as to inquire after me, I can assure him I have conjured the Stationer not to declare my Name so much as to his own Wife: not that I am ashamed of the Design, no, I glory in it; nor much of the manner of Writing; for I have seen books with the Authors names to them not much better written; neither do I fear I should be *proud* if the Book takes, and *crest-faln* if it should not; I am not a person of such a tender Constitution. *Valeat res Ludicra, si me Palma negata macrum, donata reducat opimum.*[19] But upon other pressing and important reasons. Though I am resolved not to be known, yet I intend to give you some account of my self, enough to exempt me from being so pitiful and inconsiderable a fellow, as possibly some *incensed Females* may endeavour to represent me.

I was bred a Scholar, but let none reproach me with it, for I have no more Learning left than what may become a well-bred Gentleman. I have had the opportunity (if not the advantage) of seeing all *France* and *Italy* very particularly, *Germany* and the *Spanish Netherlands en passant.* I have walkt a Corant in the hands of *Monsieur Provost*, the French Kings Dancing Master, and several times *pusht* at the *Plastron*[20] of *Monsieur Filboy le vieux.* Now I hope these qualities, joyn'd with a *white Peruke*, are sufficient to place any person *hors de la porteè*, out of the reach of Contempt.

At my return from *France*, I was advised by my Friends to settle my self in the world, that is, to Marry; when I went first amongst the Ladies upon that account, I found them very *obliging*, and as I thought *coming.*[21] I wondred mightily what might be the reason could make me so acceptable, but I afterwards found 'twas the *sent* of *France* which was then *strong* upon me; for according as that *perfume decaied*, my Mistresses grew *colder* and *colder.*

But that which precipitated me into ruine, was this following Accident: Being once in the Company of some Ladies, amongst other discourses we fell upon the comparison betwixt the *French* and *English* Nation: And here it was that I very imprudently maintained even against my own Mistress, *That a French Lacquey was not so good as an English Gentleman.*

---

[18] i.e., the bookseller's *own* name.

[19] "Goodbye to the comic stage, if for applause given or withheld, I become thinner or fatter" (Horace *Epistles* II. i. 181).    [20] practised fencing with.

[21] responsive, ready to meet advances.

The Scene was immediately chang'd, they all lookt upon me with anger and disdain; they said I was unworthy of that little breeding I had acquired, of that small parcel of wit (for they would not have me esteemed a meer Fool, because I had been so often in their Company) which nature had bestowed upon me, since I made so ill use of it as to maintain such *Paradoxes.* My Mistress for ever forbids me the House, and the next day sends me my Letters, and demands her own, *bidding me pick* up a Wife at the *Plow-tail, for 'twas impossible* any woman well-bred would ever cast her eies upon me.

I thought this Disgrace would have brought me to my grave, it impaired my health, robb'd me of my good humour. I retired from all Company as well of Men, as of Women, and have liv'd a Solitary melancholy life, and continued a Batchelour to this day.

I repented heartily, that at my return from my Travels, I did not put my self into a *Livery;* and in that Habit go and seek Entertainment at some great mans house; for 'twas impossible but good must have arrived to me from so doing. 'Twas *a la mode* to have French Servants, and no person of Quality but esteemed it a disgrace, if he had not two or three of that Nation in his Retinue: so that I had no reason to fear but that I should soon find a *Condition.*

After I had insinuated my self into one of these houses, I had just reason to expect (if I could have concealed my self from being an English man) that some young Lady with a great Portion, should run away with me, and then I had been made for ever. But if I had followed bad Courses, and Robb'd upon the high way, as the Subject of this History did, I might have expected the same *civilities* in *Prison,* the same *intercessions* for my *Life;* and if those had not prevail'd, the same *glorious Death, lying in State* in *Tangier Tavern,* and being *embalm'd* in the Ladies *tears.* And who is there worthy the name of man, that would not prefer such a Death, before a mean, solitary, and inglorious Life?

I design but two things in the writing of this Book, one is that the next *French man* that is hang'd, may not cause an uproar in this Imperial City, which I doubt not but I have effected.

The other is much a harder task, to set my Country men on even terms with the *French,* as to the *English Ladies* affections: If I should bring this about, I should esteem my self to have contributed much to the good of this Kingdome.

One Remedy there is, which possibly may conduce some thing towards it.

I have heard that there is a new invention of Transfusing[22] the bloud of one Animal into another, and that it has been experimented by putting the bloud of a Sheep into an English man. I am against that way of experiments, for should we make all *English* men *Sheep*, we should soon be a prey to the *Louvre*.

I think I can propose the making that Experiment a more advantageous way. I would have all Gentlemen, who have been a full year, or more, out of *France*, be let bloud weekly, or oftner if they can bear it; mark how much they bleed, transfuse so much *French* Lacqueys bloud into them, Replenish these last out of the English footmen, for 'tis no matter what becomes of them. Repeat this Operation *Toties Quoties*,[23] and in process of time you'l find this Event: Either the *English Gentlemen* will be as much belov'd as the *French Lacqueys*, or the *French Lacqueys* as little esteemed as the *English Gentlemen*.

But to conclude my Apology, I have certainly great reason to conceal my Name; for if I suffer'd so severely for only speaking one word, in a private Company, what Punishment will be great enough for a *Relaps'd Heretick* publishing a Book to the same purpose? I must certainly do as that *Irish* Gentleman, that let a —— *scape* in the presence of his Mistress, run my Country, shave my head, and bury my self alive in a Monastery, if there be any charitable enough to harbour a person guilty of such heinous *Crimes*.

FINIS

[22] Experiments in transfusion were actually attempted by the Royal Society during the 1660's.

[23] as often as needed.

# THE HISTORY OF THE
# GOLDEN-EAGLE

## (1672)

THE

# HISTORY

OF THE

# Golden-Eagle:

Being both delightful and
profitable.

Written by *Philaquila*.

*LONDON*,
Printed for *William Thackeray* in *Duck-Lane*, near
*West Smithfield.* 1677.

*The folklore so characteristic of much popular literature in the seventeenth century rises to a fine climax in* The History of the Golden-Eagle. *Written by someone who called himself Philaquila, the book is, surprisingly enough, a full-fledged example of the märchen, the only one I know of in the whole century. The story is organized around the quest motif so common to the genre, with three sons, two of them bad, the youngest good, seeking the golden eagle which will restore their father's health. The youngest son succeeds in the quest; because he is kind and unselfish he is granted supernatural aid denied to the others, but he is overpowered and almost beaten by the other two brothers. At the end he is rescued by the intervention, again implicitly supernatural, of a mysterious enchantress figure, and is given his due recognition and reward.*

*It would be interesting to know what Philaquila's sources, oral or written, were for this story. In any case he could hardly have done better in putting together a model märchen if he had studied the Brothers Grimm for some years. All the proper motifs are present and the atmosphere too is properly typical. There are hints at times that the action is somewhat truncated—the hero, for example, succeeds in his quest all too suddenly and easily—so that it would seem that the unknown author is exercising some kind of editorial control over his material (it is hard to believe that the story can be original), whatever it was that lay behind his tale. But even so, his feeling for his material is good enough, it would seem, to keep him from the worse temptation of making additions to his sources, a remarkable piece of restraint.*

*Besides the 1672 edition, there were two others, one dated 1677 and one undated but which may be placed around 1700. The text which follows is based on the copy of the 1677 edition at Harvard.*

### The History of the
### Golden-Eagle

*Chap. I.   How Albertus King of Arragon falling into a languishing disease, was advised by his Physicians to provide for death; the news being spread over the Countrey, many Magicians came to him, who told him, that if he could recover the Golden Eagle from the Queen of Ivyland, he should questionless recover his health.*

*Albertus* having of late buried the soul of his life, *Lysimena*, his most indulgent Queen, fell into extreme melancholy, which as it is commonly the Parent of all diseases, so it brought him into a most tedious and languishing sickness, which caused him to make moan both day and night, witness the bitter groans and passionate expressions for the loss of his departed Consort: at last, being importuned by several of his Nobles, and hourly intreated by his three Sons, *Philonzo*, *Cruentius*, and *Innocentine*, he consented to send for the chiefest Doctors in those parts to consult about the state and welfare of his body, which Doctors being arrived were presently conducted to the Kings Chamber, at whose sight the King broke out into these sad expressions:

Ye are come to look upon a declining King, ye may endeavour to use your skills, but I am confident your labours will be lost. Alas, my disease is too inward to be found out, and if ye cure me, it must be more by miracle than skill: If ye can cure an almost broken heart, or repair my half decayed lungs, or restore my near wasted breath, then draw near, but alas, my *Lysimena*—and there his sighs denying him liberty of speech, he made signs to be no more troubled, and turning from the company, and almost from his own senses, he groaned himself into a deep melancholy.

The Doctors as yet being not throughly acquainted with his disease, verily supposed him departing, but it proved otherwise; for his Sons and the rest of the Nobility informing the Doctors of his grief desired them to use their best endeavours for his recovery, which accordingly they did, but finding little hopes of life, in respect that the distemper of his mind had so much impaired the temper of his body, they only prescribed him Cordials, which indeed something revived and exhilarated his spirits, but could not give the least hopes of life, in respect that nature was much extenuated and weakned by his extraordinary melancholy.

The King, whether less insensible of his disease, or somewhat more enlivened by the prescriptions of the Doctors, desires two of the ablest of them to be brought unto him, of whom he demanded their free and absolute opinions; The Doctors after a short pause, who having more respect to conscience than gain, told him that they might prolong, but not cure; and being about to proceed into further discourse, there suddenly came in some of the Nobility and whispered with one of the Doctors, which the King perceiving, demanded the cause, to which the Nobility replyed, that there were newly arrived several Magicians, who hearing of his Majesties distemper, came out of affectionate duty to imploy their skills for his recovery; the King hearing this, dismist the Doctors, and admitted the Magicians, who being entred, and after the performance of their several duties, applyed themselves in this manner:

Most Renowned Sir, We the most humble of all your servants, being by report informed of your Majesties heavy and grievous disease, have by our industry found out a means which (though it may seem impossible to your Majesty) will without question restore you to your former health, which means (craving the favour of your Majesties patience) we shall forthwith discover.[1]

Know then, most excellent Prince, that under the jurisdiction of *Agrippina*, that most famous and invincible Queen of *Ivy-land*, there is a Golden Eagle, in whom there is a secret and infallible remedy for your disease; therefore if any of those heroick spirits which are belonging to your Majesty, will endeavour to procure this Eagle, your Majesties life will questionless be preserved: we shall not therefore trouble your Majesties ears with any further relation, but leave your Majesty to the prosecution of what we have related, only we will be bold to desire your Majesty not to be doubtful, for he that your Majesty shall least respect or expect shall perform this dangerous and almost impossible design, so we leave your Majesty to your most serious considerations.

*Chap. II.    The Magicians being gone, the King sends for his three Sons, and acquaints them with what the Magicians had told him, proffering to divide his estate between them if they could recover the Eagle from the Queen of Ivy-land, wishing them to take what treasure they would for their occasions.*

The Magicians being departed, the King immediately gave command that his three Sons should come unto him, and they as diligent to obey, as he was willing to command, forthwith presented themselves before him. The King after some discourse told them that now his days were near finished, and nature began so much to decline in him, that he was past the skill of Doctors; therefore let me advise you as a dying Father, that as ye were born brothers in Nature, so to continue in affection. Sir, replyed the eldest, if it please the Gods to dispose of you to death, we must labour for that portion of content which may be proportionable to our sorrows; for the decrees of Fate are not to be resisted, and our reason tells us, that what we cannot remedy we must patiently endure, but for my part (and I dare say as much for my brothers) I would willingly hazard my life for the prolongation of yours. Sir, I hope that you will

[1] reveal.

please to apprehend that the possessions which are like to fall to us after your death do not any way incite us either to hope or wish for your death; with that the two other Brothers, not able to contain any longer, desired their Father to imploy them in any thing whereby they might express their obedience to him. To which the King (joyful to see their passionate obedience) replyed, that there was but one way to save his life, which was to do according to the directions of the Magicians, who informed him, that if he could by any means recover the *Golden-Eagle* from the Queen of *Ivy-land*, that then he should be restored to his former health; but, says he, I find it a thing impossible, therefore I shall not trouble my self with the thoughts of obtaining it, for the Queen is of that power and strength, that if I should perswade any to attempt it, I should be guilty of their deaths, and so depart this World with a burthened conscience. But, my Sons, I am very well content to leave those slaveries which are attendants to a Crown; I can only pray for you, and that's my uttermost.

Before the King had made an end of his intended discourse, his Sons interrupted him with sighs that floated in tears, and as well as their sorrows would permit they in most humble manner desired the King to grant them a boon before his departure, to which the King pleasingly replyed, enjoy your desires, provided ye ask what is necessary for me to give; speak, what is your boon? to which they replyed:

Renowned Sir, It was not long since you were pleased to bless our ears with the discourse of the Magicians, who have assured both you and us that if the *Golden Eagle* can be recovered your health shall be renewed. Then know, Sir, that as our bodies are derivatives from you, so they are by all Laws whatsoever to be at your disposing, and here we present our selves before you, and protest with all our souls to hazard, nay lose our lives, but we will obtain the *Eagle;* for you know, Sir, that resolution backt with obedient affection knows no impossibilities. Sir, we shall not arise from our knees till you have granted our request, and at your Royal consent we will forthwith flye into action.

The King seeing them so resolved, thought it superfluous to endeavour to discourse them out of their resolutions, but told them that since their obedience made them so ready to undertake so great a hazard, his affections should prompt him, at their return, to divide all his treasure (which at that time was very great) amongst them; in the mean time he advised them to provide themselves with what money they would, and all other accoutrements necessary for their adventure, which they accordingly did.

*Chap. III.   How the Kings three Sons provided for their journey, and took leave of their Father, and departed, and what happened between them in their journey.*

The three Brothers, having prepared themselves for their journey, came in humble manner to take leave of the King, whom they found, as formerly, very much troubled with melancholy, but the eldest addressing himself unto him, began in this manner:

Royal Sir, We your most obedient Sons, in order to our dear affections more than your Royal command, present our selves to crave your blessing upon us and our designs before our departure, not despairing of our desires we humbly crave— The King, looking upon them with a countenance that imported unexpressable grief for their departure, raised himself from his Pillow, and with a stretched out arm gave them his blessing, withal advising them as they were Brothers in nature, so to continue Brothers in affection, and to have a care that neither Envy nor ambition, or ambitious Envy should raise a factious difference amongst them, but as they departed Brothers, and so consequently friends, so they should adventure and return in the like amity they departed, and so the greatest blessing a dying Father can bestow upon his departing children accompany you; but before you go, let me as a Father advise you of two things, the one is the displeasure of the Gods by the neglect of your duty to them, the other is the danger of evil company which may seduce you to many inconveniencies, and so farewel; what I want[2] in words I shall supply in thoughts.

Thus these three Brothers, having received the summ of their desires, departed from the presence of their Father, and so taking leave of their friends at Court, departed: At last, having journeyed three days, they came by the mistake of their way into a great Wood, where being in a Wilderness of doubt, they consulted what was best to do; *Philonzo* the elder Brother, beginning already to find the incumbrances of travel, exprest himself to the others as follows:

Wee see, dear Brothers, the many troubles the want of consideration brings upon us; we have (as I have weighed it in my more serious thoughts) undertaken a most dangerous, troublesome, and almost impossible design; to prevent this, how shall we advise? If we should return home, we should turn our noble undertakings to ignominy and shame, and if we proceed, without question we shall lose our lives, and what will the world say but

[2] lack.

this: they have the effect of their rashness, for the more dangerous a design is, the more it ought to be discust, but they that like *Phaeton* mount at impossibilities shall at last fall like *Phaeton* with shame and dishonour; therefore, Brothers, let me hear your advice. To which *Cruentius* the second Brother replyed:

'Tis true, rash beginnings have most commonly fatal conclusions; for my part, as yet I never weighed the business, nor the danger, but altogether depended upon your judgement as an Oracle, not dreaming but you had known the difficulty of the business. But stay, now I better consider the matter, methinks it should not be so difficult, for sure we three can conquer one *Eagle;* for, Brother, you shall catch her, and I will warrant you my Brother and I will hold her; but where shall we find her? Fie, Brother, quoth *Philonzo*, I see you as much err in the matter as I did in the manner of the business. This *Eagle* is a bird kept for her Soveraignty in a great City walled round with Brass, Pallizado'd[3] with Iron, guarded with Lyons and Dragons, and commanded by Gyants, and we must before we come to this City Encounter with several Knights which attend purposely for such attempters as we must be. Many have attempted, but never any as yet returned to tell the manner of their attempts; therefore, Brother, the business is of more intricacy than you imagine. O monstrous, cryed *Cruentius*, I am more than half dead already with the relation; talk no more of it. What, Dragons, and Bears, Lyons, and Gyants, Brazen walls, and Iron Pallizadoes? Oh how I am thundred to death! attempt it who will, for my part I will starve here rather than be eaten with Bears and Lyons, and Dragons, and—oh horrible Gyants, not I. Brother *Innocentine*, what sayest thou to these terrible things? what, art not afraid? well, I have fear enough for you both, but, good Brother, speak. To which *Innocentine*, the younger, undauntedly replyed:

As I am youngest in years, so I am last in speech, and I could wish I might be the least; but in respect I am to make answer to both your demands, I must a little exercise your patience. 'Tis true, the danger is great, therefore the more noble, but had you, my Brethren, according to my Fathers advice, importuned the Gods before you had undertaken this great design, questionless the one had not been so filled with doubts, nor the other with fears, nor I with shame for you both. You seem to be as much displeased at my words as I am at your actions; shall we begin to tire before we begin to do? for shame, let not the world have this advantage of our reputations; if we return home, we must expect to undergo a

3 fortified.

disgrace worse than death; if we dye, we die in high attempts; who knows but that the Gods may shew extraordinary favours, and smile at our designs, being we do it for our dear Fathers life? If the worst come to the worst, we can but dye, and we had better do so than live as if we lived not. But I perceive my discourse offends; I will be therefore silent.

*Chap. IV.    How Philonzo and Cruentius hearing the discourse of their younger Brother Innocentine robb'd him of his treasure, and left him bound in a Wood, where they afterwards lost themselves.*

*Cruentius* hearing his Brothers discourse, which was contrary to his expectations, told him that he was a very rash Boy, and understood not what he spoke; for, says he, shall we cast away our lives because the world should say we died nobly? Brother, says he to *Philonzo*, are we bound to be fools because he's mad? no, let's leave him to his thoughts of Honour whilst you and I consult what's best to do; so walking a distance from him, they sate down, and began thus to express themselves:

Brother *Philonzo*, I have in this short time both considered the shame and the danger, let us endeavour to haste to *Mesemptronia*, a City which I am sure cannot be far from this place, where we may refresh our selves, and have further discourse. But what shall we do, replied *Cruentius*, with yon foolish Boy? you perceive how refractory and inconsiderate he is, and makes slight of that danger which we know to be very great: If we leave him, questionless he will return home and incense the King against us; what we shall do in this I know not, but leave it to your discretion. Let's force him with us, quoth *Philonzo*, and make him do according to our wills; if not, we will threaten to kill him. No, quoth *Cruentius*, that cannot be, for then he will prie into all our actions, and make a discovery at our returns. But, Brother, quoth he, our business requires haste; let us therefore take away his treasure, and bind him, and so leave him in the Wood, for it is better one perish than two; and if the worst come to the worst, that he should be unloosed and return home, we know at our return how to perswade that what he has related is only lies to disgrace us, and by that means to insinuate the more into favour himself, and injure us. I like this advice well, quoth *Philonzo*, let us quickly put it in execution, for the night hastens; with that returning to *Innocentine*, they asked him what he intended to do, who replied, what they did not. And so you shall, quoth *Cruentius*, and so both running together laid hold on him, and without hearing him speak, bound him, and took away his treasure, and turning his Horse loose to range in the Woods, they departed. Thus lay poor *Innocentine* miserably bound, insomuch that the swelling of his hands and feet made him most sadly lament his grievous tortures. But *Philonzo* and *Cruentius* having rambled up and down the Wood for the space of two hours could by no means find the way out, insomuch that they despaired of travelling any further way out that night, but having not rode a flight-shot further, it happened that a Dog, having lost his Master, came fawning on *Cruentius*, who presently laid hold of him, and tying him in a string, followed the Dog, who forthwith brought them out of the Wood, and presently after to a Sheepherds house, where the Dog found speedy entertainment,[4] but *Philonzo* and *Cruentius* none, where we shall for a time leave them, and return to *Innocentine*, whom they left bound in the Wood.

*Chap. V.   How Innocentine was unbound by an Hermit, and how afterwards he saved a beautiful Lady from ravishment, and how the Lady requited him.*

*Innocentine* being fast bound by his unnatural Brothers lay till the approach of the evening in a most lamentable condition, till at last a Hermit coming from his Cell to take the benefit of the cool of the evening heard the sad groans of poor *Innocentine*, and being moved with pity, he addressed himself to the place (I may well say) of groans, where being come, his eye saw what his heart pitied, his heart pitied what his hand relieved, for he forthwith conducted him to his Cell, and made such preparations for him as his necessity required, so that the next morning he was in a condition to travel; but the Hermit viewing his guest read in his countenance the characters of a noble and ingenuous disposition, observing by his deportment, that he was not a man of an ordinary education, besides being led by his own inclinations, he accosts his stranger in this manner:

Sir, I Perceive that your youth and education prompts you to bashfulness, and your bashfulness hinders the liberty of your speech. I therefore heartily intreat you to inform me of your present condition, and what I want in power, I will supply in prayer for you. I will not stand to trouble you to relate the misfortunes, it is enough, and too much that I saw them, only tell me which way you intend to steer, and what you want. *Innocentine* all this while amazed at the courtesie of the Hermit, knew not presently

4 welcome.

what to answer, but as well as his late distemper attended with a multitude of thoughts would permit, he thus replied:

Most charitable Father, I could grieve that I was sorry for my last misfortune, in respect that the happiness of your acquaintance is derived from it. I will not trouble your patience with the discourse of my misfortune, only in short I am going upon a design to save the life of a renowned King, but this misfortune hath put me out of a capacity to follow my intentions. Come, says the Hermit, I know your disease, I'le be your Physician; take this cordial (giving him a bag of Gold and Jewels) and return no complemental answer, for I am bound to do it, and if you want a Steed, I have one for you which this very day stragled hither; pray take him and use him as your own. But for this Sword, which I intend for your use, pray return it, if you live; if not, conceal the vertue, for it will preserve you against all enchantments, which are now very common to my woful experience; neither need you fear whom you encounter with it, for you shall not want success. *Innocentine* not a little rejoiced at what the Hermit had told him desired liberty to depart, in order to which the Hermit conducted him to his Horse, but it fell out that the Horse was his own, which he thought his brothers had carried away with them. The Hermit, observing him look so strictly upon the Horse, told him that he could not promise him the like service from the Horse as he did from the Sword. No Sir, quoth *Innocentine*, I believe I am better acquainted with the Horse than you, for yesterday he was mine, till taken from me by misfortune; but however I cannot but express my hearty thanks to you and at my return you shall know more of me. In the mean time, let peace abide with you, let me only beg your directions towards *Green Iveland*, for I am altogether a stranger in these parts. Your ready way, quoth the Hermit, is to go to *Mesemptronia*, a City about three leagues from hence; the way is very direct through several Villages, where you may at your pleasure enquire, but there is a Forest which lies between a little Town called *Corumbus* and *Mesemptronia*, where you must have a careful eye, lest you be set upon before you can provide for resistance; this is all that I can advise you, and so farewel.

Thus they departed, and after the expence of some hours, *Innocentine* came to the Forest which the Hermit told him of, where he was no sooner entred, but he was welcomed with many loud and lamentable schreeks, which struck him into admiration;[5] but being of an undaunted spirit, and remembring the sad state he himself was in the day before, resolved to

5 wonder.

find out the place where he heard this lamentable noise; and being more directed by the ear than the eye, he at length effected his desires, for immediately in a Valley he espied two Villains about to ravish a Lady of an incomparable beauty, and being passionately exasperated, he flew upon them like lightning, but giving them leave to mount themselves, they instead of fight, presently run away, perceiving it was their Brother. *Innocentine* perceiving their flight clapt spurrs and followed them, but the Lady perceiving it, and fearful that two to one might be very disadvantagious, cryed out with what strength she had, help, help, which *Innocentine* hearing, fearing some other accident had befallen the Lady, speedily returned, but when he came he found no such matter, but the Lady being heartily glad of his return applied her self to him in this manner:

Most noble and renowned Knight, my late fright hath so disordered my thoughts that for the present I cannot return you those thanks which are due to your merits; but if you please to add one favour more to the rest, which is to conduct me to my poor habitation (from which place those Villains you saw, having surprized me in a solitary walk, dragg'd me), you will very much increase my happiness; to which request *Innocentine* condescended and in a short time came to the place, where he found a welcome entertainment: So after many Ceremonies past between them, the Lady requested to know what his name and birth was, to which *Innocentine* replied, so much confidence have I of your worth, that I will not keep the least of my thoughts from you. So composing himself, he told her his name, birth and design, and likewise told her how his Brothers had dealt with him, which he was confident were those which would have ravished her, had not he by providence preserved; the Lady hearing his relation was much astonished, but at last recalling her self from her admiration proceeded as follows:

Most magnanimous and ingenious Knight, I cannot but acknowledge my life and honour to be protected by your vertue. I shall therefore in part of a requital communicate something to you for your advantage, which in short is this:

Not far from this place there is an enchanted Castle kept by two Ladies, at which Castle (if you please to go) you shall find civil entertainment from the Ladies. One of them will much press you to marriage, but by no means consent, but promise at your return to give satisfaction to her request; tell them likewise that you have a short journey to take, but the Horse dying in the journey you are now quite destitute. Then they will presently carry you into a spacious Stable, where they will shew you many Steeds, and bid you take your choice, but refuse them all but one which seems to be the meanest there, and they will be very unwilling to lend you him. You shall know him by this sign: as soon as you come into the Stable you shall find him laid, and all the rest standing. I will not now any longer detain you, leave your Horse with me till your return, and you shall accomplish your business. Thus *Innocentine* and the Lady parted, but we will now leave him and return to the other Brothers, which are by this time come to *Mesemptronia*.

*Chap. VI.   How Philonzo and Cruentius came to the Shepheards house, but could not be entertained, and how they lay under an Oke that night, and the next morning took their journey for Mesemptronia.*

*Philonzo* and *Cruentius* being come to the Shepheards house, immediately alighted and knockt at the door, but the old Shepheard and his Wife being newly gone to bed were very unwilling to rise. At last the Shepheard hearing them grow more violent in their knocks, arose and looked out of (I cannot say the window) but out of a hole, or cranny, and asked who was there; to which *Philonzo* replied, a couple of Passengers which had lost their way in a Wood, and by a Dog which they followed were brought thither. The Shepheards Wife which but a little before was awaked out of her sleep with sighing for the loss of her Dog, starts out of her bed and cries, oh her dear *Cut*, and so runs down and lets in her Dog, and after many expressions of insufferable joy, having entertained her Dog with many a sweet kiss, she went to bed and slept very heartily, whilst *Philonzo* and *Cruentius* begg'd very earnestly for entertainment to protect them from a storm which they perceived was hastning upon them, but all their intreaties were in vain, for this Shepheard told them that he and his wife were abused not long since by a couple that desired to be entertained as they did, and therefore he would not admit them by any means. At last, when they saw their intreaties were in vain they departed, trusting themselves to the protection of an Oke, where they had not long reposed but a great tempest of thunder and lightning disturbed them of their rest, so that they forsook the place, as deeming it dangerous to lie there in such tempestuous weather; so wandring up and down all night, without any rest, in the morning they prepared for their journey, and being at last refreshed with the heat of the Sun, they spurred cheerfully along till they came within view of a (not stately but) well scituated house, not far from which they espied a beautiful Lady walking so solitary that she hardly took notice of her own thoughts. *Philonzo* riding towards her, and surprising her on a sudden, put her into such an amasement that for the present she neither knew what to do, or say, but *Philonzo* well skill'd in the rudiments of malicious impudence begins to accost her in this manner:

Madam, quoth he, I very much commend your choice; you have chosen a pleasant morning and a sweet air for your private meditations. Sir, replied the Lady, the walk and air would be more pleasant if you were further from it. I wonder a Knight, as you seem to be, should be so unadvised, or rather uncivil, to intrude without notice or acquaintance. Sir, if you are noble, shew it by your forbearance. To which replied *Philonzo:*

Madam, had you been less beautiful, I had been less ambitious, but, Madam, your beauty is the Author of my bold intrusion; but I hope you have goodness to pardon as well as I have infirmities to offend. Sir, quoth the Lady, the vanity of Courtship hath taught me to dislike a Courtier; I will therefore leave my walk to your enjoyment. Nay, quoth *Philonzo*, I cannot so suddenly dismiss you, for your beauty has made a conquest of my heart, so either return what your beauty has robb'd me of, or I must be inforced to take it. Sir, quoth the Lady, I neither know your intent nor meaning, but I expect you to be civil; therefore pray wrong not my expectations. At which words *Philonzo* beckning to his Brother *Cruentius*, that stood within sight, presently with much rigour and incivility laid hold on her, and dragg'd her into a Forest which was within half a mile, being assisted by his Brother *Cruentius*. I need not tell the Reader of the many tears, the grievous complaints, the sundry prayers this poor distressed Lady made to these inhumane Villains, but all to no purpose, for had not an unexpected Knight passed by, who hearing the schreeks of one in distress boldly approached to the place where he found these Villains endeavouring to rob her of her chastity, whom they spying perceived him to be their Brother which they left bound in the Wood, ran away, and at last arrived at *Mesemptronia*, where being come, they presently went to their Inn, and so to rest, not at the least troubled at their barbarous cruelty. The next morning approaching, they arose and commanded a plentiful dinner to be provided, and that such company as the City afforded should be invited to keep them company, being strangers, at that time, to which their Host preferring his own gain condescended, and forthwith sent for a crew of the most notorious cheats the Town could afford, who very plausibly treated the new come guests, telling them of many Courtisans the City abounded withal, which were presently sent for, and a great banquet provided, to the admiration of the diligently joyful Host. But after some days of their abode, they began to feel a consumption in their pockets, which caused them to consult of their departure.

*Chap. VII.   How Innocentine had his desire in the inchanted Castle, with a promise to return; how he recovered the Golden Eagle from the Queen of Green Ivy-land, whose Horse was turned into a man, who afterwards directed him what to do.*

After *Innocentine* perceiv'd which Steed it was which the Lady advised him to request, he was very importunate with the Ladies to let him have that Horse which was laid, to which they replyed, alas, that was the worst in the stable, desiring him to make some other choice. But he replyed that the other were too good and too lusty for him, in respect that he was a very bad Horse-man. The Ladies, seeing that he would not be denyed, endeavoured to inchant him, but their inchantments would not take effect, because the Hermits Sword was his preservative. Thus seeing all their labour in vain, they made him swear that he would return again, and he should have his desires; but to be short, having swore according to their desires, the Horse was brought forth. He leaping upon him was on a sudden carried to *Green Ivy-land*, and in his journey overthrew many Knights which waited there on purpose to encounter any that should approach; but he with his good Sword and Steed made slight of them. Then he approached to the Brazen Walls, where he was welcomed with the roaring of Lyons and Dragons, but as he brandished his Sword they fell into a dead sleep; then *Innocentine* passed freely. Not long after he came to a Fort which was guarded by Gyants, who when they perceived his approach presently came running at him with great violence, but he no sooner brandished his sword but they fell all asleep. At length, having many more difficulties, which are now too tedious to relate, he came to the place where the Queen and the Eagle was. The Queen and her attendance beholding a stranger so near her presence began to rebuke his insolency, but he brandishing his Sword, the Queen and all her attendants fell asleep, insomuch that they could not be waked. In the mean time *Innocentine* alighted and took the Eagle, with no small joy, and was departing, but his Horse would not by any means stir a foot from the place, which made *Innocentine* in a doubt what to do; but beholding the incomparable beauty of the Queen, he drew near and saluted her as she slept, after which *Innocentine* cut off a lock of the Queens hair, and left a lock of his in her bosome, and then he took a Ring of rich value from her finger, and put one of his in the same place; then finding her picture about her neck, he took that off and supplyed the place with his own. Having done these things, he writes these lines, and pins them upon the sleeve of her garment:

> *Renowned Queen, what here is done,*
> *Was acted by a Monarchs son:*
> *But before I could depart,*
> *I took your Eagle, left my heart;*
> *Accept the change, and pardon the abuse;*
> *Virtue whilst you remain will be in use.*

Having thus done, he mounts his Horse with the Eagle in his hand, and was immediately brought to the Forest where he preserved the Lady from ravishment; his steed making a stand at a great River would not go any further, notwithstanding *Innocentine* used all the skill he could with switch and spur, but at last his Horse spake and bid him forbear and alight. *Innocentine*, not a little amazed, alighted; then the Horse began to tell him that he must chop off his Head, and throw it into that River, withal bidding him not to be afraid, for he intended him no harm. But, says he, when you have thrown me in, stand with your Sword by the River, and in what shape soever you see me appear knock me down again, till I arise in the shape of a man. *Innocentine* being something amazed at this sudden and strange alteration knew not for the present what to do, but after a little pause he resolved to do it; which being done, he threw the Head into the River, and it rose up the first time like a Lion, but he presently knockt it down, then it rose up in several other shapes but he still kept it down, but at last it arose like a tall proper man, and then he helpt it out, which being done, the man bid him fear nothing but follow his advice, and give ear to him whilst he informed him of something which might conduce to his benefit. I was, saith he, a Knight inchanted in that Castle which you had me out of, and all those fair Steeds you saw were inchanted Knights. I am likewise the Husband of that Lady you preserved from the violence of your Brothers, which Brothers will meet with you before you come home, with full resolution to kill you. But fear not; hide the Ring and

Picture which you had of the Queen, and desire them not to kill you, but tell them you will never discover them to your Father; then they shall take away your Eagle and let you go. Thus as you have preserved me and mine, I will preserve you and yours.

*Chap. VIII. How Philonzo and Cruentius obtained a counterfeit Eagle in the City of Mesemptronia, and returning home met their younger Brother Innocentine, and robb'd him of his Eagle, and what after happened.*

*Philonzo* and *Cruentius*, having spent most of their money, at last agreed with some in the City to get them an Eagle, which they pretended they could do, which was not long effecting, for they got a very great Fowl, the nearest they could like an Eagle, and guilded his Feathers, and brought it to them, which they with much joy accepted, giving a large summ for it, and forthwith departed the City. But as they travelled, it was their fortune to meet their Brother *Innocentine* carrying an Eagle in a Silver Cage, at the sight whereof their Eagle trembled and dyed; but without the least salute to their Brother they run upon him and would have killed him, but he according to his advice had hid the Ring and Picture in a private place about him, which they discovered not, but took away Cage and Eagle, with full intent to kill him. But he with many passionate expressions diverted their intentions, promising them to become their Servant, and never betray them to his Father; they hearing these promises saved his life, and so he became their servant, and they journeyed together. At last coming home and carrying their Eagle in triumph, they were joyfully entertained, the King embracing the two eldest, and commanding the youngest to be immediately put to death for those lies which his Brothers had related of him, but *Innocentine* heartily begg'd of his Father that he might not be put to death, and so did his Brothers seemingly, but that he might be made inferiour to the worst servant in the house, to which the King, though unwilling, agreed. Thus was poor *Innocentine*, that deserved a just reward, cast out of his Fathers favour for ever. But it happened that not long after the Queen of *Green Ivy-land*, hearing where her Eagle was, came with a great Train to *Arragon*, and presented her self to the King, who was absolutely cured by the vertue of the *Eagle*. The Queen receiving that bountiful entertainment which her estate required, asked the King how many Sons he had, to which the King replied, two; she desired she might be allowed so great a favour as to see them. Immediately they appeared. So she called *Philonzo* and asked him if he was the man that made so gallant an attempt for her Eagle? He replied, it was his poor endeavour that obtained it. Pray, says she, let me see some assurance; did you leave me nothing, nor take nothing from me? No, replied *Philonzo*. Then quoth the Queen, you are not the man. After him was presented *Cruentius*, whom the Queen in the like manner greeted, but he replied as *Philonzo* did, that he took nothing from her nor left any thing with her. The Queen, concealing her anger, told the King that these mysteries past her imaginations, desired the King ingenuously to tell her if he had no more Sons. Renowned Queen, I must confess I had another Son, which now I own not; I think he may be living amongst the mean servants of my house, but for a Son I own him not. To which the Queen replied, she must needs see him. Alas, replied the King, I think him not worthy of my presence, much more of so renowned a Queen as your self; but to satisfie your requests, he shall be called. In the mean time the King departed, whilst *Innocentine* approached the Queens presence, to whom the Queen discourst as follows:

Are you the youngest Son of this Royal King, or no? He replied with a blushing countenance, no. What, are you his servant? He replied, no. Friend, you speak very mysteriously; discover thy self. Then know, incomparable Lady, that my Father, being incens'd against me, con-demned me to dye, but by the request of my Brothers I was preserved, and became a servant to the worst of my Fathers servants, contenting my self with these poor habiliments, which indeed were they as rich as could be imagined, were too mean to be presented before so worthy a person as, Madam, you are, and for my self, I could tremble into ashes at the sight of so excellent a creature as your vertuous self, but I shall remove so unworthy an object from your sight, and crave licence to depart. No, replied the Queen, you shall not; I have a few questions to ask you. My rudeness, most unparallel'd Lady, shall be as obedient to reply as your Grace shall be ready to demand, although I am unworthy to be the least of your creatures. The Queen hearing him express himself with so much humility and excellency of speech, the King, forgetting that his Son was there, came suddenly into the presence of the Queen, and beholding his out-cast, started back; the Queen, perceiving it, desired the King to yield her so great a favour as to stay to hear her ask his Son two or three questions. The King, not using to deny the request of such persons, sate down, whilst the Queen thus exprest her self to *Innocentine*. Was it you that took my Eagle from me; pray answer me without ceremony. To which he bowing himself replied, Madam, I did. And what token left you with me, or took from me? Madam, a lock of your hair. Where is it? replied the Queen. Next my heart, Madam, replyed *Innocentine*, and here it is. But what did you leave me? said the Queen. A lock of mine, replied *Innocentine*. Great Prince (said the Queen to the King) and here it is, but pray let your patience expect my further discourse with him. Come hither, said the Queen to bashful *Innocentine;* do you know this Picture and this Ring? Yes, Madam, and I hope your greatness knows these (shewing her the Picture and the Ring which he had took from her). Come, says the Queen, give me the Picture, and instead of the Shadow, take the Substance. I am resolved, renowned King, not to depart till I have made him possessor of all I have. Admire it not, for it is nothing but truth. The King like a man transported at first thought the Queen to be possest of a frenzy, but after more serious debate found all truth which she had related, and presently sent for his two Sons, *Philonzo* and *Cruentius*, and commands their Heads to be struck off, but *Innocentine*, seconded with his incomparable Lady, perswaded his Father to save their lives, and banish them, which the King, though unwillingly, consented to, after which he imbraced his Son, and told him, in requital of his great abuses, he would settle his Kingdom upon him. The Queen, joyful to see the King imbrace his Son, desired the King that hereafter he would please to own her as his obedient Daughter. So *Innocentine* and the Queen were shortly after married and departed into their own Country of *Ivy-land*.

FINIS

John Shirley

# LONDON'S GLORY

(1686)

# London's Glory:

## OR, THE

# HISTORY

### Of the Famous and Valiant

# London-'Prentice:

Giving an Account of his Birth, his brave Exploits in his Childhood, his coming to London, and being put Apprentice to a Turky Merchant; the Story of his Love to his Master's Daughter; and how, going for Turky, he slew a Tygar, and rescued the Great Turk's Daughter; after that, killed two Lions, prepared to devour him; and, gaining the Princess's Love, brought her to *England*, Marrying her in great splendor; with many other memorable things, to the Honour of the famous City of London, and the whole English Nation.

---

Adorned with Songs, Love-Letters, and Verses; all very Pleasant and Delightful for young Men and Maids.

London: Printed by W. O. and sold J. Deacon, in Giltspur-street.

*London's Glory represents a fairly advanced stage in the progressive vulgarization of the chivalric romance, itself a sort of debased substitute for the earlier heroic* chansons de geste. *Aurelius himself is a middle-class hero substituting for the noble knight of the earlier romances, and, though his doughtiness and moral character seem above reproach, his earlier adventures form a sort of bucolic caricature of the usual beginnings of a chivalric life. Once well launched on his career, however, Aurelius is not a bit behind his notable fictional predecessors (such as Amadis de Gaule, the Knight of the Sun, and Bevis of Hampton); in killing wild beasts single-handed, or even bare-handed, rescuing ladies, jousting, and so on, he ranks with the best. And naturally he wins the reward his excellence merits: a splendid wife and pots of money.*

*The author of this remarkable romantic hodge-podge of traditional chivalric motifs with obvious appeal to the apprentices of London and their ilk was one J. S., initials ordinarily taken as those of John Shirley (or Shurley), a professional hack writer of the 1680's, who turned out at least twenty books, both fiction and non-fiction, designed deliberately to engage the interest of the middle-class reader. Shirley produced versions of the stories of Hero and Leander and of King Arthur, both cast into the chivalric mode, a verse version of the ever-popular* Reynard the Fox, *an epitome of ecclesiastical history, the history of the wars of Hungary, and so on, all seemingly aimed at selling to respectable citizens of all ages and both sexes, his appeal ranging from the most romantic to the most practical (such as hints on daily conduct and household management for women).*

*What Shirley's sources for his fiction were is not at all clear; he may be simply giving a relatively definitive form to material derived from written or oral tradition, or he may be to a large extent original, as he seems to be in* London's Glory, *where he is probably handling an obvious sort of rise-to-riches theme in a traditional manner by drawing on his own reading of various chivalric romances. His stories seem intentionally designed by virtue of their physical appearance (black letter type with old-fashioned woodcuts), content, and even syntax to give the impression that they were of considerable antiquity. The setting, too, of* London's Glory *contributes to this effect; the action takes place in the time of Elizabeth and jousting is accepted as standard procedure at festivities.*

*The text which follows is based on the apparently unique copy in the Folger Shakespeare Library of an edition which may be dated ca. 1700. The version of the text given in this edition is slightly fuller than that of the other editions I have seen even though they are dated earlier.*

## London's Glory

*Chap. I.   The Birth and Parentage of* Aurelius, *the valiant* London
*'Prentice, Born in* Cheshire; *how he Encountred with a Serpent that
came to kill him in his Cradle, and growing up, did the like with a mighty
Bear that met him in his way from Market, and the Fame he gained.*

*England* has been behind-hand with no Nation in the World, in giving
Birth to gallant Men, Worthies and Heroes, who, by their Valour and
great Actions, have spread her Fame in every corner of the Universe,
making her beloved of her Friends, feared of her Enemies: I need not
here mention, the renowned *Bevis* of *Southampton*, King *Arthur* and his
Knights of the Round Table, the brave *Tom* of *Lincoln*, the ever-famous
*Guy* of *Warwick*, nor the valiant Knights Templers, who warred against
Infidels in the *Holy Land*, to establish the Christian Faith at the expence
of their Blood, doing Wonders in Arms, which shall preserve their Names
as long as Time shall last, since I am to treat of one whom Fortune made
her Darling, and Fame has crown'd to all Posterity with lasting wreaths
of Lawrel. To be brief then, In the Reign of the renowned Queen
*Elizabeth* of blessed Memory, who confirmed the Protestant Religion in
*England*, upheld the then sinking State of the Dutch Nation, made *Rome*
and *Spain* to tremble at her Frowns: In the famous County Palatinate of
*Chester*, commonly call'd *Cheshire*, lived a Man descended from antient
British Blood, who, marrying a vertuous Wife, was blessed with a Son,
of whose Fame all *England* has rung; nor has it been bounded here, but
passing the narrow Limits of this Isle, filled distant Lands with Admiration. In his Baptism they named him *Aurelius*, in memory of a British
Prince of that Name, who, in the defence of his Country against the
invading Romans, did Wonders in Arms, overthrowing in Battle divers
Roman Lieutenants, and destroying multitudes of their legionary Soldiers.
This Child, like *Hercules* in his Cradle, began to shew his promising
Strengh, and what great things in time he would do, when he matured
his Strength: A huge Snake that lay lurking in a hole of the House, and
used to lap the Milk in the Dairy that adjoyned to the Mansion-house,
drawn by the warmth of the Infant to the Cradle, reared his dreadful
Head, to gorge himself with innocent Blood, whilst the sleepy Nurse was
hanging her drowsy Head over the Fire, and neglected her tender Charge;
young *Aurelius*, undaunted, beheld this dreadful sight, and smiled, which
would have scared another Infant into Fits, and with his pretty hands

beat the Snake back as often as it assailed him, till with the violent motion the Cradle overturn'd, the noise of which wakned the Nurse, who suddenly turned it up, found the Infant strugling with the Snake grasped in his Hand; but fearful at the sight, instead of disengaging them, she set up such a loud throat, as made the Men that were inning their Harvest, come running with Prongs, who seeing what was the cause of her yelling, took courage, and drew away the Snake, whilst the Nurse fell into a Swound, and much ado they had to recover her; the Infant all this while lay smiling, though bit by the Arm, that the blood trickled from the Wound. This Passage being told abroad, a grave Divine came to see the Child, and being well skill'd in Astrology, kissed him, and told his Parents, That from this he foresaw that their Son would be great and fortunate, do things, tho' dangerous in the Attempt, that should make him known to the World's end. This did not a little comfort them, and put them out of the fright they were in, lest the poisonous Wound might bereave them of a Blessing, in which, next to Heaven, they placed their Happiness, and so with the use of Walwort, Poltises of Rue and Plantine, they cured it; the Wound being healed, and the danger over, they more and more rejoyced in their hopeful Issue, and as he grew up, his Beauty encreased so, that the Virgins strove who should dandle him most, and get innocent Kisses for their Labour.

When he grew up, his Parents, tho' they kept but a Farm, yet living plentiful, and bestowing much Charity on the Poor, took care to breed him up in Learning; among the Schoolboys he took so much delight to try his Strength, mastering those that were much older than himself; he delighted himself with the thoughts of noble Actions, becoming grave and serious, much above his Years, yet in publick Pastimes he would be behind none. He grew so expert in Wrestling at twelve Years old, that he would encounter with lubberly Fellows, and throw them to admiration, at Cudgels, throwing the Bar, and many other youthful Exercises; he won much Praise in shooting at the Long-bow, he might well be compared to *Robin Hood*, who rarely missed his Mark; he was very expert and much encouraged by the Gentry of the Country; and, to be brief, a hopefuller Youth was not found in the West. When he had learned as far as his Master could teach him, he was sent home with great Commendations, and often went with his Father to Fairs and Wakes to understand Company, and (as the Country-men call it) learn Behaviour, and in all Places his Discourse was so taking, that he parted not without regret: He soon learned skill in Buying and Selling, so that his Father trusted him to

Bargain and Sell, in which he was so cunning, that he brought him great Advantage thereby: One day coming home from Market, a Bear, that had been baited, broke loose and scattered both the Dogs and People, so that none durst venture to stay her in her flight; she came directly in his way, and the People that followed at a distance, cried out to him to get up a Tree to shun the fury of the ravenous Creature; but his couragious Heart scorning to stoop to base Fear, alighting from his Horse, he stood full in the way; the furious Beast to make her Passage clear, rose on end, and clasped him in her formost Paws, thinking to have overthrown him; but with his strong Arms (now not being eighteen years of Age) he girded her so hard that she roared horribly, and immediately throwing her, they realed over each other for some time, but at length catching hold of her Nose with his Teeth, a dangerous tho' successful Adventure, she roared horribly, turned on her back, and yielded to the Conquerour. By this time the People were come up in Crouds, thinking he had been slain, but, to their amazement, found he had only got some slight scratches by her Paws, and a little bite on his Shoulder; then taking a Muzzle out of one of their Hands, he put it over her Nose and Ears, and so led her tamely, tho' not without her growling, to the Place from whence she came, to the Admiration of all the Spectators.

*Chap. II.   How many fair Virgins fell in Love with him, and among others,* Lucinda, *a wealthy Herdsman's Daughter; and how her Sweethearts discovering it by a Letter she dropt, lay in wait to be revenged on* Aurelius; *how he overcame them, and served them in their kind,* &c.

The things that had befallen and been done by *Aurelius* thus early, got him great Repute amongst the young Maidens of the Country, his Beauty conspiring with his manly Limbs and proportion of his Body to inflame their Hearts, so that many a handsome Virgin longed to have him her own, and grew Love-sick for him, which appeared by their languishing Eyes, Sighs and Blushes, more than their Tongues, being restrained by Modesty, durst proclaim; among others, a very beautiful Damsel named *Lucinda*, who was courted and admired by many amorous Youths, fixed her Affection on him; it's true, she was not of noble Parentage, as most commonly Historians boast their Female-lovers to be, but her honest Parents lived by keeping and selling Cattle, Dairing,[1] and such like Rural

[1] dairying.

Affairs, and by their industry were very Wealthy: This fair Virgin infinitely doated on young *Aurelius*, Love tormented her with his burning Flames, and in vain she strugled to extinguish the sacred Fire; for, not being past her first Blushes, Modesty and Bashfulness locked up her Tongue from making known what she so much desired, and all her Language in that affair was Sighs, Blushes, and ardent Glances; but *Aurelius*, whom thirst of Fame prompted to great things, did nor would not interpret that silent talk of Lovers, yet she would not stick[2] to praise his comely Features and manly Limbs, which made them conclude some other had taken up the room of her Heart they so earnestly laboured to possess; they used all means possible to find out who this *Adonis* should be, that could charm so fair a *Venus*, and make her sigh for him, whilst they, who highly valued themselves, must sigh for a Smile in vain. They long suspected, but not certain, till an unlucky Accident discovered all: The fair Virgin seeing she could not force her Tongue to disclose her Love, thought with herself, it was better to break her Mind by a Letter, than thus to endure the scorching Torment of *Cupid*'s Tyranny; *A Letter*, says she, *will not blush, though I must almost to death, to tell what I intrust the Paper with;* and so resolving and unresolving, strugling with herself for a time, at last she resolved to write, and did so in these Words: *Dear* Aurelius, *Pardon me in your Censure for this Boldness, and spare the Blushes of a Love-sick Maid, when she tells you, constrained by no common Passion, she Loves you, and without a suitable return of Love for Love, must be ever miserable: I have slighted for your sake many that pretend to admire me, and fill my Ears with Praises of my Beauty; but whether in this they flatter me or not, the proof will lye in your Judgment; if I am scorned and slighted by you, I must unavoidably remain your disconsolate* Lucinda.

This Letter being deliver'd to a Confident of hers, in order to carry it to her dear *Aurelius*, she dropt it, and one of her Lovers coming to pay her a Visit, found it, and read it, to his no small Grief and Amazement, and soon communicated it to the rest of her Sweet-hearts, resolving to make this slight Affront a common Cause, and so unite in Revenge against this troubler of their Repose. Upon this, all of them being heartily vexed, that one whom they accounted a Boy, should steal a Heart they had laboured to possess with great expence in Gifts and Treats, much Service and obsequious Duty, and in the end, concluded she was taken more with his fair Countenance than Fortune or Beauty of the Mind; then they came to this wicked resolve, which was to way-lay him as he

[2] hesitate.

came from Market, and deform him by gashing him with Wounds, and then they doubted not but the Object of her Affection would be removed, and she would as much detest him as ever she had loved him: In order to this Villany, they, armed with Swords and Daggers, hid themselves by the side of a Wood, nor had they lain long in Ambush, but, as they wished, he came along singing merrily this Song:

> Love is folly, Melancholly
>    Does on it attend;
> *Venus* Tents I do despise,
> *Mars* alone can me suffice,
>    Where Fame does crown the end.
>
> In Battles brave the Heroes rave,
>    Whilst Victory does fly;
> Between the Hosts and Trumpets Charms,
> The mighty Globe with fierce Alarms,
>    Whilst routed Squadrons fall and die.
>
> The bloody Field does Thunder yield,
>    And crops of Iron Spears;
> The grim God of War excites,
> And rallies Fliers to the Fights,
>    Vanquishing their Fears.

Our gallant Youth being come to the place where the Ambush was laid for him was not at little surprized to see four Men leap out armed, supposing them at first to be Robbers, but by their Reproaches, saying, *Now, Villain! we complement you in* Lucinda's *Name, whom thou hast basely inchanted with Love-powder, to withdraw her Affections from us, and place them on thy self, who art not worthy of her Smiles.* He was of another opinion, and would have replied to vindicate himself, by protesting his Innocency of what they charged him with; but their blind Rage and Love-fury would not give him leave to do it, but rushing on him, they gave him many stroaks, which raised his Anger, so that (being weaponless) with his strong Arms he seized two of the forwardest of them, and grasping them fast by the Collars, brought their Heads together with such violence, that their Eyes seemed to flash Fire, and reeling, at last they fell to the ground, unable to rise for a time; then taking away one of their

Swords, he fell on with such fury, that they concluded him endued with more than Human Force; so that fainting under mighty Blows, Wounds, and loss of Bloud, they fell on their Knees and begged Mercy, intreating him for the love of God, and fair *Lucinda*, to save their Lives, and they would tell him all that moved 'em to this rash Attempt; upon this, his generous Nature ordered them immediately to disarm, and he would inflict no more Wounds on them, which they readily did, and made a full Confession to him, how they designed to have handled him if they had overcome him. *Nay*, says he, *then if you were so hot for Mischief without a Cause, it's time to cool you;* whereupon he made them unstrip, and drove them into the Wood before him, like timerous Deer, and with their Garters bound them naked to four several Trees on a row, laying every one his Cloaths by him; then pulling out his Pen and Ink, he wrote these Lines, and fixed them on the Tree above the Head of the first:

> *These valiant Heroes one poor Man assail'd,*
> *But he unarm'd, over them all prevail'd;*
> *Hot Love it seems made them so daring bold,*
> *Therefore he thought fit thus they should be cool'd.*

This done, he went home and said nothing to any body of the matter; but they having staid in the Wood, and the next day unbound by the Wood-men, they dropt such words, that, together with the lines affixed, discovered their Disgrace, and the cause they had been so treated; which flying abroad in the Villages, it was soon known who had thus handled them; so that they were jeered by every one; and fair *Lucinda* greatly rejoyced for two Causes: First, That her Lover had escaped the danger; And secondly, by this means he could not be ignorant of the Love she bore him.

*Chap. III.   How* Aurelius *was sent to* London, *and in his way fought and took two High-way Robbers; how he was put Apprentice to a* Turky *Merchant, and fell in Love with* Dorinda *his beautiful Daughter; but being slighted by her, got leave to sail for* Turky.

This Adventure got *Aurelius* much Praise; but he little regarded the Love of the fond Maid, which made her fall sick, and her Friends fearing to lose, by this means, their darling Daughter, came to treat with his Friends about a Marriage, offering a large Portion; but his Years not much suiting with Love, they finding him averse, his Parents did not much urge it to him; however, *Lucinda*, by the help of able Physicians recovered, and with her health, her love abated; so that growing more and more indifferent, a lusty Youth, Son to a rich Farmer, courting her closely, at the importunity of her Parents, she was married, which greatly rejoyced *Aurelius*, who feared she might have done some mischief to her self for being neglected by him, which would have redounded to his disgrace; however, his Parents fearing the Rivals whom he had tread as is mentioned in the foregoing Chapter, might meditate Revenge, and do him some injury one way or other, they concluded to send him to *London*, (the Metropolis of the Kingdom) and place him in some Gentile[3] Calling that might enable him to live in Wealth and Credit; and communicating it to him, bid him pitch upon what Calling he thought fit: In obedience to their Commands, he consented to it; and having an Itch for Travelling, and seeing strange Lands, chose to be a Merchant; and soon a Merchant was found, who traded to *Turky*, and with him he was placed soon, gaining the good Esteem of the whole Family, by his courteous Behaviour and Willingness to oblige. I should have told you in his way to *London*, he fought with and took two High-way Men that set upon to have robbed him, for which the County, in which he did this brave Exploite, rewarded him with an imbroidered silver Belt and a well tempered Sword, which afterward upon occasion, he used with success, as will appear in the Sequel of this History.[4]

When he had served about three Years of his time, having gained much Fame by playing several Prizes, and worsting the experienc'd Masters of Defence; he grew so in Love with Arms, that nothing charmed him more than the sound of the Trumpet, or ratling of the Martial Drum: In exercising the Pike and Musquet, he took a singular delight, exceeding in it all the Youth of the City; but whilst he followed these Practices, and every-where gained Applause, the powerful God of Love, whom he always thought to have baffled, stormed his couragious Heart, and got strong Possession in it; his Master had only one Daughter, who till this time was kept from his sight at a Boarding-school; where, having acquired many Accomplishments to add a seemly Grace to her excellent Beauty, and so lovely and charming she was in all parts that the first sight of her inflamed him; and now knowing what it was to be in Love, and the Torments that attend it, he blamed himself for stopping his Ears to *Lucinda*, and making her suffer so much upon the like score; he tryed by

---

[3] gentle(?).
[4] i.e., in what follows.

all the obliging Actions he could, to make the fair *Dorinda* (for so she was called) understand his good meaning to her; but she not exceeding fourteen, though proper of her Age, through Ignorance of what Love meant, took his civility as a duty and respect towards her, being his Master's Daughter, and concluded it no more than his Duty, though he made her several Presents; and when he waited at the Table, his Eyes were always fixed on her, his sleep went from him, and he frequently dreamed he addressed himself to her in studied Eloquence and Courtship, but she refused his Love, frowned on him, and when he went to grasp her, slided away like a shadow from his empty Arms. These he took as bad Omens of his unsuccessful Love; yet at length, summoning his Courage to his Aid, after long deliberation, he resolved to write his Mind, and lay it on her Dressing-box, that she should not miss to find the Letter; and accordingly he wrote in these words:

*Lovely* Dorinda,
  *Your Beauty, fair as the new born Light, has captivated the Heart of your poor Servant, and entangled him in the Fetters of Love; therefore humbly prostrating my self at your Feet, I beg Compassion at your Hands; The Inequality indeed may make you check my Presumption; but consider Love, that takes the Diadem from Queens, and makes them condescend to match with those of a humble Strain, pleading on my side, may make you compassionate towards him that can only live by your Smiles, and without your Favours must be miserable.*
                                      *Subscribed*, Aurelius

This fell into her Hands as he could wish, and she read it with much surprize, mixed with anger and disdain; then tore it in sunder, saying, *What, has my Father bestowed so much in breeding on me, and dares his Man, who came a Country-clown in a manner but yesterday, presume impudently to tell me he loves me, who am my Father's only Heir, a Match for a Lord, and may glitter in the Court amongst the proudest Ladies: No, no, this must not be suffered, I'll nip his sawcy Love in the Bud, and make him know his Distance.*
This said, she flung down Stairs, and finding him in the Counting-house, casting up the Books,[5] by himself, she said, *How now Aurelius, what made you so bold as to intrude into my Closet, and leave a Letter there; I think you did more than good Manners will bear you out in; but let me hear no more of your foolish Love, for if I do, you may have such cause to repent it, that you little wish for.* Thunder struck at this sharp and un-expected Repremand, whilst he laboured to force suitable words for a

[5] going over the accounts.

reply and excuse, she gave him not time, but forcing frowns on her beauteous Brow, she flung away in a Pet.

This greatly vexed *Aurelius*, and made him repent his rash leaving the Letter to fall into her Hands, but at length resolving to struggle with the Flame, and not speak of Love to her, for fear of offending, till he found a more favourable opportunity, he from that time only continued a duteous respect towards her, trying all manner of ways by his Service to oblige her, yet found her countenance estranged from him; and indeed her Father being vastly Rich, that and the Fame of her unparallel'd Beauty soon brought many young Lords and Knights to Court her; this killing sight tormented our Lover more than her disdain before had done, as now concluding he should lose the beautious Object of all his Wishes and Desires; and therefore that absence, as he fancyed, might mitigate, if not cure the violent Feavour Love tortured him withal, he took an opportunity when he found his Master in a good humour, to desire one request of him, *What is it*, said the Merchant, *if it be reasonable it shall not be denyed you?* Only Sir, *said he*, that, to improve my understanding in Merchandize, I may with your good leave go abroad and manage your Affairs for some time beyond the Seas, in the nature of your Factor. *Well mention'd*, said the Merchant, *I was thinking of this my self, and thought to ask you, how you stood inclined that way; but seeing you have freely offered it on your own accord, I am the better pleased, and shall conclude, you will be more diligent about my business, for there is nothing like a willing mind, and the next fleet that sets sail, I will provide all things necessary for your Voyage to* Constantinople *in* Turky, *the largest City in the World; for the Factor I employed there, is lately dead.* Aurelius, very well pleased at this, thanked his Master, and promised in every thing he could to do the best, faithfully to serve him.

*Chap. IV.   How* Aurelius *took leave of the Family, and left a Paper and Token for his unkind Mistress; how, sailing the Seas, he had a dreadful Fight with* Algire *and* Sally *Pirates,*[6] *the Wonders he did therein, and safely arrived at* Constantinople; *his Reception and Welcome there by the Factors; how he slew a Tygar, and rescued the* Sultan's *Daughter*, &c.

Early in the Spring, when the Seas were freed from the rage of boisterous Winds, Mr. *Tradewell*, the Merchant, fited out three Ships of his own, richly laden, which, in company of divers others, prepared to

[6] pirates from Algiers and Salli (in Morocco).

set sail; when the Maid-servants heard *Aurelius* was to go and leave them, they wept for sorrow, for they loved and valued him at a high rate; however at parting, he treated them with Wine and Sweet-meats, and left with one of them these lines, with a Jewel sealed up, to deliver to fair *Dorinda*, but with a charge not to do it, till she heard the Ship was put to Sea.

> *Lovely, but cruel Maid, too, too unkind,*
> *'Tis you that force me to the Seas and Wind;*
> *Yet I must blame my self, and needs confess,*
> *In me was found too much Unworthyness*
> *So rare a Prize to gain; I aim'd too high,*
> *Like those I'm punish'd that wou'd storm the Sky:*
> *Yet pardon me, though you will not be kind,*
> *That I must bear your Image in my Mind:*
> *That lovely Form, time never can deface,*
> *Which Infant-love, first in my Heart did place;*
> *Then be so kind, when you this Jewel see,*
> *In pitty, to vouchsafe to think on me.*

The Fleet sailed with a prosperous Gail, till they came within ten Leagues of *Gibralter*, on the *Spanish* side, and then a Storm arising, they were tossed with uncertain Winds all Night, and next Morning, to the great Terrour of most, they stood in with five *Algerine* and *Sally* Men of War; so that many began to cry out, they were utterly undone; some were for running a shoar into the first Bay or Creek, though to a certain hazard of their Lives upon those unmountable Rocks and Shoars; others for putting off in the Long-boats, and leaving the Ships and Goods a Prey to the Pirates that so they might escape Slavery; in this Consternation they came up board and board, the Admiral of *Algire* biding them strike and yield, or else to expect no quarter; to this proud Language of the *Turk*'s, *Aurelius* being on the Deck with his Sword in his Hand, answered, The Ships were laden with his Master's Goods, of which he had a charge, and that they were *English* Men on board, who did not use to be out-blustered or dared with Words; therefore if they expected any thing they must win it and wear it. Then turning to his drooping Companions, he said, *Come, pull up couragious Hearts, and let us fight for the Honour of our Nation, fam'd for Valour throughout the World; we have a stout Ship under us, and whilst she Swims above Water, let it never be said we will quit it.*

By this time the bold assailing *Turks* eagerly strove to win the Wast[7] of the Ship, in which the first that entered, with one mighty blow he struck his Head off, and down fell the Body with it into the Sea, to breakfast the Fish; this animated others, and all taking Arms, fought with prodigious fury; the great Guns in the mean while roared from either side, bellowing Thunder and breathing Fire whilst Iron Globes pierced through and through the Waves, by their violence mounted, and by the shock grew tempestuous. *Aurelius* layed about him with such violent force, that he made Arms, Legs and Heads, fly at a dismal rate; so that the *Turks* swearing by *Mahomet*, he was a Devil, and no Man, but would have ungrapled; which he perceiving, leaped on Board, and was seconded by others; hand to hand he slew the Admiral, which so dismaid the *Turks*, that they hoised all their Sails, but too late, for throwing prodigious showers of Fire upon it, soon set their tackle in a blaze, and the broad Waves shined with the light of the Flame: this Ship running foul on another, set her on Fire, and a third coming up to relieve their Fellows, met with the same fate; a fourth sunk, which made the fifth run away with all the sail she could make, to deliver her self from the like ruin, and carry home the dismal News; some of the floating *Turks* they took up and saved, the rest perished by Wounds, Fire, and Waves; and their Cries were heard half broiling in the Flames, like the Damned in Hell. The Prisoners they took, they stowed in the holds of the Ships; and lying by a few Hours, to repair the damage they had received in the Fight, they set sail, and without any further Interruption passed the Streights, and *Dardanelles* sailing directly for *Constantinople*.

The Ships no sooner arrived in the Port, but the *English* Merchants and Factors came on board, to welcome and congratulate the safe Arrival of their Country-men, and enquire of the welfare of their Friends in *England:* and great joy and feasting there was amongst them; they saluted the Port with their Guns, and were resaluted with as many; and going on shoar, he took charge of his Master's Effects in the Ware-houses on the Key, and so prudently managed Matters, that he got Reputation, and large Commendations were carried back to *England* of him: yet it moved not *Dorinda*'s haughty Mind, who sacrificed her Love to Ambition; marrying into a noble Family, though she proved unhappy in the Match, for her Husband being banished, for Conspiring against the Queen, and his Estate seized, he compelled her to accompany him, to the great grief of her Parents.

[7] waist.

*Aurelius* being as is said, in *Turky*, got great riches; and, when his leasure would permit, took his pleasure in a Chalap[8] on the shoar of the black Sea, and other pleasant Floods that are in the Neighbourhood of that famous City; when, landing by a Wood-side that descended from a Mountain, as he with some others were banquetting under a shady Palm-tree, and very merry, all on a suddain their Ears were saluted with a dismal Cry, which seemed to proceed from Female Voices (and still drew nearer) upon which apprehending the approach of some Danger, they rose up, drew their Swords, and stood on their Guards, till they should see or know what the meaning of it was; when immediately two Ladies well mounted came riding, diging the bloody Rowels of their Spurs in their Horses sides, and seeing Company, redoubled their Cries for speedy Help and Assistance to save their Lives. *Aurelius*, who as yet saw nothing pursue them, thought they had been affrighted by some Phantom, or else distracted, but they were no sooner come up, nor had time to relate the cause of their Fears and Danger, but be beheld a monsterous Tygar coming after them at full Cry, as having the scent of them in the Wind; his Companions, who were only two young Factors and a Steers-man, perswaded him as he loved his Life to hast aboard the Boat, take the Ladies with them, and leave the Horses a Prey to the ravenous Creature, seeing they could not convey them away in their Boat without danger of Sinking, not being capable of holding them; but *Aurelius* not hearkening to this, bid them put the Ladies aboard, and those that wou'd might put off in it, and see the Combate safe from Danger, for he was resolved to try his good Sword, to see if the Tygar's Skin was proof against it or not; fear soon made them all take his Counsel, and now he is left alone on the Shoar to stand the brunt. The Tygar came at him with great fury, thinking at once to have devoured him, but his undaunted Courage bore him out, for the first blow he cut off one of his fore Legs, at which he howled horribly; yet made at him again, and, wounding him in the other, quickly sheathed the Sword in his Belly, which made him loose his hold, and following that with a mighty blow he felled him and smote off his Head; his Companions in great fear beholding the Fight, now as much rejoyced to see him Vanquisher, whom they had given before for lost; his Friends embraced him, and the Ladies returned him a thousand thanks, owning the safety of their Lives had happened by his means; for this cruel Beast it seems ranging up and down the Country a long time, had destroyed many People and Cattle, being as big as an ordinary Horse; and so, with the

[8] a sloop.

Head, he returned to *Constantinople*, the Ladies quitting their Horses to go the safer way by Water, as fearing, in returning by Land, some other Danger might befal them; one of them turning aside her Veil, shewed her lovely face and lilly Hand, presenting *Aurelius* with a rich Diamond Ring, enquiring of his Country, Name, and the cause of his being in *Turky*, all which he briefly told her, the relation of which spun out the time till they landed; now this fair Lady was the Turkish *Sultan*'s Daughter, who going in disguise with her Waiting-maid to take the Air privately, and retired from State-formality, fell into this Danger, which had not Fortune thrown as it were our valiant *London* Prentice in their way had been fatal to them: And, as a further mark of her Favour, she afterward privately sent him a Vest of Cloth of Gold and Sable, and a Sword-handle studied with Rubies and other precious Stones, biding him wear it for her sake, as a Reward for the good service he had done her; but withal not to mention he had seen her, for that might be dangerous to him if not reflect on her Honour for as much as she had stolen out Veiled, and none but her Confidents knew she was missing, intimating his Companions should be cautioned the like.

*Chap. V.   How the Prince of the* Georgeans *marryed the* Sultan's *Daughter, and how* Aurelius Justing, *overthrew three mighty* Turks, *and broke the Prince's Neck with a weighty stroke, for which he was doomed to be devoured by two Lyons, which he slew, and gained his Liberty, and other matters.*

*Aurelius* bringing the Tygar's Head to *Constantinople*, the Aga of the Janisaries[9] sent for him, and demanded it of him as due to him, but withal gave him five hundred Aspers for the good Service he had done in destroying so cruel a Beast; and then it was hung up in the Arsenal among the Heads of Bears, Lyons, Leopards, Panthers, and other wild Beasts slain in Hunting, for the *Turks* naturally love that Exercise, and seek Danger for Applause, though many of them come short home.

During these Transactions, the Prince of the *Georgeans*, a vast Country, lying in the *Turkish* Territories between *Persia* and *Armenia*, came to the *Ottoman* Port, and being highly entertained by the *Sultan* for aiding the *Persians*, and doing him many good Services on the Frontiers; he at length aspired to court the beautiful *Teozara*, the Lady whom *Aurelius* had rescued, and the Sultan encouraging him in his Suit, for here the

9 the Sultan's palace guard.

Daughters have not their own chusing, but are absolutely at the disposal of their Fathers: He so prevailed, that the match was concluded, and great preparations made for the celebrating the marriage. Rich presents were sent from the Bridegroom to the Bride, and from her to him carryed publickly through the Street, for the People to behold, by Eunuches, Pages, and the great Officers of the Court; and at length, in the stately Mosque of *Sancta Sophia*, formerly a Christian Church, the Mufty, or *Mahomet*'s High-Priest, joyned their Hands; and after great Feasting, for such a Wedding usually lasts for ten or twenty Days, Martial-feats were appointed, in the nature of Justs, Tilts and Turnaments, and many gallant Men prepared to try their Prowess, and win Honour to the Nations that gave them Birth; this being known, inflamed *Aurelius*'s Heart with a thirst of Glory, and he resolved to make one amongst them; early in the Morning the City was filled with Crouds, the Trumpets and Hautboys flourishing and sounding to give warning, that the Combatants might in due time prepare to be in a readiness; and the Janizaries were appointed to make and guard the List, whilst golden Pavillions were erected for the Sultan, Sultanness, and others of the highest Rank.

In the mean while *Aurelius* had suited himself with a fine suit of Armour, furnished with a silver Launce, and the trusty Sword that was given him in *England;* the Device of his Shield was a Phenix, representing the Virgin Queen he was born under, and the Ocian chained, signifying the English Masters of the Seas; and buying a strong Horse of Thracian breed, he came prancing in to try his chance in the List; yet, seeing many forward, and being but a Stranger, and young, he gave way to them, thinking thereby to gain the greater Honour, to conquer those that had conquered others; at length, many being thrown out, three Turkish Bashaws of divers Nations were left Conquerors, who proudly, in the name of the Bridegroom, challenged any that dared to enter: *Aurelius* seeing many strange Courtiers, and none very forward, concluded this was his time to win Honour, and signalize himself at the Turkish Court; and so pricking forward his foaming Steed, gallantly enter'd. The first he encountered with, he struck full on the breast with his Launce, and tumbled him with his Heels kicking upwards over the Crupper, so that the Earth shook with his heavy fall; and much in the same manner he served the other two, one at the first, and the other at the second Course; upon which a mighty shout arose, and many wondred who this valiant Stranger should be: Some English, who was privy to his Enterprize, greatly rejoyced that their Country had bore the Honour from other

Nations: the Prince of the *Georgians* was inwardly vexed to see his Champions thus baffled, and no other attempting to enter the List in vindication of his Honour; wherefore, with the leave of his Father-in-law, the Sultan, he armed to vindicate his foiled Men; nor could the intreaties or tears of his fair Bride, stay him from the Encounter: Our Heroick English Youth, seeing him enter in golden Armour, undauntedly prepared to run the course; and they did it with such thundering speed, that the ground trembled under their Horses feet, and with such strength and fury they met, that the ends of their Launces or Spears shivered in the Air; then passing on they turned again, the Prince drew his Sword and came upon *Aurelius* e're he had time to draw his; yet, having the waighty truncheon of his spear in his hand, he met him at English Club-law, and receiving a slight wound in the shoulder, he returned the stroke with his Truncheon, charging it so forcible on the Prince's helmet behind, that he not only beat him from his Horse, but by the violent inclining, his Neck broke, so that he was taken up for dead.

This greatly enraged the Turkish Sultan, insomuch that he swore by his Father's Scalp, and the Beard of *Mahomet*, that our Youth should dye the cruel'st Death that ever was invented for Man; causing him immediately to be unarmed, and brought before him, demanding who he was, and of what Nation he was, he as undauntedly reply'd, *He was a* London *'Prentice, come over to manage his Master's Affairs, and had done this according to the rule of Justs and Law of Arms, in Honour of the Maiden Queen, to whom he was a Subject, and was ready to do more if permitted.* The Turk, amazed at this bold reply, turning to his Nobles, said, *By* Mahomet, *if all the* London *'Prentices be as stout as this, they are able to beat me out of my Empire: The* German *Armies I have so often baffled, are but Pigmies to them.* However, he ordered him to a Dungeon, where he lay three Days without any Food, only Rats and Mice which the Dungeon afforded, verily beleiving he was put there to starve to Death; in the mean while, the English Merchants and Factors did all they could to interceed for him, but the inexorable Turk would hear nothing on his behalf.

At the end of three Days, *Aurelius* over night had notice to prepare himself for death the next Morning; but was not acquainted by what means he should dye, expecting from his usage nothing but Tortures and Torments: this brought into his mind, how St. *George* broke the Dungeon, and escaped the like Fate; he tryed to do it, but finding all the sides hard Rock, and the entrance a mighty Iron-gate, wanting sutable Engins to force his way, he gave over his struggling, thinking next Morning to surprize the Keepers, when they came to take him out, and by wresting a weapon, hew his passage through them, and so escape to Sea; but then thinks he, I shall injure my Master, for all his Goods will be confiscated: whilst he was musing on these things, he heard the Bolts and Chains rattle, Ropes let down to draw him up, which he willingly embraced; and once more viewing Light, saw himself encompassed with armed Men, who led him to the Amphitheatre, where he found the Sultan and great numbers placed round in Galleries to see his Tragedy. Two Lyons it seems were prepared, the fiercest and largest in the Den, who had been kept three Days without Meat, to make them the more cruel and ravenous on their Prey: and that he should make the better Figure, the Princess, whose tender Heart would not let her be present at so woful a sight, in token of her Love, sent him privately a Shirt of Cambrick, Drawers of white Sattin, embroidered with Gold, and a crimson Cap; when upon notice from whose fair Hands they came, and being informed she was one of the Ladies he had delivered from the fury of the Tygar, he returned her the Ring she gave him, and desired, when he was dead, she would condescend to keep him in her remembrance, and whilst alive, favour him with her good wishes; and so stripping, put on the things she had sent him, as a Token of her Love.

This he had scarce done, when the Skies overcast with dismal blackness, so that the Sun yeilded but a feeble light, and soon after all Heaven thundered with a Storm, when immediately the doors of the two dreadful Dens were opened by Pullies and Chains from above in the Galleries, and two huge Lyons, with fiery Eyes came running out roaring horribly, swinging their Tails about their sides, when casting their glaring Eyes on our undaunted Youth as their Prey, they came furiously at him with open Mouths, thinking to rend him in pieces immediately, and bury him in their hungry Maws; who, resolving not to die without some tryal of Manhood, stretched out his strong Arms, and as Fortune favoured and guided them, just as they made a furious leap, to seize him in their Paws, he thrust his Fists down their Throats with such Strength and Fury,[10] that after long strugling, seizing their hearts, pulled them out by main strength; upon this, with a roar, the two furious Beasts fell dead at his Feet, and two prodigeous claps of Thunder ensued: at this all the Spectators were much afrighted, but our undaunted Youth demanded aloud if they had any more Lyons to send, he was ready to encounter them; and for the Honour of his Queen and Country, again expose his

[10] St. George, whom Aurelius here imitates, killed only *one* lion.

Life: But this valiant Act made the Sultan conclude him more than mortal Man, and ordered he should immediately be set at liberty, and rich Rewards given to him. He afterwards offered to make him great in his Court, if he would turn Mahometan, but he refused it with disdain; and so, being by his Valour freed from Danger, he went to his business.

*Chap. VI.   How the Turkish Princess fell in Love with* Aurelius; *for his sake turned Christian, and came to* England *with him with great store of Riches; of the splendor of their Wedding, and other memorable things worthy of note.*

*Aurelius* thus having encreased his Fame and Renown, no sooner was the Funerals of the Georgian Prince over with great Solemnity, but the beauteous *Teoraza* began to contemplate his Beauty and manly Courage, and to fix her mind on him, and at length growing restless in her Love, not knowing for blushes how to discover[11] it, she acquainted an English Merchant's Wife with her Love; who at first, fearing her life was in hazzard, if it should be discovered, put off the fair Princess with delays; but finding her impatient, and bringing her Jewels and Imbroyderies of Gold and Silver, to make her her Friend in this Service, at last she promised to deliver her Letter, written in few words, *viz.*

*Brave English Youth, my Preserver, I, the Sultan's Daughter, am in Love with you; I know you have Courage enough to meet me, do it this Evening in the Orange-grove behind the* Seraglio; *and I hope you will have no cause to repent your so doing.* Terazo.

*Aurelius* upon reading it was in many doubts, but considering what the Princess had already done for him, and calling to mind her excellent Beauty, resolved to go, though at the hazzard of his Life; for it had been no less than Death, had it been discovered, to make Love to a Sultaness of the Royal *Ottoman* Blood; and accordingly he met her, and she kindly received and welcomed him; for in *Turky*, nice Complements are out of fashion: And, to be brief, after some other meetings, she promised for his sake, to refuse the greatest Princes in the Empire, and turn Christian, if he would make her his Wife; it was agreed between them, that, shipping all his Master's Effects in the Fleet ready to Sail, she in disguise should go with him into *England*.

And this the Love of our brave English Youth made her enterprize in a Sailor's Habit, bringing many Caskets of Jewels and Gold with her, and

[11] reveal.

so they safely arrived in *England;* when coming home and finding his Master's Daughter marry'd. The Princess was Baptized by the Bishop of *London*, at St. *Paul*'s, and then soon after they were married in great Pomp. *Aurelius*'s Master being at the charge of the Wedding; so that the Festival lasting six Days, all the *Turky* Merchants graced the Wedding, as did the Lord-Mayor and Aldermen; and the Queen hearing of this great Princess, sent for her to Court, and kindly entertained her; and at her request, sent such prevailing Letters to *Amurath* the Turkish Sultan, that after his storming Fury was over, he began to have a liking of the Match; and, inviting his Son-in-law, without fear of harm, to Trade in his Country, and he would make him the richest Merchant in the World: Which accordingly he did, and encreased in Wealth exceedingly; having all his Goods in *Turky*, inward and outward bound (Custom free;) and for his sake the English Merchants had Priveledges granted them, and were esteemed above other Nations, which, in a good measure, continue to this day.

*Chap. VII.   How he served a* Jew *for cheating him with counterfeit Jewels, from whence the Custom of Bumping at the Post at* Bilingsgate, *on Easter Monday arose; his great Charity to the Poor; his Death, and the memorable Epitaph, placed on his Tomb.*

*Aurelius* in his Trading, still encreasing, and bringing great Riches to *England*, at length a Jew came to him, pretending he had Jewels of great Price, and he not well known in [the] Country; if he could put them off for him, he would think himself ever oblig'd to him, and would reward him to his content. *Aurelius*, who thought he meant honestly, undertook it, not regarding Rewards, and they appearing excellent in Lustre, made no farther enquiry; but believed the Man, and sold them to a great Court Lady for six hundred Pounds, which Money he gave the Jew, and he laughing in his sleeve, sneaked away to *Holland*, thinking at this rate, any thing would pass upon the English; and there making more, for they were no other than Christial[12] and such like, finely set off, came again and proposed as before; but in the mean while, the Plot had been discovered, for the Lady having occasion for Money, and going to pawn them to a Goldsmith, they were found to be Counterfits; whereupon she undeservedly reproached *Aurelius*, who told her how he came by them, and freely returned her the Money; and now he took the couzening[13] Jew to

[12] crystal, i.e., glass and hence worthless.
[13] cheating.

task, but he not having Money to satisfie him, he scorned to throw him in Goal,[14] to lye lousing and starving as many would have done, and as indeed he deserved; but living near *Billingsgate*, all the Satisfaction he took of him, was to order his four Men, each to take a Hand and a Leg, it being then Easter Monday, and carry him to a Post on the Key,[15] and there by swinging him backward and forward to bump his Arse soundly against it; and that was all the satisfaction he had for his six hundred Pounds. And in memory of this, the 'Prentices and Porters there about, keep up a Custom to do it, to any they can catch on that day near the place; concluding the Jew's Bum made not satisfaction for the Money, and so they will Bump on, till they think the Merchant's Money is out.

But to conclude, when he found himself in his declining Years, he ordered Fourscore poor People to come every morning to his door, who received twelve Pence a piece, and encreased the number, as his years encreased, to his dying day. His Princess dyed before him, for whom he built a stately Monument, in which he was also laid, and this Epitaph affixed on it:

## The Epitaph

*In* Cheshire *born, I did through Dangers wade,*
*And with Success did drive the Merchant's Trade;*
*Riches I got, and did befriend the Poor,*
*So wish I all to do who have good store:*
*The comfort of it in my life I found,*
*But now more happy in't, though under ground;*
*Eternal Life it purchases for me,*
*The best of Christian life is Charity:*
*Therefore do well for those that are in want,*
*And you will find Rewards in Heaven not scant.*

Thus Reader, have I received this antient History of the famed *London* 'Prentice (or rich Merchant) which for many Years has lain in obscurity; which no doubt will be a great encouragement to Youth, to be Virtuous and Valiant, and to those of elder Years, to hope by Industry from a small beginning, to rise to great advance; and if both succeed, I have my wish.

FINIS

[14] i.e., gaol (jail).
[15] quai.

# THE HISTORY OF
# JOHNNY ARMSTRONG

## (ca. 1700)

The Pleafant and Delightful

# HISTORY

OF THE

Renowned Northern Worthy,

## Johnny Armstrong,

O F

## *WESTMORELAND:*

SHEWING

His many Noble Deeds, in his Youth in divers Countries, in Arms againft the Turks and Sarazens in the
*Holy Land*; and how, fettling at *Guiltnock-Hall* in *Weftmore-
land*, he by his Induftry, without any Eftate in Lands or
Rents, kept Eightfcore Men to attend him, richly ap-
parelled, well-mounted, and armed : How he married a
fair Lady, a poor Knight's Daughter, and of the noble
Entertainment at his Wedding, who brought him a fair
Son : Alfo an Account of his many Victories over the Scots,
and how going to *Edenborough* upon the friendly Invitation of that King, he and his Men were all flain, valiantly
fighting, whofe Death was revenged by his Son ; with
many other matters of note.

---

**Licens'd and Enter'd according to Order.**

---

*LONDON:*
Printed by and for *W. O.* and are to be fold by the Bookfellers.

Johnny Armstrong *is again an example of popular fiction, but it is much more old-fashioned than* London's Glory. *Set in the fourteenth century (the Battle of Bannockburn mentioned in the text took place in 1314), the story, anonymous as the ballad which follows the prose text, has the quality of legend: everything in it is larger than life. The hero's openhandedness as displayed at his wedding, his generosity in helping the poor with money and protection, his pride in keeping his eightscore serving men, his great valor as shown in his epic death, all these details are related uncritically and with the loving admiration accorded only to folk heroes. Who this Johnny Armstrong was is not known, but undoubtedly he existed (Aurelius, in the previous story, clearly did not). We may surmise that he was little more than a Border raider and thief like his sixteenth-century namesake and counterpart, but he was clearly a hero to whoever composed his story and probably to a good many others also.*

*The story has indeed much of the quality of the early ballads, without of course the heightening effects provided by metrical form and extreme condensation. The prose story is nevertheless economically told, the whole narrative pointed toward the dramatic and tragic climax. The unknown narrator seeks to be as objective in his rendering as possible. He is restrained in his presentation of the abject treachery of King Robert, his comment being confined to the hint that the king would not go unpunished; almost reportorial in his account of the defense which Johnny and his men made of their lives, he gives hardly any details about the heroic quality of the fighting but merely states the facts about the outcome.*

*From the close connections between ballad and prose narrative one could easily conclude that the prose writer had simply been inspired by the verse account of the life and death of Armstrong, but the relationship is in actuality not that simple. The ballad itself is one of those which F. J. Child collected in his monumental* English and Scottish Popular Ballads,[1] *where it appears as No. 169; the text of version B is almost word for word the same as that following the prose version here. The headnote to the ballad in Child, however, connects the verses with a Johnny Armstrong who was hanged by King James V of Scotland in 1530. If the material in Child's note is reliable, then, the ballad and the prose text are dealing with two different Armstrongs, living two centuries apart, and we may well wonder why the seventeenth-century writer transfers a ballad about a sixteenth-century figure to a fourteenth-century one. Can we assume that the tradition in which our writer was working is a sounder one than that which identifies the hero with the man who died in 1530? I have no answer to this question.*

[1] Boston and New York: Houghton Mifflin Co., 1882–1898.

*The text which follows is based on the copy of the book in the Bodleian Library, Oxford.*

## The History of
## Johnny Armstrong of Westmoreland, &c.

*Chap. I.   How in his youthful Days following the Wars abroad in the* Holy Land, *and other Countries, he learned the Art of Arms, came off with great Success and Applause; and after his Return, settled at* Guiltnock-hall *in* Westmoreland; *and of the noble Entertainment he gave to his hundred and sixty Men.*

In former times when the Wars were frequent between *England* and *Scotland*, before the two Kingdoms were united in King *James* the First of *England*, and Sixth of *Scotland*, the bordering Counties, by reason of the Inroads that were made, were sometimes possessed by one Nation, and sometimes by another; so that in these Contests there happened to live in *Westmoreland* a brave jolly Man named *Johnny Armstrong*, who made it his Business to keep up the good old laudible Customs of Charity, supplying the Poor with Cloaths and Food, not denying to any that asked; so that for his Liberality he was famed everywhere and extreamly beloved by all, as well of his rich Neighbours as poor Ones; and though he had no free Estate, yet their was such a Providence upon his Industry, which he used many Ways, as in Cloathing, buying and selling Forrests of Timber, breeding Cattle, and the like, that his Store vastly encreased, insomuch that a great many wondered how he could live at the rate he did, not well knowing how his Incomes should maintain it. For building a long Hall on purpose, he had a Table every Day furnished for eightscore Men, which he not only fed, but kept cloathed, and maintained in all other Matters; having Horse and Arms upon occasion for the Defence of his Country, ready for them to Mount, taking great delight to exercise them, having been trained up a Soldier in foreign Lands, fighting against the Turks and Sarazens many Years in his youthful Days, and done great Exploits, which made him by many be stiled the Champion of the North, so that he kept the Borders very much in quiet.

His Mansion House was called *Guiltnock-hall*, and is famed to this Day for his living in it, there being small Houses standing in the Same place bearing the Name to this time; however the larger Ruins shows it has been a Place very famous in former, for upon digging, the Workmen found the Foundations very spacious; and some of them have had the Luck to light upon Earthen-pots, with the Coin of divers Kings, to the great Inriching of them, and so they called it *Johnny Armstrong's* Bounty-money. Upon these things he imployed himself till he was forty Years of Age, without being married, though several rich Offers were made to him of wealthy young Maidens; this made him consider of altering his Condition, not so much for the Desire of Marriage, as he might get an Heir to keep up the Grandure of his Hospitality, and to carry his Name to Posterity, as being descended of a very ancient and worthy Family, some of which are living to this Day.

*Chap. II.    How being setled, and living gallantly, he bethought himself of Marriage, and fell in Love with a Gentleman's Daughter of no Fortune; and of the splendid Entertainment he made; and how thereupon he was taken for the King, &c.*

His Thoughts about Marriage were no sooner known, but out of the Respect the Gentry and others in the Country had for him, many suitable Matches were proposed; but as for Riches he lightly regarded it, relying mainly on the Bounties of Providence, he resolved to choose out one Handsome, Ingenious, and Virtuous; and so it was not long e're he saw One as he was passing through a Market-Town, that he could fancy; and upon inquiry, found she was a Gentleman's Daughter, though of a mean Fortune, her Father being fallen much to Decay, by the Losses he had Received by the War between the two Nations, in his Estate and Goods: But this made no Difference between them, the Gentleman was glad to put his Daughter off so well, and *Johnny* was as well pleased he had met with a virtuous modest Woman, not without a Sufficiency of Beauty to please him well enough, and the Day being appointed, he promised to come and marry her, and so fetch her home to his House. And in order to this, he arrayed his eightscore Men in Purple, laced all with Gold and Silver Lace, with Silver hilted Swords, imbroider'd Belts, guilded Spurs, and Plumes of white Feathers in their Bonnets, and bravely mounted, he rid in most gallant Attire in the Head of them; so that the People through the Towns as he passed taking him for the King, they run before him, throwing up their Hats, and shouting; nor could they hardly [be] perswaded by himself to the contrary.

His fair Mistress was of the same Opinion, when looking out at the

Window, upon the knocking at the Gate, and seeing her Father's House surrounded with so gallant a Troop, fancying it could be none else, and that he might be a hunting in those Parts, and so came thither for Entertainment; upon this she run and waked her Father, it being yet early, and told him the King was come with a numerous Train to visit him.

*God forbid, said he; what shall we do then? We shall be undone, for all our Provisions for thy Wedding will not be a mouthful for them. Indeed the House looks fair and promising without, though my mean Fortune can allow but lean Commons.[2] Go down and tell them I am not at home, I am sick, or anything to put them off; for better so, than pretend to entertain them, when we cannot do it; better strain a Complement, than to be disgraced, or at least fast I know not how long after.*

Upon this down she went, and peeping through the Wicket, demanded what brought them to her Father's House; to which *Johnny Armstrong* replyed, My Promise to you, that I would this Day make you my Wife. Upon this, knowing his Voice, and looking wishfully on him, she could not but fancy him to be what she before had thought, till he alighted, and saluted her very kindly, assuring her he was no other than *Johnny Armstrong* of *Guiltnock-Hall* in *Westmoreland*. Upon this throwing open the Gates, she conducted him in, and run up to tell the Business, whereupon her Father coming down, kindly welcomed him. But when he saw his Train, he blessed himself, to know what he meant by bringing such a number of Men so bravely Accutered, fancying he had invited all the Gentlemen in ten Countries: But when he told him they were such as usually attended him when he went upon any important Affair, his Wonder yet more encreased, for though he had heard he had daily relieved abundance of Poor, he could not believe he could keep so many Men in that Garb.

*Chap. III.   How he was married, and of the noble Entertainment he made, the number of his Servants and Attendants, and how he invited the whole Country to his Wedding, &c.*

Now Matters being at this pass, the Pages had the care of the Horses, whilst the Men light to refresh themselves; though all the Liquor in the House was not a Morning's Draught for them, which made the old Gentleman the Father conclude that this would be a Fasting-day of a Wedding. But whilst these Doubts and Fears shook him like a Palsie,

[2] rations, daily fare.

all on a sudden arrived *Armstrong*'s Cooks and Scullions, twenty in
number, with a Carrivan of Provision ready to dress: after them his
Butlers, being eight, with another of Wine, Cyder, Ale, and other Liquor;
so that it seemed, when taken out, a Plenty sufficient to have supplied a
little City against a Siege. So to work went the Cooks, &c. whilst he and
his Bride, bravely mounted, rode attended by his Men to the Church,
making such a Show as that Country had never before seen, the People
upon notice of it, coming far and near to be Spectators, some giving out,
especially the ignorant sort, that 'Squire *Leonard*'s Daughter had married
the King for certain; for as he came out of the Church, he gave a hundred
Mark to be distributed among the Poor, which they fancied none but a
King could, or at least would do.

When they came home, after the Wine of divers Nations had gone
briskly about, they found the Tables covered with all manner of Varieties
that Sea, Earth or Air could afford, as, Fowl, Fish, Flesh, Fruits, and other
Dainties, and yet above half was not brought in, so that they were obliged,
for want of Room in the House, to have Tables spread in the Court-yard.
For the Porter was ordered to make Proclamation, That all Comers
should be welcome that Day; and so till Night they drank and feasted
plentifully; and then came his Musick and Masqueraders to divert the
Company till Bed-time; though indeed there was not Lodging for a
fortieth Part of them, so that open House was kept all Night. And he
finding the ill conveniency of staying there longer, took leave of his
Father-in-Law the next Morning, and conveyed his fair Bride home with
him in great State, and with her lived very happily, supplying her Father's
wants on all occasions with Provision and Mony, and made him live very
comfortably.

*Chap. IV.   How having carried his fair Bride home, she was magnifi-
cently entertained; How soon after he had divers Encounters with the
Scots, and thereupon a War arising between the two Nations, after the
Batle at* Bannock's *Bourn,* Westmoreland *fell into their Hands.*

Being now at home, he so settled all things in good Order in that
Country, that the King of *England* sent him Thanks for the Care he
had in protecting Passengers from Robers and Thieves, as likewise from
the plundering Scots, which he made many times go short home,[3] wherefore they mortally hated him, and layed some Designs to intrap him, but

[3] to return from an expedition with loss of men.

having his Guard of merry old true hearted Blades with him, he always came off with flying Colours: And during these Transactions his Wife was brought to Bed of a fair Son, which much rejoyced his Parents Hearts, so that holding a Feast at his Christening, all the Country came in a manner, so that the Fame of it rung far and near.

In the middle of this Joy, he had notice, that a Party of Scots were advanced within ten Miles of his Seat, ravaging and plundering the Country, so that the People came flying before them apace; but he and his Men mounting, gave them Battle on the Borders of the Country, and overthrew them with so woful a Slaughter, that very few returned to *Carlisle*, which Garrioson in those Days the Scots held, to tell of the Defeat.

These, and such like Encounters and Depradations, caused an open War between the two Nations, which had been stilled for a time; and King *Edward* of *England* marched towards *Scotland*, and entered it with a mighty Army, but very ill disciplined; for the Scotch Historians tell us, they were a hundred thousand, besides Women, Lackeys, and other Servants, many carrying their whole Families with them to settle, when *Scotland* should be over-run. But Fortune was here against the *English*, by reason of their Security and Over-confidence in their Number, for in a Mortal Battle at a place called *Bannock*'s *Bourn*,[4] *Robert* the Scots King, setting upon 'em utterly vanquished 'em with a lesser Number, killing about ten thousand of them, with the Earl of *Gloucester*, and two hundred Knights and 'Squires, and on the Scots side about six thousand were killed, with divers Nobles and Gentlemen, so that they pursuing their Success, won *Westmoreland* and *Cumberland*. Our famous *Armstrong* was not at this Battle, but was much surprized at it, and would have perswaded the retreating English, to whose Aid he was coming, to rally and face about; but wanting a Warlike Prince to lead them, and he as a private Man having no Authority with them, it proved ineffectual; and now he found himself constrained to become a Subject to the King of *Scotland*, or leave his fair Seat, which he resolved not to do, though his Wife and his Father-in-law mainly perswaded him to it, considering how much he had done against that Nation, and that he could not well expect but now it was in their Power they would not forget it: But he being of an un-daunted Courage, told them that he had been brought up a Soldier, and what he had done was according to the Law of Arms, and that even a gerous[5] Enemy could not but approve it: Besides, in a little time all

---

[4] The Battle of Bannockburn took place in 1314.

[5] generous? warlike? (not in the *Oxford English Dictionary*).

might be won back again by the English; and therefore he not being used to despair in Providence, or subject to Fear, would not remove from a Place he so dearly loved upon Suggestions of Dangers that might never happen, least the World might impute to him a Cowardice he was never guilty of.

These Words put them to Silence, and he still went on in his old generous way of living, keeping open House, and doing all the good he could even to the Poor of either Nation without Indifferency, that no Exceptions might be taken, or he be branded with Partiality.

*Chap. V.   How being perswaded to leave* Guiltnock-Hall, *and retire from the Scotish Revenge, having refused for many Reasons; and great Commotions arising by the landing of the Danes and Redshanks, he was suspected upon the false Accusation of a Lord: How the King invited him to* Edenborough *to destroy him, and he promised to go.*

During these Stirs, the Danes and Redshanks,[6] two bloody Northern Nations, made great Havock in the Western Isles of *Scotland*, where they had landed, and with them joyned some of the discontented Scots, as well Noblemen as others, so that the King knew not who to trust, since some proved treacherous on whom he seemed mostly to rely; this vexed him, and made him suspicious even of his Friends, so that he imprisoned many of them out of Fear they should joyn with the English, who were making Preparations to recover what they had so shamefully lost; or with the Northern Enemy, to whom flocked a great many Outlaws and idle Persons, who supposed in the midst of Spoil and Plunder, they should be enriched with the Goods and Chattels that others had industriously laboured for.

These Proceedings made many of the great Ones whom he sent to, refuse to come to him, least they should be clapt up as the others had been; and then what Accusations might be brought falsly against them, they knew not.

This made him clap his Hand on his Breast, looking on those that were about him, and with a sigh said, Ah! is *Scotland* so full of Treachery, that never a Man from the highest to the lowest Degree dare appear before his King when he sends for him.

Hereupon an Officer of his Houshould standing up, and then bowing low, said, May it please your Majesty, there is one, by Name *John Armstrong* in *Westmoreland*, a valiant and trusty Man, whom I doubt not

6 Scots Highlanders.

but he may do you Service. What is he, said the King, or his Abillity? Why, replyed the Officer, he lives very splendidly, gives noble Entertainment to all Comers, and yet I never heard he had any Land to maintain it. Then, said the King, he must live by Plunder and Robbery; and of such there are too many in the Kingdom already. But does he keep any Men to attend him? Yes, replyed the other, he always maintains eightscore gallant Fellows, bravely attired; and when he goes abroad, they ride with him well mounted and armed.

Whilst this Dialogue held, in came a Lord whom *Armstrong* and his Men had a little before the Fight at *Bannock's Bourn* routed on the Borders, and rescued a great Booty of Cattle taken from the poor English Country People, and challenged him to single Combat, but he durst not answer him. Of this mortal Enemy of his, the King demanded, if he knew one *Johnny Armstrong* of *Westmoreland*, and what he was? Know him, replied he, Yes, may it please your Majesty, and so does all your poor Subjects on the other, and this side *Tweed;* he has been a bitter Enemy to our Country, and it is like to be so again, when the English, who now I hear are preparing to make an Attempt upon it; and unless your Majesty can get him into your Hands, and destroy him, and the Nest of Rebels he keeps, your new Conquests can never be secured to you.

This false and malicious Report so incensed the King against this just and valiant Man, that he resolved, if possible, his Destruction, without enquiring further into the matter; purposing to go with Forces, and immediately fall upon him: But that was objected against, least upon notice of the March, he should retire into the English Territories, and become yet a more implacable Enemy: Therefore it was thought advisable in a secret Council called to that Purpose, he should be sent for to *Edenborough* under fair Pretences of Friendship, and there he and his Train he brought with him might be cut off without much Resistance.

This was agreed on as proper, whereupon the King writ to him the following Letter:

*We having heard much of the Fame of you, our dear and loving Subject, and your great Bounty, and many singular Virtues, have raised such Admiration in us, that we could do no less at this time, than take Notice of one who is beloved of the common People, and may be so greatly serviceable to us, when things go so badly; Therefore I will not command, but earnestly require you on the sight of this our Letter, to repair to us at our City of* Edenborough, *with your Attendance, where you shall be heartily welcome. And for your safe Conduct, this our Letter, with our Royal Word and solemn Promise, shall be a sufficient Pledge and Security.*

ROBERT REX

This Letter was sealed with the King's Signet, and sent with all secresie and speed, which he received as he came from Hunting; and having highly treated the Messenger, and given him his Promise to wait on the King on the Morrow, he dismissed him.

*Chap. VI.   How he went bravely attended with his eightscore Men to* Edenborough, *notwithstanding many Presages that forbid it: The Discourse he had with the King, who charging him wrongfully as a Traytor, and ordering him and his Men to be hanged, they fought with the King's Guards, and the whole City in a bloody Battle, till they were all slain but his Page; and how his little Son promised to revenge his Father's Death.*

The valiant *John Armstrong* being at this Invitation a little puzled to think what the Reason should be, and therefore communicated it to his Friends to have their Opinions; but they were as much in the dark as himself; but since he had received the King's Letter of Conduct, and passed his Word to go, they concluded (all but his Wife, who was full of Fear for him) that it would be convenient for him to fulfil his Promise.

Whereupon he ordered his Men to be ready the next Morning, and to put on their best Apparel, which were Velvet Coats lac'd with three broad Gold Laces, and Scarlet Cloaks with five of Silver, as the most modish Fashion of those times, was also to put on their gold embroidered Belts, which were made to hang over their Shoulders, and every one a Falchion[7] by his Side with a silver Handle, a Buckler of Steel, and a Plume of white Feathers in their Hats or Bonnets, the Emblem of them that they unluckily went into War and Mischief.

His Commands were not disputed, but in the Morning they were up with the Sun, and immediately had put themselves in Array to March; when all on a sudden, the glorious Luminary that shone bright at his ascending our Horizen, was clouded and overcast and thunders began to rumble in the Air, which was the Forerunner of Rain and Whirlwinds; however, there being some signs of clearing up, he resolved to set forward, but coming to take his leave of his dearly beloved Wife, and little

---

[7] a broad sword more or less curved with the edge on the convex side.

Son, and giving them many tender Kisses and Embraces, Tears trickled from his Eyes, contrary to their wonted use, and his manly Courage failed him and all on a sudden he grew sad and melancholy, without being able to give any reason for it. But his Wive's Intreaties and his Son's Tears, were too weak to stay him; so with kind Farewels they parted, as they hoped, but for a time, but it proved a long one.

As they rid through several Towns, the People flocked to see their Bravery; at last they came to the flowery Banks of *Tweed*, which parts rightly *Scotland* from *England*, and is its Boundary, over which River they passed by a Foard, and so rode on towards *Edenborough*, sending word before of his coming, least so great a Troop might make the City shut their Gates on a sudden, for fear of a Surprize.

The King no sooner had notice of this, but he placed his Guards to be ready on the first Order to execute his Commands; but when he came to his Presence so nobly attended, he began to doubt it might be a mistaken Rumour of *Armstrong*'s coming, fancying it might rather be some forreign Prince come to pay him a Visit, wherefore upon his low bowing, the King moved his Bonnet to him in a courteous manner, biding him stand up; but he was no sooner certified it was he, e're the kind Language was turned into the hateful Names of Vilain, Traytor, Enemy to *Scotland*, Thief, Robber, and much more of this unexpected Language, which something startled him; whereupon he bending one Knee to the Ground, begged Pardon if he had done any thing that had offended his Majesty; but as for his coming thither, it was in Obedience to his Letter, which promised him better Entertainment, and safe Conduct, and therefore desired to know to what end he was sent for, tendering his Service if it might be accepted. No, Traytor, replied he, in a Rage, I need not thy Service; and as for the fair Promises in my Letter, 'twas to decoy you and your Nest of Thieves hither; and lastly, the Cause of sending for you was to hang you and your Men; which shall be done by eight of the Clock to Morrow morning. At this the bold English Man rising up unconcerned, without fear desired he might Justifie himself and his Men and be cleared of the false Report his Majesty had perhaps received of them. But the Lord who first accused him and some of his Creatures incensing the King against him, it was denied, and the Guards which were about two thousand, had the Signal to drag them to Goal,[8] and the next Morning to execute them.

*Hah*, says *Armstrong*, *hast thou thus broke thy Word with me, thus basely*

[8] i.e., gaol (jail).

*to ensnare and destroy me and my Men. Well, we are Men, and like Men we will die, if it must be so, and* Scotland *shall buy our Lives at a dear rate.* Upon that, looking behind him, and encouraging his Followers to take Example by him, he drew his trusty Sword, and making at the King through the thick of his Guards struck at him with such Fury, that he had taken off his Head at the Stroak, had not he nimbly avoided it by falling on the Ground. *Armstrong*'s Men seeing their Leader engaged among so many Swords, immediately drew, and so laid about them, that all the Place was slippery with Blood; driving those that remained unslain out of the Palace, into the open Streets; whilst the Cry arose through all the City, as if it had been taken by Storm; so that at last three thousand more coming upon the Heroick *Armstrong*, being tired with the Slaughter of his Enemies, and faint with Wounds and loss of Blood, after some staggering fell to the Ground; yet calling to his Men, encouraged them to Fight on, for after he had bled a little, he would rise and help them again. This made them like enraged Lyons, so that Heaps of dead Bodies barred up their way; till at last over-powered by fresh Numbers, and seeing no way of an honourable Retreat, they all like valiant Men dyed in their Master's Cause, leaving a bloody Victory, for there fell by their Hands two thousand five hundred Citizens and Soldiers. The King the mean while was retired to a Strong-hold for Shelter; and only of *Armstrong*'s Party a little Page escaped to tell the dismal News; at which, the Mourning of his Wife and all that Country made for his untimely Fall, is more than we can relate; however, his little Son sitting on his Nurse's Knee, vowed to revenge his Death, which, being a Man, he as gallantly performed.

### *Johnny Armstrong*'s last Goodnight, *&c.*

Is there never a Man in all *Scotland*,
    from the highest estate to the lowest degree,
That can show himself now before the King,
    *Scotland* is so full of Treachery?

Yes, there is a Man in *Westmoreland*,
    and *Johnny Armstrong* they do him call,
He has no lands nor rents coming in,
    yet he keeps eightscore Men within his Hall.

He has horse and harness for them all,
    and goodly steeds that be milk-white,

With their goodly belts about their necks,
   with hats and feathers all alike.


The King he writes a loving letter,
   and with his own hand so tenderly,
And hath sent it unto *Johnny Armstrong*,
   to come and speak with him speedily.


When *John* he looked this Letter upon,
   good Lord, he lookt as blith as a Bird in a Tree,
I was never before a King in my life,
   my Father, my Grandfather, nor none of us three:


But seeing we must go before the King,
   O we will go most gallantly;
Ye shall every one have a velvet-coat,
   laid down with golden laces three.


And ye shall every one have a scarlet Cloak,
   laid down with silver laces five,
With your golden belts about your necks,
   with hats and brave feathers all alike.


But when *John* he went from *Guiltnock-hall*,
   the wind it blew hard, and full fast it did rain,
Now fare the well thou *Guiltnock-hall*,
   I fear I shall never see the again.


Now *Johnny* is to *Edenborough* gone,
   with his eightscore Men so gallantly,
And every one of them a milk white steed,
   with their bucklers and swords hanging to their knee.


But when *John* came the King before,
   with his eightscore Men so gallant to see,
The King he mov'd his Bonnet to him,
   he thought he had been a King as well as he.

O Pardon, Pardon, my Sovereign Leige,
  pardon for my eightscore Men and me,
For my Name it is *Johnny Armstrong*,
  and a Subject of yours, my Leige, said he.

Away with thee, thou false Traytor,
  no Pardon will I grant to thee,
But tomorrow morning by eight of the clock
  I will hang up thy eightscore Men and thee.

Then *Johnny* lookt over his left shoulder,
  and to his merry Men thus said he,
I have asked grace of a graceless Face,
  no Pardon there is for you or me.

Then *John* pull'd out his trusty Sword,
  and it was made of mettle so free,
Had not the King mov'd his foot as he did,
  *John* had taken his head from his fair body.

Come follow me, my merry Men all,
  we will scorn one Foot for to flye,
It shall ne'r be said we were hung like Dogs,
  we will fight it out so manfully.

Then they fought on like Champions bold,
  for their hearts were stirdy, stout and free,
Till they had kill'd the King's good Guard,
  there was none left alive but two or three.

But then rose up all *Edenborough*,
  they rose up by thousands three;
A cowardly *Scot* came *John* behind,
  and run him thorow the fair Body.

Said *John*, Fight on my merry Men all,
  I am a little wounded but am not slain,
I will lay me down for to bleed a while,
  then I'll rise and fight with you again.

Then they fought on like mad Men all,
   till many a Man lay dead upon the Plain,
For they were resolved before they would yeild,
   that every Man should there be slain:

So there they fought couragiously,
   till most of them lay dead there and slain,
But little *Musgrove* that was his Foot-page,
   with his bonny Grizel got away untain.

But when he came to *Guiltnock-hall*,
   the Lady spied him presently,
What news, what news, thou little Foot-page,
   what news from thy Master and his Company?

My news is bad, Lady, he said,
   which I do bring, as you may see,
My Master *Johnny Armstrong* is slain,
   and all his gallant Company.

Yet thou art welcome home, my bonny *Grizel*,
   full oft thou hast been fed with Corn and Hay,
But now thou shalt be fed with Bread and Wine,
   and thy sides shall be spur'd no more, I say.

O then bespake his little Son,
   as he sat on his Nurse's Knee,
If ever I live to be a Man,
   my Father's Death reveng'd shall be.

FINIS

# BATEMAN'S TRAGEDY

## (ca. 1700)

# Bateman's Tragedy;

OR, THE

## Perjur'd Bride justly Rewarded:

BEING THE

# HISTORY

OF

## The Unfortunate LOVE

OF

*German's* Wife and young *Bateman.*

London, Printed by and for C. *Brown*, and T. *Norris*, and fold by the Bookfellers of *Pye-corner* and *London-Bridge.*

*Bateman's Tragedy* is a ghost-story written for popular consumption. For all its apparent crudeness it has a good deal of strength, its anonymous author leading his reader steadily and straightforwardly from the happy opening scenes to the horror of the ending. The brief bit of moralizing at the outset makes it clear that this is to be a tragedy, but after that the opening pages mirror faithfully the standard romance traditions of earlier times; the motif of the love-sickness curable only by the presence of the beloved, for example, is reminiscent of Robert Greene. From the start the author is clearly on Bateman's side. This tragedy could have been averted, he indicates, had Isabella been faithful to her vow and to her love. It is true that he shows the pressure brought to bear upon her to break her word (and filial duty was a very strong motivation in the seventeenth century), but he brings her to condemn herself toward the end of the story by admitting explicitly that she was Bateman's by right, and not German's.

The story has obvious popular appeal. The nameless yet gruesome fate of the perjured bride, the supernatural goings-on, the macabre suicide, all blend into a fine ghost-story, the narration being conducted in a simple, unmannered prose. The main incidents, the hanging, the haunting, and the final abduction, are all shown on the title-page cut, which in itself must have formed a powerful impulse to read, if not to acquire, the book it adorned.

The ballad version which follows the prose offers slight but interesting differences from the main text. By suppressing the parental pressure on Isabella the verse makes her seem the more culpable in falling away from her love to Bateman. Since Bateman's curing her love-sickness has been here ignored, no element of gratitude is compounded in the love she feels for him and hence she is again the greater traitor against love. Moreover, the tone is now more diabolic: Bateman's spirit, that of a suicide, be it remembered, is called a "fiend," a grim reminder of his dreadful fate after death (and the odor of sulphur in the prose version is thus specifically accounted for). It is to be presumed that the unfortunate Isabella has been borne off to be his companion in Hell, a just reward for the impiety of her broken vow.

Two early editions of the text are known, both undated. The text which follows is based on what is presumably the earlier of the two, an apparently unique copy in the Folger Shakespeare Library. From what we know of the working dates of the printer and publisher a date of about 1700 seems reasonable for the book.

## Bateman's Tragedy:
## or, the Perjured Bride Justly Rewarded

*Chap. I.    How young* Bateman, *riding through* Clifton-*Town accident-
ally espied fair* Isabella, *a rich Farmer's Daughter, standing at her
Father's Door, and fell in love with her, enquiring who she was, and his
Resolves to let her know his Passion.*

We find that solemn Vows and Promises are of great Weight, and strictly
binding, by the severe notice God has taken of those that have violated
them, in punishing the Dishonour done to his Name, by various and
fearful Judgments; and that People may be more careful for the future,
not to make any Vows or solemn Promises they are prone to break, or
intend not to keep, I shall instance one dismal Example of God's Anger
in this kind so dreadful a Manner, that all *England* has not only heard it
with Admiration,[1] but stood astonished at it.

*James Bateman,* Son to a Gentleman of *Nottingham-shire,* a Person
well Educated, but (by his Father's too much Liberality,) of no great
Fortune, riding one Day through *Clifton*-Town, a few Miles from
*Nottingham,* happened to cast his Eyes on a very comely Maid, who was
standing at the Door of a seemly House, with whose innocent Looks and
pretty Features, he was, all on a sudden, so taken, that he could not but
make a full stop to gaze at her. The Maiden no sooner perceived his Eyes
were earnestly fixed on her, but colouring her Face with a rosie Blush, she
modestly retires, no less surprized with his comely Personage, than he was
with her charming Beauty; however, this being the first time they had
seen each other, neither had he Courage to make any Advances, but he
passed on about his Affairs to a Town fifteen miles beyond that, but in a
manner without a Heart, for he had left that (as Lovers term it) with his
fair Mistress.

All the Way he rode his thoughts were strangely confused, so that he
laboured to compose them, but in vain; he found now though he had
formerly made a Jest of Love, and laughed at his Companions for declaring
their Passions, that he was taken in that Net he had perswaded others so
often to break, and that the more he strugled, the faster he found himself
entangled, the Business he went about was minded but little, and his
sighs and restlessness made his Friends conclude him in much disorder;
yet he cunningly concealed the cause from them, who little suspected it,

[1] amazement.

considering his former freeness of Temper and airy course of living, that Love could be an ingredient in this sudden alteration; so that finding, however, the Contagion had seized the Mind more than the Body, they concluded it might proceed from the decay of his Fortune; whereupon, that he might not be dejected, they proffered him their assistance and service in any thing he would command them. Whilst these things passed, he was urgent to return home, and did so, enquiring by the way, who this fair Maid was, and the condition of her Parents, and found she was Daughter to a covetous old rich Farmer, who had refused many considerable Matches, in hopes to prefer her higher, by the means of her Beauty, and the many Bags he intended to bestow upon her as a Portion; and further, that he kept a very strict Hand over her to prevent her being stolen away. This struck him almost with the Horrors of Despair; yet some thing he resolved to do, but what at present he could not frame in his Mind; and so home he went, to consider prudently how to manage his Love-affair, that at the first he might not by any over-rash Address, dash all his future hopes of Happiness: In contriving which, we will leave him a while, to consider the condition wherein he left fair *Isabella*, the Farmer's Daughter.

*Chap. II. How the fair* Isabella *fell sick of Love for* Bateman, *though a Stranger, and his abode unknown to her; and how, when she was given over, he came in the Habit of a Physician, discovered himself to her, and she recovered by that means her Health, to the unspeakable Joy of her Parents.*

This beauteous Maid, who, though often courted, had stood Proof against the Sighs, Tears and Intreaties of many handsom young Batchelors, found now she stood in need of Pity herself, *Bateman*'s Idea[2] was so fixed in her Mind, that sleeping or waking, she fancied him always in her sight; she made private enquiries, by the Description she gave of him, but not any she conversed with could satisfie her in that particular, some guessing at one, and some at another, as their Fancies led them; so that Love still blowing the hidden Fire, she first grew regardless of the Domestick Affairs, of which her Father and Mother had made her Overseer; then her Appetite failed, and, after that, she fell into a languishing Disease, which caused great Heaviness in the Family: Physicians were sent for to advise withal, but all their Skill proved ineffectual; for, according to the old Proverb,

[2] image.

> *Where Love's in the Case,*
> *The Doctor's an Ass.*

So that the Father and Mother, fearing to lose their only Daughter, which they doted on, and prized above all the valuable things in the World, were in a manner at their Wits-end, wringing their Hands and shedding many woful Tears.

Whilst they were in this pitious plight, and the sighing Maiden concealed the inward Flame, that consumed her Health, had wasted her Spirits, one, in the Habit of a Physician, mounted on a stately Steed, came riding to the Gate, and desired to speak with Mr. *Gifford*, for that was the Father's Name. The old Man came quickly to him, with a heavy Countenance, and the marks of Tears on his aged Cheeks, demanding, what brought him to so sorrowful a place, and what he required? *Truly, Sir,* says he, *I came out of compassion to the Affliction of your Family, for being at an Inn in the Town, and hearing your Daughter was sick, who is your only Delight and Darling, and whose Death might bring you untimely to your Grave, divers Physicians having used their Skill in vain; if you will accept of my Advice, and she be willing to take what I shall direct, I doubt not, but by the Blessing of God upon my many Years Study in Physick, and Travels in divers Countries, so to order things that her Health will be restored in a few Days.*

The Father, upon this unexpected Visit of a Stranger, concluded it was some good Angel directed to him by a wonderful Providence, scarcely refraining from falling on his Knees, or able to speak for Joy; but, after a little recovery from this kind of Transport, he invited him in, in a loving manner; and, as this new Doctor had desired, ordered all others out of the Chamber: The Love-sick Maid no sooner fixed her Eyes on him, but she knew him, and fetching a deep sigh, fainted away; but he revived her with some Cordials he had brought: so that recovering her Senses, her Blushes overcame her Paleness, and made a very strange Alteration in her Countenance.

To be brief, he having before guessed at, and being now fully assured of the Cause of her Distemper, told her the End of his coming in that Disguise, intreating her to cheer up, and pouring out his passionate Love-expressions, mingled with Tears, to see her in such a low condition, they at last so well understand one another's Mind, that having made a few Visits to her for four or five Days, and ordered her such things as are proper to restore decayed Nature, her Health returned, and the Roses flourished again in her Cheeks, to Wonder and Admiration; at which, the Father overjoyed, embraced this seeming Physician, and offered him a handful of Gold; but he refused, only desiring leave to visit him, as he happened to pass by his House on Occasions: And so at this time they parted, with high Satisfaction on all Hands, especially of the young Couple.

*Chap. III. How being invited to her Father's House, he walked abroad with and discovered his Passion to her at large; of the Encouragement he found to proceed in his Suit, and the Prospect there was of a happy Marriage between them.*

Young *Bateman*, having thus, as he thought, made a thorough stept [*sic*] to his future Happiness, went home filled with Joy, but delayed not long to re-visit his lovely Patient in the same Habit, taking an Opportunity after Dinner, to walk with her in the Garden; where, after a turn or two, sitting down in a pleasant shady Bower, they began to talk of Love, and of the last Adventure, devouring each other in a manner with their eager Looks, kissing and using all the modest Freedom that Lovers, whose Hearts were so united and enflamed, could wish or desire; and after some interrupting Sighs had passed, clasping his Arms about her snowy Neck: *Ah! lovely* Isabella, crys he, *how blessed am I to have this Opportunity, to tell you how much and how dearly I love you; you are the only Jewel in Nature, that I prize; and could I but be possessed of your lovely self, I should think my self the happiest of all Mankind.*

At this, turning her Eyes with loveliness on him, and blushing with a Virgin-grace, she told him, that *since he had been so kind to come timely and save her Life, she thought she could do no less than recompence him any lawful and reasonable way he could desire; for though many courted her, she was engaged to none.*

Upon this encouragement, he pressing her further, and vowing eternal Love and Constancy, she not only seemed by her kind Glances, and suffering him with willingness to lay his Head in her Bosom, to give her Consent to a speedy Marriage, but likewise told him, That this being the first time he asked her to render her self up to him, it was but all the Reason in the World for Virgin modesty, and a Compliance with Custom, that he should give her some time to consider of so weighty a Matter, which should, as she assured him, turn no ways to his Prejudice; For, continued she, my Obedience to my Parents, that yet I never disobeyed, must be continued, they must know of your Pretentions; several very rich and likely Men court me at present, yet fear not my Good-liking.

This so over-joyed young *Bateman*, that he would immediately have gone to her Parents and asked that Jewel of them, whose precious Life they could not but conclude, he, next to Heaven, had saved and continued to them; but she opposed it, saying, She would prepare the way herself; and therefore the next Visit he payed, it would prove new to them, and consequently more welcome. So, rising from their Seats, they went into the House, where a splendid Treat was provided, and they sat over-against each other at the Table, feeding on Love with their Eyes with greater Contentment than on the Dainties; but, Supper ended, and Night coming on, *Bateman* took his leave; when at parting the old Farmer invited him to a Publick Entertainment, that was to be at his House the third Day following; which he accepted of, and so for that time they parted.

*Chap. IV.   How he came in his proper Garb, and with her, asked her Father's Consent; but, for want of an Estate, was refused: how one* Jerman, *who was his Rival, attempting to kill him, was wounded by him, and how he made his Escape*, &c.

I shall not trouble you with the Thoughts and Impatiency of the young Lovers, during the Intervene, but tell you this Feast was made principally to entertain a Gentleman, whose Grand-father, a little before dying, had left him a great Estate, and whose Affections were strongly placed on the fair Virgin, so that he had courted her long; but she seemed little to regard his Addresses: However, the Father and Mother, charmed with the Desire of a rich Match for their Daughter, listened to it; and had often by Perswasions, and sometimes by Threatnings, desired and commanded her Compliance; but she with as much Tenderness, and Beseeching, as often excused it, protesting her liking to a single Life, and entreating them they would not compel her to any thing against her Inclination.

The Day being come, the Guests met, and Young *Bateman*, resolving now to push on his Suit, in his own proper Garb, came very bravely attired in the Habit of a Gentleman. The Entertainment was very splendid, Sea, Earth, and Air contributed their Stores to furnish out the Table with all manner of Dainties, as, Fish, Flesh, Fowl, Fruits, &c. nor was Musick, or any thing requisite wanting: But that which dash'd part of the Merriment, was, that fair *Isabella*, placing herself over against

*Bateman*, the other Lover, whose Name was *German*, and, by his Years and Observations in Love-intreagues, understanding the Language of their Eyes, in their often Gazings, the Blushes coming and going in his Mistress's Face, and many other Signs that *Cupid* has lively painted perspicuous to Lovers; his Fancy hit upon the Truth, *viz.* That they were deeply in Love with each other; whereupon his Countenance changed to a Sullen and Melancholly, and, throwing by what was before him, he abruptly retired from the Table, ordering his Servant to make ready his Horse in order to be gone.

The Father and Mother were startled at this, and knew not what should be the Occasion of so sudden an Alteration, in a Person who had professed so much Love to their Daughter, and on whom he resolved to bestow her, and thereupon followed him into a private Room, to be better satisfied in the Cause of his [Distaste],[3] or Discontent, and was soon satisfied in it; whereupon taking his Daughter aside, he told her what had been suggested by *German*. To which she modestly replied, *Seeing the Gentleman had saved her Life, when others had failed, she thought in Con-'science she could do no less than to give him her Love in Requital, and was resolved, if ever she married, to be his Wife.* This startled the old Man more and more, and *Bateman* mistrusting what had happened, coming in in the interim, and being demanded by the Father, if he made Love to his Daughter, boldly owning it, and desired his Consent to have her in Marriage.

*How!* says the old Man, *You that are a Stranger, make Love to my Daughter, and without my Knowledge? You may, for all your fine Gegaws, be a Beggar, for ought I know: I intend to give her a great Fortune, and therefore resolve to have her married to one that can settle a good Joynter[4] on her: Pray, what Estate have you?*

*Truly,* replied *Bateman, I am rich in Love towards her, but for Estate I cannot boast of much; I was born a Gentleman, but without the Fortune to maintain it; my Parents were unfortunate and left me but Little, yet I hope that Little, with your Blessing, and our Love, will woo Providence to be so kind, that our Endeavours may not fail to make us Happy, and you not repine, to give me this fair Creature to be my Wife.*

Upon this, he was going to take her by the Hand, and Seal his Love with a Kiss; but the old Dad stept between them, in an angry manner, crying, *Poh, poh; stand off, Sir; a Gentleman without an Estate is like a*

[3] original reads "Distaff."
[4] jointure; money or land settled on a wife at marriage.

*Pudding without Fat; you have indeed done my Daughter a Kindness in recovering her Health, but for having her to your Wife, I must beg your Pardon, she is Meat for your Betters.*

Upon this, *Bateman*'s Anger began to arise into some little Reproaches, but whilst he was upbraiding his expected Father with Ingratitude, in rushes *German*, who had heard in the next Room what had passed, with his drawn Sword, and made a full Pass at him; but he nimbly put it aside, and drawing, wounded him in the Breast, whereupon he fell dead to the Ground; and thereupon *Bateman* was forced to make his Escape, to gain time for further Consideration of what was to be done.

*Chap. V.   How, being banished her Father's house, his loved Mistress, upon sending a Letter, came to him in Disguise, in a Neighbouring Wood, and there they sealed their Love, by Solemn Vows, and breaking a piece of Gold between them.*

Fair *Isabella*, upon this unexpected accident, being left all in Tears as well as the rest of the Family in Fear and Confusion, Surgeons were sent for, who, upon searching the Wound, gave Hopes of their Patient's Recovery; yet *Bateman*, fearing the worst, absented himself from his Dwelling, and got, one Evening, a travelling Pedler, for a good Reward, to deliver a Letter to his Mistress, which he did, under the Colour of coming to her Father's House, to proffer his Wares; which was, to intreat her, if she had any Pity on the Sufferings of an unfortunate Man, not only to forgive what he did in Defence of his own Life, but to meet in a Neighbouring Wood at such an Hour.

She had no sooner read it, but, resolving to answer his Desire she escaped in the Disguise of a Milk-maid, dressing herself with the Maid's Apparel; when they met, (it's in vain for us to go about to describe the Raptures of Joy that was between them) she gave him an Account of all that had happened, and how *German* was likely to recover: But long they dwelt not on this Theme, before they fell to that of Love, renewing their Vows of eternal Love and Constancy, that nothing but Death should be able to seperate them; and, to bind it, he broke a piece of Gold, giving her the one half, and keeping the other himself; and then with Tears and tender Kisses they parted; she, at the Farewel, which proved a sad one, intreated him to travel a few Weeks, and give her Notice where he was secretly, and she would send him word, as to the recovery, or danger of his Rival; to which he consented with much alacrity

*Chap. VI.   How, upon her coming back, her going was discovered, and
she confined to her Chamber, which* German *courting her with Tears,
Presents, and the Proffer of a great Estate; she, at the Instance of her
Parents, renounced her Vows, sent back the broken Gold, and married*
German, *whereupon* Bateman *hanged himself.*

The beautious Virgin, during her Absence, having been missed at
home, and much enquired after, at her return, by reason of the un-
seasonableness of the time, was suspected of what had happen'd; and
altho' she modestly denied it, she was confined to her Chamber, and an
old Nurse set upon her as a Guard; so that *Bateman*'s Letters were
intercepted, and she lost the opportunity of writing to him. In the mean
while, *German* was recovered, and [admitted][5] to court her, whose
addresses for a long time she resisted: but at last, O the Inconstancy of
Women! notwithstanding her Vows to be *Bateman*'s, *Alive or Dead*, and
many other Protestations, the Glittering of the Miser's Gold, the Perswasions & Threats of her Father, and her Mother's Tears, with fine
Treats & rich Presentations, prevailed with her to alter her Mind; and,
by Instigation of these three to write to *Bateman* a Letter, wherein she
detested his Love; which, however, she could not do, without blotting
the Paper with Tears, and great Reluctancy of Mind. This Letter found
him many Miles off a-hunting; but, upon the reading it, his Spirits was
dashed, and a chill struck to his Heart: However, though he knew her
Hand, he flattered himself in believing it was to punish him for his so
long absence, or that she was compelled to do it; however, fearing the
worst, he hasted the next Morning to *Clifton*, and hearing the Bells
ringing merrily, his Heart misgave him; however, he had the Courage to
enquire the Cause, which proved a fatal One.

That Morning he was informed she was married to his Rival; then in a
rage he began to curse his Stars, and all Woman-kind; oft he thought to
fall on his Sword; but then Desire of Revenge interposed, not to fall
alone, but to Sacrifice the Bridegroom, and then himself: After somewhat
milder Resolutions came into his Mind, that he in this should give cause
of Grief to his Mistress; yet, to let know his Resentments, he sent her a
Letter with the half piece of Gold in it which found her [at] Dinner, and
made her be taken away sick from the Table; however, she was comforted
with Cordial, Joy of a Bridial-night, riding in a Coach, and great Estate,
passed it over, and to Bed they went when Night came.

[5] original reads "admired."

*Bateman*, receiving no answer, took it as a farther Slight, and so entring on a desperate Resolve, he stole into the House privately, as knowing the way, and hiding himself in a Closet by the Bridal Chamber-door, hanged himself before the Door, where he was found, to their great Horror and Amazement, upon opening the Door the next Morning, with this Distitch on his breast:

> *False Woman, of thy Vows and Oaths have dread,*
> *For thou art mine by them, alive or dead.*

*Chap. VII.    How, upon* Bateman's *hanging himself before her Chamber-door, she grew melancholy, always fancying she saw him with a ghastly face, putting her in mind of her broken Vows; and how, after being delivered of a Child, a Spirit carried her away.*

This not only Discomposed the Mirth of the Wedding, and made the Bride exceeding melancholy, but the ensuing Night dreadful Cries and Screeks were heard, as if Hell had been brooke loose, blazing Lights oft flashed in the Eyes of the new-married Pair, as they lay entwined in each others Arms followed with a dreadful Cry, *Thou art mine dead or alive.* This made them hastily remove to the Husband's House some miles distant; but the same Hunting pursued them, and where-ever she went, she thought the Spirit of *Bateman* appeared to her, holding the broken Gold in a String, and upbraiding her with her Breach of Faith: The Curtains were often drawn violently when they were in Bed, and the former Cry continued, till at last, she proving with Child, the Spirit came in a more furious manner, to bid her prepare to go with him, as soon as she was delivered; at which, weary of her Life, stretching out her Arms she cried, *I am thine by right, and am ready to go along with thee.*

*No*, replied he, *the innocent Babe in thy Womb protects thee, that I cannot have thee till thou art Delivered.*

Thus she continued in Sorrow and Fear, having many Divines to pray with her, but it availed not; for the time of her Delivery being come, which she desired might be prolonged, tho' in Pain, her Mother and divers other Women watched with her, which she earnestly begged of to pray, and not by any Means to fall asleep; however, a sudden Drowsiness about Midnight, in spight of all they could do, overcame them, till wakened with a dreadful Cry, they found the Candles out, and feeling for the Child-bed-woman, she was missing; the Casement being burst in pieces, and a strong smell of Sulpher left in the Room. The Town's People affirmed, they heard great Cries and Screeks in the Air, accompanied with a Clap of Thunder, and a Clap of Lightning about that time; however, she was never after heard on, though much sought for.

A Godly Warning to all Maidens by the Example of God's Judgment shewed on *Jerman*'s Wife of *Clifton*, in the County of *Nottingham*, who lying in Child-bed, was borne away, and never heard of after.

To the Tune of, *The Lady's Fall*, &c.

You dainty Dames so finely fram'd
   of Beauty's chiefest mould,
And you that trip it up and down,
   like lambs in *Cupid*'s fold,
Here is a lesson to be learn'd,
   a lesson in my mind,
For such as will prove false in love,
   and bear a faithless mind:

Not far from *Nottingham* of late,
   in *Clifton*, as I hear,
There dwelt a fair and comely Dame,
   for beauty without Peer;
Her cheeks were like the crimson rose,
   yet as you may perceive,
The fairest face the falsest heart,
   and soonest will deceive.

This gallant Dame she was belov'd
   of many in that place,
And many sought in marriage-bed
   her body to imbrace:
At last a proper handsome Youth,
   young *Bateman* call'd by name,
In hopes to make a married Wife,
   unto this Maiden came.

Such love and likeing there was found,
  that he from all the rest,
Had stol'n away the Maiden's heart,
  and she did love him best;
Then plighted promise secretly
  did pass between them two,
That nothing could but Death itself,
  this true love's knot undo.

He brake a piece of gold in twain,
  one half to her he gave,
*The other as a pledge*, quoth he,
  *dear Heart, my self will have.*
*If I do break my vow*, quoth she,
  *while I remain alive,*
*May never thing I take in hand*
  *be seen at all to thrive.*

This passed on for two months space,
  and then this Maid began
To settle love, and liking too
  upon another Man:
One *Jerman*, who a Widower was,
  her Husband needs must be,
Because he was of greater wealth,
  and better in degree.

Her vows and promise lately made,
  to *Bateman* she deny'd;
And in despight of him and his
  she utterly defy'd:
*Well then*, quoth he, *if it be so,*
  *that you will me forsake,*
*And like a false and forsworn Wretch*
  *another Husband take:*

*Thou shalt not live one quiet hour,*
  *for surely I will have*
*Thee either now alive or dead,*
  *when I am laid in grave;*

*Thy faithless mind thou shalt repent,*
*therefore be well assur'd,*
*When for thy sake thou hear'st report,*
*what torments I endur'd.*

But mark how *Bateman* dy'd for love,
and finisht up his life,
That very day she marry'd was,
and made old *Jerman*'s Wife;
For with a strangling-cord, God wot,
great moan was made therefor,
He hang'd himself in desperate sort,
before the Bride's own door.

Whereat such sorrow pierc'd her heart,
and troubled sore her mind,
That she could never after that,
one day of comfort find;
And wheresoever she did go,
her fancy did surmise,
Young *Bateman*'s pale and ghastly Ghost
appear'd before her eyes.

When she in bed at night did lye
betwixt her Husband's arms,
In hope thereby to sleep and rest,
in safety without harms;
Great cries, & grievous groans she heard,
a voice that sometimes said,
*O thou art she that I must have,*
*and will not be deny'd.*

But she being big with Child,
was for the Infant's sake,
Preserved from the Spirit's power,
no vengeance could it take:
The Babe unborn did safely keep,
as God appointed so,

His Mother's body from the Fiend,
    that sought her overthrow.

But being of her Burden eas'd,
    and safely brought to bed,
Her care and grief began anew,
    and farther sorrow bred:
And of her Friends she did intreat,
    desiring them to stay,
*Out of the bed,* quoth she, *this night,*
    *I shall be born away.*

*Here comes the Spirit of my Love,*
    *with pale and gastly face,*
*Who till he bear me hence away,*
    *will not depart this place;*
*Alive or dead I am his by right,*
    *and he will surely have,*
*In spight of me, and all the World,*
    *what I by promise gave.*

*O watch with me this night, I pray,*
    *and see you do not sleep;*
*No longer than you be awake,*
    *my body can you keep.*
All promised to do their best,
    yet nothing could suffice,
In middle of the night to keep
    sad slumber from their eyes.

So being all full fast asleep,
    to them unknown which way,
The Child-bed-woman that woful night
    from thence was born away;
And to what place no Creature knew,
    nor to this day can tell;
As strange a thing as ever yet
    in any Age befel.

You Maidens that desire to love,
   and would good Husbands chuse,
To him that you do vow to love,
   by no means do refuse.
For God that hears all secret oaths,
   will dreadful vengeance take,
On such that of a wilful vow
   do slender reckoning make.

FINIS